Sweet Tooth

Sweet Tooth

Ian McEwan

JONATHAN CAPE
LONDON

Published by Jonathan Cape 2012

2 4 6 8 10 9 7 5 3 1

Ian McEwan is an unlimited company registered
in England and Wales no. 7473219

First published in Great Britain in 2012 by
Jonathan Cape
Random House, 20 Vauxhall Bridge Road,
London SW1V 2SA

www.vintage-books.co.uk

Addresses for companies within The Random House Group Limited can be found at:
www.randomhouse.co.uk/offices.htm

The Random House Group Limited Reg. No. 954009

A CIP catalogue record for this book is available from the British Library

Hardback ISBN 9780224097376
Trade paperback ISBN 9780224097383

The Random House Group Limited supports The Forest Stewardship Council (FSC®),
the leading international forest certification organisation. Our books carrying the
FSC label are printed on FSC® certified paper. FSC is the only forest certification
scheme endorsed by the leading environmental organisations, including Greenpeace.
Our paper procurement policy can be found at www.randomhouse.co.uk/environment

Typeset in Palatino by Palimpsest Book Production Limited,
Falkirk, Stirlingshire

Printed and bound in Great Britain by
Clays Ltd, St Ives PLC

To Christopher Hitchens
1949–2011

If only I had met, on this search, a single clearly evil person.

Timothy Garton Ash, *The File*

1

My name is Serena Frome (rhymes with plume) and almost forty years ago I was sent on a secret mission for the British security service. I didn't return safely. Within eighteen months of joining I was sacked, having disgraced myself and ruined my lover, though he certainly had a hand in his own undoing.

I won't waste much time on my childhood and teenage years. I'm the daughter of an Anglican bishop and grew up with a sister in the cathedral precinct of a charming small city in the east of England. My home was genial, polished, orderly, book-filled. My parents liked each other well enough and loved me, and I them. My sister Lucy and I were a year and a half apart and though we fought shrilly during our adolescence, there was no lasting harm and we became closer in adult life. Our father's belief in God was muted and reasonable, did not intrude much on our lives and was just sufficient to raise him smoothly through the Church hierarchy and install us in a comfortable Queen Anne house. It overlooked an enclosed garden with ancient herbaceous borders that were well known, and still are, to those who know about plants. So, all stable, enviable, idyllic even. We grew up inside a walled garden, with all the pleasures and limitations that implies.

The late sixties lightened but did not disrupt our existence. I never missed a day at my local grammar school unless I was ill. In my late teens there slipped over the garden wall some heavy petting, as they used to call it, experiments with tobacco, alcohol and a little hashish, rock and roll records, brighter colours and warmer relations all round. At seventeen my friends and I were timidly and delightedly rebellious, but we did our school work, we memorised and disgorged the irregular verbs, the equations, the motives of fictional characters. We liked to think of ourselves as bad girls, but actually we were rather good. It pleased us, the general excitement in the air in 1969. It was inseparable from the expectation that soon it would be time to leave home for another education elsewhere. Nothing strange or terrible happened to me during my first eighteen years and that is why I'll skip them.

Left to myself I would have chosen to do a lazy English degree at a provincial university far to the north or west of my home. I enjoyed reading novels. I went fast – I could get through two or three a week – and doing that for three years would have suited me just fine. But at the time I was considered something of a freak of nature – a girl who happened to have a talent for mathematics. I wasn't interested in the subject, I took little pleasure in it, but I enjoyed being top, and getting there without much work. I knew the answers to questions before I even knew how I had got to them. While my friends struggled and calculated, I reached a solution by a set of floating steps that were partly visual, partly just a feeling for what was right. It was hard to explain how I knew what I knew. Obviously, an exam in maths was far less effort than one in English literature. And in my final year I was captain of the school chess team. You must exercise some historical imagination to understand what it meant for a girl in those times to travel to a neighbouring school and knock from his perch some condescending smirking squit of a boy. However, maths and chess, along with hockey, pleated skirts and hymn-singing, I considered mere school stuff. I reckoned it was time to put away these childish things when I began to think about applying to university. But I reckoned without my mother.

She was the quintessence, or parody, of a vicar's then a bishop's wife – a formidable memory for parishoners' names and faces and gripes, a way of sailing down a street in her Hermès scarf, a kindly but unbending manner with the daily and the gardener. Faultless charm on any social scale, in any key. How knowingly she could level with the tight-faced, chain-smoking women from the housing estates when they came for the Mothers' and Babies' Club in the crypt. How compellingly she read the Christmas Eve story to the Barnardo's children gathered at her feet in our drawing room. With what natural authority she put the Archbishop of Canterbury at his ease when he came through once for tea and Jaffa cakes after blessing the restored cathedral font. Lucy and I were banished upstairs for the duration of his visit. All this – and here is the difficult part – combined with utter devotion and subordination to my father's cause. She promoted him, served him, eased his way at every turn. From boxed socks and ironed surplice hanging in the wardrobe, to his dustless study, to the profoundest Saturday silence in the house when he wrote his sermon. All she demanded in return – my guess, of course – was that he love her or, at least, never leave her.

But what I hadn't understood about my mother was that buried deep beneath this conventional exterior was the hardy little seed of a feminist. I'm sure that word never passed her lips, but it made no difference. Her certainty frightened me. She said it was my duty as a woman to go to Cambridge to study maths. As a woman? In those days, in our milieu, no one ever spoke like that. No woman did anything 'as a woman'. She told me she would not permit me to waste my talent. I was to excel and become extraordinary. I must have a proper career in science or engineering or economics. She allowed herself the world-oyster cliché. It was unfair on my sister that I was both clever and beautiful when she was neither. It would compound the injustice if I failed to aim high. I didn't follow the logic of this, but I said nothing. My mother told me she would never forgive me and she would never forgive herself if I went off to read English and became no more than a slightly better educated housewife than she was. I was in danger of *wasting my life*. Those were her words, and they represented an admission. This was the only time she expressed or implied dissatisfaction with her lot.

Then she enlisted my father – 'the Bishop' was what my sister and I called him. When I came in from school one afternoon my mother told me he was waiting for me in his study. In my green blazer with its heraldic crest and emblazoned motto – *Nisi Dominus Vanum* (Without the Lord All is in Vain) – I sulkily lolled in his clubbish leather armchair while he presided at his desk, shuffling papers, humming to himself as he ordered his thoughts. I thought he was about to rehearse for me the parable of the talents, but he took a surprising and practical line. He had made some enquiries. Cambridge was anxious to be seen to be 'opening its gates to the modern egalitarian world'. With my burden of triple misfortune – a grammar school, a girl, an all-male subject – I was certain to get in. If, however, I applied to do English there (never my intention; the Bishop was always poor on detail) I would have a far harder time. Within a week my mother had spoken to my headmaster. Certain subject teachers were deployed and used all my parents' arguments as well as some of their own, and of course I had to give way.

So I abandoned my ambition to read English at Durham or Aberystwyth, where I am sure I would have been happy, and went instead to Newnham College, Cambridge, to learn at my first tutorial, which took place at Trinity, what a mediocrity I was in mathematics. My Michaelmas term depressed me and I almost left. Gawky boys, unblessed by charm or other human attributes like empathy and generative grammar, cleverer cousins of the fools I had smashed at chess, leered as I struggled with concepts they took for granted. 'Ah, the serene Miss Frome,' one tutor would exclaim sarcastically as I entered his room each Tuesday morning. '*Serenissima*. Blue-eyed one! Come and enlighten us!' It was obvious to my tutors and fellow students that I could not succeed precisely because I was a good-looking girl in a mini-skirt, with blonde hair curling past her shoulder blades. The truth was that I couldn't succeed because I was like nearly all the rest of humanity – not much good at maths, not at this level. I did my best to transfer out to English or French or even anthropology, but no one wanted me. In those days the rules were tightly observed. To shorten a long, unhappy story, I stuck it out and by the end managed a third.

If I've rushed through my childhood and teenage years, then I'll certainly condense my time as an undergraduate. I never went in a punt, with or without a wind-up gramophone, or visited the Footlights – theatre embarrasses me – or got myself arrested at the Garden House riots. But I lost my virginity in my first term, several times over it seemed, the general style being so wordless and clumsy, and had a pleasant succession of boyfriends, six or seven or eight over the nine terms, depending on your definitions of carnality. I made a handful of good friends from among the Newnham women. I played tennis and I read books. All thanks to my mother, I was studying the wrong subject, but I didn't stop reading. I'd never read much poetry or any plays at school, but I think I had more pleasure out of novels than my university friends, who were obliged to sweat over weekly essays on *Middlemarch* or *Vanity Fair*. I raced through the same books, chatted about them perhaps, if there was someone around who could tolerate my base level of discourse, then I moved on. Reading was my way of not thinking about maths. More than that (or do I mean less?), it was my way of not thinking.

I've said I was fast. *The Way We Live Now* in four afternoons lying on my bed! I could take in a block of text or a whole paragraph in one visual gulp. It was a matter of letting my eyes and thoughts go soft, like wax, to take the impression fresh off the page. To the irritation of those around me, I'd turn a page every few seconds with an impatient snap of the wrist. My needs were simple. I didn't bother much with themes or felicitous phrases and skipped fine descriptions of weather, landscapes and interiors. I wanted characters I could believe in, and I wanted to be made curious about what was to happen to them. Generally, I preferred people to be falling in and out of love, but I didn't mind so much if they tried their hand at something else. It was vulgar to want it, but I liked someone to say 'Marry me' by the end. Novels without female characters were a lifeless desert. Conrad was beyond my consideration, as were most stories by Kipling and Hemingway. Nor was I impressed by reputations. I read anything I saw lying around. Pulp fiction, great literature and everything in between – I gave them all the same rough treatment.

What famous novel pithily begins like this? *The temperature hit ninety degrees the day she arrived*. Isn't it punchy? Don't you know it? I caused amusement among my Newnham friends studying English when I told them that *Valley of the Dolls* was as good as anything Jane Austen ever wrote. They laughed, they teased me for months. And they hadn't read a line of Susann's work. But who cared? Who really minded about the unformed opinions of a failing mathematician? Not me, not my friends. To this extent at least I was free.

The matter of my undergraduate reading habits is not a digression. Those books delivered me to my career in intelligence. In my final year my friend Rona Kemp started up a weekly magazine called *?Quis?*. Such projects rose and fell by the dozen, but hers was ahead of its time with its high–low mix. Poetry and pop music, political theory and gossip, string quartets and student fashion, *nouvelle vague* and football. Ten years later the formula was everywhere. Rona may not have invented it but she was among the first to see its attractions. She went on to *Vogue* by way of the *TLS* and then to an incendiary rise and fall, starting new magazines in Manhattan and Rio. The double question marks in this, her first title, were an innovation that helped ensure a run of eleven issues. Remembering my Susann moment, she asked me to write a regular column, 'What I Read Last Week'. My brief was to be 'chatty and omnivorous'. Easy! I wrote as I talked, usually doing little more than summarising the plots of the books I had just raced through, and, in conscious self-parody, I heightened the occasional verdict with a row of exclamation marks. My light-headed alliterative prose went down well. On a couple of occasions strangers approached me in the street to tell me so. Even my facetious maths tutor made a complimentary remark. It was the closest I ever came to a taste of that sweet and heady elixir, student fame.

I had written half a dozen jaunty pieces when something went wrong. Like many writers who come by a little success, I began to take myself too seriously. I was a girl with untutored tastes, I was an empty mind, ripe for a takeover. I was waiting, as they said in some of the novels I was reading, for Mr Right to come along and sweep me off my feet. My Mr Right was a stern Russian. I discovered an author and a subject and became an enthusiast. Suddenly I had a theme, and a mission to persuade. I began to indulge myself with lengthy rewrites. Instead of talking straight onto the page, I was doing second and then third drafts. In my modest view, my column had become a vital public service. I got up in the night to delete whole paragraphs and draw arrows and balloons across the pages. I went for important walks. I knew my popular appeal would dwindle, but I didn't care. The dwindling proved my point, it was the heroic price I knew I must pay. The wrong people had been reading me. I didn't care when Rona remonstrated. In fact, I felt vindicated. 'This isn't exactly chatty,' she said coolly as she handed back my copy in the Copper Kettle one afternoon. 'This isn't what we agreed.'

She was right. My breeziness and exclamation marks had dissolved as anger and urgency narrowed my interests and destroyed my style.

My decline was initiated by the fifty minutes I spent with Aleksandr Solzhenitsyn's *One Day in the Life of Ivan Denisovich* in the new translation by Gillon Aitken. I picked it up straight after finishing Ian Fleming's *Octopussy*. The transition was harsh. I knew nothing of the Soviet labour camps and had never heard the word 'gulag'. Growing up in a cathedral precinct, what did I know of the cruel absurdities of communism, of how brave men and women in bleak and remote penal colonies were reduced to thinking day by day of nothing else beyond their own survival? Hundreds of thousands transported to the Siberian wastes for fighting for their country in a foreign land, for having been a prisoner of war, for upsetting a party official, for being a party official, for wearing glasses, for being a Jew, a homosexual, a peasant who owned a cow, a poet. Who was speaking out for all this lost humanity? I had never troubled myself with politics before. I knew nothing of the arguments and disillusionment of an older generation. Nor had I heard of the 'left opposition'. Beyond school, my education had been confined to some extra maths and piles of paperback novels. I was an innocent and my outrage was moral. I didn't use, and hadn't even heard, the word 'totalitarianism'. I probably would have thought it had something to do with refusing a drink. I believed I was seeing through a veil, that I was breaking new ground as I filed dispatches from an obscure front.

Within a week I'd read Solzhenitsyn's *The First Circle*. The title came from Dante. His first circle of hell was reserved for Greek philosophers and consisted, as it happened, of a pleasant *walled garden* surrounded by hellish suffering, a garden from which escape and access to paradise was forbidden. I made the enthusiast's mistake of assuming that everyone shared my previous ignorance. My column became a harangue. Did smug Cambridge not know what had gone on, was still going on, three thousand miles to the east, had it not noticed the damage this failed utopia of food queues, awful clothes and restricted travel was doing to the human spirit? What was to be done?

?Quis? tolerated four rounds of my anti-communism. My interests extended to Koestler's *Darkness at Noon*, Nabokov's *Bend Sinister* and that fine treatise by Milosz, *The Captive Mind*. I was also the first person in the world to understand Orwell's *Nineteen Eighty-Four*. But my heart was always with my first love, Aleksandr. The forehead that rose like an Orthodox dome, the hillbilly pastor's wedge of beard, the grim, gulag-conferred authority, his stubborn immunity to politicians. Even his religious convictions could not deter me. I forgave him when he said that men had forgotten God. *He* was God. Who could match him? Who could deny him his Nobel Prize? Gazing at his photograph, I wanted to be his lover. I would have served him as my mother did my father. Box his socks? I would have knelt to wash his feet. With my tongue!

In those days, dwelling on the iniquities of the Soviet system was routine for Western politicians and editorials in most newspapers. In the context of student life and politics, it was just a little distasteful. If the CIA was against communism, there must be something to be said for it. Sections of the Labour Party still held a candle for the ageing, square-jawed Kremlin brutes and their grisly project, still sang the Internationale at the annual conference, still dispatched students on goodwill exchanges. In the Cold War years of binary thinking, it would not do to find yourself agreeing about the Soviet Union with an American President waging war in Vietnam. But at that teatime rendezvous in the Copper Kettle, Rona, even then so polished, perfumed, precise, said it was not the politics of my column that troubled her. My sin was to be earnest. The next issue of her magazine didn't carry my byline. My space was taken up by an interview with the Incredible String Band. And then *?Quis?* folded.

* * *

9

Within days of my sacking I started on a Colette phase, which consumed me for months. And I had other urgent concerns. Finals were only weeks away and I had a new boyfriend, a historian called Jeremy Mott. He was of a certain old-fashioned type – lanky, large-nosed, with an outsized Adam's apple. He was unkempt, clever in an understated way, and extremely polite. I'd noticed quite a few of his sort around. They all seemed to be descended from a single family and come from public schools in the north of England, where they were issued with the same clothes. These were the last men on earth still wearing Harris tweed jackets with leather patches on the elbows and trim on the cuffs. I learned, though not from Jeremy, that he was expected to get a first and that he had already published an article in a scholarly journal of sixteenth-century studies.

He turned out to be a tender and considerate lover, despite his unfortunate, sharply angled pubic bone, which first time hurt like hell. He apologised for it, as one might for a mad but distant relative. By which I mean he was not particularly embarrassed. We settled the matter by making love with a folded towel between us, a remedy I sensed he had often used before. He was truly attentive and skilful, and could keep going for as long as I wanted, and beyond, until I could bear no more. But his own orgasms were elusive, despite my efforts, and I began to suspect that there was something he wanted me to be saying or doing. He wouldn't tell me what it was. Or rather, he insisted that there was nothing to tell. I didn't believe him. I wanted him to have a secret and shameful desire that only I could satisfy. I wanted to make this lofty, courteous man all mine. Did he want to smack my backside, or have me smack his? Was he wanting to try on my under-wear? This mystery obsessed me when I was away from him, and made it all the harder to stop thinking about him when I was supposed to be concentrating on the maths. Colette was my escape.

One afternoon in early April, after a session with the folded towel in Jeremy's rooms, we were crossing the road by the old Corn Exchange, I in a haze of contentment and some related pain from a pulled muscle in the small of my back, and he – well, I wasn't sure. As we walked along I was wondering whether I should broach the subject once more. He was being pleasant, with his arm heavily around my shoulders as he told me about his essay on the Star Chamber. I was convinced that he wasn't properly fulfilled. I thought I heard it in the tightness of his voice, his nervous pace. In days of lovemaking he had not been blessed with a single orgasm. I wanted to help him, and I was genuinely curious. I was also troubled by the thought that I might be failing him. I aroused him, that much was clear, but perhaps he didn't quite desire me sufficiently. We went past the Corn Exchange in the twilight chill of a damp spring, my lover's arm was about me like a fox fur, my happiness faintly compromised by a muscular twinge and only a little more by the enigma of Jeremy's desires.

Suddenly, from out of an alley, there appeared before us under the inadequate street lighting Jeremy's history tutor, Tony Canning. When we were introduced he shook my hand, and held on to it far too lingeringly, I thought. He was in his early fifties – about my father's age – and I knew only what Jeremy had already told me. He was a professor, a one-time friend of the Home Secretary, Reggie Maudling, who had been to dine in his college. The two men had fallen out one drunken evening over the policy of internment without trial in Northern Ireland. Professor Canning had chaired a commission on historical sites, sat on various advisory boards, was a trustee of the British Museum and had written a highly regarded book about the Congress of Vienna.

He was of the great and good, a type vaguely familiar to me. Men like him came to our house to visit the Bishop from time to time. They were annoying of course to anyone under twenty-five in that post-sixties period, but I rather liked them too. They could be charming, even witty, and the whiff they trailed of cigars and brandy made the world seem orderly and rich. They thought much of themselves, but they didn't seem dishonest, and they had, or gave the impression they had, a strong sense of public service. They took their pleasures seriously (wine, food, fishing, bridge, etc.) and apparently some had fought an interesting war. I had memories of childhood Christmases when one or two of them would tip my sister and me a ten bob note. Let these men rule the world. There were others far worse.

Canning had a relatively subdued grand manner, perhaps to match his modest public roles. I noted the wavy hair, finely parted, and moist fleshy lips and a small cleft in the centre of his chin, which I thought was endearing because I could see, even in poor light, that he had some trouble shaving it clean. Ungovernable dark hairs protruded from the vertical trough of skin. He was a good-looking man.

When the introductions were over, Canning asked me some questions about myself. They were polite and innocent enough – about my degree, Newnham, the principal, who was a good friend of his, my home town, the cathedral. Jeremy cut in with some small talk and then Canning interrupted in turn to thank him for showing him my last three articles for *?Quis?*.

He turned to me again. 'Bloody good pieces. You've quite a talent, my dear. Are you going into journalism?'

?Quis? was a student rag, not intended for serious eyes. I was gratified by the praise, but too young to know how to take a compliment. I mumbled something modest but it sounded dismissive, then I clumsily tried to correct myself and became flustered. The professor took pity on me and invited us to tea and we accepted, or Jeremy did. And so we followed Canning back across the market towards his college.

His rooms were smaller, dingier, more chaotic than I expected, and I was surprised to see him making a mess of the tea, partly rinsing the chunky brown-stained mugs and slopping hot water from a filthy electric kettle over papers and books. None of this fitted with what I came to know of him later. He sat behind his desk, we sat on armchairs and he continued to ask questions. It could have been a tutorial. Now that I was nibbling his Fortnum & Mason chocolate biscuits, I felt obliged to answer him more fully. Jeremy was encouraging me, nodding stupidly at everything I said. The professor asked about my parents, and what it was like growing up 'in the shadow of a cathedral' – I said, wittily, I thought, that there was no shadow because the cathedral was to the north of our house. Both men laughed and I wondered if my joke had implied more than I understood. We moved on to nuclear weapons and calls in the Labour Party for unilateral disarmament. I repeated a phrase I'd read somewhere – a cliché I realised later. It would be impossible 'to put the genie back in the bottle'. Nuclear weapons would have to be managed, not banned. So much for youthful idealism. Actually, I had no particular views on the subject. In another context, I could have spoken up for nuclear disarmament. I would have denied it, but I was trying to please, to give the right answers, to be interesting. I liked the way Tony Canning leaned forwards when I spoke, I was encouraged by his little smile of approbation, which stretched but did not quite part his plump lips, and his way of saying 'I see' or 'Quite . . .' whenever I paused.

Perhaps it should have been obvious to me where this was leading. In a tiny, hothouse world of undergraduate journalism, I'd announced myself as a trainee Cold Warrior. It must be obvious now. This was Cambridge, after all. Why else would I recount the meeting? At the time the encounter had no significance for me at all. We had been on our way to a bookshop and instead we were taking tea with Jeremy's tutor. Nothing very strange in that. Recruitment methods in those days were changing, but only a little. The Western world may have been undergoing a steady transformation, the young may have thought they had discovered a new way of talking to each other, the old barriers were said to be crumbling from the base. But the famous 'hand on the shoulder' was still applied, perhaps less frequently, perhaps with less pressure. In the university context certain dons continued to look out for promising material and pass names on for interview. Certain successful candidates in the Civil Service exams were still taken aside and asked if they had ever thought of 'another' department. Mostly, people were quietly approached once they'd been out in the world a few years. No one ever needed to spell it out, but background remained important, and having the Bishop in mine was no disadvantage. It's often been remarked how long it took for the Burgess, Maclean and Philby cases to dislodge the assumption that a certain class of person was more likely to be loyal to his country than the rest. In the seventies those famous betrayals still resounded, but the old enlistment methods were robust.

Generally, both hand and shoulder belonged to men. It was unusual for a woman to be approached in that much-described, time-honoured way. And though it was strictly true that Tony Canning ended up recruiting me for MI5, his motives were complicated and he had no official sanction. If the fact that I was young and attractive was important to him, it took a while to discover the full pathos of that. (Now that the mirror tells a different story, I can say it and get it out of the way. I really was *pretty*. More than that. As Jeremy once wrote in a rare effusive letter, I was 'actually rather gorgeous'.) Even the elevated greybeards on the fifth floor, whom I never met and rarely saw in my brief period of service, had no idea why I'd been sent to them. They hedged their bets, but they never guessed that Professor Canning, an old MI5 hand himself, thought he was making them a gift in the spirit of expiation. His case was more complex and sadder than anyone knew. He would

14

change my life and behave with selfless cruelty as he prepared to set out on a journey with no hope of return. If I know so little about him even now, it's because I accompanied him only a very small part of the way.

2

My affair with Tony Canning lasted a few months. At first I was also seeing Jeremy, but by late June, after finals, he moved to Edinburgh to start work on a PhD. My life became less fraught, though it still troubled me that I hadn't cracked his secret by the time he left and couldn't give him satisfaction. He had never complained or looked sorry for himself. Some weeks later he wrote a tender, regretful letter to say that he had fallen in love with a violinist he'd heard one evening at the Usher Hall playing a Bruch concerto, a young German from Düsseldorf with an exquisite tone, especially in the slow movement. His name was Manfred. Of course. If I'd been a little more old-fashioned in my thinking, I would have guessed it, for there was a time when every man's sexual problem had only one cause.

How convenient. The mystery was solved, and I could stop worrying about Jeremy's happiness. He was sweetly concerned for my feelings, even offering to travel down and meet me to explain things. I wrote back to congratulate him, and felt mature as I exaggerated my delight for his benefit. Such liaisons had only been legal for five years and were a novelty to me. I told him that there was no need to come all the way to Cambridge, that I'd always have the fondest memories, that he was the loveliest of men, and I looked forward to meeting Manfred one day, please let's keep in touch, Goodbye! I would have liked to thank him for introducing me to Tony, but I saw no point in creating suspicion. Nor did I tell Tony about his former student. Everyone knew as much as they needed to know to be happy.

And we were. We kept our tryst each weekend in an isolated cottage not far from Bury St Edmunds in Suffolk. You turned off a quiet narrow lane onto an indistinct track that crossed a field, you stopped at the edge of an ancient pollarded wood, and there, hidden by a tangle of hawthorn bushes, was a small white picket gate. A flagstone path curved through an overgrown country garden (lupins, hollyhocks, giant poppies) to a heavy oak door studded with rivets or nails. When you opened that door you were in the dining room, a place of giant flagstones and wormholed beams half buried in the plaster. On the wall opposite was a bright Mediterranean scene of whitewashed houses and sheets drying on a line. It was a watercolour by Winston Churchill, painted in Marrakech during a break from the Conference in 1943. I never learned how it came into Tony's possession.

Frieda Canning, an art dealer who travelled abroad a good deal, didn't like coming here. She complained about the damp and the smell of mildew and the dozens of tasks associated with a second home. As it happened, the smell vanished as soon as the place warmed up, and it was her husband who did all the tasks. They required special knowledge and skills: how to light the stubborn Rayburn stove and force open the kitchen window, how to activate the bathroom plumbing and dispose of the broken-backed mice in the traps. I didn't even have to cook much. For all his sloppy tea-making, Tony fancied himself in the kitchen. I was sometimes his sous-chef, and he taught me a good deal. He cooked in the Italian style, learned during four years as a lecturer at an institute in Siena. His back played up, so at the beginning of each visit I humped hessian sacks of food and wine through the garden from his ancient MGA parked in the field.

It was a decent summer by English standards and Tony set a stately pace to the day. We often ate our lunch in the shade of an ancient cotoneaster in the garden. Generally, when he woke from his after-lunch nap, he took a bath and then, if it was warm, he read in a hammock slung between two birch trees. And, if it was really hot, he sometimes suffered from nosebleeds and had to lie on his back indoors with a flannel and ice cubes pressed to his face. Some evenings we took a picnic into the woods, with a bottle of white wine wrapped in a crisp tea towel, wine glasses in a cedarwood container, and a flask of coffee. This was high table *sur l'herbe*. Saucers as well as cups, damask tablecloth, porcelain plates, silverware and one collapsible aluminium and canvas chair – I carried everything without complaint. Later in the summer we didn't go far along the footpaths because Tony said it hurt to walk, and he tired easily. In the evenings he liked to play opera on an old gramophone and though he urgently explained the characters and intrigues of *Aida, Così Fan Tutte* and *L'Elisir d'Amore*, those reedy yearning voices meant little to me. The quaint hiss and crackle of the blunted needle as it gently rose and fell with the warp of the album sounded like the ether, through which the dead were hopelessly calling to us.

He liked talking to me about his childhood. His father had been a naval commander in the first war and was an expert yachtsman. In the late twenties, family holidays consisted of island hopping in the Baltic and this was how his parents came across and bought a stone cottage on the remote island of Kumlinge. It became one of those childhood paradise places burnished by nostalgia. Tony and his older brother roamed free, building fires and camps on the beaches, rowing out to an uninhabited islet to steal sea-bird eggs. He had cracked box-camera snaps to prove that the dream was real.

One afternoon in late August we went into the woods. We often did, but on this occasion Tony turned off the footpath and I blindly followed. We barged through the undergrowth, and I assumed we were going to make love in some secret place he knew. The leaves were dry enough. But he was thinking only of mushrooms, ceps. I concealed my disappointment and learned the identifying tricks – pores not gills, a fine filigree on the stem, no staining when you pushed your thumb into the flesh. That evening he cooked up a big pan of what he preferred to call porcini, with olive oil, pepper, salt and pancetta, and we ate them with grilled polenta, salad and red wine, a Barolo. This was exotic food in the seventies. I remember everything – the scrubbed pine table with dented legs of faded duck-egg blue, the wide faience bowl of slippery ceps, the disc of polenta beaming like a miniature sun from a pale green plate with a cracked glaze, the dusty black bottle of wine, the peppery rugola in a chipped white bowl, and Tony making the dressing in seconds, tipping oil and squeezing half a lemon in his fist even, so it seemed, as he carried the salad to the table. (My mother concocted her dressings at eye level, like an industrial chemist.) Tony and I ate many similar meals at that table, but this one can stand for the rest. What simplicity, what taste, what a man of the world! That night the wind was up and the bough of an ash thumped and scraped across the thatched roof. After dinner there would be reading, then talking to be sure, but only after lovemaking, and that only after another glass of wine.

As a lover? Well, obviously not as energetic and inexhaustible as Jeremy. And though Tony was in good shape for his age, I was a little put out first time to see what fifty-four years could do to a body. He was sitting on the edge of the bed, bending to remove a sock. His poor naked foot looked like a worn-out old shoe. I saw folds of flesh in improbable places, even under his arms. How strange, that in my surprise, quickly suppressed, it didn't occur to me that I was looking at my own future. I was twenty-one. What I took to be the norm – taut, smooth, supple – was the transient special case of youth. To me, the old were a separate species, like sparrows

19

or foxes. And now, what I would give to be fifty-four again! The body's largest organ bears the brunt – the old no longer fit their skin. It hangs off them, off us, like a room-for-growth school blazer. Or pyjamas. And in a certain light, though it may have been the bedroom curtains, Tony had a yellowish look, like an old paperback, one in which you could read of various misfortunes – of over-eating, scars from knee and appendicitis operations, of a dog bite, a rock-climbing accident and a childhood disaster with a breakfast frying pan which had left him bereft of a patch of pubic hair. There was a white four-inch scar to the right of his chest reaching towards his neck, whose history he would never explain. But if he was slightly . . . foxed, and resembled at times my frayed old teddy back home in the cathedral close, he was also a worldly, a gentlemanly lover. His style was courtly. I warmed to the way he undressed me, and draped my clothes over his forearm, like a swimming-pool attendant, and the way he sometimes wanted me to sit astride his face – as new to me as rugola salad, that one.

I also had reservations. He could be hasty, impatient to get on to the next thing – the passions of his life were drinking and talking. Later, I sometimes thought he was selfish, definitely old school, racing towards his own moment, which he always gained with a wheezy shout. And too obsessed by my breasts, which were lovely then, I'm sure, but it didn't feel right to have a man the Bishop's age fixated in a near infantile way, virtually nursing there with a strange whimpering sound. He was one of those English-men wrenched aged seven from Mummy and driven into numbing boarding-school exile. They never acknowledge the damage, these poor fellows, they just live it. But these were minor complaints. It was all new, an adventure that proved my own maturity. A knowing, older man doted on me. I forgave him everything. And I loved those soft-cush-ioned lips. He kissed beautifully.

Still, I liked him most when he was back in his clothes,

with his fine parting restored (he used hair oil and a steel comb), when he was great and good once more, settling me in an armchair, deftly drawing the cork from a Pinot Grigio, directing my reading. And there was something I've since noticed over the years – the mountain range that separates the naked from the clothed man. Two men on one passport. Again, it hardly mattered, it was all one – sex and cooking, wine and short walks, talking. And we were also studious. In the early days, in the spring and early summer of that year, I was working for my finals. Tony could give me no help there. He sat across from me, writing a monograph about John Dee.

He had scores of friends but, of course, he never invited anyone round when I was there. Only once did we have visitors. They came one afternoon in a car with a driver, two men in dark suits, in their forties, I guessed. Rather too curtly, Tony asked me if I would go for a longish walk in the woods. When I came back an hour and a half later, the men had gone. Tony gave no explanation and that night we went back to Cambridge.

The cottage was the only place where we saw each other. Cambridge was too much of a village; Tony was too well known there. I had to hike with my holdall to a remote corner of town on the edge of a housing estate and wait in a bus shelter for him to come by in his ailing sports car. It was supposed to be a convertible but the concertina metal bits that supported the canvas top were too rusted to fold back. This old MGA had a map light on a chrome stem, and quivering dials. It smelled of engine oil and friction heat, the way a 1940s Spitfire might. You felt the warm tin floor vibrate beneath your feet. It was a thrill to step out of the bus queue, resentfully observed by ordinary passengers, while I turned from frog to princess and stooped to crawl in beside the professor. It was like getting into bed, in public. I shoved my bag into the tiny space behind me, and felt the seat's cracked leather snag faintly against the silk of my blouse – one he

21

had bought me in Liberty's – as I leaned across to receive my kiss.

When exams were over Tony said he was taking charge of my reading. Enough novels! He was appalled by my ignorance of what he called 'our island story'. He was right to be. I'd studied no history at school beyond the age of fourteen. Now I was twenty-one, blessed with a privileged education, but Agincourt, the Divine Right of Kings, the Hundred Years War were mere phrases to me. The very word 'history' conjured a dull succession of thrones and murderous clerical wrangling. But I submitted to the tutelage. The material was more interesting than maths and my reading list was short – Winston Churchill and G.M. Trevelyan. The rest my professor would talk me through.

My first tutorial was conducted in the garden under the cotoneaster. I learned that since the sixteenth century the foundation of English then British policy in Europe was the pursuit of the balance of power. I was required to read up on the Congress of Vienna of 1815. Tony was insistent that an equilibrium between nations was the foundation of a lawful international system of peaceful diplomacy. It was vital that nations held one another in check.

I often did my reading alone after lunch while Tony took his nap – these sleeps became longer as the summer wore on and I should have taken notice. Initially, I impressed him with my speed-reading. Two hundred pages in a couple of hours! Then I disappointed him. I couldn't answer his questions clearly, I wasn't retaining information. He made me go back through Churchill's version of the Glorious Revolution, tested me, groaned theatrically – You bloody sieve! – made me read again, asked more questions. These oral exams happened during walks in the woods, and over glasses of wine after the suppers he cooked. I resented his persistence. I wanted us to be lovers, not teacher and pupil. I was annoyed with him as well as myself when I didn't know the answers. And then, a few querulous sessions later, I began to feel some pride, and not simply in my improved performance. I started to take note of the story itself. Here was something precious and it seemed as if I'd discovered it on my own, like Soviet oppression. Wasn't England at the end of the seventeenth century the freest and most inquisitive society the world had ever known? Wasn't the English Enlightenment of more consequence than the French? Wasn't it right that England should have set itself apart to struggle against the Catholic despotisms on the Continent? And surely, we were the inheritors of that freedom.

I was easily led. I was being groomed for my first interview, which was to take place in September. He had an idea of the kind of Englishwoman they would want to take on, or that he would want, and he worried that my narrow education would let me down. He believed, wrongly as it turned out, that one of his old students would be among my interviewers. He insisted I read a newspaper every day, by which of course he meant *The Times*, which in those days was still the august paper of record. I hadn't bothered much with the press before, and I had never even heard of a leader. Apparently, this was the 'living heart' of a newspaper. At first glance, the prose resembled a chess problem. So I was hooked. I admired those orotund and lordly pronouncements on matters of public concern. The judgements were somewhat opaque and never above a reference to Tacitus or Virgil. So mature! I thought any of these anonymous writers was fit to be World President.

And what were the concerns of the day? In the leaders, grand subordinate clauses orbited elliptically about their starry main verbs, but in the letters pages no one was in any doubt. The planets were out of kilter and the letter writers knew in their anxious hearts that the country was sinking into despair and rage and desperate self-harm. The United Kingdom had succumbed, one letter announced, to a frenzy of *akrasia* – which was, Tony reminded me, the Greek word for acting against one's better judgement. (Had I not read

23

Plato's *Protagoras*?) A useful word. I stored it away. But there *was* no better judgement, nothing to act against. Everyone had gone mad, so everyone said. The archaic word 'strife' was in heavy use in those rackety days, with inflation provoking strikes, pay settlements driving inflation, thick-headed, two-bottle-lunch management, bloody-minded unions with insurrectionary ambitions, weak government, energy crises and power cuts, skinheads, filthy streets, the Troubles, nukes. Decadence, decay, decline, dull inefficiency and apocalypse . . .

Among the favoured topics in letters to *The Times* were the miners, 'a workers' state', the bipolar world of Enoch Powell and Tony Benn, flying pickets, and the Battle for Saltley. A letter from a retired rear admiral said the country resembled a rusting battleship holed below the waterline. Tony read the letter over breakfast and shook his copy noisily at me – newsprint was crinkly and loud back then.

'Battleship?' he fumed. 'It isn't even a corvette. This is a bloody rowing boat going down!'

That year, 1972, was just the beginning. When I started reading the paper the three-day week, the next power cuts, the government's *fifth* state of emergency were not so far ahead of us. I believed what I read, but it seemed remote. Cambridge looked much the same, and so did the woods around the Cannings' cottage. Despite my history lessons I felt I had no stake in the nation's fate. I owned one suitcase of clothes, fewer than fifty books, some childhood things in my bedroom at home. I had a lover who adored me and cooked for me and never threatened to leave his wife. I had one obligation, a job interview – *weeks* away. I was free. So what was I doing, applying to the Security Service to help maintain this ailing state, this sick man of Europe? Nothing, I was doing nothing. I didn't know. A chance had come my way and I was taking it. Tony wanted it so I wanted it and I had little else going on. So why not?

Besides, I still regarded myself as accountable to my parents and they were pleased to hear that I was considering a respectable wing of the Civil Service, the Department of Health and Social Security. It may not have been the atom-smashing my mother had in mind, but its solidity in turbulent times must have soothed her. She wanted to know why I had not come to live at home after finals, and I was able to tell her that a kindly older tutor was preparing me for my 'board'. It made sense, surely, to take a tiny cheap room by Jesus Green and 'work my socks off', even at weekends.

My mother might have expressed some scepticism, if my sister Lucy hadn't created a diversion by getting herself into such trouble that summer. She was always louder, feistier, a bigger risk-taker, and had been far more convinced than I was by the liberating sixties as they limped into the next decade. She was also two inches taller now and was the first person I ever saw wearing 'cut-off' jeans. Loosen up, Serena, be free! Let's go travelling! She caught hippiedom just as it was going out of fashion, but that's how it was in provincial market towns. She was also telling the world that her sole aim in life was to be a doctor, a general practitioner or perhaps a paediatrician.

She pursued her ambitions by a roundabout route. That July she was a foot passenger off the Calais to Dover ferry and was interrupted by a customs official, or rather, by his dog, a barking bloodhound suddenly excited by the aroma of her backpack. Inside, wrapped in unlaundered T-shirts and dog-proof layers of plastic, was half a pound of Turkish hashish. And inside Lucy, though this was also not declared, was a developing embryo. The identity of the father was uncertain.

My mother had to devote a good portion of every day for the next few months to a quadruple mission. The first was to save Lucy from prison, the second, to keep her story out of the newspapers, the third, to prevent her being sent down from Manchester, where she was a second-year medical student, and the fourth, after not much agonising, was to arrange the termination. As far as I could tell from my crisis visit home (Lucy smelling of patchouli and sobbing as she crushed me in her sun-tanned arms), the Bishop was prepared to bow his head and take whatever the heavens had prepared for him. But my mother was already at the controls, fiercely activating the networks that extend locally and nationally from any twelfth-century cathedral. For example, the Chief Constable for our county was a regular lay preacher and knew of old his counterpart, the Chief Constable of Kent. A Conservative Association friend was acquainted with the Dover magistrate before whom Lucy made her first appearance. The editor of our local paper was wanting to get his tone-deaf twin sons into the cathedral choir. Pitch of course was relative, but nothing could be taken for granted, and it was, my mother assured me, *all jolly hard work*, and none of it more so than the abortion, medically routine but, to Lucy's surprise, deeply upsetting. Eventually she received a six-month suspended sentence, nothing appeared in the press, and a Mancunian university rector or some such eminence was assured of my father's support on an arcane matter at the upcoming Synod. My sister returned to her studies in September. Two months later she dropped out.

So I was left in peace during July and August to loll about Jesus Green, reading Churchill, bored, waiting for the weekend and the hike to the bus stop on the city boundary. It would not be long before I enshrined the summer of '72 as a golden age, a precious idyll, but it was only Friday to Sunday evening that held the pleasures. Those weekends were an extended tutorial in how to live, how and what to eat and drink, how to read newspapers and hold up my end of an argument and how to 'gut' a book. I knew I had an interview coming up, but it never crossed my mind to ask why Tony took such trouble over me. If I had I would have probably thought that such attentions were part of what it meant to have an affair with an older man.

Of course, the situation couldn't last and it all came apart during a stormy half-hour by a busy main road, two days before I was due at my interview in London. The precise sequence of events is worth recording. There was a silk blouse, the one I've already mentioned, bought for me by Tony in early July. It was well chosen. I liked the expensive feel of it on a warm evening and Tony told me more than once how he liked the plain loose cut of it on me. I was touched. He was the first man in my life to buy me an article of clothing. A sugar daddy. (I don't think the Bishop had ever been in a shop.) It was an old-fashioned thing, this present, with a touch of kitsch about it, and awfully girlish, but I loved it. When I wore it I was in his embrace. The pale blue copperplate words on the label appeared distinctly erotic – 'wild silk hand wash'. Round the neck and cuffs were bands of *broderie anglaise*, and two pleats on the shoulder were matched by two little tucks at the back. This gift was an emblem, I suppose. When it was time to come away, I would bring it back to my bedsit, wash it in the basin, and iron and fold it so that it would be ready for the next visit. Like me.

But on this occasion in September we were in the bedroom and I was packing my things away when Tony interrupted what he was saying – he was talking about Idi Amin of Uganda – to tell me to chuck the blouse in the laundry basket along with one of his shirts. It made sense. We would be back soon and the housekeeper, Mrs Travers, would be in the following day to take care of everything. Mrs Canning was in Vienna for ten days. I remembered the moment well because it gave me such pleasure. That our love was routine, taken for granted, with an immediate future measured in three or four days was comforting. I was often lonely in Cambridge, waiting for Tony's call to the payphone in the hallway. In a passing moment of something like wifely entitlement, I lifted the wicker lid and dropped my blouse on top of his shirt and thought no more about it. Sarah Travers came in three times a week from the nearest village. We once spent a pleasant half-hour shelling peas together at the kitchen table and she told me about her son, gone off to be a hippie in Afghanistan. She said it with pride, as though he'd joined the army for a necessary and dangerous war. I didn't like to think about it too closely, but I assumed she had seen a succession of Tony's women friends pass through the cottage. I don't think she cared, as long as she was paid.

Back on Jesus Green four days went by and I heard nothing. Obediently, I read up on the Factory Acts and the Corn Laws and studied the newspaper. I saw some friends who were passing through, but never wandered far from the phone. On the fifth day I went to Tony's college, left a note with the porter and hurried home, worried that I might have missed his call. I couldn't ring him – my lover had taken care not to give me his home phone number. He rang that evening. His voice was flat. Without greeting, he instructed me to be at the bus stop the following morning at ten. I was halfway through asking him a plaintive question when he hung up. Naturally, I didn't sleep much that night. Amazing to think that I lay awake worrying about *him*, when I should have known in my silly heart that I was for the chop.

At dawn I took a bath and made myself fragrant. By seven I was ready. What a hopeful fool, to have packed a bag with the underwear he liked (black of course, and purple) and plimsolls for walking in the woods. I was at the bus stop by nine twenty-five, worried that he'd be early and disappointed not to find me there. He came around ten fifteen. He pushed open the passenger door and I crawled in, but there was no kiss. Instead he kept both hands on the wheel and pulled away hard from the kerb. We drove ten miles or so and he wouldn't speak to me. His knuckles were white from his grip and he would only look ahead. What was the matter? He wouldn't tell me. And I was frantic, intimidated by the way he swung his little car out across the lanes, overtaking recklessly on rises and bends, as if to warn me of the storm to come.

He doubled back towards Cambridge on a roundabout and

pulled into a lay-by off the A45, a place of oily, littered grass with a kiosk on worn bare ground that sold hot dogs and burgers to lorry drivers. At this time in the morning the stall was shuttered and padlocked and no one else was parked there. We got out. It was the worst kind of day at the end of summer – sunny, windy, dusty. To our right was a widely spaced row of parched sycamore saplings and on the other side of it the traffic was whining and roaring. It was like being on the edge of a race track. The lay-by was a couple of hundred yards long. He set off along it and I kept by his side. To talk we almost had to shout.

The first thing he said was, 'So your little trick didn't work.'

'What trick?'

I quickly turned over the recent past. Since there was no trick, I was suddenly hopeful that there was a simple matter we could straighten out in seconds. We could be laughing about this, I even thought. We could be making love before noon.

We reached the point where the lay-by joined the road. 'Get this clear,' he said, and we stopped. 'You'll never get between Frieda and me.'

'Tony, *what trick*?'

He turned back again in the direction of his car and I followed. 'Bloody nightmare.' He was talking to himself.

I called out over the din. 'Tony. Tell me!'

'Aren't you pleased? Last night we had our worst row in twenty-five years. Aren't you excited by your success?'

Even I, inexperienced and baffled and horrified as I was, could sense the absurdity of this. He was going to tell me in his own way, so I said nothing and waited. We walked back past his car and the closed-up kiosk. To our right was a hedge of high dusty hawthorns. Gaily coloured sweet wrappers and crisp packets were trapped in the spiky branches. There was a used condom, ridiculously long, lying on the grass. A fine place to end an affair.

'Serena, how could you be so stupid?'

I did feel stupid. We stopped again and I said in a quavering voice I couldn't control, 'I honestly don't understand.'

'You wanted her to find your blouse. Well, she found your blouse. You thought she'd be furious and you were right. You thought you could break up my marriage and move in but you were wrong.'

The injustice of this overwhelmed me and it was hard to speak. Somewhere just behind and above the root of my tongue my throat was beginning to tighten. In case there were tears I turned away quickly. I didn't want him to see.

'Of course, you're young and all that. But you should be ashamed.'

When I found it, I hated my croaky pleading voice. 'Tony, you said to put it in your laundry basket.'

'Come on now. You know I said nothing of the sort.'

He said it gently, almost lovingly, like a caring father, one I was about to lose. We should have been having a row, bigger than any he'd ever had with Frieda, I should have been flying at him. But inconveniently I thought I was about to start crying and I was determined not to. I don't cry easily, and when I do I want to be alone. But that soft plummy voice of authority pierced me. It was so confident and kind that I was close to believing it. I already sensed I could never alter his recollection of the previous Sunday or prevent him from dismissing me. I also knew I was in danger of behaving as though I was guilty. Like a shoplifter, crying with relief at being caught. So unfair, so hopeless. I couldn't speak to make my case. Those hours of waiting by the phone and the sleepless night had undone me. The back of my throat went on tightening, other muscles lower down my neck joined in, tugging at my lips, trying to stretch them over my teeth. Something was going to snap, but I couldn't let it, not in front of him. Not when he was so wrong. The only way to hold it down and keep my dignity was to remain silent. To speak would have been to let go. And I was desperate to speak. I needed to tell him how unjust he was being, how he was risking everything between us for a lapse in memory. It was one of those familiar occasions when the mind wants one thing, the body another. Like wanting sex during an exam, or being sick at a wedding. The more I struggled in silence to stay on top of my feelings, the more I hated myself and the calmer he became.

'It was underhand, Serena. I thought you were better than that. I don't find this easy to say, but I'm deeply disappointed.'

He went on in this way while I remained with my back turned. How he had trusted me, encouraged me, had high hopes for me, and I had let him down. It must have been easier for him, talking to the back of my head, not having to look me in the eye. I was beginning to suspect that this was not about a simple mistake, a commonplace failure of memory in a busy, important older man. I thought I saw it all plainly enough. Frieda had come back early from Vienna. For some reason, perhaps a nasty hunch, she had gone out to the cottage. Or they had gone there together. In the bedroom was my laundered blouse. Then came the scene in Suffolk or London, and her ultimatum – get rid of the girl, or march. So Tony had made the obvious decision. But here's the point. He had made another choice too. He had decided to cast himself as the victim, the wronged, the deceived, the rightly furious. He had persuaded himself that he had said nothing to me about the laundry basket. The memory had been erased, and for a purpose. But now he didn't even know he'd erased it. He wasn't even pretending. He actually believed in his disappointment. He really did think that I had done something devious and mean. He was protecting himself from the idea that he'd had a choice. Weak, self-deluding, pompous? All those, but above all, a failure of *reasoning*. High table, monographs, government commissions – meaningless. His reasoning had deserted him. As I saw it, Professor Canning was suffering from a gross intellectual malfunction.

I groped for a tissue in the tight pocket of my jeans and

blew my nose with a sad honking sound. I still could not trust myself to speak.

Tony was saying, 'You know where this all has to lead, don't you?'

Still in his soft-voiced therapeutic mode. I nodded. I knew exactly. He told me anyway. As he did, I watched a van draw up at speed and stop with a clever drifting skid on the gravel by the kiosk. Pop music was playing loudly from the cabin. A young guy with a ponytail and drummer's T-shirt that showed off his muscled brown arms got out and slung two big polythene bags of hamburger buns onto the dirt by the kiosk. Then he was gone with a roar and a cloud of blue smoke which the wind brought straight to us. Yes, I was being dumped, like the buns. I suddenly understood why we were here in this lay-by. Tony was expecting a scene. He didn't want to have it in his tiny car. How would he eject a hysterical girl from the passenger seat? So why not have it here, where he could drive away and leave me to hitch a ride back into town?

Why should I tolerate that? I walked away from him towards his car. I knew what I had to do. We could both remain in the lay-by. Forced into my company for an extra hour, he might be brought to his senses. Or not. It didn't matter. I had my plan. I reached the driver's door, pulled it open and took the keys from the ignition. His whole life on a chunky ring, a big busy masculine array of Chubbs, Banhams and Yales, his office, his house, his second home, his mailbox, safe and second car, and all the other parts of his existence he had kept from me. I drew back my arm to throw the ensemble over the hawthorn hedge. If he could find a way in, let him go through the field on hands and knees among the cows and shit puddles and look for the keys to his life while I watched.

After three years of Newnham tennis my throw would have been reasonably strong. But I wasn't able to show it off. My arm was at the limit of its backswing when I felt his fingers curl round my wrist and tighten. He had the keys off me in seconds. He wasn't rough and I put up no struggle. He pushed round me and got into his car without speaking. He had said enough, and besides, I had just confirmed the worst of his expectations. He tossed my bag onto the ground, slammed the door and started the engine. Now that I had my voice back, what did I say? Again, I was pathetic. I didn't want him to leave. I called stupidly through the car's canvas top, 'Tony, stop pretending that you don't know the truth.'

How ridiculous. Of course he wasn't pretending. That was precisely his failure. He gunned the engine a couple of times in case there was anything else I wanted to say that needed drowning out. Then he pulled forward – slowly at first, concerned perhaps that I would throw myself over the windscreen or under the wheels. But I stood there like a tragic fool and I watched him go. I saw his brake lights come on as he slowed to join the traffic. Then he was gone, and it was over.

3

I didn't cancel my appointment with MI5. I had nothing else in my life now, and with Lucy's affairs settled for the moment, even the Bishop was encouraging about my career prospects in Health and Social Security. Two days after the lay-by scene I went to my interview in Great Marlborough Street, on the western edge of Soho. I waited on a hard chair set down for me by a mutely disapproving secretary in a dim corridor with a concrete floor. I don't think I'd ever been in such a depressing building. Along from where I sat was a row of iron-framed windows formed out of the sort of bubbled glass bricks I associated with basements. But it was the dirt, inside and out, not the bricks, that deterred the light. On the window ledge nearest me were piles of newspapers covered in black grit. I wondered whether the job, if I was offered it, would turn out to be a form of sustained punishment administered at a distance by Tony. There was a complex odour drifting up a stairwell. I passed the time trying to identify its multiple sources. Perfume, cigarettes, ammonia-based cleaning fluid and something organic, perhaps once edible.

My first interview, with a brisk and friendly woman called Joan, consisted mostly of form-filling and answering simple biographical questions. An hour later I was back in the same room with Joan and an army type called Harry Tapp, who had a sandy toothbrush moustache and chain-smoked from a slim gold case. I took to his old-fashioned clipped voice, and the way he softly drummed the yellow fingers of his right hand whenever he spoke and rested them when he listened. In the course of fifty minutes the three of us colluded in the construction of a character profile for me. I was essentially a mathematician with other suitable interests. But how on earth had I ended up with a third? I lied or distorted as required and said that in my final year I had, quite foolishly, given my workload, become interested in writing, in the Soviet Union and in the work of Solzhenitsyn. Mr Tapp was intrigued to hear my views, which I recited, having read through my old pieces as advised by my departed lover. And beyond university, the self I invented was derived entirely from my summer with him. Who else did I have? Sometimes I *was* Tony. I had a passion, it turned out, for the English countryside, in particular Suffolk, and for one glorious ancient pollarded wood, where I liked to ramble and pick ceps in the autumn. Joan knew about ceps and while Tapp looked on impatiently, we quickly swapped recipes. She had never heard of pancetta. Tapp asked me if I had ever taken an interest in encryption. No, but I confessed a weakness for current affairs. We hurried through the issues of the day – the miners' and dockers' strikes, the Common Market, the mayhem in Belfast. I spoke the language of a *Times* leader, echoing patrician, thoughtful-sounding opinions that could hardly be opposed. For example, when we arrived at the 'permissive society' I cited *The Times*'s view that the sexual freedom of individuals had to be balanced against the needs of children for security and love. Who could take a stand against that? I was getting into my stride. Then there was my passion for English history. Again, Harry Tapp perked up. What in particular? The Glorious Revolution. Ah now, that was very interesting indeed! And then, later, who was my intellectual hero? I talked of Churchill, not as a politician, but as a historian (I summarised the 'incomparable' account of Trafalgar), as the

Nobel Laureate for Literature, and then as the watercolourist. I'd always had a particular fondness for the little-known *Marrakech Rooftop Laundry*, which I believed was now in a private collection.

Prompted by something that Tapp said, I daubed onto my self-portrait a passion for chess without mentioning that I hadn't played in more than three years. He asked me if I was familiar with the Zilber–Tal endgame of 1958. I wasn't but I could plausibly elaborate on the famous Saavedra position. In fact, I had never in my life been so clever as during that interview. And not since my articles in *?Quis?* had I been so pleased with myself. There was little I could not talk about. I could give my ignorance on any matter a certain shine. My voice was Tony's. I spoke like a master of a college, the chairman of a government committee of inquiry, a country squire. Join MI5? I was ready to lead it. It was no surprise then, after I had been asked to leave the room and called back five minutes later, to hear Mr Tapp tell me he had decided to offer me a job. What else could he do?

For several seconds I didn't take in what he was saying. And when I did, I thought he was teasing or testing me. I was to fill the post of junior assistant officer. I already knew that in Civil Service rankings this was the lowest of the low. My principal duties would be in filing, indexing and related library work. With hard work and in time, I might rise to assistant officer. I didn't allow my expression to betray what I suddenly understood – that I'd made a terrible mistake, or Tony had. Or that this really was the punishment he had devised for me. I was not being recruited as an 'officer'. Not a spy then, no front-line work. Pretending to be pleased, I enquired tentatively, and it was confirmed by Joan as a routine fact of life: men and women had separate career tracks and only men became officers. Of course, of course, I said. Of course I knew that. I was the clever young woman who knew everything. I was too proud to let them see how misinformed I had been or how put out I was. I heard myself accept with enthusiasm. Marvellous!

Thank you! I was given a start date. Can't wait! We stood and Mr Tapp shook my hand and drifted away. As Joan walked me down to the entrance, she explained that his offer was subject to the usual vetting procedures. If I was accepted, I would be working over in Curzon Street. I would be obliged to sign the Official Secrets Act and be bound by its strict provisions. Of course, I kept saying. Marvellous. Thank you.

I left the building in a disturbed and dark state of mind. Even before I said goodbye to Joan I'd decided I didn't want the job. It was an insult, a lowly secretarial position at two-thirds the usual rate. With tips I could have earned double as a waitress. They could keep their job. I'd write them a note. However disappointing, that at least seemed clear. I felt emptied out, I had no idea what I was supposed to be doing or where I should go. My money was running out for my Cambridge room. No choice then but to go back to my parents, become a daughter again, a child, and face the Bishop's indifference and my mother's organising zeal. Worse though than that prospect was this sudden fit of lover's grief. Impersonating Tony for an hour and raiding memories of our summer for my own use had brought the affair to life in my thoughts. I had talked myself into understanding the full measure of my loss. It was as though we'd been having a long conversation and he'd abruptly turned away, leaving me with an overpowering sense of his absence. I missed him and yearned for him, and knew I'd never get him back.

Desolate, I went slowly along Great Marlborough Street. The job and Tony were twin aspects of one thing, a summer's sentimental education, and it had disintegrated around me in forty-eight hours. He was back with his wife and his college, and I had nothing. No love, no job. Only the chill of loneliness. And the sorrow was compounded by the memory of the way he'd turned on me. So unfair! I glanced across the road and by a nasty coincidence found myself approaching the mock Tudor facade of Liberty's, where Tony had bought the blouse.

Trying not to feel crushed, I quickly turned down Carnaby Street and picked my way through the crowds. Whining guitar music and the scent of patchouli from a basement shop made me think of my sister and all the trouble at home. Ranks of 'psychedelic' shirts and Sergeant Pepper-ish tasselled military suits hung on long racks on the pavement. Available for like-minded hordes desperate to express their individuality. Well, my mood was sour. I went down Regent Street, then turned left, penetrating deeper into Soho, and walked along streets filthy with litter and abandoned snacks, ketchup-streaked burgers and hotdogs and cartons squelched into the pavement and gutter, and rubbish sacks heaped around lamp posts. The word 'adult' was everywhere in red neon. In windows, items on mock-velvet plinths, whips, dildoes, erotic ointments, a studded mask. A fat guy in a leather jacket, some kind of strip-joint barker, called out to me from a doorway a single indistinct word that sounded like Toy! Perhaps it was Oi! Someone whistled at me. I hurried on, careful to look no one in the eye. I was still thinking of Lucy. Unfair to associate this quarter with her, but the new spirit of liberation that had got my sister arrested and pregnant had also permitted these shops (and, I might have added, my own affair with an older man). Lucy had told me more than once that the past was a burden, that it was time to tear everything down. A lot of people were thinking that way. A seedy, careless insurrection was in the air. But thanks to Tony I now knew with what trouble it had been assembled, Western civilisation, imperfect as it was. We suffered from faulty governance, our freedoms were incomplete. But in this part of the world our rulers no longer had absolute power, savagery was mostly a private affair. Whatever was under my feet in the streets of Soho, we had raised ourselves above filth. The cathedrals, the parliaments, the paintings, the courts of law, the libraries and the labs – far too precious to pull down.

Perhaps it was Cambridge and the cumulative effect of so many ancient buildings and lawns, of seeing how kind time was to stone, or perhaps I simply lacked youthful courage and was cautious and prim. But this inglorious revolution wasn't for me. I didn't want a sex shop in every town, I didn't want my sister's kind of life, I didn't want history put to the torch. Come travelling? I wanted to travel with civilised men like Tony Canning, who took for granted the importance of laws and institutions and thought constantly of how to improve them. If only he wanted to travel with *me*. If only he wasn't such a bastard.

The half-hour it took me to wander from Regent Street to the Charing Cross Road arranged my fate for me. I changed my mind, I decided to take the job after all and have order and purpose in my life and some independence. There may have been a passing touch of masochism in my decision – as a rejected lover I deserved no more than to be an office skivvy. And nothing else was on offer. I could leave behind Cambridge and its association with Tony, and I could lose myself in London's crowds – there was something pleasingly tragic about that. I would tell my parents I had a proper Civil Service job in the Department of Health and Social Security. It turned out that I needn't have been so secretive, but at the time it rather thrilled me to mislead them.

I returned to my bedsit that afternoon, gave notice to my landlord and began to pack up my room. The following day I arrived home in the cathedral close with all my belongings. My mother was delighted for me and embraced me lovingly. To my astonishment, the Bishop gave me a twenty-pound note. Three weeks later I started my new life in London.

Did I know Millie Trimingham, the single mother who would one day become Director General? When, in later years, it became permissible to tell everyone that you once worked for MI5, I was often asked this question. If it irritated me it was because I suspected it concealed another: with my Cambridge connections why didn't I rise nearly as high? I joined three years after she did, and, it's true, I started out

following her path, the one she describes in her memoir –
same grim building in Mayfair, same training section in a
long, thin, ill-lit room, same tasks, both meaningless and
intriguing. But when I joined in 1972 Trimingham was already
a legend among the new girls. Remember, we were in our
early twenties, she was in her mid-thirties. My new friend
Shirley Shilling pointed her out to me. Trimingham was at
the end of a corridor, back-lit by a grubby window, a wedge
of files under one arm, in urgent conference with an anonymous man who looked to be from the cloudy summits of
authority. She seemed at ease, almost an equal, clearly
empowered to make a joke, causing him to give out a shout
of a laugh and place his hand on her forearm briefly, as if
to say, restrain that wit of yours or you'll make my life
impossible.

She was admired by us new-joiners because we'd heard
that she'd mastered the filing system and the intricacies of
the Registry so quickly that she was moved on in less than
two months. Some said it was weeks, even days. We believed
there was a hint of rebellion in the clothes she wore, bright
prints and scarves, authentic, bought in Pakistan, where
she'd worked for the Service in some lawless outpost. This
was what we told ourselves. We should have asked her. A
lifetime later I read in her memoir that she did clerical work
in the Islamabad office. I still don't know if she took part in
the Women's Revolt of that year, when female graduates
in MI5 started campaigning for better prospects. They wanted
to be allowed to run agents themselves, like male desk officers.
My guess is that Trimingham would have been sympathetic
to the aims, but wary of collective action, speeches and reso-
lutions. I've never understood why word of the Revolt never
reached our intake. Perhaps we were considered too junior.
Above all, it was the spirit of the age that slowly changed
the Service, but she was the first to break out, first to dig the
hole in the ceiling of the women's block. She did it quietly,
with tact. The rest of us scrambled up noisily behind her. I

was one of the last. And when she had been transferred out of the training section, it was to confront the hard new future – IRA terrorism – whereas many of us who followed lingered a while, fighting the old battles with the Soviet Union.

Most of the ground floor was taken up by the Registry, that vast memory bank where more than three hundred well-born secretaries toiled like slaves on the pyramids, processing file requests, returning or distributing files to desk case officers round the building and sorting incoming material. The system was thought to work so well that it held out far too long against the computer age. This was the last redoubt, the ultimate tyranny of paper. Just as an army recruit is made to embrace his new life by peeling spuds and scouring the parade ground with a toothbrush, so I passed my first few months compiling members' lists of provincial branches of the Communist Party of Great Britain and opening files on all those not already accounted for. My special concern was Gloucestershire. (In her time, Trimingham had Yorkshire.) In my first month I opened a file on the headmaster of a grammar school in Stroud who had attended an open meeting of his local branch one Saturday evening in July 1972. He wrote his name on a sheet of paper that was circulated by the comrades, but then he must have decided not to join. He was on none of the subscription lists that had been procured for us. But I chose to start a file on him because he was in a position to influence young minds. This was on my own initiative, my very first, and that's why I remember his name, Harold Templeman, and his year of birth. If Templeman had decided to get out of schoolmastering (he was only forty-three) and apply for a Civil Service job that brought him into contact with classified information, the vetting procedure would have led someone to his file. Templeman would have been questioned about that evening in July (surely he would have been impressed) or his application would have been dismissed and he would never have known why. Perfect. In theory, at least. We were still learning the demanding protocols that determined what was acceptable material for a file. During the early months of 1973 such a closed, functioning system, however pointless, was a comfort to me. All twelve of us working in that room knew well enough that any agent run by the Soviet Centre was never going to announce himself to us by joining the Communist Party of Great Britain. I didn't care.

On my way to work I used to reflect on the immensity that separated my job description from the reality. I could say to myself – since I could say it to no one else – that I worked for MI5. That had a certain ring. Even now it stirs me a little, to think of that pale little thing wanting to do her bit for the country. But I was just one more office girl in a mini-skirt, jammed in with the rest, thousands of us pouring down the filthy connecting Tube tunnels at the change for Green Park, where the litter and grit and stinking subterranean gales that we took as our due slapped our faces and restyled our hair. (London is so much cleaner now.) And when I got to work, I was still an office girl, typing straight-backed on a giant Remington in a smoky room like hundreds of thousands across the capital, fetching files, deciphering male hand-writing, hurrying back from my lunch break. I even earned less than most. And just like the working girl in a Betjeman poem Tony once read to me, I too washed my smalls in the hand basin of my bedsit.

As a clerical officer of the lowest grade my first week's pay after deductions was fourteen pounds thirty pence, in the novel decimal currency, which had not yet lost its unserious, half-baked, fraudulent air. I paid four pounds a week for my room, and an extra pound for electricity. My travel cost just over a pound, leaving me eight pounds for food and all else. I present these details not to complain, but in the spirit of Jane Austen, whose novels I had once raced through at Cambridge. How can one understand the inner life of a character, real or fictional, without knowing the state of her finances? *Miss Frome, newly installed in diminutive lodgings*

*at number seventy St Augustine's Road, London North West
One, had less than one thousand a year and a heavy heart.*
I managed week to week, but I did not feel part of a
glamorous clandestine world.

Still, I was young, and maintaining a heavy heart all
moments of the day was beyond me. My chum, at lunch
breaks and evenings out, was Shirley Shilling, whose alliterative name in the dependable old currency caught something
of her plump lop-sided smile and old-fashioned taste for
fun. She was in trouble with our chain-smoking supervisor,
Miss Ling, in the very first week for 'taking too long in the
lavatory'. Actually, Shirley had hurried out of the building
at ten o'clock to buy herself a frock for a party that night,
had run all the way to Marks & Spencer in Oxford Street,
found the very thing, tried it on, tried the next size up, paid
and got a bus back – in twenty minutes. There would have
been no time at lunch because she planned to try on shoes.
None of the rest of us new girls would have dared so much.

So what did we make of her? The cultural changes of the
past several years may have seemed profound but they had
clipped no one's social antennae. Within a minute, no, less,
by the time Shirley had uttered three words, we would have
known that she was of humble origins. Her father owned a
bed and sofa shop in Ilford called Bedworld, her school was
a giant local comprehensive, her university was Nottingham.
She was the first in her family to stay on at school past the
age of sixteen. MI5 may have been wanting to demonstrate
a more open recruitment policy, but Shirley happened to be
exceptional. She typed at twice the speed of the best of us,
her memory – for faces, files, conversations, procedures – was
sharper than ours, she asked fearless, interesting questions.
It was a sign of the times that a large minority of the girls
admired her – her mild Cockney had a touch of modern
glamour, her voice and manner reminded us of Twiggy or
Keith Richards or Bobby Moore. In fact her brother was a
professional footballer who played for the Wolverhampton

Wanderers reserves. This club, so we were obliged to learn, had reached the final of the new-fangled UEFA Cup that year. Shirley was exotic, she represented a confident new world.

Some girls were snobbish about Shirley, but none of us was as worldly and cool. Many of our intake would have been presentable at court to Queen Elizabeth as debutantes if the practice hadn't been terminated fifteen years earlier. A few were the daughters or nieces of serving or retired officers. Two-thirds of us had degrees from the older universities. We spoke in identical tones, we were socially confident and could have passed muster at a country house weekend. But there was always a trace of an apology in our style, a polite impulse to defer, especially when one of the senior officers, one of the ex-colonial types, came through our crepuscular room. Then most of us (I exclude myself, of course) were the mistresses of the lowered gaze and the compliant near-smile. Among the new-joiners a low-level unacknowledged search was on for a decent husband from the right sort of background.

Shirley, however, was unapologetically loud and, being in no mood to marry, looked everyone in the eye. She had a knack or weakness for laughing boisterously at her own anecdotes – not, I thought, because she found herself funny, but because she thought that life needed celebrating and wanted others to join in. Loud people, especially loud women, always attract enemies and Shirley had one or two who despised her heartily, but in general she breezed her way into our affections, mine especially. It may have helped her, not to have been threateningly beautiful. She was large, at least thirty pounds overweight, size sixteen to my ten, and she actually told us that the word we must use of her was 'willowy'. Then she laughed. Her round, somewhat pudgy face was rescued, even blessed, by being rarely at rest, she was so animated. Her best feature was the slightly unusual combination of black hair, naturally curled, with pale freckles across the bridge of her nose, and greyish-blue eyes. And her smile tilted downwards to the right, giving her a look I can't quite find the word for. Somewhere between *rakish* and *game*. Despite her limited circumstances, she had been around more than most of us. In the year after university she hitchhiked alone to Istanbul, sold her blood, bought a motorbike, broke her leg, shoulder and elbow, fell in love with a Syrian doctor, had an abortion, and was brought home to England from Anatolia on a private yacht in return for a little on-board cooking.

But from my point of view none of these adventures was as exotic as the notebook she carried with her always, a childish pink plastic-covered thing with a short pencil tucked into the spine. For a while she wouldn't say what she wrote, but one evening in a Muswell Hill pub she owned up to jotting down 'the clever or funny or daft stuff' people said. She also wrote 'tiny stories about stories' and otherwise just 'thoughts'. The notebook was always within reach and she'd write in it mid-conversation. The other girls in the office teased her about it, and I was curious to know if she had wider writing ambitions. I talked to her about the books I was reading, and though she listened politely, even intently, she never offered an opinion of her own. I wasn't sure she did any reading at all. Either that or she was protecting a big secret.

She lodged just a mile to the north of me in a tiny third-floor room that overlooked the thunderous Holloway Road. Within a week of introducing ourselves we started meeting in the evenings. Soon afterwards I discovered that our friendship had earned us the office nickname 'Laurel and Hardy', the reference being to our relative sizes, not a taste for slapstick. I didn't tell Shirley. It never occurred to her that a night out should take place anywhere other than in pubs, by preference noisy ones with music. She had no interest in the places round Mayfair. Within a few months I was familiar with the human ecology, the gradations of decency and decay, of the pubs around Camden, Kentish Town and Islington.

45

It was in Kentish Town, on our first excursion, that I saw
in an Irish pub a terrible fight. In films a punch to the jaw is
banal but it's extraordinary to witness in reality, though the
sound, the bony crunch, is far more muted and wet. To a
sheltered young woman, it looked reckless beyond belief, so
careless of retaliation, of prospects, of life itself, those fists
that wielded a pick-axe by day for Murphy the builders, pile-
driving into a face. We watched from our bar stools. I saw
something curve through the air past a beer-pump handle
– a button or a tooth. More people were joining in, there was
a fair amount of shouting, and the barman, a handy-looking
fellow himself with a caduceus tattooed above his wrist, was
speaking into the phone. Shirley put an arm about my shoulders and propelled me towards the door. Our rum and cokes
with melting ice were behind us on the bar.

'Police on their way, might want witnesses. Best to go.'
Out in the street we remembered her coat. 'Ah forget it,'
she said with a wave of her hand. She was already walking
on. 'I *'ate* that coat.'

We weren't looking for men on our nights out. Instead, we
talked a good deal – about our families, about our lives so
far. She spoke of her Syrian doctor, I spoke of Jeremy Mott,
but not of Tony Canning. Office gossip was strictly forbidden,
even to us lowly beginners, and it was a matter of pride to
obey instructions. Besides, I had the impression that Shirley
was already doing more important work than me. It was bad
form to ask. When our pub conversation was interrupted,
when men did approach us, they came looking for me and
got Shirley instead. I was content to be mute at her side as
she took over. They couldn't get past the banter and laughter,
the bright chatty questions about what they did and where
they were from, and they retreated after subsidising a round
or two of rum and cokes. In the hippy pubs around Camden
Lock, which was not yet a tourist attraction, the long-haired
men were more insidious and persistent with softer come-ons
about their inner feminine spirit, the collective unconscious,

the transit of Venus and related hokum. Shirley repelled them with uncomprehending friendliness while I shrank from these reminders of my sister.

We would be in that part of town for the music, drinking our way towards the Dublin Castle on Parkway. Shirley had a boyish passion for rock and roll and in the early seventies the best bands played in pubs, often cavernous Victorian establishments. I surprised myself by developing a passing taste for this racy, unpretentious music. My bedsit was dull and I was glad to have something to do in the evenings apart from reading novels. One evening, when we knew each other better, Shirley and I had a conversation about our ideal man. She told me about her dream, an introspective bony guy, just over six feet, jeans, black T-shirt, cropped hair and hollow cheeks and a guitar round his neck. We must have seen two dozen versions of this archetype as she escorted me to all pub venues between Canvey Island and Shepherd's Bush. We heard Bees Make Honey (my favourite), Roogalator (hers) – and Dr Feelgood, Ducks Deluxe, Kilburn and the High Roads. Not like me at all, to be standing in a sweaty crowd with a half pint in my hand, my ears buzzing with the din. It gave me some innocent pleasure to think how horrified the counter-culture crowd around us would be, to know that we were the ultimate enemy from the 'straight' grey world of MI5. Laurel and Hardy, the new shock troops of internal security.

4

Towards the end of winter in 1973 I received a letter forwarded by my mother from my old friend Jeremy Mott. He was still in Edinburgh, still happy with his doctoral work and his new life of semi-secretive affairs, each one ending, so he claimed, without much trouble or remorse. I read the letter one morning on my way to work on one of the rare occasions when I'd managed to push through the packed fetid carriage and find myself a seat. The important paragraph began halfway down the second page. To Jeremy it would have been no more than an item of serious gossip.

You remember my tutor, Tony Canning. We went to his rooms once for tea. Last September he left his wife, Frieda. They were married for more than thirty years. No explanation apparently. There'd been rumours around the college that he'd been seeing a younger woman out at his cottage in Suffolk. But that wasn't it. The word was he dumped her too. I had a letter from a friend last month. He heard it from the Master's mouth. All this has been an open secret around the college but no one thought to tell me. Canning was ill. Why not say it? He had something badly wrong and he was beyond treatment. In October he resigned his fellowship and took himself off to an island in the Baltic, where he rented a small house. He was looked after by a local woman, who may have been a little more than a housekeeper. Towards the end he was moved to a cottage hospital on another island. His son visited him there and Frieda went too. I'm assuming you didn't see the obituary in *The Times* in February. I'm sure I would have heard from you if you had. I never knew he was in the SOE towards the end of the war. Quite the hero, parachuting into Bulgaria by night and getting seriously wounded in the chest during an ambush. Then four years in MI5 in the late forties. Our fathers' generation – their lives were so much more meaningful than ours, don't you think? Tony was awfully good to me. I wish someone had let me know. At least I could have written to him. Why don't you come and cheer me up? There's a sweet little spare room off the kitchen. But I think I've told you that before.

Why not say it? Cancer. In the early seventies it was only just coming to an end, the time when people used to drop their voices at the word. Cancer was a disgrace, the victim's that is, a form of failure, a smear and a dirty defect, of personality rather than flesh. Back then I'm sure I'd have taken for granted Tony's need to creep away without explanation, to winter with his awful secret by a cold sea. The sand dunes of his childhood, bitter winds, treeless inland marshes, and Tony walking by the empty beach hunched in his donkey jacket with his shame, his nasty secret and his increasing need for another nap. Sleep coming in like a tide. Of course he needed to be alone. I'm sure I didn't question any of that. What impressed and shocked me was the planning. Telling me to put my blouse in the laundry basket, then pretending to forget that he had in order to make himself obnoxious to me so I wouldn't follow him and complicate his last months. Did it really have to be so elaborate? Or severe?

On my way to work I blushed to remember how I'd thought

my reasoning about feelings was superior to his. I blushed just before I started to cry. Passengers nearest me on the crowded Tube decently looked away. He must have known how much past I would have to rewrite when I heard the real story. There must have been some comfort in believing that I would forgive him then. That seemed very sad. But why had there been no posthumous letter, explaining, remembering something between us, saying goodbye, acknowledging me, giving me something to live with, anything to replace our last scene? For weeks afterwards I tormented myself with suspicions that such a letter would have been intercepted by the 'housekeeper' or Frieda.

Tony in exile, trudging the lonely beaches, without the playmate-brother who'd shared the carefree years – Terence Canning was killed in the D-Day landings – and without his college, his friends, his wife. Above all, without me. Tony could have been looked after by Frieda, he could have been in the cottage or in his bedroom at home, with his books, with visits from his friends and his son. Even I could have sneaked in somehow, disguised as a former student. Flowers, champagne, family and old friends, old photographs – wasn't that how people try to organise their deaths, at least when they were not fighting for breath or writhing in pain or dumbly immobilised by terror?

In the weeks that followed, I replayed scores of small moments. Those afternoon naps that made me so impatient, that grey morning face I couldn't bear to look at. At the time I'd thought it was simply how it had to be, when you were fifty-four. There was one exchange in particular I kept returning to – those few seconds in the bedroom by the laundry basket when he was telling me about Idi Amin and the expelled Ugandan Asians. It was a big story at the time. The vicious dictator was driving his countrymen out, they had British passports, and Ted Heath's government, ignoring the outrage in the tabloids, was insisting, decently enough, that they must be allowed to settle here. That was Tony's view too. He interrupted himself and without drawing breath said quickly, 'Just drop it in there with mine. We'll be back soon.' Just that, a mundane domestic instruction, and then he continued with his line of thought. Now wasn't that ingenious, when his body was already failing and his plans were taking shape? To orchestrate the moment, see a chance and take it on the wing. Or work something up afterwards. Perhaps less of a trick, more a habit of mind picked up in his time with the SOE. A trick of the trade. As a device, a deception, it was cleverly managed. He threw me off and I was too injured to pursue him. I don't think I really loved him at the time, during those months out at the cottage, but when I heard of his death I soon convinced myself that I did. The trick, his deceit, was far more duplicitous than any married man's love affair. Even then, I admired him for it, but I couldn't quite forgive him.

I went to Holborn public library, where back issues of *The Times* were kept, and looked up the obituary. Idiotically, I skimmed it, scanning it for my name, and then I started again. A whole life in a few columns, and not even a photograph. The Dragon School in Oxford, Marlborough, then Balliol, the Guards, action in the Western Desert, an unexplained gap, and then SOE as Jeremy had described it, followed by four years in the Security Service from 1948. How uncurious I'd been about Tony's war and post war, though I knew he had good connections in MI5. The piece briefly summarised the fifties onwards – journalism, books, public service, Cambridge, death.

And for me, nothing changed. I went on working in Curzon Street while I tended the little shrine of my secret grief. Tony had chosen my profession for me, lent me his woods, ceps, opinions, worldliness. But I had no proof, no tokens, no photograph of him, no letters, not even a scrap of a note because our meetings were arranged by phone. Diligently, I'd returned all the books he lent me as I read them, except one, R.H. Tawney's *Religion and the Rise of Capitalism*. I looked for it everywhere, and went back many times to search forlornly in the same places again. It had sun-faded soft green boards with a cup stain that looped through the author's initials, and a simple 'Canning' in imperious purple ink on the first endpaper, and throughout, on almost every page, his marginalia in hard pencil. So precious. But it had melted away, as only books can, perhaps when I moved out of my Jesus Green room. My surviving keepsakes were a carelessly donated bookmark, of which more later, and my job. He had dispatched me to this grubby office in Leconfield House. I didn't like it, but it was the legacy and I could not have tolerated being anywhere else.

Working patiently, without complaint, humbly submitting to the disparagements of Miss Ling – this was how I kept the flame. If I failed to be efficient, if I arrived late or complained or thought about leaving MI5, I would have been letting him down. I persuaded myself of a great love in ruins, and so I racked up the pain. *Akrasia!* Whenever I took extra care in turning some desk officer's scrawl into an error-free typed memo in triplicate, it was because it was my duty to honour the memory of the man I had loved.

There were twelve in our intake, including three men. Of these, two were married businessmen in their thirties and of no interest to anyone. There was a third, Greatorex, on whom ambitious parents had conferred the name Maximilian. He was about thirty, had jutting ears and was extremely reticent, whether from shyness or superiority none of us was certain. He'd been transferred across from MI6 and was already desk officer status, merely sitting in with us new-joiners to see how our systems worked. The other two men, the business types, were also not so far now from officer status. Whatever I'd felt at the interview, I no longer minded so much. As our chaotic training proceeded, I absorbed the general spirit of the place and, taking my cue from the other girls, began to accept that in this small part of the adult world, and unlike in the rest of the Civil Service, women were of a lower caste.

We were spending even more time now with the scores of other girls in the Registry, learning the strict rules of file retrieval and discovering, without being told, that there were concentric circles of security clearance and that we languished in outer darkness. The clattering temperamental trolleys on their tracks delivered files to the various departments around the building. Whenever one of them went wrong, Greatorex knew how to fix it with a set of miniature screwdrivers he kept on him. Among the more snobbish girls this earned him the nickname 'Handyman', confirming him as a ridiculous prospect. That was fortunate for me because, even in my condition of mourning, I was beginning to take an interest in Maximilian Greatorex.

Occasionally, in the late afternoon, we would be 'invited' to attend a lecture. It would have been unthinkable not to go. The subject never wandered far from communism, its theory and practice, the geo-political struggle, the naked intent of the Soviet Union to attain world dominance. I'm making these talks sound more interesting than they were. The theory and practice element was by far the largest, and most of that was theory. This was because the talks were given by an ex-RAF man, Archibald Jowell, who had gone into the whole thing, perhaps in an evening class, and was anxious to share what he knew of dialectics and related concepts. If you were to close your eyes, as many did, you could easily imagine that you were at a Communist Party meeting in somewhere like Stroud, for it was not Jowell's intention or remit to demolish Marxist–Leninist thought, or even express scepticism. He wanted us to understand the mind of the enemy 'from the inside', and to know thoroughly the theoretical base from which it worked. Coming at the end of a day of typing and of trying to learn what constituted a file-worthy fact in the mind of the fearsome Miss Ling, Jowell's earnest, haranguing delivery had a deadly, soporific effect on most of the intake. Everyone believed that to be caught out in a shameful moment when neck muscles relax and the head snaps forward might damage career prospects. But believing was not quite enough. Heavy eyelids in the late afternoon had their own logic, their own peculiar weight.

So what was wrong with me that I sat upright and alert for the entire hour on the edge of my chair, legs crossed, notebook pressed against my bare knee as I wrote my notes? I was a mathematician and a former chess player, and I was a girl in need of comfort. Dialectical materialism was a safely enclosed system, like the vetting procedures, but more rigorous and intricate. More like an equation of Leibniz or Hilbert. Human aspirations, societies, history, and a method of analysis in an entanglement as expressive and inhumanly perfect as a Bach fugue. Who could sleep through it? The answer was everyone but myself and Greatorex. He would sit a knight's move ahead of me and to my left, with the visible page of his notebook covered in dense loopy writing.

Once, my attention drifted from the lecture as I considered him. It was the case that his ears protruded from strange hillocks of bone at the sides of his skull and those ears were awfully pink. But the effect was much exaggerated by his old-fashioned haircut, the standard military short back and sides, a style which revealed a deep groove down his nape. He reminded me of Jeremy and, less comfortably, of some of the undergraduate mathematicians at Cambridge, the ones who had humiliated me in tutorials. But his facial appearance was misleading, for his body looked lean and strong. In my thoughts I restyled his hair, growing it out so that it filled the space between the tips of his ears and his head, and covered the top of his collar, perfectly permissible now even in Leconfield House. The mustard-coloured check tweed jacket should go. Even from my oblique angle I could see that his tie knot was too small. He needed to start calling himself Max and keep his screwdrivers in a drawer. He was writing in brown ink. That too would have to change.

'And so I return to my starting point,' ex-Flight Commander Jowell was saying in conclusion. 'Ultimately the power and endurance of Marxism, as with any other theoretical scheme, rests with its capacity to seduce intelligent men and women. And this one most certainly can. Thank you.'

Our bleary group roused itself to stand respectfully as the lecturer left the room. When he was gone Max turned and looked right at me. It was as if the vertical groove at the base of his skull was telepathically sensitive. He knew I'd been rearranging his entire being.

I was the one who looked away.

He indicated the pen in my hand. 'Taking lots of notes.'

I said, 'It was fascinating.'

He started to say something, then changed his mind and with an impatient downward gesture with his hand he turned from me and left the room.

But we became friends. Because he reminded me of Jeremy, I lazily assumed that he preferred men, though I hoped I was wrong. I hardly expected him to speak of it, especially in these offices. The security world despised homosexuals, at least outwardly, which made them vulnerable to blackmail, which made them unemployable in the intelligence services and therefore despicable. But while I fantasised about Max I could at least tell myself that I must be getting over Tony. And Max, as I tried to make everyone call him, was a good addition. I thought at first we might make a threesome around town with Shirley, but she told me he was creepy and not to be trusted. And he didn't like pubs or cigarette smoke, or loud music, so we often sat after work on a bench in Hyde Park or Berkeley Square. He couldn't talk about it and I wouldn't ask, but my impression was that he'd worked for a while at Cheltenham, in signals intelligence. He was thirty-two and lived alone in one part of the wing of a country house near Egham, on a bend in the Thames. He said more than once I should come and visit, but there was never a specific invitation. He came from a family of academics, was educated at Winchester and

Harvard, where he did a law degree and then another in psychology, but he was haunted by the idea that he had made the wrong choices, that he should have been studying something practical like engineering. At one point he had thought of apprenticing himself to a watch designer in Geneva, but his parents talked him out of it. His father was a philosopher, his mother a social anthropologist, and Maximilian was their only child. They wanted him to have a life of the mind and thought he shouldn't be fiddling about with his hands. After a short unhappy spell teaching at a crammer, some freelance journalism and travelling, he came into the Service through a business friend of an uncle.

It was a warm spring that year and our friendship blossomed with the trees and shrubs around our various benches. Early on, in my eagerness, I ran ahead of our intimacy and asked if pressure from academic parents bearing down on an only child might have caused him to be shy. The question offended him, as though I'd insulted his family. He had a typically English distaste for psychological explanation. His manner was stiff as he explained that he didn't recognise himself in the term. If he held back with strangers it was because he believed that it was best to go carefully until he understood what he was dealing with. He was perfectly at ease with people he knew and liked. And so it turned out. Gently prompted, I told him everything – my family, my Cambridge, my poor maths degree, my column in *?Quis?*.

'I heard about your column,' he said, to my surprise. Then he added something that pleased me. 'The word around the place is that you've read everything worth reading. You're up on modern literature and all that.'

It was a release to talk to someone at last about Tony. Max had even heard of him, and remembered a government commission, a history book and one or two other scraps, one of which was a public argument over funding for the arts.

'What did you say his island was called?'

At that point, my mind emptied. I had known the name

so well. It was synonymous with death. I said, 'It's suddenly gone from me.'

'Finnish? Swedish?'

'Finnish. In the Åland archipelago.'

'Was it Lemland?'

'Doesn't sound right. It'll come to me.'

'Let me know when it does.'

I was surprised by his insistence. 'Why does it matter?'

'D'you know, I've been around the Baltic a bit. Tens of thousands of islands. One of the best-kept secrets of modern tourism. Thank God everybody flees south in summer. Clearly, your Canning was a man of taste.'

We left it at that. But a month or so later, we were sitting in Berkeley Square trying to reconstruct the lyrics of the famous song about a nightingale singing there. Max had told me he was a self-taught pianist who liked to play show tunes and soppy crooning songs from the forties and fifties, music as unfashionable then as his haircut. I happened to know this particular song from a school revue. We were partly singing, partly speaking the charming words, *I may be right, I may be wrong/But I'm perfectly willing to swear/That when you turned and smiled at me/A nightingale . . .* when Max broke off and said, 'Was it Kumlinge?'

'Yes, that's it. How did you know?'

'Well, I've heard it's very beautiful.'

'I think he liked the isolation.'

'He must have.'

As the spring wore on I grew even fonder of Max, to the point of mild obsession. When I wasn't with him, when I was out in the evening with Shirley, I felt incomplete and restless. It was a relief to be back at work, where I could see him across the desks, his head bent over his papers. But that was never enough and soon I would be trying to arrange our next encounter. It had to be faced, I had a taste for a certain ill-dressed, old-fashioned kind of man (Tony didn't count), big-boned and thin and awkwardly intelligent. There was

something remote and upright in Max's manner. His automatic restraint made me feel clumsy and overemphatic. I
worried that he didn't actually like me and was too civil to
say so. I imagined that he had all manner of private rules,
hidden notions of correctness that I was constantly trans-
gressing. My unease sharpened my interest in him. What
animated him, the subject that breathed warmth into his
manner, was Soviet communism. He was a Cold Warrior of
a superior sort. Where others loathed and raged, Max believed
that good intentions had combined with human nature to
devise a tragedy of sullen entrapment. The happiness and
fulfilment of hundreds of millions across the Russian empire
had been fatally compromised. No one, not even its leaders,
would have chosen what they now had. The trick was to offer
escape by degrees, without loss of face, by patient coaxing
and incentives, by building trust while standing firm against
what he called a truly terrible idea.

He was certainly not the sort I could question about his
love life. I wondered if he had a male lover living with him
in Egham. I even formed an idea of going down there to take
a look. That's how bad things were getting. Wanting what I
assumed I could not have heightened my feelings. But I also
wondered if he might, like Jeremy, be able to give a woman
pleasure without getting much for himself. Not ideal, not
reciprocal, but it wouldn't be so bad for me. Better than pointless longing.

We were walking in the park one early evening after work.
The subject was the Provisional IRA – I suspected he had
some insider knowledge. He was telling me about an article
he'd read when, on an impulse, I took his arm and asked if
he wanted to kiss me.

'Not particularly.'

'I'd like you to.'

We stopped in the centre of the path where it went between
two trees, obliging people to squeeze around us. It was a
deep, passionate kiss, or a good imitation of one. I thought

he might be compensating for a lack of desire. When he drew away, I tried to pull him back towards me, but he resisted.

'That's it for now,' he said, touching the tip of my nose with his forefinger, acting the firm parent talking down to a demanding child. So, playing along, I made a sulky moue and meekly put my hand in his and we walked on. I knew the kiss was going to make things harder for me, but at least we were holding hands for the first time. He disengaged a few minutes later.

We sat on the grass, well away from other people, and returned to the Provos. There had been bombs in Whitehall and at Scotland Yard the previous month. The Service was continuing to reorganise itself. A handful, the more promising handful, Shirley included, of our intake had been moved on from nursery-level Registry work, and had probably been absorbed into the new concern. Rooms had been taken over, meetings went on late behind closed doors. I had been left behind. I displaced my frustration by complaining, as I had before, about being stuck with the old battle. The lectures were fascinating in the way a dead language was. The world was securely settled into its two camps, I argued. Soviet communism had as much evangelical fervour for expansion as you'd find in the Church of England. The Russian empire was repressive and corrupt, but comatose. The new threat was terrorism. I'd read an article in *Time* magazine and regarded myself as well informed. It wasn't just the Provisional IRA, or the various Palestinian groups. Underground anarchist and far-left factions across mainland Europe were already setting off bombs and kidnapping politicians and industrialists. The Red Brigades, the Baader–Meinhof Group, and in South America the Tupamaros and scores like them, in the United States the Symbionese Liberation Army – these blood-thirsty nihilists and narcissists were well connected across borders and soon they'd represent an internal threat here. We'd had the Angry Brigade, others far worse would follow. What were we doing, still piling most of our resources into cat-and-mouse business with irrelevant time-servers in Soviet trade delegations?

Most of our resources? What could a mere trainee know about allocations within the Service? But I tried to make myself sound confident. I was stirred up by a kiss, I wanted to impress Max. He was watching me closely, tolerantly amused.

'I'm glad you're up on your grisly factions. But, Serena, the year before last we threw out a hundred and five Soviet agents. They were crawling all over us. Educating Whitehall to do the right thing was a big moment for the Service. The gossip was that it was awfully difficult to bring the Home Secretary on board.'

'He was Tony's friend until they . . .'

'It all came out of Oleg Lyalin's defection. He was supposed to be responsible for organising sabotage in the UK in the event of a crisis. There was a statement in the Commons. You must have read about it at the time.'

'Yes, I remember.'

Of course I didn't. The expulsions had failed to make it into my *?Quis?* columns. I didn't then have Tony around to make me read newspapers.

'My point is,' Max said, 'that comatose isn't quite right, is it?'

He was still regarding me in a particular way, as if he expected the conversation to lead somewhere significant.

I said, 'I suppose not.' I was feeling uneasy, all the more so because I sensed that he intended me to be. Our friendship was so recent and sudden. I knew nothing about him and now he looked like a stranger to me, his outsized ears cupped in my direction like radar dishes to catch my softest, least honest whisper, his thin, intense face tightly concentrated on mine. I worried that he wanted something from me and that, even if he got it, I wouldn't know what it was.

'Would you like me to kiss you again?'

It was as long as the first, this stranger's kiss, and because it broke the tension between us, all the more pleasurable. I felt myself relaxing, even *dissolving*, the way people do in romantic novels. I could no longer bear to think that he was pretending.

He drew back and said quietly, 'Did Canning ever mention Lyalin to you?' Before I could reply, he kissed me again, just a glancing touch of lips and tongues. I was tempted to say yes because it was what he wanted.

'No, he didn't. Why are you asking?'

'Just curious. Did he introduce you to Maudling?'

'No. Why?'

'I would have been interested to hear your impressions, that's all.'

We kissed again. We were reclining on the grass. My hand was on his thigh and I let it slip towards his groin. I wanted to know if he was genuinely aroused by me. I didn't want him to be a brilliant pretender. But just as my fingertips were inches from the hard proof, he twisted away, extracted himself and stood, then stooped to brush dried grass from his trousers. The gesture looked fussy. He offered a hand to pull me up.

'I should get my train. I'm cooking dinner for a friend.'

'Oh, really.'

We walked on. He had caught the hostility in my voice and his touch on my arm was tentative, or apologetic. He said, 'Did you ever go to Kumlinge to visit his grave?'

'No.'

'Did you read the obituary?'

Because of this 'friend' our evening was going nowhere.

'Yes.'

'Was it *The Times* or *Telegraph*?'

'Max, are you interrogating me?'

'Don't be silly. I'm just terribly nosy. Please forgive me.'

'Then leave me alone.'

We walked in silence. He didn't know what to say. An only child, a boys' boarding school – he didn't know how to talk to a woman when things went awry. And I said nothing. I was angry, but I didn't want to drive him away. I was calmer by the time we stopped to say our goodbyes on the pavement just beyond the park railings.

'Serena, you do realise that I'm becoming very attached to you.'

I was pleased, I was very pleased, but I didn't show it and said nothing, waiting for him to say more. He seemed about to, then he changed the subject.

'By the way. Don't be impatient about the work. I happen to know there's a really interesting project coming through. Sweet Tooth. Right up your street. I've put in a good word for you.'

He didn't wait for a response. He pursed his lips and shrugged, then set off along Park Lane in the direction of Marble Arch, while I stood there watching him, wondering whether he was telling the truth.

5

My room in St Augustine's Road faced north over the street with a view into the branches of a horse chestnut tree. As it came into leaf that spring the room grew darker by the day. My bed, which was about half the size of the room, was a rickety affair with walnut veneer headboard and mattress of boggy softness. With the bed came a musty yellow candlewick bedcover. I took it to the launderette a couple of times but never completely purged it of a clammy intimate scent, of dog perhaps, or very unhappy human. The only other furniture was a chest of drawers with a tilting bevelled mirror on top. The whole piece stood in front of a miniature fireplace, which exuded a sour, sooty smell on warm days. With the tree in full blossom there wasn't enough natural light to read by when it was cloudy, so I bought an art deco lamp for 30p from a junk shop on the Camden Road. A day later I went back and paid £1.20 for a compact boxy armchair to read in without having to sink into the bed. The shop owner carried the chair home for me on his back, half a mile and up two flights of stairs for what we agreed was the price of a pint – 13p. But I gave him 15p.

Most of the houses in the street were subdivided and unmodernised, though I don't remember anyone using that word then or thinking in those terms. Heating was by electric fire, the floors were covered in ancient brown lino in the corridors and kitchen, and elsewhere with floral carpeting that was sticky underfoot. Small improvements probably dated from the twenties or thirties – the wiring was contained in dusty pipes screwed to the walls, the telephone confined to the draughty hallway, the electric immersion heater, fed by a hungry meter, delivered water at near boiling point to a tiny cold bathroom with no shower, shared by four women. These houses had not yet escaped their inheritance of Victorian gloom, but I never heard anyone complain. As I remember it, even in the seventies ordinary people who happened to live in these old places were only just beginning to wake up to the idea that they could be more comfortable further out of town if prices here kept on rising. The houses in the back streets of Camden Town awaited a new and vigorous class of people to move in and get to work, installing radiators and, for reasons no one could explain, stripping the pine skirting and floorboards and every last door of all vestiges of paintwork or covering.

I was lucky in my housemates – Pauline, Bridget, Tricia – three working-class girls from Stoke-on-Trent, who knew each other from childhood, passed all their school exams and somehow remained together during their legal training, which was almost complete. They were boring, ambitious, ferociously tidy. The house ran smoothly, the kitchen was always clean, the tiny fridge was full. If there were boyfriends, I never saw them. No drunkenness, no drugs, no loud music. In those days, a more likely household would have had people like my sister in it. Tricia was studying for the bar, Pauline was specialising in company law and Bridget was going into property. They each told me in their different defiant ways that they were never going back. And they weren't speaking of Stoke in purely geographical terms. But I didn't enquire too closely. I was adapting to my new job and wasn't much interested in their class struggle or upward mobility. They thought I was a dull civil servant, I thought they were dull trainee solicitors. Perfect. We had different schedules and we rarely ate together. No one bothered much with the sitting room – the only comfortable communal space. Even the TV was mostly silent. They studied in their rooms in the evening, I read in mine, or I went out with Shirley.

I kept up the reading in the same old style, three or four books a week. That year it was mostly modern stuff in paperbacks I bought from charity and second-hand shops in the High Street or, when I thought I could afford it, from Compendium near Camden Lock. I went at things in my usual hungry way, and there was an element of boredom too, which I was trying to keep at bay, and not succeeding. Anyone watching me might have thought I was consulting a reference book, I turned the pages so fast. And I suppose I was, in my mindless way, looking for a something, version of myself, a heroine I could slip inside as one might a pair of favourite old shoes. Or a wild silk blouse. For it was my best self I wanted, not the girl hunched in the evenings in her junk-shop chair over a cracked-spine paperback, but a fast young woman pulling open the passenger door of a sports car, leaning over to receive her lover's kiss, speeding towards a rural hideout. I would not admit to myself that I should have been reading a lower grade of fiction, like a mass-market romance. I had finally managed to absorb a degree of taste or snobbery from Cambridge, or from Tony. I no longer promoted Jacqueline Susann over Jane Austen. Sometimes my alter ego shimmered fleetingly between the lines, she floated towards me like a friendly ghost from the pages of Doris Lessing, or Margaret Drabble or Iris Murdoch. Then she was gone – their versions were too educated or too clever, or not quite lonely enough in the world to be me. I suppose I would not have been satisfied until I had in my hands a novel about a girl in a Camden bedsit who occupied a lowly position in MI5 and was without a man.

I craved a form of naive realism. I paid special attention, I craned my readerly neck whenever a London street I knew was mentioned, or a style of frock, a real public person, even a make of car. Then, I thought, I had a measure, I could gauge the quality of the writing by its accuracy, by the extent to which it aligned with my own impressions, or improved upon them. I was fortunate that most English writing of the time was in the form of undemanding social documentary. I wasn't impressed by those writers (they were spread between South and North America) who infiltrated their own pages as part of the cast, determined to remind the poor reader that all the characters and even they themselves were pure inventions and that there was a difference between fiction and life. Or, to the contrary, to insist that life was a fiction anyway. Only writers, I thought, were ever in danger of confusing the two. I was a born empiricist. I believed that writers were paid to pretend, and where appropriate should make use of the real world, the one we all shared, to give plausibility to whatever they had made up. So, no tricksy haggling over the limits of their art, no showing disloyalty to the reader by appearing to cross and recross in disguise the borders of the imaginary. No room in the books I liked for the double agent. That year I tried and discarded the authors that sophisticated friends in Cambridge had pressed on me – Borges and Barth, Pynchon and Cortázar and Gaddis. Not an Englishman among them, I noted, and no women of any race. I was rather like people of my parents' generation who not only disliked the taste and smell of garlic, but distrusted all those who consumed it.

During our summer of love Tony Canning used to tell me off for leaving books lying around open and face down. It ruined the spine, causing a book to spring open at a certain page, which was a random and irrelevant intrusion on a writer's intentions and another reader's judgement. And so he presented me with a bookmark. It wasn't much of a gift. He must have pulled it out of the bottom of a drawer. It was a strip of green leather with crenellated ends and embossed in gold with the name of some Welsh castle or ramparts. It was holiday gift-shop kitsch from the days when he and his wife were happy, or happy enough to take excursions together. I only faintly resented it, this tongue of leather that spoke so insidiously of another life elsewhere, without me. I don't think I ever used it then. I memorised my page number and stopped damaging spines. Months after the affair I found the bookmark lying curled and sticky with a chocolate wrapper at the bottom of a duffel bag.

I've said that after his death I had no love tokens. But I had this. I cleaned it up, straightened it out, and started to treasure and use it. Writers are said to have superstitions and little rituals. Readers have them too. Mine was to hold my bookmark curled between my fingers and stroke it with my thumb as I read. Late at night, when the time came to put my book away, my ritual was to touch the bookmark to my lips, and set it between the pages before closing the book and putting it on the floor by my chair, where I could reach for it easily next time. Tony would have approved.

One evening in early May, more than a week after our first kisses, I stayed later than usual talking with Max in Berkeley Square. He'd been in a particularly communicative mood, telling me about an eighteenth-century clock he thought he might write about one day. By the time I got back to St Augustine's Road the house was dark. I remembered that this was the second day of some obscure legal holiday. Pauline, Bridget and Tricia, for all their disavowals, had gone back to Stoke for a long weekend. I put on the lights in the hall and in the passage to the kitchen. I bolted the front door and went up towards my room. I suddenly missed that trio of sensible girls from the north and the wedge of light under the doors of their rooms, and I was uneasy. But I was sensible too. I had no supernatural fears, and I scoffed at reverential talk of intuitional knowledge and a sixth sense. My raised pulse, I reassured myself, was due to my exertions on the stairs. But when I reached my own door, I paused on the threshold before turning on the overhead light, restrained by the faintest of anxieties at being alone in a large old house. There had been a pavement knifing in Camden Square a month before, a motiveless attack by a thirty-year-old schizophrenic man. I was sure there was no intruder in the house, but news of a terrible event like that acts on you viscerally, in ways you're hardly aware of. It sharpens the senses. I stood still and listened and heard, beyond the tinnitus hiss of silence, the city's hum and, nearer, creaks and clicks as the shell of the building cooled and contracted in the night air.

I reached out and pushed down the Bakelite switch and saw immediately that the room was undisturbed. Or so I thought. I stepped in, put down my bag. The book I'd been reading the night before – *Eating People is Wrong*, by Malcolm Bradbury – was in its proper position, on the floor by the chair. But the bookmark was lying on the seat of my armchair. And no one had been in the house since I'd left that morning.

Naturally, my first assumption was that I had broken with my ritual the night before. Easy enough when you're tired. I could have stood and let the bookmark fall as I crossed to the basin to wash. My memory, however, was distinct. The novel was short enough for me to read in two sittings. But my eyes were heavy. I was less than halfway when I kissed the scrap of leather and placed it between pages ninety-eight and ninety-nine. I even recalled the last phrase I read because I glanced at it again before I closed the book. It was a line of dialogue. 'Intelligentsias are by no means always liberal in outlook.'

I went about the room looking for other signs of disturbance. Since I had no bookshelves, my books were in piles against the wall, divided between the read and the unread. On top of the latter, next in line, was A.S. Byatt's *The Game*. All was in order. I went through the chest of drawers, through my wash bag, I looked at the bed and under it – nothing had been moved or stolen. I came back to the chair and stared down a good while, as if that would solve the mystery. I knew I should go downstairs and look for signs of a break-in, but I didn't want to. The title of Bradbury's novel stared up at me and seemed now an ineffective protest against a prevailing ethic. I picked up the book and riffled through the pages and found the place where I had left off. Out on the landing I leaned over the banister and heard nothing unusual, but I still did not dare go down.

There was no lock or bolt on my door. I dragged the chest of drawers across it and went to bed with the light on. For most of the night I lay on my back with the covers pulled up to my chin, listening, thinking in circles, waiting for the dawn to come like a soothing mother and make things better. And when it did, they were. At first light I was persuaded that tiredness had fogged my memory, that I was confusing the intention with the act, that I had put the book down without the bookmark. I'd been frightening myself with my own shadow. Daylight seemed then to be the physical manifestation of common sense. I needed some rest because the next day I had an important lecture to attend. Enough ambiguity had gathered around the bookmark to let me sleep the two and half hours before the alarm went off.

The next day I earned a black mark from MI5, or rather, Shirley Shilling earned it for me. I was the sort of girl who could occasionally speak her mind, but my stronger impulse was for advancement and for approval from my seniors. Shirley had something combative, even reckless, about her that was alien to my nature. But we were a duo, after all, Laurel and Hardy, and perhaps it was inevitable that I would be drawn into the general ambience of her cockiness and be cast as the sidekick who was bound to take the blame.

It happened in the afternoon when we attended the lecture in Leconfield House, with the title 'Economic Anarchy, Civic Unrest'. The meeting was well attended. By an unspoken convention, whenever we had a distinguished visitor, the seating arranged itself by status. Right up in the front were various grand figures from the fifth floor. Three rows back was Harry Tapp, sitting with Millie Trimingham. Two rows behind them was Max, talking to a man I'd never seen before. Then there were the packed ranks of women below assistant desk officer status. And finally, Shirley and I, the naughty girls, had the back row to ourselves. I, at least, had a notebook at the ready.

The Director General came forward to introduce the visiting speaker, a brigadier, as someone with long experience in counter-insurgency, who was now in a consultative role with the Service. From scattered parts of the room there was applause for a military man. He spoke with a trace of the clipped manner we associate now with old British movies and 1940s wireless commentaries. There were still a few around among our seniors who exuded that flinty seriousness derived from their experience of a prolonged and total war.

But the brigadier also had a taste for the occasional flowery phrase. He said he was aware that there was a good number of ex-servicemen in the room and he hoped they would forgive him for stating facts well known to them but not to others. And the first of those facts was this – our soldiers were fighting a war, but no politician had the courage to give it that name. Men sent in to keep apart factions divided by obscure and ancient sectarian hatred found themselves attacked by both sides. Rules of engagement were such that trained soldiers were not allowed to respond in the way they knew best. Nineteen-year-old squaddies from Northumberland or Surrey, who may once have thought their mission was to come and protect the Catholic minority from the Protestant ascendancy, lay bleeding their lives, their futures, into the gutters of Belfast and Derry while Catholic children and teenage yobs taunted them and cheered. These men were being felled by sniper fire, often from tower blocks, and generally by IRA gunmen working under cover of coordinated riot or street disturbance. As for last year's Bloody Sunday, the Paras were under intolerable pressure from those same well-tried tactics – Derry hooligans backed up by sniper fire. The Widgery Report last April, produced with commendable speed, had confirmed the facts. That said, it was clearly an operational error to have an aggressive and highly motivated outfit like the Paras policing a civil-rights march. It should have been the task of the Royal Ulster Constabulary. Even the Royal Anglians would have been a calmer influence.

But it was done, and the net effect of killing thirteen civilians on that day was to endear both wings of the IRA to the world. Money, arms and recruits were as rivers of honey in spate. Sentimental and ignorant Americans, many of Protestant rather than Catholic descent, were feeding the fires with their foolish dollars donated to the Republican cause through fundraisers like NORAID. Not until the United States had its own terrorist attacks would it even begin to understand. To right the tragedy of Derry's wasted lives, the Official IRA slaughtered five cleaning ladies, a gardener and a Catholic priest in Aldershot, while the Provisionals murdered mothers and children in Belfast's Abercorn restaurant, some of them Catholics. And during the national strike our boys confronted ugly Protestant mobs, spurred on by the Ulster Vanguard, as nasty a bunch as one could hope to meet. Then the ceasefire, and when that failed, utter savagery dispensed to the Ulster public by psychopathic gun and bomb toters of both persuasions, and thousands of armed robberies and indiscriminate nail bombings, knee cappings, punishment beatings, five thousand seriously injured, several hundred killed by loyalist and Republican militias, and quite a few by the British army – though not, of course, intentionally. Such were the tallies for 1972.

The brigadier sighed theatrically. He was a big man, with eyes too small for the bony mass of his head. Neither a life-time of spit and polish nor his tailored dark suit and breast pocket handkerchief could contain the shaggy, shambling six-foot-three bulk of him. He appeared ready to dispatch a score of psychopaths with his own bare hands. Now, he told us, the Provisional IRA had organised itself into cells on the mainland in classic terrorist style. After eighteen months of lethal attacks, the word was they were about to get worse. The pretence of going for purely military assets had long been dropped. The game was terror. As in Northern Ireland, children, shoppers, ordinary working men were all suitable targets. Bombs in department stores and pubs would have even more impact in the context of the widely anticipated social breakdown brought on by industrial decline, high unemployment, rising inflation and an energy crisis.

It was to our collective dishonour that we had failed to expose the terrorist cells or disrupt their lines of supply. And this was to be his main point – there was one overriding reason for our failure, which was the lack of coordinated intelligence. Too many agencies, too many bureaucracies defending their corners, too many points of demarcation, insufficient centralised control.

The only sound was a creak of chairs and whispers, and I saw in front of me a restrained movement of heads tilting or turning minimally, of shoulders canting slightly towards a neighbour. The brigadier had touched upon a common complaint in Leconfield House. Even I had heard some of it, from Max. No flow of information across the borders of the jealous empires. But was our visitor going to tell the room what it wanted to hear, was he on our side? He was. He said MI6 was operating where it was not supposed to be, in Belfast and Londonderry, in the United Kingdom. With its remit of foreign intelligence, Six had a historical claim which dated back before Partition and was now irrelevant. This was a domestic issue. The territory therefore belonged to Five. Army Intelligence was over-staffed, mired in procedural antecedents. The RUC Special Branch, which considered itself the owner of the turf, was clumsy, under-resourced and, more to the point, part of the problem – a Protestant fiefdom. And who else could have made such a mess of internment in '71?

Five had been right to keep its distance from the dubious interrogation techniques, torture in anyone's book. Now it was doing its best in a crowded field. But even if each agency was staffed by geniuses and paragons of efficiency, four in collaboration could never defeat the monolithic entity of the Provisional IRA, one of the most formidable terrorist groups the world had ever known. Northern Ireland was a vital concern of domestic security. The Service must get a grip and advance its claim through the Whitehall corridors, suborn the other players to its will, become the rightful inheritor of the estate, and move in on the root of the problem.

There was no applause, partly because the brigadier's tone was close to exhortation, and that sort of thing didn't go down well here. And everyone knew that an assault on Whitehall's corridors would hardly be enough. I didn't take notes during the discussion between the brigadier and the Director General. From the question session I recorded only one of the questions, or ran a couple together as representative of the general drift. They came from the ex-colonial officers – one in particular I remember was Jack MacGregor, who had a dry, gingerish look and the tightly swallowed vowels of a South African, though he originally came from Surrey. He and some of his colleagues were particularly interested in the proper response to social breakdown. What would be the role of the Service? And what about the army? Could we stand aside and watch public order break down in the event that the government couldn't hold the line?

The Director General answered – curtly and with excessive politeness. The Service was accountable to the Joint Intelligence Committee and the Home Secretary, the army to the Ministry of Defence, and that was how it would remain. The emergency powers were sufficient to meet any threat and were something of a challenge to democracy in themselves.

A few minutes later, the question returned in a more pointed form from another ex-colonial. Suppose at the next general election a Labour government was returned. And suppose its left wing made common cause with radical union elements and one saw a direct threat to parliamentary democracy. Surely some form of contingency planning would be in order.

I wrote down the DG's exact words. 'I rather think I've made the position perfectly clear. Restoring democracy, as it's called, is what the army and security services might do in Paraguay. Not here.'

I thought the DG was embarrassed to have what he would have thought of as ranchers and tea planters reveal their colours before an outsider, who was nodding gravely.

It was at this point that Shirley startled the room by calling out from her back-row seat next to mine, 'These berks want to stage a coup!'

There was a collective gasp and all heads turned to look at us. She had broken several rules at a stroke. She had spoken unbidden by the Director General, and had used a dubious word like 'berk', whose provenance as rhyming slang some must have known. She had thereby insulted decorum and two desk officers far senior to herself. She had been uncouth in front of a visitor. And, she was lowly, and she was a woman. And, worst of all, she was probably right. None of that would have mattered to me but for the fact that Shirley sat nonchalantly before the collective glare, while I blushed, and the more I blushed the more certain everyone was that I was the one who had spoken. Aware of what they were thinking, I blushed even more, until my neck was hot. Their eyes were no longer fixed on us, but on me. I wanted to crawl under my chair. My shame rose in my throat for the crime I had not committed. I fiddled with my notebook – those notes I had hoped would earn me respect – and lowered my eyes, stared at my knees and so provided yet more evidence of my guilt.

The Director General brought the occasion back to its formal proprieties by thanking the brigadier. There was applause, the brigadier and the DG left the room and people stood to go, and turned to look at me again.

Suddenly Max was right in front of me. He said quietly, 'Serena, that wasn't a good idea.'

I turned to appeal to Shirley but she was in the crowd going out through the door. I don't know how I came by such a masochistic code of honour that prevented me from insisting I wasn't the one who had called out. And yet I was sure that by now the DG would be asking for my name, and someone like Harry Tapp would be telling him.

Later, when I caught up with Shirley and confronted her, she told me the whole thing was trivial and hilarious. I shouldn't worry, she told me. It would do me no harm for people to think I had a mind of my own. But I knew that the opposite was true. It would do me a lot of harm. People at our level were not supposed to have minds of their own. This was my first black mark, and it was not the last.

6

I was expecting a reprimand, but instead my moment came
– I was sent out of the building on a secret mission, and
Shirley went with me. We received our instructions one
morning from a desk officer called Tim Le Prevost. I'd seen
him about the place but he'd never spoken to us before. We
were summoned to his office and invited to listen carefully.
He was a small-lipped tightly buttoned chap with narrow
shoulders and a rigid expression, almost certainly ex-army.
A van was parked in a locked garage off a Mayfair street half
a mile away. We were to drive to an address in Fulham. It
was a safe house, of course, and in the brown envelope he
tossed across his desk were various keys. In the back of the
van we would find cleaning materials, a Hoover and vinyl
aprons, which we were to put on before we set off. Our cover
was that we worked for a firm called Springklene.

When we arrived at our destination we were to give the
place 'a damned good going over', which would include
changing the sheets on all the beds and cleaning the windows.
Clean linen had already been delivered. One of the mattresses
on a single bed needed to be turned. It should have been
replaced long ago. The lavatories and bath needed particular
attention. The rotten food in the fridge was to be disposed
of. All ashtrays were to be emptied. Le Prevost enunciated

these homely details with much distaste. Before the day was out, we were to go to a small supermarket on the Fulham Road and buy basic provisions and three meals a day for two persons for three days. A separate trip was to be made to an off-licence, where we should buy four bottles of Johnnie Walker Red Label. We were to settle for nothing else. Here was another envelope with fifty pounds in fivers. He wanted receipts and change. We were to remember to triple lock the front door on our way out with the three Banhams. Above all, we should never in our lives mention this address, not even to colleagues in this building.

'Or,' Le Prevost said, with a twist of his little mouth, 'do I mean *especially*?'

We were dismissed and when were out of the building, heading along Curzon Street, it was Shirley, not me, who was scathing.

'Our *cover*,' she kept saying in a loud whisper. 'Our bloody cover. Cleaning ladies pretending to be *cleaning ladies*!'

It was an insult, of course, though less of one then than it would be now. I didn't say the obvious, that the Service could hardly bring in outside cleaners to a safe house, any more than it could call on our male colleagues – they were not only too grand, but they would have made a terrible job. I surprised myself with my stoicism. I think I must have absorbed the general spirit of camaraderie and cheerful devotion to duty among the women. I was becoming like my mother. She had the Bishop, I had the Service. Like her I had my own strong-minded inclination to obey. I did worry, however, whether this was the job that Max had said was right up my street. If it was, I'd never talk to him again.

We found the garage and put on our aprons. Shirley, wedged in tight behind the wheel, was still muttering muti-nously as we pulled out into Piccadilly. The van was pre-war – it had spoked wheels and a running board and must have been among the last of the sit-up-and-beg contraptions on the road. The name of our firm was written on the sides in art deco lettering. The 'k' of 'Springklene' was done up as a gleeful housemaid wielding a feather duster. I thought we looked far too conspicuous. Shirley drove with surprising confidence, swinging us at speed round Hyde Park Corner and demonstrating a flashy technique with the gear stick, known, she told me, as double declutching, necessary on such an ancient crate.

The flat occupied the ground floor of a Georgian house in a quiet side street and was grander than I expected. All the windows were barred. Once we were in with our mops, fluids and buckets, we made a tour. The squalor was even more depressing than Le Prevost had implied and was of the obvious male sort, right down to a once-sodden cigar stub on the edge of the bath, and a foot-high pile of *The Times*, with some copies roughly quartered, moonlighting as lavatory paper. The sitting room had an abandoned late-night air – drawn curtains, empty bottles of vodka and scotch, heaped ashtrays, four glasses. There were three bedrooms, the smallest of which had a single bed. On its mattress, which was stripped, was a wide patch of dried blood, just where a head might rest. Shirley was loudly disgusted, I was rather thrilled. Someone had been intensively interrogated. Those Registry files were connected to real fates.

As we went round taking in the mess, she continued to complain and exclaim, and clearly wanted me to join in. I tried, but my heart wasn't in it. If my small part in the war against the totalitarian mind was bagging up decaying food and scraping down hardened bathtub scum, then I was for it. It was only a little duller than typing up a memo.

It turned out that I had a better understanding of the work involved – odd, considering my cosseted childhood with nanny and daily. I suggested we did the filthiest stuff first, lavatories, bathroom, kitchen, clearing the rubbish, then we could start on the surfaces, then the floors and finally the beds. But before all else, we turned the mattress, for Shirley's sake. There was a radio in the sitting room and we decided that it would be consistent with our cover to have pop music playing. We went at it for two hours, then I took one of the fivers and went out to buy the wherewithal for a tea break. On the way back I used some change to feed the parking meter. When I returned to the house, Shirley was perched on the edge of one of the double beds, writing in her little pink book. We sat in the kitchen, drank tea, smoked and ate chocolate biscuits. The radio was playing, there was fresh air and sunlight through the open windows and Shirley was restored to a good mood and told me a surprising story about herself while she finished off all the biscuits.

Her English teacher at the Ilford comprehensive, a force in her life the way certain teachers can be, was a Labour councillor, probably ex-Communist Party, and it was through him that she found herself at the age of sixteen on an exchange with German students. That is, she went to communist East Germany with a school group, to a village an hour's bus ride from Leipzig.

'I thought it was going to be shit. Everyone said it would be. Serena, it was fucking paradise.'

'The GDR?'

She lodged with a family on the edge of the village. The house was an ugly, cramped two-bedroom bungalow but there was a half-acre of orchard and a stream, and not far away a forest big enough to get lost in. The father was a TV engineer, the mother a doctor, and there were two little girls under five years who fell in love with the lodger and used to climb into her bed early in the morning. The sun always shone in East Germany – it was April, and by chance there was a heatwave. There were expeditions into the forest to hunt for morels, there were friendly neighbours, everyone encouraged her German, someone had a guitar and knew some Dylan songs, there was a good-looking boy with three fingers on one hand who was keen on her. He took her to Leipzig one afternoon to see a serious football match.

'No one had much. But they had enough. At the end of

ten days I thought, no, this really works, this is better than Ilford.'

'Maybe everywhere is. Especially in the countryside. Shirley, you could have had a good experience just outside Dorking.'

'Honestly, this was different. People cared about each other.'

What she was saying was familiar. There had been pieces in the newspaper and a TV documentary reporting in triumph that East Germany had finally overtaken Britain in living standards. Years later, when the Wall came down and the books were opened, it turned out to be nonsense. The GDR was a disaster. The facts and figures people had believed, and had wanted to believe, were the Party's own. But in the seventies, the British mood was self-lacerating, and there was a general willingness to assume that every country in the world, Upper Volta included, was about to leave us far behind.

I said, 'People care about each other here as well.'

'Well, fine. We all care about each other. So what are we fighting against?'

'A paranoid one-party state, no free press, no freedom to travel. A nation as prison camp, that sort of thing.' I heard Tony at my shoulder.

'*This* is a one-party state. Our press is a joke. And the poor can't travel anywhere.'

'Oh, Shirley, really!'

'Parliament's our single party. Heath and Wilson belong to the same elite.'

'What nonsense!'

We had never talked politics before. It had always been music, families, personal tastes. I assumed that all my colleagues had roughly the same sort of views. I was looking at her closely to see if she was teasing me. She looked away, reached roughly across the table for another cigarette. She was angry. I didn't want a full-on row with my new friend. Lowering my tone I said softly, 'But if you think that, Shirley, why join this lot?'

'I dunno. Partly to please my dad. I mean, I've told him it's the Civil Service. I didn't think they'd let me in. When they did everyone was proud. Including me. It felt like a victory. But you know how it is – they had to have one non-Oxbridge type. I'm just your token prole. So.' She stood. 'Better get on with our crucial work.'

I stood too. The conversation was embarrassing and I was glad it was over.

'I'll finish off in the sitting room,' she said, and then paused in the kitchen doorway. She looked a sad figure, bulging under her plastic apron, her hair, still damp from her exertions before our tea break, sticking to her forehead.

She said, 'Come on, Serena, you can't think all this is so simple. That we just happen to be on the side of the angels.'

I shrugged. Actually, in relative terms I thought we were, but her tone was so scathing that I didn't want to say so. I said, 'If people had a free vote across Eastern Europe, including your GDR, they'd kick the Russians out, and the CP wouldn't stand a chance. They're there by force. That's what I'm against.'

'You think people here wouldn't kick the Americans off their bases? You must have noticed – the choice isn't on offer.'

I was about to reply when Shirley snatched up her duster and a lavender canister of spray-on polish and left, calling out as she went down the hall, 'You've soaked up all the propaganda, girl. Reality isn't always middle class.'

Now I was angry, too angry to speak. In the last minute or so Shirley had upped her Cockney accent, the better to use some notion of working-class integrity against me. How dare she condescend like that? Reality isn't always middle class! Intolerable. Her 'reality' had been ludicrously glottal. How could she traduce our friendship and say she was my token prole? And I'd never given a moment's thought to the college she was at, except to think that I would have been happier at hers. As for her politics – the outworn orthodoxy of *idiots*. I felt I could have run after her and shouted at her.

My mind was filled with withering retorts, and I wanted to use them all at once. But I stood in silence and walked around the kitchen table a couple of times, then I picked up the vacuum cleaner, a heavy-duty affair, and went to the small bedroom, the one with the bloody mattress.

That was how I came to clean the room so thoroughly. I went at it in a fury, running the conversation over and over again, merging what I'd said with what I wished I'd said. Just before our break I had filled a bucket to clean the wood-work round the windows. I decided I would clean the skirting boards first. And if I was going to be kneeling on the floor, I would need to vacuum the carpet. To do that properly I carried out into the corridor a few pieces of furniture – a bedside locker and two wooden chairs that were by the bed. The only electric socket in the room was low down on the wall under the bed and a reading lamp was already plugged in. I had to lie on my side on the floor and reach in at full stretch. No one had cleaned under there in a long time. There were dust balls, a couple of used tissues and one dirty white sock. Because the plug was a tight fit it took an effort to pull and jiggle it clear. My thoughts were still on Shirley and what I would say to her next. I'm a coward in important confronta-tions. I suspected we would both choose the English solution and pretend that the conversation had never happened. That made me angrier still.

Then my wrist brushed against a piece of paper concealed by one of the legs of the bed. It was triangular, no more than three inches along the hypotenuse, torn from the right-hand top corner of *The Times*. On one side was the familiar lettering – 'Olympic Games: Complete programme, page 5'. On the reverse, faint pencil writing under one of the straight edges. I backed out and sat down on the bed to take a closer look. I peered and understood nothing until I realised I was holding the scrap upside down. What I saw first were two letters in lower case. 'tc'. The line of the tear sliced right through the word below. The writing was faint, as though there had been minimal downward pressure, but the letters were clearly formed: 'umlinge'. Just before the 'u' was a stroke that could only have been the foot of the letter 'k'. I turned the piece of paper upside down again, hoping to make the letters do something else for me, demonstrate that I was simply projecting. But there was no ambiguity. His initials, his island. But not his handwriting. In a matter of seconds my mood had shifted from intense irritation to a more complex mix – of bafflement and unfocused anxiety.

Naturally, one of my first thoughts was of Max. He was the only one I knew who knew the name of the island. The obituary had made no mention of it and Jeremy Mott probably didn't know. But Tony had plenty of old connections in the Service, though very few were active now. Perhaps a couple of very senior figures. They surely wouldn't have known of Kumlinge. As for Max, I sensed it would be a bad idea to ask him for an explanation. I would have been giving away something I should hold on to. He wouldn't tell me the truth if it didn't suit him. If he knew anything worth telling, then he had already deceived me by keeping silent. I thought back to our conversation in the park and his persistent questions. I looked at the scrap of paper again. It looked old, faintly yellowish. If this was a significant mystery, I didn't have enough information to solve it. Into this vacancy came an irrelevant thought. The 'k' on the side of our van was the missing letter, dressed up like a housemaid – just like me. Yes, everything was connected! Now that I was being really stupid, it was almost a relief.

I stood up. I was tempted to turn the mattress back just to look at the blood again. It was right under where I'd just been sitting. Was it as old as the piece of paper? I didn't know how blood aged. But that was it, here was the simplest formulation of the mystery and the core of my unease: did the name of the island and Tony's initials have anything to do with the blood?

I put the paper in the pocket of my apron and went along

the hallway to the lavatory, hoping I didn't run into Shirley. I locked the door, knelt by the pile of newspapers and began sorting through it. Not every day was there – the safe house must have stood empty for longish periods. So the copies reached back many months. The Munich games were last summer, ten months ago. Who could forget, eleven Israeli athletes massacred by Palestinian guerrillas? I found the copy with the missing corner only a couple of inches from the bottom and pulled it clear. There was the first half of the word 'programme'. August 25th, 1972. 'Unemployment at its highest level for August since 1939'. I faintly remembered the story, not for the jobless headline but for the article about my old hero Solzhenitsyn across the top of the page. His 1970 Nobel Prize acceptance speech had just surfaced. He attacked the United Nations for failing to make acceptance of the declaration of human rights a condition of membership. I thought that was right, Tony thought it was naive. I was stirred by the lines about 'the shadows of the fallen' and 'the vision of art that sprang from the pain and solitude of the Siberian waste'. And I especially liked the line, 'Woe to the nation whose literature is disturbed by the intervention of power.'

Yes, we'd spent some time talking about that speech, and disagreeing. And that would have been not long before our parting scene in the lay-by. Might he have come here afterwards when his plans for retreat had already taken shape? But why? And whose blood? I had solved nothing, but I felt clever in making progress. And feeling clever, I've always thought, is just a sigh away from being cheerful. I heard Shirley coming and quickly put the pile in order, flushed the lavatory, washed my hands and opened the door.

I said, 'We should remember to put lavatory rolls on the list.'

She was standing well back along the corridor and I don't think she heard me. She was looking contrite and I felt suddenly warm towards her.

'I'm sorry about just now. Serena, I don't know why I do this. Bloody stupid. I go right over the top for the sake of argument.' And then she added as a jokey softener, 'It's only because I like you!'

I noted that she deliberately sounded the 't' of 'right', in itself a muted apology.

I said, 'It was nothing,' and meant it. What had passed between us was nothing to what I had just found. I'd already decided not to discuss it. I'd never said much to her about Tony. I'd saved all that for Max. I might have got this the wrong way round, but there was nothing to be gained from confiding in her now. The piece of paper was tucked deep into my pocket. We chatted in our usual friendly way for a while and then we went back to work. It was a long day and we were not completely done, cleaning and shopping, until after six. I came away with the August copy of *The Times* in case I could learn more from it. When we dropped off the van in Mayfair that evening and parted, I thought Shirley and I were once more the best of friends.

7

The following morning I received an eleven o'clock invitation to Harry Tapp's office. I was still expecting to have my wrists slapped for Shirley's indiscretion at the lecture. At ten to eleven I went to the ladies' to check on my appearance and as I combed my hair I imagined myself taking the train home after being sacked, and preparing a story for my mother. Would the Bishop even notice I'd been away? I went up two floors to a part of the building that was new to me. It was only slightly less dingy – the corridors were carpeted, the cream and green paint on the walls was not peeling. I tapped timidly on a door. A man came out – he looked even younger than me – and told me in a nervous, pleasant way that I should wait. He indicated one of the bright orange plastic moulded chairs that were then spreading through the offices. A quarter of an hour passed before he appeared again and held the door open for me.

In a sense, this was when the story began, at the point at which I entered the office and had my mission explained. Tapp was sitting behind his desk and nodded expressionlessly at me. There were three others in the room besides the fellow who had shown me in. One, by far the oldest, with swept-back silver hair, was sprawled in a scuffed leather armchair, the others were on hard office chairs. Max was there and pursed his lips in greeting. I wasn't surprised to see him and simply smiled. There was a large combination safe in one corner. The air was thick with smoke and moist with breath. They had been in conference a good while. There were no introductions.

I was shown onto one of the hard seats and we sat in a horseshoe facing the desk.

Tapp said, 'So, Serena. How are you settling in?'

I said I thought I had settled in well and that I was happy with the work. I was aware that Max knew it wasn't so, but I didn't care. I added, 'Am I here because you think I'm not up to scratch, sir?'

Tapp said, 'It wouldn't take five of us to tell you that.'

There were low chuckles all round and I took care to join in. 'Up to scratch' was a phrase I'd never used before.

There followed a session of small talk. Someone asked me about my lodgings, another about my commute. There was a discussion about the irregularities of the Northern line. Canteen food was gently mocked. The more this went on, the more nervous I became. The man in the armchair said nothing, but he was watching me over the steeple he formed with his fingers, with his thumbs tucked under his chin. I tried not to look in his direction. Guided by Tapp, the conversation shifted to the events of the day. Inevitably, we came to the Prime Minister and the miners. I said that free trade unions were important institutions. But their remit should be the pay and conditions of their members. They should not be politicised and it was not their business to remove democratically elected governments. This was the right answer. I was prompted to speak of Britain's recent entry to the Common Market. I said I was for it, that it would be good for business, dissolve our insularity, improve our food. I didn't really know what to think, but decided it was better to sound decisive. This time I knew that I'd parted company with the room. We progressed to the Channel Tunnel. There had been a White Paper, and Heath had just signed a preliminary agreement with Pompidou. I was all for it – imagine catching the London–Paris express! I surprised myself with a burst of enthusiasm. Again, I was alone. The man in the armchair grimaced and looked away. I guessed that in his youth he had been prepared to give his life to defend the realm against the political passions of Continentals. A tunnel was a security threat.

So we went on. I was being interviewed, but I had no idea to what end. Automatically I strove to please, more so whenever I sensed that I was not succeeding. I assumed that the whole business was being conducted for the benefit of the silver-haired man. Apart from that single look of displeasure, he communicated nothing. His hands remained in their praying position, with the tips of his forefingers just touching his nose. It was a conscious effort not to look at him. I was annoyed with myself for wanting his approval. Whatever he had in mind for me, I wanted it too. I wanted him to want me. I couldn't look at him, but when my gaze moved across the room to meet the eye of another speaker, I caught just a glimpse, and learned nothing.

We came to a break in the conversation. Tapp indicated a lacquered box on the desk and cigarettes were offered around. I expected to be sent out of the room as before. But some quiet signal must have emanated from the silvery gentleman because Tapp cleared his throat to mark a fresh start and said, 'Well then, Serena. We understand from Max here that on top of your maths you're rather well up on modern writing – literature, novels, that sort of thing – bang up to date on, what's the word?'

'Contemporary literature,' Max supplied.

'Yes, awfully well read and quite in with the scene.'

I hesitated, and said, 'I like reading in my spare time, sir.'

'No need for "sir". And you're up to date on this contemporary stuff that's coming out now.'

'I read novels in second-hand paperbacks mostly, a couple

of years after they've appeared in hardback. The hardbacks are a bit beyond my budget.'

This hair-splitting distinction seemed to baffle or irritate Tapp. He leaned back in his chair and closed his eyes for several seconds and waited for the confusion to disperse. He didn't open them again until he was halfway through his next sentence. 'So if I said to you the names of Kingsley Amis or David Storey or . . .' he glanced down at a sheet of paper, 'William Golding, you'd know exactly what I was talking about.'

'I've read those writers.'

'And you know how to talk about them.'

'I think so.'

'How would you rank them?'

'Rank them?'

'Yes, you know, best to worst.'

'They're very different kinds of writer . . . Amis is a comic novelist, brilliantly observant with something quite merciless about his humour. Storey is a chronicler of working-class life, marvellous in his way and, uh, Golding is harder to define, probably a genius . . .'

'So then?'

'For pure reading pleasure I'd put Amis at the top, then Golding because I'm sure he's profound, and Storey third.'

Tapp checked his notes, then looked up with a brisk smile. 'Exactly what I've got down here.'

My accuracy evinced a rumble of approval. It didn't seem much of an achievement to me. There were, after all, only six ways to organise such a list.

'And do you know personally any of these writers?'

'No.'

'Do you know any writers at all, or publishers or anyone else connected with the business?'

'No.'

'Have you ever actually met a writer, or been in a room with one?'

'No, never.'

'Or written to one, as it were, a fan letter?'

'No.'

'Any Cambridge friends determined to be writers?'

I thought carefully. Among the Eng Lit set at Newnham there had been a fair amount of longing in this direction, but as far as I knew my female acquaintance had settled for various combinations of finding respectable jobs, marrying, getting pregnant, disappearing abroad or retreating into the remnants of the counter-culture in a haze of pot smoke.

'No.'

Tapp looked up expectantly. 'Peter?'

At last the man in the armchair lowered his hands and spoke. 'I'm Peter Nutting by the way. Miss Frome, have you ever heard of a magazine called *Encounter*?'

Nutting's nose was revealed as beakish. His voice was a light tenor – somehow surprising. I thought I had heard of a nudist lonely-hearts small-ads news-sheet of that name, but I wasn't sure. Before I could speak he continued, 'It doesn't matter if you haven't. It's a monthly, intellectual stuff, politics, literature, general cultural matters. Pretty good, well respected, or it was, with a fairly wide range of opinion. Let's say centre left to centre right, and mostly the latter. But here's the point. Unlike most intellectual periodicals it's been sceptical or downright hostile when it comes to communism, especially of the Soviet sort. It spoke up for the unfashionable causes – freedom of speech, democracy and so on. Actually, it still does. And it soft-pedals rather on American foreign policy. Ring any bells with you? No? Five or six years ago it came out, in an obscure American magazine and then the *New York Times* I think it was, that *Encounter* was funded by the CIA. There was a stink, a lot of arm-waving and shouting, various writers took flight with their consciences. The name Melvin Lasky means nothing to you? No reason why it should. The CIA has been backing its own highbrow notion of culture since the end of the forties. They've generally worked at one remove through various foundations. The idea has been to try to lure left-of-centre European intellectuals away from the Marxist perspective and make it intellectually respectable to speak up for the Free World. Our friends have sloshed a lot of cash around by way of various fronts. Ever hear of the Congress of Cultural Freedom? Never mind.

'So that's been the American way and basically, since the *Encounter* affair, it's a busted flush. When a Mr X pops up from some giant foundation offering a six-figure sum, everyone runs screaming. But still, this is a culture war, not just a political and military affair, and the effort's worthwhile. The Soviets know it and they spend on exchange schemes, visits, conferences, the Bolshoi Ballet. That's on top of the money they channel into the National Union of Mineworkers strike fund by way of . . .'

'Peter,' Tapp murmured, 'let's not go down that pit again.'

'All right. Thank you. Now the dust is settling, we've decided to push ahead with our own scheme. Modest budget, no international festivals, no first-class flights, no twenty-pantechnicon orchestral tours, no bean feasts. We can't afford it and we don't want to. What we intend is pinpointed, long-term and cheap. And that's why you're here. Are there any questions so far?'

'No.'

'You might know of the Information Research Department over at the Foreign Office.'

I didn't, but I nodded.

'So you'll know this kind of thing has a long history. IRD have worked with us and MI6 for years, cultivating writers, newspapers, publishers. George Orwell on his deathbed gave IRD a list of thirty-eight communist fellow-travellers. And IRD helped *Animal Farm* into eighteen languages and did a lot of good work for *Nineteen Eighty-Four*. And some marvellous publishing ventures over the years. Ever heard of Background Books? – that was an IRD outfit, paid for with the Secret Vote. Superb stuff. Bertrand Russell, Guy Wint, Vic Feather. But these days . . .'

He sighed and looked around the room. I sensed a common grievance.

'IRD has lost its way. Too many silly ideas, too close to Six – in fact, one of their own is in charge. D'you know, Carlton House Terrace is full of nice hard-working girls like you, and when people from Six visit, some fool has to run ahead through the offices shouting, "Faces to the wall, everybody!" Can you imagine such a thing? You can bet those girls peep through their fingers, eh?'

He looked around expectantly. There were obliging chuckles.

'So we want to start afresh. Our idea is to concentrate on suitable young writers, academics and journalists mostly, people at the start of their careers, when they need financial support. Typically, they'll have a book they want to write and need to take time off from a demanding job. And we thought it might be interesting to have a novelist on the list . . .'

Harry Tapp cut in, unusually excited. 'Makes it a little less heavy, more, you know, a bit of light-hearted fun. Frothy. Someone the newspapers will take an interest in.'

Nutting continued. 'Since you like that sort of thing, we thought you might want to be involved. We're not interested in the decline of the West, or down with progress or any other modish pessimism. Do you see what I mean?'

I nodded. I thought I did.

'Your corner's going to be a little trickier than the rest. You know as well as I do, it's not straightforward to deduce an author's views from his novels. That's why we've been looking for a novelist who also writes journalism. We're looking out for the sort who might spare a moment for his hard-pressed fellows in the Eastern bloc, travels out there perhaps to lend support or sends books, signs petitions for persecuted writers, engages his mendacious Marxist colleagues here, isn't afraid to talk publicly about writers in prison in Castro's Cuba. Generally swims against the orthodox flow. It takes courage, Miss Frome.'

'Yes, sir. I mean, yes.'

'Especially if you're young.'

'Yes.'

'Free speech, freedom of assembly, legal rights, democratic process – not much cherished these days by a lot of intellectuals.'

'No.'

'We need to encourage the right people.'

'Yes.'

A silence settled on the room. Tapp offered round cigarettes from his case, first to me, then to the rest. We all smoked and waited for Nutting. I was aware of Max's eyes on me. When I met his look he made the slightest inclination of his head, as if to say, 'Keep it up.'

With some initial difficulty, Nutting levered himself out of his armchair, went across to Tapp's desk and picked up the notes. He turned the pages until he found what he wanted.

'The people we're looking for will be of your generation. They'll cost us less, that's for sure. The sort of stipend we'll be offering through our front organisation will be enough to keep a chap from having to do a day job for a year or two, even three. We know we can't be in a hurry and that we're not going to see results next week. We're expecting to have ten subjects, but all you need to think about is this one. And one proposal . . .'

He looked down through half-moon specs that hung by a cord around his neck.

'His name is Thomas Haley, or T.H. Haley as he prefers it in print. Degree in English at the University of Sussex, got a first, still there now, studied for an MA in international relations under Peter Calvocoressi, now doing a doctorate in literature. We took a peek at Haley's medical record. Nothing much to report. He's published a few short stories and some journalism. He's looking for a publisher. But he also needs to find himself a proper job once his studies are over. Calvocoressi rates him highly, which should be enough

93

for anyone. Benjamin here has put together a file and we'd like your opinion. Assuming you're happy, we'd like you to get on the train to Brighton and take a look at him. If you give the thumbs up, we'll take him on. Otherwise, we'll look somewhere else. It'll be on your say-so. You'll precede your visit, of course, with an introductory letter.'

They were all watching me. Tapp, whose elbows rested on his desk, had made his own finger-steeple. Then, without parting his palms, he drummed his fingers together soundlessly.

I felt obliged to make some form of intelligent objection. 'Won't I be like your Mr X, popping up with a chequebook? He might run at the sight of me.'

'At the sight of you? I rather doubt it, my dear.'

Again, low chuckles all round. I blushed and was annoyed. Nutting was smiling at me and I made myself smile back.

He said, 'The sums are going to be attractive. We'll channel funds through a cut-out, an existing Foundation. Not a huge or well-known outfit, but it's one where we have some reliable contacts. If Haley or any of the others decides to check, it'll stand up nicely. I'll let you know its name as soon as it's settled. Obviously, you'll be the Foundation's representative. They'll let us know when letters come for you. And we'll get you some of their headed paper.'

'Wouldn't it be possible to simply make some friendly recommendations to the, you know, the government department that hands out money to artists?'

'The Arts Council?' Nutting let out a pantomime shout of a bitter laugh. Everyone else was grinning. 'My dear girl. I envy your innocence. But you're right. It should have been possible! It's a novelist in charge of the literature section, Angus Wilson. Know of him? On paper just the sort we could have worked with. Member of the Athenaeum, naval attaché in the war, worked on secret stuff in the famous Hut Eight on the uh, at, well, I'm not allowed to say. I took him to lunch, then saw him a week later in his office. I started to explain what I wanted. D'you know, Miss Frome, he all but threw me out of a third-floor window.'

He had told this story before and delighted in telling it again, embellished.

'One moment he was behind his desk, nice white linen suit, lavender bow tie, clever jokes, the next his face was puce and he had hold of my lapels and was pushing me out of his office. What he said I can't repeat in front of a lady. And camp as a tent peg. God knows how they let him near naval codes in 'forty-two.'

'There you go,' Tapp said. 'It's filthy propaganda when we do it, and then they're sold out at the Albert Hall for the Red Army Chorus.'

'Max here rather wishes Wilson *had* tossed me out of the window,' Nutting said, and to my surprise winked at me. 'Isn't that right, Max?'

'I've had my say,' Max said. 'Now I'm on board.'

'Good.' Nutting nodded at Benjamin, the young man who had shown me in. He opened the folder on his lap.

'I'm sure this is everything he's published. Not easy to track down, some of it. I suggest you look at the journalism first. I should direct your attention towards an article he wrote for the *Listener*, deploring the way newspapers romanticise villains. It's mostly about the Great Train Robbery – he objects to the word "great" – but there's a robust aside about Burgess and Maclean and the number of deaths they were responsible for. You'll see he's a member of the Readers and Writers Educational Trust, an organisation that supports dissidents in Eastern Europe. He wrote a piece for the Trust's journal last year. You might look at the longish article he wrote for *History Today* about the East German uprising of 'fifty-three. There's a goodish piece about the Berlin Wall in *Encounter*. Generally, the journalism is sound. But it's the short stories you'll be writing to him about, and they're his thing. Five in all, as Peter said. Actually, one in *Encounter*, and then things you've never heard of – the *Paris Review*, the *New American Review*, *Kenyon Review* and *Transatlantic Review*.'

'Geniuses with the titles, these creative types,' Tapp said.

'Worth noting that those four are based in the States,' Benjamin went on. 'An Atlanticist at heart. We've asked around and people describe him as promising. Though one insider told us that's a standard description for any young writer. He's been turned down three times by a Penguin short-story series. He's also been turned down by the *New Yorker*, the *London Magazine* and *Esquire*.'

Tapp said, 'As a matter of interest, how did you come by all this?'

'It's a long story. First I met a former . . .'

'Keep going,' Nutting said. 'I'm due upstairs at eleven thirty. And by the way. Calvocoressi has told a friend that Haley's a personable fellow, decently turned out. So, a good role model for the young. I'm sorry, Benjamin. Carry on.'

'A well-known publishing house has said they like the stories but won't publish them in a collection until he comes up with a novel. Short stories don't sell. Publishers usually do these collections as a favour to their well-established authors. He needs to write something longer. This is important to know because a novel takes a while and it's hard to do when you've got a full-time job. And he's keen to write a novel, says he has an idea for one apparently. Another thing, he doesn't have an agent and is looking for one.'

'*Agent?*'

'Altogether different fish, Harry. Sells the work, does the contracts, takes a cut.'

Benjamin handed me the folder. 'That's about it. Obviously, don't leave it lying around.'

The man who had not yet spoken, a greyish shrunken-looking fellow with oily centre-parted hair, said, 'Are we expecting to have at least a little influence over what any of these people write?'

Nutting said, 'It would never work. We have to trust in our

choices and hope Haley and the rest turn out well and become, you know, important. This is a slow-burn thing. We aim to show the Americans how it's done. But there's no reason why we can't give him a leg-up along the way. You know, people who owe us a favour or three. In Haley's case, well, sooner or later one of our own is going to be chairing this new Booker Prize committee. And we might look into that agent business. But as for the stuff itself, they have to feel free.'

He was standing up and looking at his watch. Then he looked at me. 'Any more background questions, Benjamin's your man. Operationally, it's Max. The codename is Sweet Tooth. Right then? That'll be all.'

I was taking a risk, but I had begun to feel indispensable. Over-confident, perhaps. But who else in this room apart from me had ever, as an adult, read a short story in his leisure time? I couldn't hold back. I was eager and hungry. I said, 'This is a little awkward for me, and no offence to Max, but if I'm working directly to him, I wonder if it might be helpful if I could have some clarification of my own status.'

Peter Nutting sat down again. 'My dear girl. What can you mean?'

I stood in front of him humbly, as I used to in front of my father in his study. 'It's a great challenge and I'm thrilled to be asked. The Haley case is fascinating, and it's also delicate. You're asking me, in effect, to run Haley. I'm honoured. But agent-running . . . well, I'd like to be clear then about where I stand.'

There followed an embarrassed silence of the sort only a woman can impose on a roomful of men. Then Nutting muttered, 'Well, yes, quite . . .'

He turned in desperation to Tapp. 'Harry?'

Tapp slipped his gold cigarette case into the inside pocket of his jacket as he stood. 'Simple, Peter. You and I will go downstairs after lunch and talk to Personnel. I don't foresee any objection. Serena can be made up to assistant desk officer. It's time she was.'

'There you are, Miss Frome.'

'Thank you.'

We all stood. Max was looking at me with what I thought was new respect. I heard a singing sound in my ears, like a polyphonic chorus. I had been in the Service only nine months and even if I was among the last in my intake to be promoted, I'd reached as high as any woman could go. Tony would have been so proud of me. He would have taken me out for a celebratory dinner at his club. Wasn't it the same as Nutting's? The least I could do, I thought, as we filed out of Tapp's office, was to phone my mother and let her know how well I was doing at the Department of Health and Social Security.

8

I settled myself into my armchair, angled my new reading lamp and took up my bookmark fetish. I had a pencil at the ready, as though preparing for a tutorial. My dream had come true – I was studying English, not maths. I was free of my mother's ambitions for me. The folder was on my lap, buff coloured, HMSO, closed with loops of string. What a transgression, and how privileged I was, to have a file at home. It had been hammered into us in our early training – files were sacred. Nothing was to be removed from a file, no file was to be removed from the building. Benjamin had accompanied me to the front entrance, and was made to open up the folder to prove that it wasn't a Registry Personal File, even though it was the same colour as one. As he explained to the P Branch duty officer on the desk, it was mere background information. But that night it gave me pleasure to think of it as the Haley file.

I count those first hours with his fiction as among the happiest in my time at Five. All my needs beyond the sexual met and merged: I was reading, I was doing it for a higher purpose that gave me professional pride, and I was soon to meet the author. Did I have doubts or moral qualms about the project? Not at that stage. I was pleased to have been chosen. I thought I could do the job well. I thought I might earn praise from the higher floors in the building – I was a girl who liked to be praised. If someone had asked, I would have said we were nothing more than a clandestine Arts Council. The opportunities we offered were as good as any.

The story had been published in the *Kenyon Review* in the winter of 1970 and the whole issue was there, with a protruding purchase slip from a specialist bookshop in Longacre, Covent Garden. It concerned the formidably named Edmund Alfredus, an academic teacher of medieval social history who becomes in his mid-forties a Labour MP in a tough east London constituency, having been a local councillor there for a dozen years. He's well to the left of his party and *something of a trouble-maker, an intellectual dandy, a serial adulterer and a brilliant public speaker* with good connections to powerful members of the Tube train drivers' union. He happens to have an identical twin brother, Giles, a milder figure, an Anglican vicar with a pleasant living in rural West Sussex within cycling distance of Petworth House, where Turner once painted. His small, elderly congregation gathers in *a pre-Norman church whose pargeted uneven walls bore the palimpsests of Saxon murals depicting a suffering Christ overlaid by a gyre of ascending angels, whose awkward grace and simplicity spoke to Giles of mysteries beyond the reach of an industrial, scientific age.*

They are also beyond the reach of Edmund, a strict atheist who in private is scornful of Giles's comfortable life and improbable beliefs. For his part, the vicar is embarrassed that Edmund has not outgrown his adolescent bolshevik views. But the brothers are close and usually manage to avoid religious or political disputes. They lost their mother to breast cancer when they were eight and were sent away by their emotionally remote father to boarding prep school, where they clung to each other for comfort, and so were bound for life.

Both men married in their late twenties and have children. But a year after Edmund takes his seat in the House of

Commons, the patience of his wife, Molly, breaks on account of one affair too many and she throws him out. Looking for shelter from the storm of domestic ruin and divorce proceedings, and nascent press interest, Edmund heads to the Sussex vicarage to spend a long weekend, and here is where the story proper begins. Brother Giles is in distress. That Sunday he is due to deliver the sermon in his church in the presence of the Bishop of Ch—, well known for being a prickly, intolerant sort. (Naturally, I projected my father into the role.) His Grace will not be pleased to be told that the vicar, whose performance he intends to inspect, has come down with a bad dose of flu complicated by laryngitis.

On his arrival, Edmund is directed by the vicar's wife, his sister-in-law, straight up to the old nursery on the top floor, where Giles has been quarantined. Even in their forties and for all their differences, the Alfredus twins share a taste for mischief. With Giles sweating, and croaking to be heard, they confer for half an hour and make their decision. For Edmund it's a useful distraction from the trouble at home, to spend all the next day, Saturday, learning the liturgy and the order of service and thinking about his sermon. The theme, announced to the bishop in advance, is from I Corinthians 13, the famous verses in the King James translation declaring that of faith, hope and charity, 'the greatest of these is charity'. Giles has insisted that in line with modern scholarship, Edmund is to substitute 'love' for 'charity'. No disagreement here. As a medievalist, Edmund knows his Bible, and he admires the Authorised Version. And yes, he is happy to talk of love. On Sunday morning he puts on his brother's surplice and, after combing his hair in imitation of Giles's neat side parting, slips out of the house and makes his way across the graveyard to the church.

News of the bishop's visit *had swollen the congregation to almost forty*. Prayers and hymns follow in the usual order. Everything proceeds smoothly. An ancient canon, *his gaze wrenched downward by osteoporosis*, assists efficiently in the service without noticing that Giles is Edmund. At the correct moment Edmund mounts the carved stone pulpit. Even the ageing regulars in the pews are aware that their soft-spoken vicar appears particularly confident, forthright even, no doubt keen to impress the distinguished visitor. Edmund begins by repeating from the first reading selected passages from Corinthians, speaking the lines with actorly rotundity – close, some might have thought, if they had ever been to a theatre (so Haley adds in aside), to a parody of Olivier. Edmund's words resound in the near-empty church, and with tongue thrust between teeth he relishes the 'th' sound in the verbs. *Love suffereth long, and is kind; love envieth not; love vaunteth not itself, is not puffed up, doth not behave itself unseemly, seeketh not her own, is not easily provoked, thinketh no evil; rejoiceth not in iniquity, but rejoiceth in the truth . . .*

Then he begins a passionate disquisition on love, driven in part by shame at his recent betrayals and sorrow for the wife and two children he has left behind, and the warm memories of all the good women he has known, and by the sheer pleasure in performance that a good public speaker feels. The generous acoustic and his raised position in the pulpit also help him to fresh turns of rhetorical extravagance. Deploying the very debating skills that have helped bring out the Tube train drivers on three one-day strikes in as many weeks, he sets out the case that love as we know and celebrate it today is a Christian invention. In the harsh Iron Age world of the Old Testament, ethics were pitiless, its jealous God was ruthless and His most cherished values were revenge, domination, enslavement, genocide and rape. Here some noted the bishop swallowing hard.

Against such a background, Edmund says, we see how radical the new religion was in putting love at its centre. Uniquely in human history, a quite different principle of social organisation was proposed. In fact, a new civilisation takes root. However short it may fall of these ideals, a fresh direction is set. Jesus's idea is irresistible and irreversible.

Even unbelievers must live within it. For love doesn't stand alone, nor can it, *but trails like a blazing comet, bringing with it other shining goods – forgiveness, kindness, tolerance, fairness, companionability and friendship, all bound to the love which is at the heart of Jesus's message.*

It is not done, in an Anglican church in West Sussex, to applaud a sermon. But when Edmund has finished, having quoted from memory lines of Shakespeare, Herrick, Christina Rossetti, Wilfred Owen and Auden, the impulse to cheer is palpable in the pews. The vicar, in sonorous falling tones which breathe wisdom and sadness down the nave, leads the congregation into prayer. When the bishop straightens, purplish from the effort of leaning forwards, he's beaming and everyone else, the retired colonels and horse breeders and the ex-captain of the polo team and all their wives beam too, and beam again as they file out through the porch, where they shake Edmund's hand. The bishop actually pumps his hand, is fulsome, then, mercifully, regrets he has another appointment and cannot stay for coffee. The canon shuffles off without a word, and soon everyone is heading towards their Sunday lunch, and Edmund, feeling the lightness of triumph in his step, fairly skips through the graveyard, back to the vicarage to tell his brother all about it.

Here, on the eighteenth of thirty-nine pages, was a space between the paragraphs adorned with a single asterisk. I stared into it to prevent my gaze slipping down the page and revealing the writer's next move. Sentimentally, I hoped that Edmund's high-flown talk of love would deliver him back to his wife and children. Not much chance of that in a modern story. Or he might talk himself into becoming a Christian. Or Giles could lose his faith when he hears how his congregation is stirred by clever rhetoric from the mouth of an atheist. I was drawn to the possibility of the narrative following the bishop home to witness him that night lying in the bath, brooding steamily on what he had heard. That was because

I didn't want my father the Bishop to disappear from the scene. In fact, the ecclesiastical trappings entranced me – the Norman church, the smells of brass polish, lavender wax, old stone and dust that Haley evoked, the black, white and red bell ropes behind the font with the wonky oak lid held together by iron rivets and ties across a massive split, and above all the vicarage with the chaotic back hall beyond the kitchen, where Edmund dumps his bag on the chessboard lino, and the nursery on the top floor, just like ours. I felt faintly homesick. If only Haley had gone, or made Edmund go, into the bathroom to see the waist-high tongue-and-groove panelling painted baby blue and the giant bath, stained by blue-green algae beneath the taps, standing four-square on rusty lion's feet. And into the lavatory, where a faded bathtime duck hung from the end of the cistern chain. I was the basest of readers. All I wanted was my own world, and myself in it, given back to me in artful shapes and accessible form.

I was drawn to mild-mannered Giles by the same associations, but it was Edmund I wanted. Wanted? To travel with. I wanted Haley to examine Edmund's mind for me, to open it up for my inspection, and to explain it to me, man to woman. Edmund reminded me of Max, and of Jeremy. And of Tony most of all. These clever, amoral, inventive, destructive men, single-minded, selfish, emotionally cool, coolly attractive. I think I preferred them to the love of Jesus. They were so necessary, and not only to me. Without them we would still be living in mud huts, waiting to invent the wheel. Three-crop rotation would never have come to pass. Such impermissible thoughts at the dawn of feminism's second wave. I stared into the asterisk. Haley had got under my skin, and I wondered if he was one of those necessary men. I felt violated by him, and homesick and curious, all at once. So far I hadn't made a single pencil mark. It wasn't fair that such a shit as Edmund should give a brilliant cynical speech and be praised, but it was right, it seemed true. That image of him dancing in joy among the graves on his way back to tell his brother how well he has performed suggested hubris. Haley was intimating that punishment or downfall must follow. I didn't want it to. Tony had been punished and that was enough for me. Writers owed their readers a duty of care, of mercy. The *Kenyon Review*'s asterisk was beginning to rotate beneath my fixed gaze. I blinked it to a standstill and read on.

It had not occurred to me that with almost half of the story told, Haley would introduce another important character. But she was there all through the service, sitting at the end of the third row, right against the wall by the piled-up hymnbooks, unnoticed by Edmund. Her name is Jean Alise. It is quickly established that she is thirty-five, lives locally, is a widow and somewhat wealthy, is devout, more so since the death of her husband in a motorbike accident, has some psychiatric illness in her past and is, of course, beautiful. Edmund's sermon has a profound, even devastating, effect upon her. She loves its message and understands its truth, she loves the poetry and is powerfully drawn to the man who speaks it. She stays up all that night wondering what to do. She doesn't actually want to, but she's falling in love and is prepared to go to the vicarage and say so. She cannot help it, she's ready to wreck the vicar's marriage.

At nine the following morning she rings the vicarage doorbell and it is Giles in his dressing gown who answers. He's making the beginnings of a recovery, but he's still pale and shaky. To my relief, Jean knows right away that this is not her man. She establishes that there is a brother and follows him to London, to the address that Giles has innocently provided. It's a small furnished flat in Chalk Farm, where Edmund is setting up a temporary base while he goes through his divorce.

It's a stressful time and he is not able to resist a beautiful woman who appears desperate to give him everything he wants. She stays for an unbroken two weeks and Edmund makes passionate love to her – Haley describes their intimacy in detail I found difficult. Her clitoris is *monstrous, the size of a prepubertal boy's penis.* He has never known such a generous lover. Jean soon decides that she is bound to Edmund for the rest of her life. Once she has learned that her man is an atheist, she understands that the task granted to her is to bring him to the light of God. Wisely, she doesn't mention her mission and bides her time. It takes her only a few days to forgive him the blasphemous impersonation of his brother.

Edmund meanwhile is reading and re-reading in private a letter from Molly which hints strongly at a reconciliation. She loves him, and if he could only cease his affairs there might be a way they could be a family again. The children are missing him sorely. It is going to be hard to extricate himself, but he knows what he must do. Fortunately, Jean pops down to her moated house in Sussex to attend to her horses and dogs and other matters. Edmund arrives at the family home and has an hour with his wife. It goes well, she looks wonderful, he makes promises he is certain he can keep. The children come home from school and they have tea together. It's like old times.

When he tells Jean the next day, over a fry-up breakfast in a local greasy spoon, that he is going back to his wife, he sets off a frightening psychiatric episode. He didn't realise up until this point quite how fragile her mental health is. After breaking the plate he was eating off, she runs screaming from the cafe into the street. He decides not to go after her. Instead, he hurries to the flat and packs up his belongings, leaves what he thinks is a kindly note to Jean and moves back in with Molly. The bliss of reunion lasts three days, until Jean re-enters his life with a vengeance.

The nightmare begins with her calling at the house and making a scene in front of Molly and the kids. She writes letters to Molly as well as Edmund, she accosts the children on their way to school, she phones several times every day and often in the small hours. Daily she stands outside the house, waiting to talk to any member of the family who dares come out. The police will do nothing because they say that Jean is not breaking any law. She follows Molly to her work – she's a headmistress at a primary school – and makes one of her awesome scenes in the playground.

Two months pass. *A stalker can as easily bind a family in solidarity as break it apart.* But in the Alfredus marriage, the bonds are still too weak, the damage of past years has not yet been repaired. This affliction, Molly tells Edmund in their final heart to heart, is what he has brought down on their family. She must protect the children as well as her own sanity and her job. Once more, she asks him to leave. He acknowledges an intolerable situation. As he steps out of the house with his bags, Jean is waiting for him on the pavement. He hails a cab. After a violent scuffle, witnessed by Molly from a bedroom window, Jean forces her way in beside her man, whose face she has badly scratched. He weeps for his marriage all the way to Chalk Farm, back to the apartment she has kept on as a shrine to their love. He is not aware of her comforting arm around his shoulder and her promise to love him and be with him always.

Now they are together, she is sane, practical and loving. For a while it is hard to imagine those terrible episodes ever took place, and it is easy in his distress, submitting to her kindly ministrations, to become her lover again. But now and then *she drifted up towards the dark clouds where these tornadoes of emotion were formed.* Even the legal confirmation of his divorce fails to bring Jean contentment. He dreads her explosive moments and does everything he can to avert them. What sets her off? When she suspects he is thinking of, or looking at, another woman, when he stays too late at the House for an all-night sitting, when he's out drinking with his left-wing friends, when he delays yet again the registry-office wedding. *He hated confrontations and was innately lazy, so by degrees her jealous eruptions trained him to her will.* It happens slowly. He finds it easier to stay away from old lovers who have become friends, or from female colleagues in general, easier to ignore the division bell and the demands of the Whips' Office and his constituents, and easier in fact to marry than face the consequences – those terrifying storms – of continuing to put off the day.

In the 1970 election that brings Edward Heath to power, Edmund loses his seat and is taken aside by his agent and told that the Party will not nominate him next time round. The newly married couple move to her lovely home in Sussex. He has become financially dependent on Jean. He carries no weight these days with the Tube train drivers' union or other friends on the left. Just as well, because his opulent surroundings embarrass him. Visits from his children seem to precipitate nasty scenes and so, by degrees, he joins *that sorry legion of passive men who abandon their children in order to placate their second wives.* Easier too to attend weekly church services than have yet more shouting matches. As he advances into his fifties he begins to take an interest in the roses within the estate's walled garden and becomes an expert on the carp in the moat. He learns to ride, though he can never shake off the feeling that he looks ridiculous on a horse. However, his relations with his brother Giles have never been better. As for Jean, in church when she sees through furtive partly opened eyes Edmund kneeling at her side during the blessing that follows the Reverend Alfredus's sermon, she knows that *though the way had been hard and she had suffered for her pains, she was bringing her husband ever closer to Jesus and this, her single most important achievement in life, had only been possible through the redeeming and enduring power of love.*

There it was. Only as I reached the end did I realise that I had failed to take in the title. 'This is love'. He seemed too worldly, too knowing, this twenty-seven-year-old who was to be my innocent target. Here was a man who knew what it was to love a destructive woman afflicted by mood storms, a man who had noted the lid of an ancient font, who knew that the wealthy stocked their moats with carp and the downtrodden kept their stuff in supermarket trolleys – both supermarkets and trolleys were recent additions to life in Britain. If Jean's mutant genitalia were not an invention but a memory, then I already felt belittled or outclassed. Was I a touch jealous of his affair?

I was packing away the file, too tired to face another story. I'd experienced a peculiar form of wilful narrative sadism. Alfredus may have earned the narrowing of his life, but Haley had driven him into the ground. Misanthropy or self-loathing – were they entirely distinct? – must be part of his make-up. I was discovering that the experience of reading is skewed when you know, or are about to know, the author. I had been inside a stranger's mind. Vulgar curiosity made me wonder if every sentence confirmed or denied or masked a secret intention. I felt closer to Tom Haley than I would if he'd been a colleague in the Registry these past nine months. But if I sensed intimacy, it was hard to say exactly what I knew. I needed an instrument, some measuring device, the narrative equivalent of movable compass points with which to gauge the distance between Haley and Edmund Alfredus. The author may have been keeping his own demons at arm's length. Perhaps Alfredus – not a necessary man after all – represented the kind of person Haley feared he could become. Or he may have punished Alfredus in the spirit of moral primness for adultery and presuming to impersonate a pious man. Haley might be a prig, even a religious prig, or he could be a man with many fears. And priggishness and fear could be twin aspects of a single larger character defect. If I hadn't wasted three years being bad at maths at Cambridge, I might have done English and learned how to read. But would I have known how to read T.H. Haley?

9

The following night I had a date with Shirley at the Hope and Anchor in Islington to hear Bees Make Honey. I was half an hour late. She was sitting alone at the bar smoking, hunched over her notebook, with a couple of inches of beer in her pint glass. It was warm outside but it had been raining heavily and the place had a canine smell of damp jeans and hair. Amp lights glowed in a corner where a lone roadie was setting up. The crowd, which probably included the band and their pals, was hardly more than two dozen. In those days, at least in my circle, even women didn't embrace on greeting. I slipped onto the bar stool beside Shirley and ordered drinks. It was still something back then for two girls to assume a pub was as much theirs as any man's and to drink at the bar. In the Hope and Anchor and a handful of other places in London no one cared. The revolution had arrived and you could get away with it. We pretended to take it for granted, but it was still a kick. Elsewhere across the kingdom they would have taken us for whores, or treated us as though we were.

At work we ate our lunches together but there was still something between us, a little piece of gritty residue from that brief dispute. If her politics were so infantile or bone-headed, how much of a friend could she be? But at other times I believed that time would settle the matter and that, by simple contagion at work, her political views would mature. Sometimes *not* talking is the best way through a difficulty. The fad for personal 'truth' and confrontation was doing great damage in my view and blighting many friendships and marriages.

Not long before our date, Shirley had gone missing from her desk for most of one day and part of the next. She wasn't ill. Someone had seen her getting into the lift and had seen the button she pushed. The gossip was she'd been summoned to the fifth floor, the misty heights where our masters conducted their unknowable business. The gossip also hinted that since she was smarter than the rest of us, she was up for some unusual form of promotion. From the large debutante faction this provoked some amiable snobbery of the 'Oh, if only *I'd* been born into the working class' sort. I checked my own feelings. Would I feel jealous at being left behind by my best friend? I thought I would.

When she was back among us she ignored questions and told us nothing, didn't even lie, which was taken by most as confirmation of superior advancement. I wasn't so sure. Her plumpness sometimes made her expression hard to read, her subcutaneous fat being the mask she lived behind. Which would have made this line of work a good choice for her, if only the women were sent out to do more than clean houses. But I thought I knew her well enough. There was no triumph there. Did I feel just a tiny bit relieved? I thought so.

This was our first meeting outside the building since then. I was determined not to ask questions about the fifth floor. It would have looked undignified. Besides, I now had my own assignment and promotion, even if they emanated from two floors below hers. She switched to gin and orange, a large one, and I had the same. In low voices we talked office gossip for the first quarter of an hour. Now that we were no longer new girls, we felt at liberty to ignore some of the rules. There was a substantial new item. One of our intake, Lisa

– Oxford High, St Anne's, bright and charming – had just announced her engagement to a desk officer called Andrew – Eton, King's, boyish and intellectual. It was the fourth such alliance in nine months. If Poland had joined NATO it would not have caused more excitement in the ranks than these bilateral negotiations. Part of the interest was speculating who would be next. 'Who whom?' as some Leninist wag put it. Early on, I'd been spotted on the bench in Berkeley Square with Max. I used to feel a thrill in my stomach when I heard our names fed through the mill, but lately we'd been dropped for more tangible outcomes. So Shirley and I discussed Lisa and the consensus that her wedding date was too remote, and then touched on Wendy's prospects with a figure who may have been too grand – her Oliver was an assistant head of section. But I thought there was something flat or routine in our exchange. I sensed that Shirley was putting something off, lifting her glass too frequently, as if summoning her courage.

Sure enough, she ordered another gin, took a swig, hesitated, then said, 'I have to tell you something. But first you have to do something for me.'

'Yes.'

'Smile, like you were just now.'

'What?'

'Just do as I say. We're being watched. Put on a smile. We're having a happy conversation. OK?'

I stretched my lips.

'You can do better than that. Don't freeze.'

I tried harder, I nodded and shrugged, trying to look animated.

Shirley said, 'I've been sacked.'

'Impossible!'

'As of today.'

'Shirley!'

'Just keep smiling. You mustn't tell anyone.'

'OK, but why?'

'I can't tell you everything.'

'You can't have been sacked. It doesn't make sense. You're better than all of us.'

'I could have told you somewhere private. But our rooms aren't secure. And I want them to see me talking to you.'

The lead guitarist had strapped on his guitar. He and the drummer were with the roadie now, all three bent over some piece of equipment on the floor. There was a howl of feedback, quickly subdued. I stared at the crowd, knots of people with their backs to us, mostly men, standing about with their pints waiting for the band to start. Could one or two be from A4, the Watchers? I was sceptical.

I said, 'Do you really think you're being followed?'

'No, not me. *You*.'

My laughter was genuine. 'That's ridiculous.'

'Seriously. The Watchers. Ever since you joined. They've probably been into your room. Put in a mike. Serena, don't stop smiling.'

I turned back to the crowd. Shoulder-length hair for men was by then a minority taste, and the terrible moustaches and big sideburns were still some while ahead. So, plenty of ambiguous-looking types, plenty of candidates. I thought I could see a possible half-dozen. Then, suddenly, everyone in the room looked a possibility.

'But Shirley. Why?'

'I thought you could tell me.'

'There's nothing. You've made this up.'

'Look, I've got something to tell you. I did something stupid and I'm really ashamed. I don't know how to say it. I was going to do it yesterday, then my nerve failed. But I need to be honest about this. I've fucked up.'

She took a deep breath and reached for another cigarette. Her hands were shaking. We looked over towards the band. The drummer was sitting in, adjusting the hi-hat, showing off a tricky little turn with the brushes.

Shirley said at last, 'Before we went to clean that house,

113

they called me in. Peter Nutting, Tapp, that creepy kid, Benjamin someone.'

'Jesus. Why?'

'They laid it on. Said I was doing well, possibility of promotion, softening me up like. Then they said they knew we were close friends. Nutting asked if you ever said anything unusual or suspicious. I said no. They asked what we talked about.'

'Christ. What did you say?'

'I should have told them to get stuffed. I didn't have the courage. There was nothing to hide so I told them the truth. I said we talked about music, friends, family, the past, chit-chat, nothing much at all.' She looked at me a touch accusingly. 'You would've done the same.'

'I'm not sure.'

'If I'd said nothing they'd have been even more suspicious.'

'All right. Then what?'

Tapp asked me if we ever spoke about politics and I said no. He said he found that hard to believe, I said it was a fact. We went round and round for a bit. Then they said OK, they were going to ask me something delicate. But it was very important and they'd be deeply appreciative, etc., if I could see my way to oblige, on and on, you know the greasy way they talk.'

'I think so.'

'They wanted me to get into a political conversation with you, and to come on like a real closet leftie, draw you out and see where you stood and . . .'

'Let them know.'

'I know. I'm ashamed. But don't get sour. I'm trying to be straight with you. And remember to smile.'

I stared at her, at her fat face and its scattered freckles. I was trying to hate her. Almost there. I said, '*You* smile. Faking's your thing.'

'I'm sorry.'

'So that whole conversation . . . you were on the job.'

'Listen, Serena, I voted for *Heath*. So yes, I was on the job, and I hate myself for it.'

'That workers' paradise near Leipzig was a lie?'

'No, it was a real school trip. Boring as shit. And I was homesick, wept like a baby. But listen, you did all right, you said all the right things.'

'Which you reported back!'

She was looking at me sorrowfully, shaking her head. 'That's the point. I didn't. I went to see them that evening and told them I couldn't do it, I wasn't playing. I didn't even tell them we'd had the conversation. I said I wasn't going to inform on a friend.'

I looked away. Now I was really confused, because I rather wished she had told them what I'd said. But I couldn't say that to Shirley. We drank our gin in silence for half a minute. The bass player was on now and the thing on the floor, some sort of junction box, was still giving trouble. I glanced around. No one in the pub was looking in our direction.

I said, 'If they know that we're friends they must have guessed that you'd tell me what they asked you to do.'

'Exactly. They're sending you a message. Perhaps they're warning you off something. I've been straight with you. Now you tell me. Why are they interested in you?'

Of course, I had no idea. But I was angry with her. I didn't want to look ignorant – no, more than that, I wanted her to believe that there were matters I preferred not to discuss. And I wasn't sure I believed anything she was saying.

I turned the question back to her. 'So they sacked you because you wouldn't inform on a colleague? That doesn't sound plausible to me.'

She took a long time getting out her cigarettes, offering one, lighting them. We ordered more drinks. I didn't want another gin, but my thoughts were too disordered, I couldn't think of what else to have. So we had the same again. I was almost out of money.

'Well,' she said, 'I don't want to talk about it. So there you

115

are. This career is over. I never thought it would last anyway. I'm going to live at home and look after my dad. He's acting a bit confused lately. I'll help out in the shop. And I might even do some writing. But listen. I wish you'd tell me what was going on.'

And then, in a sudden gesture of affection, conjuring up the old days of our friendship she took the lapel of my cotton jacket and shook it. Shaking sense into me. 'You've got yourself caught up in something. It's crazy, Serena. They look and talk like a bunch of stuffed shirts, and they *are*, but they can be mean. It's what they're good at. They're *mean*.'

I said, 'We'll see.'

I was anxious and completely baffled, but I wanted to punish her, make her worry about me. I could almost fool myself that I really had a secret.

'Serena. You can tell me.'

'Too complicated. And why should I tell you anything? What could you do about it anyway? You're bottom of the heap like me. Or you were.'

'Are you talking to the other side?'

It was a shocking question. In that reckless tipsy moment I wished I did have a Russian controller and a double life, and dead-letter drops on Hampstead Heath, or better, that I was a double agent, feeding useless truths and destructive lies into an alien system. At least I had T. H. Haley. And why would they give me him if I was under suspicion?

'Shirley, *you're* the other side.'

Her reply was lost to the opening chords of 'Knee Trembler', an old favourite with us, but we didn't enjoy it this time round. It was the end of our conversation. Stalemate. She wouldn't tell me why she was sacked, I wouldn't tell her the secret I didn't have. A minute later, she slid from her bar stool and left without saying or miming goodbye. I wouldn't have responded anyway. I sat there a while, trying to enjoy the band, trying to calm myself and think straight. When I'd finished my gin, I drank the remains of Shirley's. I didn't know which upset me more, my good friend or my employers snooping on me. Shirley's betrayal was unforgivable, my employers' frightening. If I was under suspicion, there must have been an administrative error, but that didn't make Nutting and Co any less frightening. It was no comfort to learn they had sent the Watchers into my room and that, in a moment's incompetence, someone had dropped my bookmark.

Without a pause the band cruised straight into their second song, 'My Rockin' Days'. If they really were there, down among the punters and their pints, the Watchers would have been far closer to the speakers than I was. I guessed that this wouldn't have been their kind of music. Those stolid A4 types would be more the easy-listening sort. They'd hate this throbbing jangling din. There was some comfort in that, but not in much else.

I decided to go home and read another story.

No one knew how Neil Carder came by his money or what he was doing living alone in an eight-bedroom Highgate mansion. Most neighbours who passed him occasionally in the street didn't even know his name. He was a plain-looking fellow in his late thirties, with a narrow pale face, very shy and with an awkward manner, and no gift for the kind of easy small talk that might have led him towards the beginnings of some local acquaintance. But he caused no trouble, and kept his house and garden in good order. If his name came up in the rounds of gossip, what generally featured was the large white 1959 Bentley he kept parked outside the house. What was a mousy fellow like Carder doing with a showy vehicle like that? Another item of speculation was the young, cheerful, colourfully dressed Nigerian house-keeper who came in six days a week. Abeje shopped, laundered, cooked, she was attractive, and was popular with the watchful housewives. But was she also Mr Carder's lover? It seemed so unlikely that people were tempted to think it might even be true. Those pale silent men, you never knew . . . But then, they were never seen together, she was never in his car, she always left just after teatime and waited at the top of the street for her bus back to Willesden. If Neil Carder had a sex life it was indoors and strictly nine till five.

The circumstances of a brief marriage, a large and surprising inheritance and an inward, unadventurous nature had combined to empty Carder's life. It had been a mistake to buy so large a house in an unfamiliar part of London, but he couldn't motivate himself to move out and buy another. What would be the point? His few friends and Civil Service colleagues had been repelled by his sudden enormous wealth. Perhaps they were jealous. Either way, people were not queuing up to help him spend his money. Beyond the house and car he had no great material ambitions, no passionate interests he could at last fulfil, no philanthropic impulses, and travelling abroad didn't appeal. Abeje was certainly a bonus, and he fantasised about her a fair bit, but she was married with two small children. Her husband, also a Nigerian, had once kept goal for the national soccer team. One glance at a snapshot of him and Carder knew he was no match, he was not Abeje's type.

Neil Carder was a dull fellow and his life was making him duller. He slept late, checked on his portfolio and spoke with his stockbroker, read a bit, watched TV, walked on the Heath now and then, occasionally went to bars and clubs, hoping to meet someone. But he was too shy to make approaches and nothing ever happened. He felt he was held in suspension, he was waiting for a new life to begin, but he felt incapable of taking an initiative. And when at last it did begin, it was in a most unexceptional way. He was walking along Oxford Street, at the Marble Arch end, on his way from his dentist in Wigmore Street when he passed a department store with immense plate-glass windows behind which was an array of mannequins in various poses, modelling evening wear. He paused a moment to look in, felt self-conscious, walked on a few paces, hesitated, and went back. The dummies – he came to hate that term – were disposed in such a way as to suggest a sophisticated gathering at cocktail hour. One woman leaned forwards, as though to divulge a secret, another held up a stiff white arm in amused disbelief, a third, languorously bored, looked across her shoulder towards a doorway, where a rugged fellow in dinner jacket leaned with his unlit cigarette.

But Neil wasn't interested in any of these. He was looking at a young woman who had turned away from the entire group. She was contemplating an engraving – a view of Venice – on the wall. But not quite. Through an error of alignment by the window dresser, or, as he suddenly found himself imagining, *a degree of stubbornness in the woman herself, her gaze was off the picture by several inches and was angled straight into the corner. She was pursuing a thought, an idea, and she didn't care how she appeared.* She didn't want to be there. She wore an orange silk dress of simple folds and, unlike all the rest, she was barefoot. Her shoes – they must have been her shoes – were lying on their sides by the door, discarded as she came in. She loved freedom. In one hand she held *a small black and orange beaded purse, while the other trailed at her side, wrist turned outwards as she lost herself to her idea. Or perhaps a memory. Her head was slightly lowered to reveal the pure line of her neck. Her lips were parted, but only just, as though she was formulating a thought, a word, a name . . . Neil.*

He shrugged himself out of his daydream. He knew it was absurd and walked on purposefully, glancing at his watch to convince himself that he did indeed have a purpose. But he didn't. All that waited for him was the empty house in Highgate. Abeje would have gone by the time he got home. He wouldn't even have the benefit of the latest bulletin on her toddler children. He forced himself to keep walking, well aware that a form of madness was lying in wait, for an idea was forming, and becoming pressing. It said something for his strength of mind that he made it all the way to Oxford

Circus before he turned around. Not so good, though, that he hurried all the way back to the store. This time he felt no embarrassment standing by her, gazing into this private moment of hers. What he saw now was her face. So thoughtful, so sad, so beautiful. She was so apart, so alone. The conversation around her was shallow, she had heard it all before, these were not her people, this was not her milieu. How was she to break out? It was a sweet fantasy and an enjoyable one, and at this stage Carder had no difficulty acknowledging that it *was* a fantasy. That token of sanity left him all the freer to indulge himself as the shopping crowds stepped around him on the pavement.

Later, he was not able to remember actually weighing up or making a decision. With a sense of a destiny already formed, he went into the shop, spoke to one person, was referred up to another, then a more senior third who refused outright. Quite out of order. A sum was mentioned, eyebrows were raised, a superior summoned, the sum was doubled and the matter agreed. By the end of the week? No, it had to be now, and the dress must come too, and he wished to buy several others of the correct size. *The assistants and the managers stood around him. Here they had on their hands, not for the first time, an eccentric. A man in love. All present knew that a mighty purchase was under way.* For such dresses were not cheap, and nor were several pairs of matching shoes, and the shot silk underwear. And then – how calm and decisive the fellow was – the jewellery. And, an afterthought, the perfume. All done in two and a half hours. A delivery van was made immediately available, the address in Highgate was written down, the payment made.

That evening, no one saw her arrive in the arms of the driver.

At this point I got myself out of my reading chair and went downstairs to make tea. I was still a little drunk, still troubled by my conversation with Shirley. I felt that I would doubt my own sanity if I started looking for a hidden microphone in my room. I also felt vulnerable to Neil Carder's loose grip on reality. It could loosen my own. And was he yet another character to be ground under Haley's narrative heel for getting everything wrong? With some reluctance, I carried my tea upstairs and sat on the edge of my bed, willing myself to pick up another of Haley's pages. Clearly, the reader was intended to have no relief from the millionaire's madness, no chance to stand outside it and see it for what it was. There was no possibility of this clammy tale ending well.

At last I returned to the chair and learned that the mannequin's name was Hermione, which happened to be the name of Carder's ex-wife. She had walked out on him one morning after less than a year. That evening, while Hermione lay naked on the bed, he cleared a wardrobe for her in the dressing room and hung her clothes and stowed her shoes. He took a shower, then they dressed for dinner. He went downstairs to arrange on two plates the meal Abeje had prepared for him. It only needed reheating. Then he went back to the bedroom to fetch her down to the splendid dining room. They ate in silence. In fact, she didn't touch her food and wouldn't meet his eye. He understood why. The tension between them was almost unbearable – one reason why he drank two bottles of wine. *He was so drunk he had to carry her up the stairs.*

What a night! He was one of those men *for whom passivity in a woman was a goad, a piercing enticement.* Even in rapture he saw the boredom in her eyes that brought him to fresh heights of ecstasy. Finally, not long before dawn, they rolled apart, sated, immobilised by a profound exhaustion. Hours later, aroused by sunlight through the curtains, he managed to turn onto his side. It touched him profoundly that she had slept the night through on her back. *He delighted in her stillness. Her inwardness was so intense that it rolled back upon itself to become its opposite, a force that overwhelmed and consumed him and drove his love onwards to constant sensuous obsession.* What had started as an idle fantasy outside a shop window was now an intact inner world, a vertiginous reality he preserved with the fervour of a religious fanatic. He couldn't allow himself to consider her inanimate because his pleasure in love depended on a masochistic understanding that she was *ignoring him, she disdained him and thought he was not worthy of her kisses, of her caresses, or even of her conversation.*

When Abeje came in to tidy and clean the bedroom, she was surprised to find Hermione in a corner staring out of the window, wearing a dress of torn silk. But the housekeeper was pleased to discover in one of the wardrobes a rack of fine dresses. She was an intelligent woman of the world and she had been aware of, and somewhat oppressed by, her employer's lingering, ineffectual gaze as she went about her work. Now he had a lover. What a relief. If his woman imported a dummy to hang her clothes on, who cared? As the extreme disorder of the bedlinen suggested, and as she relayed it in her native Yoruba that night to embolden her muscular husband, *They are truly singing.*

Even in the most richly communicative and reciprocal love affairs, it is nearly impossible to sustain that initial state of rapture beyond a few weeks. Historically, a resourceful few may have managed months. *But when the sexual terrain is tended by one mind alone, one lonely figure tilling the frontiers of a wilderness, the fall must come in days.* What nourished Carder's love – Hermione's silence – was bound to destroy it. She had been living with him less than a week when he observed a shift in her mood, a near imperceptible recalibration of her silence that contained the faint but constant note, almost beyond hearing, of dissatisfaction. Driven by this tinnitus of doubt, he strove harder to please her. That night, when they were upstairs, a suspicion passed through his mind and he experienced a thrill – it really was a thrill – of horror. *She was thinking about someone else.* She had that same look he had observed through the store window as she stood apart from the guests and gazed into the corner. She wanted to be elsewhere. When he made love to her, the agony of this realisation was inseparable from the pleasure, sharp as a surgeon's scalpel, that seemed to slice his heart in two. But it was only a suspicion after all, he thought as he retreated to his side of the bed. He slept deeply that night.

What revived his doubts the next morning was a parallel shift in Abeje's attitude as she served him his breakfast (Hermione always stayed in bed until noon). His housekeeper was both brisk and evasive. She wouldn't meet his eye. The coffee was lukewarm and weak and when he complained, he thought she was surly. When she brought in another pot, hot and strong, so she said as she put it down, it came to him. It was simple. The truth was always simple. They were lovers, Hermione and Abeje. Furtive and fleeting. Whenever he was out of the house. For who else had Hermione seen since she arrived? Hence that look of distracted longing. Hence Abeje's abrupt performance this morning. Hence everything. He was a fool, an innocent fool.

The unravelling was swift. That night the surgeon's knife was sharper, cut deeper, with a twist. And he knew Hermione knew. He saw it in the blankness of her terror. *Her crime was his reckless empowerment. He tore into her with all the savagery of disappointed love, and his fingers were round her throat as she came, as they both came. And when he was done, her arms and legs and head had parted company with her torso, which he dashed against the bedroom wall. She lay in all corners, a ruined woman.* This time there was no consoling sleep. In the morning he concealed her body parts in a plastic sack and carried her and all her belongings to the dustbins. In a daze he wrote a note (he was in no mood for further confrontation) to Abeje to inform her of her dismissal 'forthwith' and left on the kitchen table her wages to the end of the month. He went for a long and purging walk across the Heath. That night, Abeje opened up the plastic bags she had retrieved from the bins and modelled the outfits for her husband – the jewels and shoes as well as the silky frocks. She told him haltingly in his native Kanuri (they had married out of their tribes), *She left him and it broke him up.*

Thereafter, Carder lived alone and 'did' for himself and

shrank into middle age with minimal dignity. The whole experience bequeathed him nothing. There were no lessons for him, no reckoning, *for though he, an ordinary fellow, had discovered for himself the awesome power of the imagination, he tried not to think of what had happened. He decided to banish the affair utterly, and such is the efficiency of the compartmentalised mind, he succeeded. He forgot all about her. And he never lived so intensely again.*

10

Max had told me his new office was smaller than a broom cupboard, but it was slightly larger. More than a dozen brooms could have been stored vertically between the desk and the door, and a few more between his chair and the walls. However, there was no space for a window. The room formed a narrow triangle, with Max squeezed in at the apex while I sat with my back to the base. The door wouldn't close properly, so there was no real privacy. Since it opened inwards, I would have had to stand and push my chair under the desk if someone had wanted to come in. On the desk was a pile of headed paper with Freedom International Foundation's address in Upper Regent Street, and a Picassoesque ascending dove holding an open book in its beak. We each had in front of us a copy of the Foundation's brochure, whose cover bore the single word 'freedom' at a slant in uneven red lettering that suggested a rubber stamp. Freedom International, a registered charity, promoted 'excellence and freedom of expression in the arts everywhere in the world'. It was not easily dismissed. It had subsidised or supported by translation or roundabout means writers in Yugoslavia, Brazil, Chile, Cuba, Syria, Romania and Hungary, a dance troupe in Paraguay, journalists in Franco's Spain and Salazar's Portugal and poets in the Soviet Union. It had given money to an actors' collective in Harlem, New York, a baroque orchestra in Alabama, and successfully campaigned for the abolition of the Lord Chamberlain's power over the British theatre.

'It's a decent outfit,' Max said. 'I hope you'll agree. They take their stands everywhere. No one's going to confuse them with those IRD apparatchiks. Altogether more subtle.'

He was wearing a dark blue suit. Far better than the mustard jacket he'd been wearing every other day. And because he was growing his hair, his ears looked less protuberant. The only light source in the room, a high single bulb under a tin shade, picked out his cheekbones and the bow of his lips. He looked sleek and beautiful and quite incongruous in the narrow room, like an animal trapped in an undersized cage.

I said, 'Why was Shirley Shilling sacked?'

He didn't blink at the change of subject. 'I was hoping you might know.'

'Something to do with me?'

'Look, the thing about working in places like this . . . you have all these colleagues, they're pleasant, charming, good backgrounds and all that. Unless you do operations together you don't know what they're up to, what their work is and whether they're any good at it. You don't know whether they're beaming idiots or friendly geniuses. Suddenly they're promoted or sacked and you've no idea why. That's how it is.'

I didn't believe he knew nothing. There was a silence as we let the matter rest. Since Max told me by the gates of Hyde Park that he was becoming attached to me we had spent very little time together. I sensed he was moving up the hierarchy, out of my reach.

He said, 'I got the impression at the meeting the other day that you don't know much about IRD. Information Research Department. It doesn't officially exist. Set up in 'forty-eight, part of the Foreign Office, works out of Carlton Terrace, the idea being to feed information about the Soviet Union into the public domain through friendly journalists, news agencies, put out fact sheets, issue rebuttals, encourage

126

certain publications. So – labour camps, no rule of law, rotten standards of living, repression of dissent, usual stuff. Generally helping out the NCL, the non-communist left, and anything to puncture fantasies here about life in the East. But IRD is drifting. Last year it was trying to persuade the left that we need to join Europe. Ridiculous. And thank God we're taking Northern Ireland off them. It did good work in its day. Now it's too bloated and crude. And rather irrelevant. The word is that it's going to be cut soon. But what matters in this building is that IRD's become the creature of MI6, got itself sucked into black propaganda, deception exercises that deceive no one. Their reports come out of dodgy sources. IRD and its so-called Action Desk have been helping Six to relive the last war. It's Boy Scout nonsense they go in for. That's why everyone in Five likes that "faces to the wall" story Peter Nutting told.'

I said, 'Is it true?'

'I doubt it. But it makes Six look idiotic and pompous, so it goes down well here. Anyway, the idea with Sweet Tooth is to strike out on our own, independently of Six or the Americans. Having a novelist was an afterthought, Peter's whim. Personally, I think it's a mistake – too unpredictable. But this is what we're doing. The writer doesn't have to be a Cold War fanatic. Just be sceptical about utopias in the East or looming catastrophe in the West – you know the sort of thing.'

'What happens when the writer discovers we've been paying his rent? He's going to be furious.'

Max looked away. I thought I'd asked a stupid question. But after a moment's silence he said, 'The link between us and Freedom International works at several removes. Even if you knew exactly where to look, you'd have your work cut out. The calculation is that, if anything comes out, writers will prefer to avoid the embarrassment. They'll stay quiet. And if they don't, we'll explain there are ways of proving that they always knew where the money was coming from.

And the money will keep on flowing. A fellow can get used to a certain way of living and be reluctant to lose it.'

'Blackmail then.'

He shrugged. 'Look, the IRD in its heyday never told Orwell or Koestler what to put in their books. But it did what it could to make sure their ideas got the best circulation around the world. We're dealing with free spirits. We don't tell them what to think. We enable them to do their work. Over there free spirits used to be marched to the gulags. Now Soviet psychiatry's the new State terror. To oppose the system is to be criminally insane. Here we've got some Labour Party and union people and university profs and students and so-called intellectuals who'll tell you the US is no better—'

'Bombing Vietnam.'

'Well, all right. But across the Third World there are whole populations who think the Soviet Union has something to teach them about liberty. The fight isn't over yet. We want to encourage the right good thing. As Peter sees it, Serena, you love literature, you love your country. He thinks this is perfect for you.'

'But you don't.'

'I think we should stick to non-fiction.'

I couldn't work him out. There was something impersonal in his manner. He didn't like Sweet Tooth, or my bit of it, but he was calm about it, even bland. He was like a bored shop assistant encouraging me to buy a dress he knew wasn't right. I wanted to throw him off balance, bring him closer. He was taking me through the details. I was to use my real name. I was to go to Upper Regent Street and meet the Foundation staff. As they understood it, I worked for the organisation called Word Unpenned, which was donating funds to Freedom International to distribute to recommended writers. When I eventually travelled to Brighton I was to make sure that I took nothing with me that would connect me to Leconfield House.

I wondered if Max thought I was stupid. I interrupted him and said, 'What if I like Haley?'

'Fine. We'll sign him up.'

'I mean, really like him.'

He looked up sharply from his check list. 'If you think you'd rather not take this on . . .' His tone was cold and I was pleased.

'Max,' I said, 'it was a joke.'

'Let's talk about your letter to him. I'll need to see a draft.'

So we discussed that and other arrangements and I realised that as far as he was concerned, we were no longer close friends. I could no longer ask him to kiss me. But I wasn't prepared to accept that. I picked up my handbag from the floor and opened it and took out a packet of paper tissues. It was only the year before that I'd stopped using cotton handkerchiefs with broderie anglaise edging and my initials monogrammed in pink in one corner – a Christmas present from my mother. Paper tissues were becoming ubiquitous, like supermarket trolleys. The world was starting to become seriously disposable. I dabbed at a corner of my eye, trying to make my decision. Resting curled in my bag was the triangle of paper with the pencil marks. I'd changed my mind. It was exactly the right thing to do, to show it to Max. Or it was exactly the wrong thing. There was nothing in between.

'Are you all right?'

'Touch of hayfever.'

Finally I thought what I had thought many times before, that it was better, or at least more interesting, to have Max lie to me, than to know nothing at all. I took out the fragment of newsprint and slid it across the desk towards him. He glanced at it, turned it over, turned it back, set it down and looked fixedly at me.

'Well?'

I said, 'Canning and the island whose name you so cleverly guessed.'

'Where did you get it?'

129

'If I tell you, are you going to be straight with me?'

He said nothing, so I told him anyway, about the Fulham safe house and the single bed and its mattress.

'Who was with you?'

I told him and he said 'Ah' quietly into his hands. Then he said, 'So they sacked her.'

'Meaning?'

He pulled his hands apart in a gesture of helplessness. I wasn't cleared to know.

'May I hold on to this?'

'Certainly not.' I snatched it off the desk before he could move his hand and stowed it in my bag.

He softly cleared his throat. 'Then we should move to the next item. The stories. What are you going to say to him?'

'Very excited, brilliant new talent, extraordinary range, lovely sinuous prose, deeply sensitive, especially about women, seems to know and understand them from the inside, unlike most men, dying to know him better and—'

'Serena, enough!'

'And sure that he has a great future, one that the Foundation would like to be a part of. Especially if he'll consider writing a novel. Prepared to pay – how much?'

'Two thousand a year.'

'For how many—'

'Two years. Renewable.'

'My God. How's he going to refuse?'

'Because a complete stranger will be sitting on his lap licking his face. Be cooler. Make him come to you. The Foundation is interested, considering his case, lots of other candidates, what are his future plans, etc?'

'Fine. I play hard to get. Then I'll give him everything.'

Max sat back, folded his arms, glanced at the ceiling and said, 'Serena, I'm sorry you're upset. I honestly don't know why Shilling was sacked, I don't know about your piece of paper. That's it. But look, it's only fair that I tell you something about myself.'

He was about to tell me what I already suspected, that he was a homosexual. Now I was ashamed. I hadn't wanted to force a confession out of him.

'I'm telling you because we've been good friends.'

'Yes.'

'But it mustn't leave this room.'

'No!'

'I'm engaged to be married.'

I suspected that in the fraction of a second it took me to rearrange my expression, he glimpsed the heart of my confusion.

'But that's fantastic news. Who's—'

'She's not in Five. Ruth's a doctor at Guy's. Our families have always been very close.'

My words were out before I could snatch them back. 'An arranged marriage!'

But Max only laughed shyly and there may have been the hint of a blush, hard to detect in the yellowish light. So perhaps I was right, the parents who had chosen his studies, who wouldn't let him work with his hands, had chosen his wife. Remembering that vulnerability in him I felt the first chill of sorrow. I had missed out. And there was self-pity too. People told me I was beautiful and I believed them. I should have been wafted through life with the special dispensation that beauty bestows, discarding men at every turn. Instead, they abandoned me, or died on me. Or married.

Max said, 'I thought I should tell you.'

'Yes. Thanks.'

'We won't be announcing it for another couple of months.'

'Of course not.'

Max briskly squared his notes against the desk. The distasteful business was concluded and we could continue. He said, 'What did you really think of the stories? That one about the twin brothers.'

'I thought it was very good.'

'I thought it was awful. I couldn't believe that an atheist

would know his Bible. Or dress up as a vicar to deliver a sermon.'

'Brotherly love.'

'But he's not capable of any sort of love. He's a cad, and he's weak. I couldn't see why we should care about him or what happens to him.'

My impression was that we were really talking about Haley, not Edmund Alfredus. There was something strained in Max's tone. I thought I'd succeeded in making him jealous. I said, 'I thought he was extremely attractive. Clever, brilliant public speaker, sense of mischief, took interesting risks. Just no match for – what's her name? – Jean.'

'I couldn't believe in her at all. These destructive men-eating women are just fantasies of a certain kind of man.'

'What kind of man is that?'

'Oh I don't know. Masochistic. Guilty. Or self-hating. Perhaps you can tell me when you get back.'

He stood to indicate the meeting was over. I couldn't tell whether he was angry. I wondered whether in some perverse way he thought it was my fault he was getting married. Or perhaps he was angry with himself. Or my arranged marriage remark had offended him.

'Do you really think Haley's not right for us?'

'That's Nutting's department. What's odd is sending you down to Brighton. We don't usually get our own involved like this. The usual way would be to get the Foundation to send someone, do it all at one remove. Besides, I think the whole thing's, well, anyway, it's not my, um . . .'

He was leaning forward on his fingertips which were splayed against the desk and he seemed to be indicating the door behind me by faintly inclining his head. Throwing me out with minimal effort. But I didn't want the conversation to end.

'There's one other thing, Max. You're the only one I could say this to. I think I'm being followed.'

'Really? Quite an achievement at your level.'

I ignored this sneer. 'I'm not talking about Moscow Centre. I mean the Watchers. Someone's been in my room.'

Since my conversation with Shirley, I'd looked around carefully on the way home, but I'd seen nothing suspicious. But I didn't know what to look for. It wasn't part of our training. I had some vague notions derived from films and I'd doubled back on myself in the street, and I'd peered into hundreds of rush-hour faces. I'd tried getting on the Tube and straight off, and achieved nothing beyond a longer journey to Camden.

But I achieved my purpose now, for Max was sitting down and the conversation resumed. His face had gone hard, he looked older.

'How do you know?'

'Oh, you know, things out of place in my room. I suppose the Watchers can be rather clumsy.'

He looked at me steadily. I was already beginning to feel foolish.

'Serena, be careful. If you pretend to know more than you do, if you pretend to knowledge that hardly tallies with a few months in the Registry, you'll give the wrong impression. After the Cambridge Three and George Blake, people are still nervous and a bit demoralised. They jump to conclusions rather too quickly. So stop acting as though you know more than you do. You end up getting followed. In fact, I think that's your problem.'

'Is this a guess or something you know?'

'It's a friendly warning.'

'So I really am being followed.'

'I'm a relatively lowly figure here. I'd be the last to know. People have seen us around together . . .'

'Not any more, Max. Perhaps our friendship was harming your career prospects.'

It was shallow stuff. I couldn't quite admit to myself how upset I was by the news of his engagement. His self-control irritated me. I wanted to provoke and punish him and

133

here it was, I had my wish, he was on his feet, fairly quivering.

'Are women really incapable of keeping their professional and private lives apart? I'm trying to help you, Serena. You're not listening. Let me put it another way. In this work the line between what people imagine and what's actually the case can get very blurred. In fact that line is a big grey space, big enough to get lost in. You imagine things – and you can make them come true. The ghosts become real. Am I making sense?'

I didn't think he was. I was on my feet with a clever retort ready, but he'd had enough of me. Before I could speak he said more quietly, 'Best to go now. Just do your own work. Keep things simple.'

I was intending to make a stormy exit. But I had to slide my chair under his desk and squeeze round it to get out, and when I was out in the corridor I couldn't slam the door behind me because it was warped in its frame.

11

This was a bureaucracy and delay followed as though by policy directive. My draft letter to Haley was submitted to Max, who made alterations to this as well as my second attempt, and, when at last a third was passed on to Peter Nutting and to Benjamin Trescott, I waited almost three weeks for their notes. They were incorporated, Max put in some final touches, and I posted the fifth and final version five weeks after my first. A month went by and we heard nothing. Enquiries were made on our behalf and eventually we learned that Haley was abroad for research. It was not until late September that we had his reply, scrawled at a slant on a lined sheet torn from a notepad. It looked deliberately insouciant. He wrote that he would be interested to know more. He was making ends meet by working as a postgraduate teacher, which meant he now had an office on the campus. Better to meet there, he said, because his flat was rather cramped.

I had a short final briefing with Max.

He said, 'What about that *Paris Review* story, the one about the shop-window dummy?'

'I thought it was interesting.'

'Serena! It was completely implausible. Anyone that deluded would be in the secure wing of a psychiatric institution.'

'How do you know he isn't?'

135

'Then Haley should have let the reader know.'

He told me as I was leaving his office that three Sweet Tooth writers had accepted the Freedom International stipend. I was not to let him or myself down by failing to nail down a fourth.

'I thought I had to play hard to get.'

'We've fallen behind everyone else. Peter's getting impatient. Even if he's no good, just sign him up.'

It was a pleasant break in routine to travel down to Brighton one unseasonably warm morning in mid-October, to cross the cavernous railway station and smell the salty air and hear the falling cries of herring gulls. I remembered the word from a summer Shakespeare production of *Othello* on the lawn at King's. A gull. Was I looking for a gull? Certainly not. I took the dilapidated three-carriage Lewes train and got out at the Falmer stop to walk the quarter mile to the redbrick building site called the University of Sussex, or, as it was known in the press for a while, Balliol-by-the-Sea. I was wearing a red mini-skirt and black jacket with high collar, black high heels and a white patent leather shoulder bag on a short strap. Ignoring the pain in my feet, I swanked along the paved approach to the main entrance through the student crowds, disdainful of the boys – I regarded them as boys – shaggily dressed out of army surplus stores, and even more so of the girls with their long plain centre-parted hair, no make-up and cheesecloth skirts. Some students were barefoot, in sympathy, I assumed, with peasants of the undeveloped world. The very word 'campus' seemed to me a frivolous import from the USA. As I self-consciously strode towards Sir Basil Spence's creation in a fold of the Sussex Downs, I felt dismissive of the idea of a new university. For the first time in my life I was proud of my Cambridge and Newnham connection. How could a serious university be *new*? And how could anyone resist me in my confection of red, white and black, intolerantly scissoring my way towards the porters' desk, where I intended to ask directions?

I entered what was probably an architectural reference to a quad. It was flanked by shallow water features, rectangular ponds lined with smooth river-bed stones. But the water had been drained off to make way for beer cans and sandwich wrappers. From the brick, stone and glass structure ahead of me came the throb and wail of rock music. I recognised the rasping, heaving flute of Jethro Tull. Through the plate-glass windows on the first floor I could see figures, players and spectators, hunched over banks of table football. The students' union, surely. The same everywhere, these places, reserved for the exclusive use of lunk-headed boys, mathematicians and chemists mostly. The girls and the aesthetes went elsewhere. As a portal to a university it made a poor impression. I quickened my pace, resenting the way my stride fell in with the pounding drums. It was like approaching a holiday camp.

The paved way passed under the students' union and here I turned through glass doors to a reception area. At least the porters in their uniforms behind a long counter were familiar to me – that special breed of men with their air of weary tolerance, and gruff certainty of being wiser than any student had ever been. With the music fading behind me, I followed their directions, crossed a wide open space, went under giant concrete rugby posts to enter Arts Block A and came out the other side to approach Arts Block B. Couldn't they name their buildings after artists or philosophers? Inside, I turned down a corridor, noting the items posted on the teachers' doors. A tacked-up card that said, 'The world is everything that is the case', a Black Panthers poster, something in German by Hegel, something in French by Merleau-Ponty. Show-offs. Right at the end of a second corridor was Haley's room. I hesitated outside it before knocking.

I was at the corridor's dead-end, standing by a tall, narrow window that gave onto a square of lawn. The light was such that I had a watery reflection of myself, so I took out a comb and quickly tidied my hair and straightened my collar. If I was slightly nervous it was because in the past weeks I had

137

become intimate with my own private version of Haley, I had read his thoughts on sex and deceit, pride and failure. We were on terms already and I knew they were about to be reformed or destroyed. Whatever he was in reality would be a surprise and probably a disappointment. As soon as we shook hands our intimacy would go into reverse. I had re-read all the journalism on the way down to Brighton. Unlike the fiction it was sensible, sceptical, rather schoolmasterish in tone, as if he'd supposed he was writing for ideological fools. The article on the East German uprising of 1953 began 'Let no one think the Workers' State loves its workers. It hates them', and was scornful of the Brecht poem about the government dissolving the people and electing another. Brecht's first impulse, in Haley's account, was to 'toady' to the German State by giving public support to the brutal Soviet suppression of the strikes. Russian soldiers had fired directly into the crowds. Without knowing much about him, I'd always assumed that Brecht had sided with the angels. I didn't know if Haley was right, or how to reconcile his plain-speaking journalism with the crafty intimacy of the fiction, and I assumed that when we met I would know even less.

A feistier piece excoriated West German novelists as weak-minded cowards for ignoring in their fiction the Berlin Wall. Of course they loathed its existence, but they feared that saying so would seem to align them with American foreign policy. And yet it was a brilliant and necessary subject, uniting the geo-political with personal tragedy. Surely, every British writer would have something to say about a London Wall. Would Norman Mailer ignore a wall that divided Washington? Would Philip Roth prefer not to notice if the houses of Newark were cut in two? Would John Updike's characters not seize the opportunity of a marital affair across a divided New England? This pampered, over-subsidised literary culture, protected from Soviet repression by the pax Americana, preferred to hate the hand that kept it free. West German writers pretended the Wall didn't exist and thereby lost all moral authority. The title of the essay, published in *Index on Censorship*, was 'La Trahison des Clercs'.

With a pearly pink painted nail I tapped lightly on the door and, at the sound of an indistinct murmur or groan, pushed it open. I was right to have prepared myself for disappointment. It was a slight figure who rose from his desk, slightly stooped, though he made the effort to straighten his back as he stood. He was girlishly slender, with narrow wrists and his hand when I shook it seemed smaller and softer than mine. Skin very pale, eyes dark green, hair dark brown and long, and cut in a style that was almost a bob. In those first few seconds I wondered if I'd missed a transsexual element in the stories. But here he was, twin brother, smug vicar, smart and rising Labour MP, lonely millionaire in love with an inanimate object. He wore a collarless shirt made of flecked white flannel, tight jeans with a broad belt and scuffed leather boots. I was confused by him. The voice from such a delicate frame was deep, without regional accent, pure and classless.

'Let me clear these things away so you can sit.'

He shifted some books from an armless soft chair. I thought, with a touch of annoyance, that he was letting me know that he had made no special preparations for my arrival.

'Was your journey down all right? Would you like some coffee?'

The journey was pleasant, I told him, and I didn't need coffee.

He sat down at his desk and swivelled his chair to face me, crossed an ankle over a knee and with a little smile opened out his palms in an interrogative manner. 'So, Miss Frome . . .'

'It rhymes with plume. But please call me Serena.'

He cocked his head to one side as he repeated my name. Then his eyes settled softly on mine and he waited. I noted the long eyelashes. I'd rehearsed this moment and it was easy enough to lay it all out for him. Truthfully. The work of

139

Freedom International, its wide remit, its extensive global reach, its open-mindedness and lack of ideology. He listened to me, head still cocked, and with a look of amused scepticism, his lips quivering slightly as though at any moment he was ready to join in or take over and make my words his own, or improve upon them. He wore the expression of a man listening to an extended joke, anticipating an explosive punchline with held-in delight that puffs and puckers his lips. As I named the writers and artists the Foundation had helped, I fantasised that he had already seen right through me and had no intention of letting me know. He was forcing me to make my pitch so he could observe a liar at close hand. Useful for a later fiction. Horrified, I pushed the idea away and forgot about it. I needed to concentrate. I moved on to talk about the source of the Foundation's wealth. Max thought Haley should be told just how rich Freedom International was. The money came from an endowment by the artistic widow of a Bulgarian immigrant to the USA who had made his money buying and exploiting patents in the twenties and thirties. In the years following his death, his wife bought up Impressionist paintings after the war from a ruined Europe at pre-war prices. In the last year of her life she had fallen for a culturally inclined politician who was setting up the Foundation. She left her and her husband's fortune to his project.

Everything I had said so far had been the case, easily verified. Now I took my first tentative step into mendacity. 'I'll be quite frank with you,' I said. 'I sometimes feel Freedom International doesn't have enough projects to throw its money at.'

'How flattering then,' Haley said. Perhaps he saw me blush because he added, 'I didn't mean to be rude.'

'You misunderstand me, Mr Haley . . .'

'Tom.'

'Tom. Sorry. I put that badly. What I meant was this. There are plenty of artists being imprisoned or oppressed by unsavoury governments. We do everything we can to help these people and get their work known. But, of course, being censored doesn't necessarily mean a writer or sculptor is any good. For example, we've found ourselves supporting a terrible playwright in Poland simply because his work is banned. And we'll go on supporting him. And we've bought up any amount of rubbish by an imprisoned Hungarian abstract impressionist. So the steering committee has decided to add another dimension to the portfolio. We want to encourage excellence wherever we can find it, oppressed or not. We're especially interested in young people at the beginning of their careers . . .'

'And how old are you, Serena?' Tom Haley leaned forward solicitously, as if asking about a serious illness.

I told him. He was letting me know he was not to be patronised. And it was true, in my nervousness I had taken on a distant, official tone. I needed to relax, be less pompous, I needed to call him Tom. I realised I wasn't much good at any of this. He asked me if I'd been at university. I told him, and said the name of my college.

'What was your subject?'

I hesitated, I tripped over my words. I hadn't expected to be asked, and suddenly mathematics sounded suspect and without knowing what I was doing I said, 'English.'

He smiled pleasantly, appearing pleased at finding common ground. 'I suppose you got a brilliant first?'

'A two one actually.' I didn't know what I was saying. A third sounded shameful, a first would have set me on dangerous ground. I had told two unnecessary lies. Bad form. For all I knew, a phone call to Newnham would establish there had been no Serena Frome doing English. I hadn't expected to be interrogated. Such basic preparatory work, and I'd failed to do it. Why hadn't Max thought of helping me towards a decent watertight personal story? I felt flustered and sweaty, I imagined myself jumping up without a word, snatching up my bag, fleeing from the room.

Tom was looking at me in that way he had, both kindly

and ironic. 'My guess is that you were expecting a first. But listen, there's nothing wrong with a two one.'

'I was disappointed,' I said, recovering a little. 'There was this, um, general, um . . .'

'Weight of expectation?'

Our eyes met for a little more than two or three seconds, and then I looked away. Having read him, knowing too well one corner of his mind, I found it hard to look him in the eye for long. I let my gaze drop below his chin and noticed a fine silver chain around his neck.

'So you were saying, writers at the beginning of their careers.' He was self-consciously playing the part of the friendly don, coaxing a nervous applicant through her entrance interview. I knew I had to get back on top.

I said, 'Look, Mr Haley . . .'

'Tom.'

'I don't want to waste your time. We take advice from very good, very expert people. They've given a lot of thought to this. They like your journalism, and they love your stories. Really love them. The hope is . . .'

'And you. Have you read them?'

'Of course.'

'And what did you think?'

'I'm really just the messenger. It's not relevant what I think.'

'It's relevant to me. What did you make of them?'

The room appeared to darken. I looked past him, out of the window. There was a grass strip, and the corner of another building. I could see into a room like the one we were in, where a tutorial was in progress. A girl not much younger than me was reading aloud her essay. At her side was a boy in a bomber jacket, bearded chin resting in his hand, nodding sagely. The tutor had her back to me. I turned my gaze back into our room, wondering if I was not overdoing this significant pause. Our eyes met again and I forced myself to hold on. Such a strange dark green, such long child-like lashes, and thick black eyebrows. But there was hesitancy in his gaze, he was about to look away, and this time the power had passed to me.

I said very quietly, 'I think they're utterly brilliant.'

He flinched as though someone had poked him in the chest, in the heart, and he gave a little gasp, not quite a laugh. He went to speak but was stuck for words. He stared at me, waiting, wanting me to go on, tell him more about himself and his talent, but I held back. I thought my words would have more power for being undiluted. And I wasn't sure I could trust myself to say anything profound. Between us a certain formality had been peeled away to expose an embarrassing secret. I'd revealed his hunger for affirmation, praise, anything I might give. I guessed that nothing mattered more to him. His stories in the various reviews had probably gone unremarked, beyond a routine thanks and pat on the head from an editor. It was likely that no one, no stranger at least, had ever told him that his fiction was brilliant. Now he was hearing it and realising that he had always suspected it was so. I had delivered stupendous news. How could he have known if he was any good until someone confirmed it? And now he knew it was true and he was grateful.

As soon as he spoke, the moment was broken and the room resumed its normal tone. 'Did you have a favourite?'

It was such a stupid, sheepish excuse of a question that I warmed to him for his vulnerability. 'They're all remarkable,' I said. 'But the one about the twin brothers, "This Is Love", is the most ambitious. I thought it had the scale of a novel. A novel about belief and emotion. And what a wonderful character Jean is, so insecure and destructive and alluring. It's a magnificent piece of work. Did you ever think of expanding it into a novel, you know, filling it out a bit?'

He looked at me curiously. 'No, I didn't think of filling it out a bit.' The deadpan reiteration of my words alarmed me.

'I'm sorry, it was a stupid . . .'

'It's the length I wanted. About fifteen thousand words. But I'm glad you liked it.'

Sardonic and teasing, he smiled and I was forgiven, but my advantage had dimmed. I had never heard fiction quantified in this technical way. My ignorance felt like a weight on my tongue.

I said, 'And "Lovers", the man with the shop-window mannequin, was so strange and completely convincing, it swept everyone away.' It was now liberating to be telling outright lies. 'We have two professors and two well-known reviewers on our board. They see a lot of new writing. But you should have heard the excitement at the last meeting. Honestly, Tom, they couldn't stop talking about your stories. For the first time ever the vote was unanimous.'

The little smile had faded. His eyes had a glazed look, as though I was hypnotising him. This was going deep.

'Well,' he said, shaking his head to bring himself out of the trance. 'This is all very pleasing. What else can I say?' Then he added, 'Who are the two critics?'

'We have to respect their anonymity, I'm afraid.'

'I see.'

He turned away from me for a moment and seemed lost in some private thought. Then he said, 'So, what is it you're offering, and what do you want from me?'

'Can I answer that by asking you a question? What will you do when you've finished your doctorate?'

'I'm applying for various teaching jobs, including one here.'

'Full time?'

'Yes.'

'We'd like to make it possible for you to stay out of a job. In return you'd concentrate on your writing, including journalism if you want.'

He asked me how much money was on offer and I told him. He asked for how long and I said, 'Let's say two or three years.'

'And if I produce nothing?'

'We'd be disappointed and we'd move on. We won't be asking for our money back.'

He took this in and then said, 'And you'd want the rights in what I do?'

'No. And we don't ask you to show us your work. You don't even have to acknowledge us. The Foundation thinks you're a unique and extraordinary talent. If your fiction and journalism get written, published and read, then we'll be happy. When your career is launched and you can support yourself we'll fade out of your life. We'll have met the terms of our remit.'

He stood up and went round the far side of his desk and stood at the window with his back to me. He ran his hand through his hair and muttered something sibilant under his breath that may have been 'Ridiculous', or perhaps, 'Enough of this'. He was looking into the same room across the lawn. Now the bearded boy was reading his essay while his tutorial partner stared ahead of her without expression. Oddly, the tutor was speaking on the phone.

Tom returned to his chair and crossed his arms. His gaze was directed across my shoulder and his lips were pressed shut. I sensed he was about to make a serious objection.

I said, 'Think it over for a day or two, talk to a friend . . . Think it through.'

He said, 'The thing is . . .' and he trailed away. He looked down at his lap and he continued. 'It's this. Every day I think about this problem. I don't have anything bigger to think about. It keeps me awake at night. Always the same four steps. One, I want to write a novel. Two, I'm broke. Three, I've got to get a job. Four, the job will kill the writing. I can't see a way round it. There isn't one. Then a nice young woman knocks on my door and offers me a fat pension for nothing. It's too good to be true. I'm suspicious.'

'Tom, you make it sound simpler than it is. You're not passive in this affair. The first move was yours. You wrote these brilliant stories. In London people are beginning to talk

145

about you. How else do you think we found you? You've made your own luck with talent and hard work.'

The ironic smile, the cocked head – progress.

He said, 'I like it when you say brilliant.'

'Good. Brilliant, brilliant, brilliant.' I reached into my bag on the floor and took out the Foundation's brochure. 'This is the work we do. You can come to the office in Upper Regent Street and talk to the people there. You'll like them.'

'You'll be there too?'

'My immediate employer is Word Unpenned. We work closely with Freedom International and are putting money their way. They help us find the artists. I travel a lot or work from home. But messages to the Foundation office will find me.'

He glanced at his watch and stood, so I did too. I was a dutiful young woman, determined to achieve what was expected of me. I wanted Haley to agree now, before lunch, to be kept by us. I would break the news by phone to Max in the afternoon and by tomorrow morning I hoped to have a routine note of congratulation from Peter Nutting, unemphatic, unsigned, typed by someone else, but important to me.

'I'm not asking you to commit to anything now,' I said, hoping I didn't sound like I was pleading. 'You're not bound to anything at all. Just give me the say-so and I'll arrange a monthly payment. All I need is your bank details.'

The say-so? I'd never used that word in my life. He blinked in assent, but not to the money so much as to my general drift. We were standing less than six feet apart. His waist was slender and through some disorder in his shirt I caught a glimpse below a button of skin and downy hair above his navel.

'Thanks,' he said. 'I'll think about it very carefully. I've got to be in London on Friday. I could look in at your office.'

'Well then,' I said and put out my hand. He took it, but it wasn't a handshake. He took my fingers in his palm and stroked them with his thumb, just one slow pass. Exactly that, a pass, and he was looking at me steadily. As I took my hand away, I let my own thumb brush along the length of his forefinger. I think we may have been about to move closer when there was a hearty, ridiculously loud knock on the door. He stepped back from me as he called, 'Come in.' The door swung open and there stood two girls, centre-parted blonde hair, fading suntans, sandals and painted toenails, bare arms, sweet expectant smiles, unbearably pretty. The books and papers under their arms didn't look at all plausible to me.

'Aha,' Tom said. 'Our *Faerie Queene* tutorial.'

I was edging round him towards the door. 'I haven't read that one,' I said.

He laughed, and the two girls joined in, as if I'd made a wonderful joke. They probably didn't believe me.

12

I was the only passenger in my carriage on the early after-noon train back to London. As we left the South Downs behind and sped across the Sussex Weald, I tried to work off my agitation by walking up and down the aisle. I sat for a couple of minutes, then I was back on my feet. I blamed myself for a lack of persistence. I should have waited out the hour until his teaching was over, forced him to have lunch with me, gone through it all again, got his consent. But that wasn't it really. I'd come away without his home address. Nor that. Something may or may not have started between us, but it was just a touch – almost nothing at all. I should have stayed and built on it, left with a little more, a bridge to our next meeting. One deep kiss on that mouth that wanted to do my talking for me. I was bothered by the memory of the skin between the shirt buttons, the pale hair in a whorl around the edges of the navel, and the light and slender childlike body. I took up one of his stories to re-read but my attention soon slipped. I thought of getting off at Haywards Heath and going back. Would I have been so troubled if he hadn't caressed my fingers? I thought I would. Might the touch of his thumb have been entirely accidental? Impossible. He meant it, he was telling me. *Stay*. But when the train stopped, I didn't move, I didn't trust myself. Look what happened, I thought, when I threw myself at Max.

Sebastian Morel is a teacher of French at a large comprehensive school near Tufnell Park, north London. He is married to Monica and they have two children, a girl and a boy aged seven and four, and they live in a rented terraced house near Finsbury Park. Sebastian's work is *tough, pointless and ill-paid*, the pupils are insolent and unruly. Sometimes he spends his entire day trying to keep order in class and handing out punishments he doesn't believe in. He marvels at how irrelevant knowledge of rudimentary French is to the lives of these kids. *He wanted to like them, but he was repelled by their ignorance and aggression and the way they jeered at and bullied any of their number who dared to show an interest in learning. In this way they kept themselves down.* Nearly all of them will leave school as soon as they can and get unskilled jobs or get pregnant or make do with unemployment benefit. He wants to help them. Sometimes he pities them, sometimes he struggles to suppress his contempt.

He is in his early thirties, *a wiry man of exceptional strength*. At university in Manchester, Sebastian was a keen mountaineer and led expeditions in Norway, Chile and Austria. But these days he no longer gets out onto the heights because his life is too constrained, there is never enough money or time and his spirits are low. *His climbing gear was stowed in canvas bags in a cupboard under the stairs, well behind the Hoover and mops and buckets.* Money is always a problem. Monica trained as a primary school teacher. Now she stays at home to look after the children and the house. She does it well, she is a loving mother, the children are adorable, but she suffers from bouts of restlessness and frustration that mirror Sebastian's. Their rent is outrageous for such a small house in a dingy street and their marriage of nine years is dull, flattened by worries and hard work, marred by the occasional row – usually about money.

One dark late afternoon in December, three days before the end of term, he is mugged in the street. Monica has asked him to go to the bank at lunchtime to draw out seventy pounds from the joint account so that she can buy presents and Christmas treats. It is almost all they have by way of savings. He has turned into his own road, which is narrow and poorly lit, and is a hundred yards from his front door when he hears steps behind him and feels a tap on his shoulder. He turns and *standing before him was a kid of sixteen or so, West Indian, holding a kitchen knife, a big one with a serrated blade. For a few seconds the two stood close, less than three feet apart, staring at each other in silence.* What troubles Sebastian is the boy's agitation, the way the knife trembles in his hands, the terror in his face. Things could easily get out of control. In a quiet shaky voice the boy asks for his wallet. Sebastian raises his hand slowly to the inside pocket of his coat. He is about to give away his children's Christmas. He knows he is stronger than the kid and he calculates that as he holds out his wallet he could strike out, hit him hard on the nose and snatch the knife off him.

But it is more than the kid's agitation that restrains Sebastian. *There was a general view, strongly held in the staffroom, that crime, especially burglary and mugging, was caused by social injustice.* Robbers are poor, they've never had the right chances in life and can hardly be blamed for taking what isn't theirs. This is Sebastian's view too, though he's never given the matter much thought. In fact, it isn't even a view, it's a general atmosphere of tolerance that surrounds decent educated people. Those who complain about crime are likely to complain also about graffiti and litter in the streets and hold a whole set of distasteful views on immigration and the unions, tax, war and hanging. *It was important therefore, for the sake of one's self-respect, not to mind too much about being mugged.*

So he hands over his wallet and the thief runs away. Instead of going straight home Sebastian walks back towards the High

Street and goes to the police station to report the incident. As he speaks to the desk sergeant, he feels a bit of a cad or a snitch, for the police are clearly agents of the system that forces people to steal. His discomfort increases in the face of the sergeant's grave concern, and the way he keeps asking about the knife, the length of the blade, and whether Sebastian was able to see anything of the handle. Of course, armed robbery is a very serious offence. That kid could go to jail for years. Even when the sergeant tells him that there was a fatal stabbing only the month before of an old lady who tried to hang on to her purse, Sebastian's unease is not dispelled. He shouldn't have mentioned the knife. As he walks back along the street, he regrets his automatic impulse to report the matter. He's becoming middle-aged and bourgeois. He should have taken responsibility for himself. He is no longer the sort of guy who puts his life on the line and climbs up sheer faces of granite, trusting his agility, strength and skill.

Because he is beginning to feel weakness and trembling in his legs he goes into a pub and with the loose change in his pocket is just about able to afford a large scotch. He downs it in one, and then he goes home.

The mugging marks a decline in his marriage. Though Monica never says so, it is clear she doesn't believe him. It's the old story. He's come home stinking of drink, protesting that someone has run off with the holiday money. The Christmas is wretched. They have to borrow from her haughty brother. Her distrust kindles his resentment, they are distant with each other, they have to pretend to be jolly on Christmas Day for the sake of their children, and that seems to heighten the bleakness that comes down to trap them into silence. *The idea that she thought he was a liar was like a poison in his heart.* He works hard, he is loyal and faithful and keeps no secrets from her. How dare she doubt him! One evening when Naomi and Jake are in bed, he challenges her to tell him that she believes him about the mugging. She is immediately angry, and won't say whether she does or not. Instead, she changes the subject, a trick in argument, he thinks bitterly, she is supremely good at and one he should learn himself. She is sick of her life, she tells him, sick of being financially dependent on him, of being stuck at home all day while he is out advancing his career. Why have they never considered the possibility of him doing the housework and looking after the children while she resumes her career?

Even as she says all this he is thinking what an attractive prospect it is. He could turn his back on those awful kids, who never keep quiet or stay in their seats in his classes. He could stop pretending to care whether they ever spoke a word of French. And he likes being with his children. He would get them to their school and playgroup, then take a couple of hours for himself, perhaps fulfil an old ambition and get some writing done before picking up Jake and giving him lunch. Then an afternoon of childcare and light housework. Bliss. Let her be the wage slave. But they are having a row and he is in no mood to make conciliatory offers. He brings Monica back sharply to the mugging. He challenges her again to call him a liar, he tells her to go to the police station and read his statement. In reply, she leaves the room, slamming the door hard behind her.

A sour peace prevails, the holidays end and he goes back to work. It's as bad as ever at school. The kids are absorbing from the culture at large a cocky spirit of rebellion. *Hash, spirits and tobacco were playground currencies*, and teachers, including the headmaster, are confused, half believing that this atmosphere of insurrection is a token of the very freedom and creativity they are supposed to be imparting, and half aware that nothing is being taught or learned and the school is going to the dogs. The 'sixties', whatever they were, have entered this decade wearing a sinister new mask. *The same drugs that were said to have brought peace and light to middle-class students were now shrinking the prospects of the hard-edged urban poor.* Fifteen-year-olds come to Sebastian's classes stoned or drunk or both. Kids younger than them have taken LSD in the playground and have to be sent home. Ex-pupils sell drugs at the school gates, standing there openly with their wares alongside the mums and their pushchairs. The headmaster dithers, everyone dithers.

At the end of the day Sebastian is often hoarse from raising his voice in class. Walking home slowly is his one comfort, when he can be alone with his thoughts as he makes his way from one bleak setting to another. It's a relief that Monica is out at evening classes four times a week – yoga, German lessons, angelology. Otherwise, they step around each other at home, speaking only to manage the household. He sleeps in the spare room, explaining to the children that his snoring keeps Mummy awake. He is ready to give up his job so that she can go back to hers. But he can't forget that she thinks he's the sort of man who can drink away the children's Christmas. And then lie about it. Clearly, there is a far deeper problem. Their trust in each other has vanished and their marriage is in crisis. Swapping roles with her would be merely cosmetic. The thought of divorce fills him with horror. *What wrangling and stupidity would follow! How could they inflict such pain and sadness on Naomi and Jake?* It is his and Monica's responsibility to sort this matter out. But he does not know how to begin. Whenever he thinks of that boy and the kitchen knife in his hand, the old anger returns. Monica's refusal to believe him, to believe in him, has broken a vital bond and seems to him a monstrous betrayal.

And then there is the money: there is never enough money. In January their twelve-year-old car needs a new clutch. This in turn delays the repayment to Monica's brother – the debt is not settled until early March. It is a week later, while Sebastian is in the staff room at lunchtime, that he is approached by the school secretary. His wife is on the phone and needs to speak to him urgently. *He hurried to the office nauseous with dread. She had never phoned him at work before, and it could only be very bad news, perhaps something to do with Naomi or Jake.* So it's with some relief that he hears her tell him that there has been a break-in that morning at the house. After dropping off the children, she went to her doctor's appointment, then to the shops. When she got home the front door was ajar. The burglar had got in round the back garden, broken a window at the rear of the house, lifted a catch and climbed in, gathered up the stuff and gone out by the front. What stuff? *She listed it all tonelessly.* His precious 1930s Rolleiflex, bought years ago with the proceeds of a French prize he won at Manchester. Then, their transistor radio and his Leica binoculars, and her hairdryer. She pauses, and then she tells him, in that same flat voice, that all his climbing gear has been taken too.

At that point he feels the need to sit down. The secretary, who has been hovering, tactfully leaves the office and closes the door. *So much good stuff carefully accumulated over the years, and so much of sentimental value, including a rope he once used to save a friend's life during a descent in a storm in the Andes.* Even if the insurance covers it all, which Sebastian doubts, he knows he will never replace his mountaineering equipment. There was too much of it, there are too many other priorities. His youth has been stolen. *With his upright, goodhearted tolerance deserting him, he imagined his hands closing around the thief's windpipe.* Then he shakes his head to dismiss the fantasy. Monica is telling him that the police have already been round. There is blood on the broken windowpane. But it looks like the thief wore gloves, as there are no fingerprints. He tells her that there must have been two burglars at least, to lift all his gear out of the cupboard and carry it quickly from the house. *Yes, she agreed in her affectless voice that there must have been two.*

At home that evening he can't resist punishing himself by opening the cupboard under the stairs and gazing at the space where his equipment was. *He restored the buckets and mops and brushes to their upright position, then he went upstairs to look in his sock drawer, where he had kept his camera.* The thieves knew what to take, though the hairdryer matters less since there are two. This latest setback, this assault on their domestic privacy, does nothing to bring Sebastian and Monica closer. After a brief discussion they agree not to tell the children about the break-in and she goes off to her class. In the days that follow he feels so low he can barely bring himself to make the insurance claim. The full-colour handbook boasts of 'solid protection' but the small print in the schedule is miserly and punitive. Only a fraction of the camera's value is covered, and the climbing gear not at all because he failed to itemise it.

Their dreary co-existence resumed. A month after the burglary, the same school secretary seeks out Sebastian at break to tell him that there's a gentleman to see him in the school office. In fact he is waiting for Sebastian in the corridor, holding a raincoat over his arm. He introduces himself as Detective Inspector Barnes and he has a matter to discuss. Would Mr Morel care to drop by the police station after work?

A few hours later he is back at the front desk where he reported the mugging before Christmas. He is obliged to wait for half an hour before Barnes is free. The DI apologises as he shows him up three flights of concrete stairs and ushers him into a small darkened room. *There was a fold-down screen on a wall and a film projector in the centre of the room balanced on what looked like a bar stool. Barnes showed Sebastian a seat and began his account of a successful sting.* A year ago the police rented a run-down shop in a side street and staffed it with a couple of plainclothes officers. The shop bought secondhand goods from the public, the idea being to film thieves as they came in with stolen goods. With a number of prosecutions now under way, the cover has been blown and the shop has closed. But there are one or two loose ends. He dims the lights.

A hidden camera is positioned behind the 'shop assistant' and gives a view of the door onto the street and, in the foreground, the counter. Sebastian has already guessed that he is about to see the young guy who mugged him come into

155

the shop. With a successful identification, he'll be done for armed robbery, and that will be fine. But Sebastian's guess is wildly wrong. The person who comes in with a holdall and sets down on the counter a radio, a camera and a hairdryer is his wife. There she is, in the coat he bought her some birthdays ago. By chance she turns and looks towards the camera, as if she has seen Sebastian and is saying, Watch this! Soundlessly, she exchanges a few words with the assistant and together they go outside and come back moments later dragging three heavy canvas bags. The car must be parked right outside. The shop assistant peers inside each of the bags, then goes back behind the counter, glances over the items. There follows what must be a negotiation over prices. *Monica's face was lit by a bar of fluorescent light. She seemed animated, even elated in a nervous sort of way. She smiled a lot and at one point even laughed at a joke the plainclothes policeman made.* A price is agreed, banknotes are counted out, and Monica turns to leave. *At the door she stopped to make a parting remark, something more elaborate than a goodbye, and then she was gone and the screen went black.*

The DI switches off the projector and turns up the lights. His manner is apologetic. They could have prosecuted, he says. Wasting police time, perverting the course of justice, that sort of thing. But clearly this is a delicate domestic matter and Sebastian will have to decide for himself what to do. The two men go down the stairs and out into the street. As he shakes Sebastian's hand the DI says he is terribly sorry, he can see that this is a difficult situation and he wishes him all the best with it. Then, before he goes back into the station, he adds that *it was the view of the police team working in the shop, who had recordings of what was said at the counter, that 'Mrs Morel probably needed help'.*

On the way home – has he ever walked more slowly? – he would have stopped in that same pub for another fortifying drink, but he does not have on him even the price of a half pint. Perhaps it's just as well. He needs a clear head and clean breath. It takes him an hour to walk the mile to his house.

She is cooking with the children when he comes in. *He lingers in the doorway of the kitchen watching his little family at work on a cake. It was terribly sad, the way Jake and Naomi's precious heads bobbed so eagerly at their mother's murmured instructions.* He goes upstairs and lies on the bed in the spare room, staring at the ceiling. He feels heavy and tired and wonders if he is suffering from shock. And yet, despite the awful truth he has learned that day, he is troubled now by something new and equally shocking. Shocking? Is that the right word?

When he was downstairs just now watching Monica and the children, there was a moment when she glanced back over her shoulder at him. Their eyes met. He knows her well enough, he has seen that look many times before and has always welcomed it. It promises much. It is a tacit suggestion that when the moment is right, when the children are asleep, they should seize their chance and obliterate all thoughts of domestic duties. In the new circumstances, with what he knows now, he should be repelled. But he is excited by that glance because it came from a stranger, from a woman he knows nothing about beyond her obvious taste for destruction. *He had seen her in a silent movie and realised that he had never understood her.* He had got her all wrong. She was no longer his familiar. In the kitchen *he had seen her with fresh eyes and realised, as though for the first time, how beautiful she was. Beautiful and mad. Here was someone he had just met, at a party say, noticed her across a crowded room, the sort of woman who, with a single unambiguous look, offers a dangerous and thrilling invitation.*

He has been doggedly faithful throughout his marriage. His fidelity now seems like one more aspect of the general constriction and failure in his life. His marriage is over, there can be no going back, for how can he live with her now? How can he trust a woman who has stolen from him and lied? It's over. But here is the chance of an affair. An affair with madness. If she needs help, then this is what he can offer.

That evening he plays with the children, cleans the hamster's cage with them, gets them into their pyjamas, and reads to them three times over, once together, then to Jake on his own, then to Naomi. It is at times like these that his life makes sense. How soothing it is, the scent of clean bedlinen and minty toothpaste breath, and his children's eagerness to hear the adventures of imaginary beings, and how touching, to watch the children's eyes grow heavy as they struggle to hang on to the priceless last minutes of their day, and finally fail. All the while he is aware of Monica moving about downstairs, he hears the distinctive clunk of the oven door a few times and is aroused by the simple distracting logic: if there is to be food, if they are eating together, then there will be sex.

When he goes down, their tiny sitting room has been tidied, the usual junk has been cleared from the dining table and there is candlelight, Art Blakey on the hi-fi, a bottle of wine on the table and a roast chicken in an earthenware dish. *When he remembered the police film – his thoughts kept returning to it – he hated her. And when she came in from the kitchen in fresh skirt and blouse, bearing two wine glasses, he wanted her.* What is missing now is the love, or the guilty memory of love, or the need for it, and that is a liberation. She has become another woman, devious, deceitful, unkind, even cruel, and he is about to make love to her.

During the meal they avoid talk of the ill-feeling that has stifled their marriage for months. They don't even talk about the children as they so often do. Instead they talk about success-ful family holidays in the past, and holidays they will take with the children when Jake is a little older. It is all false, none of it will ever happen. *Then they talked politics, of strikes and the state of emergency and the sense of impending ruin in parliament, in cities, in the country's sense of itself – they talked of all the ruin but their own*. He watches her closely as she talks, and knows that every word is a lie. Doesn't she think it extraordinary, as he does, that after all this silence they are behaving as though nothing has happened? She is counting on sex to put everything right. He wants her all the more. And more again when she asks in passing about the insurance claim and expresses concern. *Amazing. What an actress. It was as if she was alone and he was watching her through a peep-hole.* He has no intention of confronting her. If he did, they would surely row, because she would deny everything. Or she would tell him that her financial dependence forced her to desperate measures. And he would have to point out that all their accounts are jointly held and that he has as little money as she does. But this way they will make love and he at least will know that it is for the very last time. *He would make love to a liar and a thief, to a woman he would never know. And she in turn would convince herself that she was making love to a liar and a thief. And doing so in the spirit of forgiveness.*

In my opinion Tom Haley spent too long over this farewell chicken dinner, and it seemed especially drawn out on a second reading. It wasn't necessary to mention the vegetables, or to tell us that the wine was a Burgundy. My train was approaching Clapham Junction as I turned the pages to locate the finale. I was tempted to skip it altogether. I made no claims to sophistication – I was a simple sort of reader, temperamentally bound to consider Sebastian as Tom's double, the bearer of his sexual prowess, the receptacle of his sexual anxieties. I became uneasy whenever one of his male characters became intimate with a woman, with *another* woman. But I was curious too, I had to watch. If Monica was daffy as well as deceitful (what was this angelology business?) then there was something obtuse and dark in Sebastian. His decision not to confront his wife about her deception may have been a cruel exercise of power for sexual ends, or a simple matter of cowardice, of an essentially English preference to avoid a scene. It didn't reflect well on Tom.

Over the years, uxorious repetition has streamlined the process and they are *swiftly naked and embracing on the bed*. They have been married long enough to be thorough experts on each other's needs, and the ending of long weeks of *froideur* and abstinence surely contribute a certain bonus, but it can't explain away the passion that overwhelms them now. *Their customary, companionable rhythms were violently discarded*. They are hungry, ferocious, extravagant and loud. At one point little Naomi in the next room *let out a cry in her sleep, a pure silvery rising wail in the dark that they mistook at first for a cat*. The couple freeze and wait for her to settle.

And then came the final lines of 'Pawnography', with the characters perched uneasily on ecstasy's summit. The desolation was to follow, off the page. The reader was spared the worst.

> *The sound was so icy and bleak that he imagined his daughter had seen in her dreams the unavoidable future, all the sorrow and confusion to come, and he felt himself shrink in horror. But the moment passed, and soon Sebastian and Monica sank again, or they rose, for there seemed to be no physical dimensions in the space they swam or tumbled through, only sensation, only pleasure so focused, so pointed it was a reminder of pain.*

13

Max was taking a week's holiday in Taormina with his
fiancée, so there could be no immediate debriefing
when I returned to the office. I lived in a state of suspension.
Friday came and there was no word from Tom Haley. I decided
that if he'd visited the office in Upper Regent Street that day,
he must have made a firm decision against seeing me. On
Monday I picked up a letter from a PO Box service in Park
Lane. A Freedom International secretary had typed a memo
confirming that Mr Haley had come by on Friday in the late
morning, stayed an hour, asked many questions and seemed
impressed by the Foundation's work. I should have felt
encouraged, and I suppose I was in a remote sort of way. But
mostly I felt I'd been dumped. Haley's thumb action, I
decided, was reflexive, the sort of move he tried on any
woman he thought he had a chance with. I schemed sulkily,
imagining that when he finally told me he would deign to
accept the Foundation's money, I would wreck his chances
by telling Max that he had turned us down and that we
should look for someone else.

At work the one topic was the war in the Middle East.
Even the most light-headed of the society girls among the
secretaries was drawn into the daily drama. People were
saying that with the Americans lining up behind Israel and

the Soviets behind Egypt and Syria and the Palestinian cause, there was potential for the sort of proxy war that could bring us a step closer to a nuclear exchange. A new Cuban Missile Crisis! A wall map went up in our corridor with sticky plastic beads representing the opposing divisions and arrows to show their recent movements. The Israelis, reeling from the surprise attack on Yom Kippur, began to pull themselves together, the Egyptians and Syrians made some tactical errors, the United States airlifted weapons to their ally, Moscow issued warnings. All this should have excited me more than it did, daily life should have had a keener edge. Civilisation threatened by nuclear war, and I'm brooding about a stranger who caressed my palm with his thumb. Monstrous solipsism.

But I wasn't only thinking of Tom. I was also worrying about Shirley. Six weeks had passed since our parting at the Bees Make Honey gig. She had left her place, her desk at the Registry, at the end of a working week without saying goodbye to anyone. Three days later a new new-joiner was in her place. Some of the girls who had gloomily predicted Shirley's promotion were now saying that she was forced to leave because she was *not one of us*. I'd been too angry with my old friend to seek her out. At the time I was relieved that she crept away without a fuss. But as the weeks passed, the sense of betrayal faded. I began to think that in her place I would have done the same. Perhaps with greater willingness, given my hunger for approval. I suspected that she'd been wrong – I wasn't being followed. But I was missing her, her boisterous laugh, the heavy hand on my wrist when she wanted to confide, her carefree taste for rock and roll. By comparison, the rest of us at work were timid and buttoned up, even when we were gossiping or teasing each other.

My evenings now were empty. I came home from work, took my groceries from 'my' corner of the fridge, cooked my supper, passed the time with the solicitors if they happened to be around, then read in my room in my boxy little armchair until eleven, my bedtime. That October I was absorbed by the short stories of William Trevor. The constrained lives of his characters made me wonder how my own existence might appear in his hands. The young girl alone in her bedsit, washing her hair in the basin, daydreaming about a man from Brighton who didn't get in touch, about the best friend who had vanished from her life, about another man she had fallen for whom she must meet tomorrow to hear about his wedding plans. How grey and sad.

A week after my meeting with Haley I walked from Camden to the Holloway Road with all kinds of foolish hopes, and apologies at the ready. But Shirley had abandoned her room and had left no forwarding address. I didn't have her parents' address in Ilford and they wouldn't give it to me at work. I looked up Bedworld in the Yellow Pages and spoke to an unhelpful assistant. Mr Shilling could not come to the phone, his daughter didn't work there and might or might not be away. A letter addressed to her care of Bedworld might or might not reach her. I wrote a postcard, unnaturally cheery, pretending nothing had happened between us. I asked her to get in touch. I didn't expect a reply.

I was due to meet Max on his first day back at work. That morning I had a miserable time getting to the office. Everyone did. It was cold and the rain fell in that steady, pitiless way it has in a city, letting you know it could go on for a month. There was a bomb scare on the Victoria line. The Provisional IRA had phoned a newspaper and given a special code. So I walked the last mile to the office, past queues for buses, too long to be worth joining. Part of the fabric of my umbrella had come away from the spokes, which gave me the appearance of a Chaplinesque tramp. My court shoes had cracks in the leather that sucked in the damp. On the news-stands every front page carried the story of OPEC's 'oil price shock'. The West was being punished with a hefty rise for supporting Israel. Exports to the US were embargoed. The leaders of the mineworkers' union were holding a special meeting to discuss how best they could exploit the situation. We were doomed.

The skies grew darker over the Conduit Street crowds shuffling along, hunched into their raincoats, trying to keep their umbrellas out of each other's faces. It was only October and barely four degrees above freezing – a taste of the long winter to come. I thought back gloomily to the talk I'd attended with Shirley, and how every vile prediction was coming true. I remembered those turned heads, those accusing looks, my black mark, and my old anger against her revived and my mood darkened further. Her friendship had been a pretence, I was a dupe, I belonged in another line of work. I wished I was still in my soft sagging bed with the pillow over my head.

I was already late but I checked the PO Box first before running round the corner to Leconfield House. I spent a quarter of an hour in the women's bathroom, trying to dry my hair on the roller towel and wiping the puddle stains from my tights. Max was a lost cause but I had my dignity to protect. I was ten minutes late when I squeezed into his triangular office, conscious of how cold and wet my feet were. I watched him across his desk as he arranged his files and made a show of being business-like. Did he look different after a week of making love in Taormina to Dr Ruth? He'd had a haircut before coming back to work and his ears had reverted to jug formation. There was no gleam of new confidence in his eyes, or dark patches beneath them. Beyond the new white shirt and a tie of a darker blue and a new dark suit, I saw no transformation. Was it just possible that they took separate rooms to save themselves for their wedding night? Not from what I knew of medical types and their long and rowdy apprenticeships. Even if Max, in obedience to some improbable instruction from his mother, had made a half-hearted attempt to hang back, Dr Ruth would have eaten him alive. The body, in all its frailty, was her profession. Well, I still wanted Max, but I also wanted Tom Haley and that was protection of a sort, if I ignored the fact that he wasn't interested in me.

'So,' he said at last. He looked up from the Sweet Tooth file and waited.

'How was Taormina?'

'Do you know, it rained every day we were there.'

He was telling me they had stayed in bed all day. As if acknowledging the fact he added quickly, 'So we saw the inside of a lot of churches, museums, that kind of thing.'

'Sounds fun,' I said in a flat tone.

He glanced up sharply, ready to detect irony but, I think, saw none.

He said, 'Have we heard back from Haley?'

'Not yet. The meeting went well. Clearly needs the money. Can't quite believe his luck. Came up to town last week to check out the Foundation. I guess he's mulling it over.'

It was odd how, in putting it this way, I cheered myself up. Yes, I thought. I should try to be more sensible.

'What was he like?'

'Very welcoming actually.'

'No, I mean, what *is* he like?'

'No fool. Highly educated, very driven about his writing, obviously. Students adore him. Good-looking in an unusual sort of way.'

'I've seen his photograph,' Max said. It occurred to me that he might be regretting his mistake. He could have made love to me and *then* announced his engagement. I felt I had a duty to my self-respect to flirt with Max, make him sorry for passing me over.

'I was hoping for a postcard from you.'

'Sorry, Serena. I never write them – just not in the habit.'

'Were you happy?'

The directness of the question took him by surprise. I was gratified to see him flustered. 'Yes, yes we were in fact. Very happy. But there's . . .'

'But?'

'There's something else . . .'

'Yes?'

'We can talk about holidays and all that later. But before I tell you about it, still on Haley, give him another week, then write to him and say we need to hear from him straight away, or else the offer is withdrawn.'

'Fine.'

He closed the file. 'The thing is this. Remember Oleg Lyalin?'

'You mentioned him.'

'I shouldn't know any of this. And you certainly shouldn't. But it's gossip. It's going the rounds. I think you might as well know. He was a great coup for us. He wanted to come across in 'seventy-one but apparently we kept him in place here in London for a few extra months. Five was about to arrange his defection when he was picked up by Westminster police for drunk driving. We got to him before the Russians did – they would have certainly killed him. He came across to us with his secretary, his lover. He was a KGB officer connected to their sabotage department. Pretty low-level guy, something of a thug apparently, but priceless. He confirmed our worst nightmare, that there were dozens, scores of Soviet intelligence officers working here under diplomatic immunity. When we threw out the hundred and five – and by the way, Heath was a trouper on that, whatever they're saying about him now – it seemed to take Moscow Centre completely by surprise. We didn't even tell the Americans, and that caused a stink which hasn't quite settled down yet. But the important thing was that it showed that we no longer had a mole at any significant level. Nothing since George Blake. Huge relief all round.

'We'll probably go on talking to Lyalin until the end of his life. There are always loose ends, things in the past, old stories with a new angle, procedural stuff, structures, order of battle and so on. There was one particular minor mystery, a cryptonym no one could crack because the information was too vague. It was an Englishman codenamed Volt, active in the very late forties until the end of 'fifty, working for us, not

Six. The interest was the hydrogen bomb. Not really our department. Nothing spectacular like Fuchs, nothing technical. Not even long-range planning or logistics. Lyalin saw the Volt material when he was still in Moscow. It didn't add up to much, but he knew the source was Five. He saw some speculative things, you know, "What if" papers, what the Americans call scenarios. What we call smart weekends in country houses. Hot air. What happens when the Chinese get the bomb, what price a pre-emptive strike, what's the optimum stockpile assuming no cost restraints and kindly pass the port.'

It was at this point I guessed what was coming. Or my body knew. My heart was going a little harder.

'Our people spent months on this, but we had too little on Volt to match the payroll or anyone's biography. Then last year someone came over to the Americans through Buenos Aires. I don't know what our friends learned. I do know they were slow passing it across, still huffy about the expulsions, I expect. Whatever they gave us, it was enough.'

He paused. 'You know where this is leading, don't you?'

I went to say 'Yes', but my tongue couldn't move itself in time. What came out was a grunt.

'So this is what's going round. Twenty-odd years ago Canning was passing documents to a contact. It lasted fifteen months. If there was more damaging stuff, we don't know about it. We don't know why it stopped. Perhaps it was disappointment all round.'

While I was in my well-sprung royal blue pram with silver spokes, still an only child, wheeled in bonneted splendour from the Rectory to the village shops, Tony was doing business with his contact, trying out a few phrases in Russian in that show-off way he had. I saw him in a bus-station greasy spoon, pulling from the inside pocket of a double-breasted suit a folded brown envelope. Perhaps an apologetic smile and shrug because the material was not first grade – he liked to be the best. But I couldn't quite see his face. In the past few months, whenever I summoned it, the image dissolved before the inner eye. Perhaps that was why I'd been less tormented. Or, other way round, my fading grief had begun to erase his features.

But not his voice. The inner ear is the more acute organ. I could play Tony's voice in my mind like turning on a radio. A way he had of resisting until the very end the rising pitch of a question, the hint of a 'w' sound for an 'r', and certain phrases of demurral – 'If you say so', 'I wouldn't put it like that', 'Well, up to a point' and 'Hang on' – and the college-claret plumminess, his way of being so sure that he would never think or say anything stupid or extreme. Only the considered, balanced view. Which was why it was easy to summon up his explanation over breakfast in the cottage, early summer sunshine pouring through the open door with its countless inexplicable rivets, across the flagstones, to illuminate the lime-white lath and plaster of the dining room's far wall, where the Churchill watercolour hung. And on the table between us, muddy coffee made in a special way, by 'the jug method' with a pinch of salt thrown in, and undercooked toast like stale bread piled on a pale green plate with a spidery glaze and bitter thick-cut marmalade made by the housekeeper's sister.

I heard it plainly, Tony's justification, which, his tone would suggest, only a fool dared oppose. My dear girl. I hope you remember our first tutorial. These terrifying new weapons can only be restrained by a balance of power, by mutual fear, mutual respect. Even if it means yielding secrets to a tyranny it would be preferable to the lopsided dominion of American swagger. Kindly recall the voices from the American right after 1945 urging the nuclear extermination of the Soviet Union while it still had no means of retaliation. Who could ignore that insidious logic? If Japan had possessed such a weapon there would have been no horrors of Hiroshima. Only a balance of power can keep the peace. I did what I had to. The Cold War was upon us. The world had arranged itself into hostile camps. I wasn't alone in thinking the way I did. However grotesque its abuses, let the Soviet Union be similarly armed. Let small minds accuse me of unpatriotic betrayal, the rational man acts for global peace and the continuance of civilisation.

'Well,' Max said. 'Don't you have anything to say?'

His tone suggested that I was complicit or somehow responsible. I allowed a short silence to neutralise his question. I said, 'Did they confront him before he died?'

'I don't know. All I have is the gossip that trickles down from the fifth floor. They certainly had time – about six months.'

I was remembering the car that came with the two men in suits, and the walk I was obliged to take in the woods, and our sudden return to Cambridge. In those first few minutes after Max's revelation I didn't feel much at all. I understood the importance of it, I knew that there were emotions lying in wait for me, but I would have to be alone to confront them. For now I felt protected by an unreasonable hostility to Max, by my impulse to blame the messenger. He talked down Tom Haley at every opportunity and now he was demolishing my former lover, trying to strip the men out of my life. He could have kept the Canning story to himself. It was only a rumour and, even if it was true, there was no operational reason for me to be told. It was a rare case of prospective and retrospective jealousy running side by side. If he couldn't have me, then no one could, not even from the past.

I said, 'Tony wasn't a communist.'

'I expect he dabbled in the thirties like everyone else.'

'He was in the Labour Party. He hated the show trials and the purges. He always said he would have voted for king and country in that Oxford union debate.'

Max shrugged. 'I can see it's hard.'

But he couldn't, and nor could I just yet.

I went from Max's room straight to my desk, determined to numb myself with the tasks in hand. It was too soon to be thinking. Or rather, I didn't dare think. I was in shock and I set about my tasks like an automaton. I was working with a desk officer called Chas Mount, a genial sort, ex-army, a former computer salesman who was happy to give me proper responsibilities. I had at last graduated to Ireland. We had two agents in the Provisionals – there may have been more but I wasn't aware of them. And these two were not aware of each other. They were sleepers, expected to spend some years rising through the military hierarchy, but almost immediately we'd had a flood of information from one of the men relating to chains of arms supply. We needed to expand and rationalise the files by creating sub-groupings and opening new files on the suppliers and middlemen, with cross-references and a degree of duplicated material that would lead any misplaced enquiry to the right place. We knew nothing about our agents – to us they were only 'Helium' and 'Spade', but I often thought about them, the dangers they ran and how safe I was back here in the dingy office I so often complained about. They would be Irish Catholic certainly, meeting in tiny front parlours in Bogside or in function rooms in pubs, aware that one slip, one obvious inconsistency could cost a bullet in the back of the head. And the body dumped in the street so that everyone could see what happened to informers. They would have to live the part in order to be convincing. Already, to protect his cover, Spade had seriously injured two British soldiers in an ambush and been involved in the deaths of members of the RUC and the torture and murder of a police informant.

Spade, Helium, and now Volt. After a couple of hours trying to block out Tony, I went to the women's lavatory, locked myself in a cubicle and sat there a while, and attempted to take in the news. I wanted to cry, but my turmoil had dry elements of anger and disappointment. It was all so long ago and he was dead, but the act seemed to me as fresh as yesterday. I thought I knew his arguments, but I couldn't accept them. You let down friends and colleagues, I heard myself tell him at that same sunlit breakfast. It's a matter of dishonour, and when it gets out, which it's bound to, this will be the one act you'll be remembered for. Everything else you achieved will be irrelevant. Your reputation will rest only on this, because ultimately reality is social, it's among others that we have to live and their judgements matter. Even, or especially, when we're dead. Your entire existence now will be reduced in the minds of the living to something seedy and underhand. No one will doubt that you wanted to do more harm than you did, that you would have handed over complete blueprints if you could have got your hands on them. If you thought that your actions were so noble and rational, why not present them openly and argue your case in public and face the consequences? If Stalin could murder and starve twenty million of his own for the sake of the revolution, who's to say he couldn't sacrifice more for the same cause in a nuclear exchange? If a dictator values life so much less than an American President, where is your balance of power?

Arguing with a dead man in a lavatory is a claustrophobic experience. I came out of the cubicle, splashed my face with cold water and tidied myself up, then went back to work. By lunchtime I was desperate to get out of the building. The rain had stopped and the pavements gleamed cleanly in the surprising sunlight. But there was a biting wind and there was no possibility of wandering idly through the park. I went briskly along Curzon Street, full of irrational thoughts. I was angry with Max for bringing me the news, angry with Tony for failing to live, for abandoning me with the burden of his mistakes. And because he had steered me into my career – I now thought of it as more than a job – I felt myself to be contaminated by his disloyalty. He had added his name to an inglorious list – Nunn May, the Rosenbergs, Fuchs – but unlike them had given away nothing of significance. He was a footnote in the history of nuclear spying, and I was a footnote to his treachery. I'd been diminished. Clearly, Max thought so. Another reason to be angry with *him*. And I was angry with myself for being a fool about him, for thinking that this stuffy jug-eared idiot could ever have brought me happiness. What luck it was for me, to be inoculated by his ridiculous engagement.

I went through Berkeley Square, where we'd remembered the nightingale song, and turned right down Berkeley Street towards Piccadilly. By Green Park station I saw the headlines on the noon edition of the evening newspapers. Petrol rationing, energy crisis, Heath to address the nation. I didn't care. I walked towards Hyde Park Corner. I was too upset to be hungry for lunch. There was a curious burning sensation in the balls of my feet. I wanted to run or kick. I wanted a game of tennis with a ferocious opponent, one I could beat. I wanted to shout at someone – that was it, I wanted a full-on row with Tony and then to leave him before he had a chance to leave me. The wind blew harder, right into my face as I turned into Park Lane. Rain clouds were piling up over Marble Arch, getting ready to drench me again. I walked faster.

I was passing the PO Box office so I went in, partly to get out of the cold. I'd checked only hours before and I had no real expectation of a letter, but there it suddenly was, in my hand, postmarked Brighton and yesterday's date. I fumbled with it, I pulled the envelope apart like a child on Christmas Day. Let one thing be right today, I thought as I went to stand by the glass door to read. *Dear Serena*. And it *was* right. It was more than right. He apologised for taking his time. He liked meeting me, he had given careful thought to my offer. He was accepting the money and he was grateful, it was an amazing opportunity. And then there was a new paragraph. I brought the letter closer to my face. He'd used a fountain pen, crossed out a word, made a smudge. He wanted to impose a condition.

If you don't mind, I'd like us to keep in regular contact – for two reasons. The first is that I'd prefer this generous Foundation to have a human face, so the money that comes to me each month is not simply an impersonal, bureaucratic matter. Second, your appreciative remarks meant a lot to me, more than I can say in a note like this. I'd like to be able to show you my work from time to time. I promise I won't be looking for constant praise and encouragement. I'd like your honest criticism. Naturally, I'd want to feel free to ignore any notes of yours that don't seem right to me. But the main thing is that by having your occasional input I wouldn't be writing into a void, and that's important if I'm starting out on a novel. As far as hand-holding goes, it won't be much of an imposition. Just a cup of coffee now and then. I'm nervous about writing something longer, more so now that there's some expectation laid upon me. I want to be worthy of this investment you're making in me. I'd like the Foundation people who chose me to feel that they made a decision they can be proud of.

I'm coming to London on Saturday morning. I could meet you in the National Portrait Gallery at ten by Severn's painting of Keats. Don't worry, if I haven't heard from you and you're not there, I won't rush to any conclusions.

Best wishes, Tom Haley

14

By five o'clock that Saturday afternoon we were lovers. It didn't run smoothly, there was no explosion of relief and delight in the meeting of bodies and souls. It wasn't ecstatic, the way it was for Sebastian and Monica, the thieving wife. Not at first. It was self-conscious and awkward, it had a theatrical quality, as if we were aware of the expectations of an unseen audience. And the audience was real. As I opened the front door of number seventy and showed Tom in, my three solicitor housemates were grouped at the foot of the stairs, mugs of tea in hand, clearly wasting time before making their way back to their rooms and an afternoon of legal grind. I closed the door behind us with a loud slam. The women from the north stared at my new friend with undisguised interest as he stood there on the doormat. There was a fair amount of meaningful grinning and shuffling as I made my reluctant introductions. If we'd arrived five minutes later no one would have seen us. Too bad.

Rather than conduct Tom to my bedroom pursued by their looks and nudges, I took him through to the kitchen and waited for them to disperse. But they lingered. While I made tea I could hear them murmuring in the hall. I wanted to ignore them and have a conversation of our own, but my mind was a blank. Sensitive to my discomfort Tom filled the silence by telling me about the Camden Town of Dickens's *Dombey and Son*, the line north from Euston station, the colossal cutting dug by Irish navvies that forced its way through the poorest neighbourhoods. He even had a line or two by heart and his words defined my own confusion. 'There were a hundred thousand shapes and substances of incompleteness, wildly mingled out of their places, upside down, burrowing in the earth, aspiring in the air, mouldering in the water, and unintelligible as any dream.'

At last my housemates went back to their desks, and after a few minutes we climbed the creaky stairs with our own mugs of tea. The silence behind each of their doors as we passed them on the way up seemed intensely alert. I was trying to remember whether my bed also creaked and how thick my bedroom walls were – hardly sensual thoughts. Once Tom was installed in my room, in my reading armchair while I sat on the bed, it seemed a better idea to go on talking.

At this at least we were already adept. We had passed an hour in the Portrait Gallery showing each other our favourites. Mine was Cassandra Austen's sketch of her sister, his, William Strang's Hardy. Looking at pictures with a stranger is an unobtrusive form of mutual exploration and mild seduction. It was an easy slide from aesthetics to biography – the subject's obviously, but also the painter's, at least, the scraps we knew. And Tom knew far more than I did. Basically, we gossiped. There was an element of showing off – this is what I like, this is the kind of person I am. It was no great commitment to say that Branwell Brontë's painting of his sisters was deeply unflattering, or that Hardy told people he was often mistaken for a detective. Somehow, between paintings, we joined arms. It wasn't clear whose initiative it was. I said, 'The hand-holding has begun,' and he laughed. It was probably then, as we linked fingers, that we assumed we would end up in my room.

He was easy company. He didn't have the compulsion of so many men on a date (this was now a date) to want to make you laugh at every turn, or point at things and sternly explain them, or constrain you with a string of polite questions. He was curious, he listened, he offered a story, he accepted one. He was relaxed in the to and fro of conversation. We were like tennis players warming up, rooted to our baselines, sending fast but easy balls down the centre of the court to our opponent's forehand, taking pride in our obliging accuracy. Yes, tennis was on my mind. I hadn't played in almost a year.

We went to the gallery cafe for a sandwich and it was here that everything could have fallen apart. The conversation had moved off paintings – my repertoire was tiny – and he had started to talk about poetry. This was unfortunate. I'd told him I had a good degree in English and now I couldn't remember when I last read a poem. No one I knew read poetry. Even at school I had managed to avoid it. We never 'did' poetry. Novels, of course, a couple of Shakespeare plays. I nodded encouragingly as he told me what he'd been re-reading. I knew what was coming and I was trying to think of a ready answer, with the consequence that I wasn't listening to him. If he asked, could I say Shakespeare? At that moment I couldn't name a single poem by him. Yes, there were Keats, Byron, Shelley, but what did they write that I was supposed to like? There were modern poets, of course I knew their names, but nervousness was whiting out my thoughts. I was in a snowstorm of mounting anxiety. Could I make the case that the short story was a kind of poem? Even if I came up with a poet, I would have to name a particular work. There it was. Not a poem in the world that I could name. Not at this moment. He had asked something, he was staring at me, waiting. *The boy stood on the burning deck*. Then he repeated his question.

'What do you think of him?'

'He's not really my kind of . . .' Then I stopped. I had only two options – to be revealed as a fraud or to own up. 'Look, I've got a confession to make. I was going to tell you at some point. It might as well be now. I lied to you. I didn't get an English degree.'

'You went straight from school to work?' He said this encouragingly and was looking at me in that way I remembered from our interview, both kindly and teasing.

'I've a degree in maths.'

'From Cambridge? Christ. Why conceal that?'

'I thought my opinion of your work would matter less to you. It was stupid, I know. I was pretending to be the person I once wanted to be.'

'And who was that?'

So I told him the whole story of my speed-reading fiction compulsion, of my mother turning me away from studying English, my academic misery at Cambridge, and of how I continued reading, and still did. How I hoped he would forgive me. And how I really loved his work.

'Listen, a maths degree is far more demanding. You've got the rest of your life to read poetry. We can start with the poet I was just talking about.'

'I've forgotten his name already.'

'Edward Thomas. And the poem – a sweet, old-fashioned thing. Hardly the stuff of poetic revolutions. But it's lovely, one of the best-known, best-loved poems in the language. It's marvellous you don't know it. You've got so much ahead of you!'

We had already paid for our lunch. He stood abruptly and took my arm and propelled me out of the building, up the Charing Cross Road. What could have been a disaster was drawing us closer, even though it now meant that my date was telling me things in the traditional manner. We stood in a corner of a basement of a second-hand bookshop in St Martin's Court, with an old hardback *Collected Thomas* opened by Tom for me at the right page.

Obediently, I read it, and looked up. 'Very nice.'

'You can't have read it in three seconds. Take it slowly.'

There wasn't much to take. Four verses of four short lines.

A train makes an unscheduled stop at an obscure station, no one gets on or off, someone coughs, a bird sings, it's hot, there are flowers and trees, hay drying in the fields and lots of other birds. And that was it.

I closed the book and said, 'Beautiful.'

His head was cocked and he was smiling patiently. 'You don't get it.'

'Of course I do.'

'Then tell it to me.'

'What do you mean?'

'Say it back to me, everything in it that you can remember.'

So I told him all I knew, almost line by line, and even remembered the haycocks, cloudlets, willows and meadow-sweet, as well as Oxfordshire and Gloucestershire. He seemed impressed and he was looking at me oddly, as if he was making a discovery.

He said, 'There's nothing wrong with your memory. Now try to remember the feelings.'

We were the only customers downstairs in the shop and there were no windows and only two dim bulbs, without shades. There was a pleasant dusty soporific smell, as though the books had stolen most of the air.

I said, 'I'm sure there isn't a single mention of a feeling.'

'What's the first word of the poem?'

'Yes.'

'Good.'

'It goes, "Yes, I remember Adlestrop."'

He came closer. 'The memory of a name and nothing else, the stillness, the beauty, the arbitrariness of the stop, birdsong spread out across two counties, the sense of pure existence, of being suspended in space and time, a time before a cata-clysmic war.'

I angled my head and his lips brushed mine. I said very quietly, 'The poem doesn't mention a war.'

He took the book from my hands as we kissed, and I remembered that when Neil Carder kissed the mannequin for the very first time, her lips *were hard and cool from a lifetime of trusting no one.*

I made my lips go soft.

Later we doubled back on ourselves, crossed Trafalgar Square, towards St James's Park. Here, as we strolled past staggering toddlers with fistfuls of bread for the mallards, we talked about our sisters. His, Laura, once a great beauty, was seven years older than Tom, had studied for the bar, had had a brilliant future, then by degrees, with this or that difficult case and difficult husband, became an alcoholic and lost everything. Her descent was complicated by some near-successful attempts at recovery, heroic comebacks in the courtroom, until drink pulled her back down again. There were various dramas that used up the last of the family's patience. And finally, a car accident in which the youngest of her children, a five-year-old girl, lost a foot. There were three children by two fathers. Laura had fallen through every safety net the modern liberal State could devise. Now she was living in a hostel in Bristol, but the management was ready to throw her out. The children were looked after by their fathers and stepmothers. There was a younger sister, Joan, married to a Church of England vicar, who also looked out for them, and two or three times a year Tom took his two nieces and nephew on holiday.

His parents were also marvellous with their grandchildren. But Mr and Mrs Haley had lived through twenty years of shock, false hopes, embarrassments and night-time emergencies. They dreaded her next phone call and lived in a condition of constant sadness and self-blame. However much they loved Laura, however they kept alive on the mantelpiece the essence of what she had been in the silver-framed photos of her tenth birthday and degree ceremony and first wedding, even they could not deny she had become a terrible person, terrible to look at, to listen to, terrible to smell. Terrible to remember the calm intelligence, then hear her wheedling self-pity and lies and sodden promises. The family had tried everything in the way of coaxing, then gentle confrontation, then outright blaming, and clinics and therapies and hopeful new drugs. The Haleys had spent almost all they had in tears and time and money, and there was really nothing to do now but concentrate their affection and resources on the children and wait for their mother to be permanently hospitalised, and die.

In the race to such ruin as Laura's, my sister Lucy could hardly compete. She had dropped out of her medical degree and was back living near our parents, even as she discovered in herself, through therapy, a bitter reserve of anger against my mother for arranging the abortion. In every town there's a cadre who refuse or fail, sometimes quite happily, to move on to the next stage, the next place. Lucy found a snug community of old school friends who had returned too soon from forays on the hippie trail, or to art college or universities, and were settling down to a marginal life in their pleasant home town. Despite the crises and states of emergency, these were good years for staying out of a job. Without asking too many impertinent questions, the State paid the rent and granted a weekly pension to artists, out-of-work actors, musicians, mystics, therapists and a network of citizens for whom smoking cannabis and talking about it was an engrossing profession, even a vocation. The weekly handout was fiercely defended as a hard-won right, though everyone, even Lucy, knew in their hearts that it had not been devised to keep the middle classes in such playful leisure.

Now that I was a taxpayer with a meagre income, my scepticism about my sister ran deep. She was clever, brilliant at biology and chemistry at school, and she was kind, she had the human touch. I wanted her to be a doctor. I wanted her to want what she used to want. She lived rent-free with another woman, a circus-skills instructor, in a Victorian terraced cottage renovated by the local council. She signed on, smoked dope, and for three hours a week on Saturday mornings sold rainbow-coloured candles from a stall in the city-centre market. On my last visit home she had talked of the neurotic, competitive 'straight' world she had left behind. When I suggested that this was the world that supported her work-free existence she laughed and said, 'Serena, you're so right wing!'

While I was filling in the background and telling Tom this story I was fully aware that he was about to become a State pensioner too, on a grander scale, from the Secret Vote, that portion of government expenditure that parliament may never scrutinise. But T.H. Haley was going to work hard and produce great novels, not rainbow candles or tie-dye T-shirts. As we made our three or four turns about the park, I did feel queasy about withholding information from him, but it helped to remember that he'd visited our cut-out, the Foundation, and had approved of it. No one was going to tell him what to write or think or tell him how he should live. I had helped bring freedom to a genuine artist. Perhaps the great patrons of the Renaissance felt the way I did. Generous, above imme-diate earthly concerns. If that seems a grand claim, remember that I was feeling a little drunk and lit up by the afterglow of our long kiss in the bookshop basement. We both were. Talking about our less fortunate sisters was our unintentional way of marking our own happiness, of keeping our feet on the ground. Otherwise we might have floated off above Horse Guards Parade, away over Whitehall and across the river, especially after we stopped under an oak, still hoarding its load of rusty dry leaves, and he pressed me against its trunk and we kissed again.

This time I put my arms round him and felt beneath the tightness of his belted jeans the sinewy slenderness of his waist and, below, the hard muscle of his buttocks. I felt weak and sick, my throat was parched and I wondered if I was getting flu. I wanted to lie down with him and stare into his face. We decided to go to my place, but we couldn't face public transport and we couldn't afford a taxi. So we walked. Tom carried my books, the Edward Thomas and his other gift, the *Oxford Book of English Verse*. Past Buckingham Palace

to Hyde Park Corner, along Park Lane, past my work street
– which I failed to point out – then a long trudge up the
Edgware Road, passing the new Arab restaurants, eventually
turning right onto St John's Wood Road, past Lord's cricket
ground, along the top of Regent's Park and into Camden
Town. There are far quicker ways, but we didn't notice or
care. We knew what we were walking towards. Mostly, not
thinking about it made the walking easier.

In the usual way of young lovers, we talked about our
families, placing ourselves for each other in the scheme of
things, counting up our comparative luck. At one point Tom
said he wondered how I found it possible to live without
poetry.

I said, 'Well, you can show me how to be unable to live
without poetry.' Even as I said this I was reminding myself
that this could be a one-off and that I should be prepared.

I knew the outline of his family's story from the profile
Max had given me. Tom's luck had been not too bad at all,
give or take a Laura and an agoraphobic mother. We shared
the protected prosperous lives of post-war children. His father
was an architect working in the town planning department
of Kent County Council and about to retire. Like me, Tom
was the product of a good grammar school. Sevenoaks. He
chose Sussex over Oxford and Cambridge because he liked
the look of the courses ('themes not surveys'), and had arrived
at a stage of life when it was interesting to upset expectations.
I couldn't quite believe him when he insisted that he had no
regrets. His mother was a peripatetic piano teacher until her
growing fear of stepping outdoors confined her to lessons at
home. A glimpse of sky, of a corner of a cloud was enough
to bring her to the edge of a panic attack. No one knew what
brought the agoraphobia on. Laura's drinking came later.
Tom's sister Joan, before her marriage to the vicar, had been
a dress designer – the source of the shop-window dummy as
well as the Rev. Alfredus, I thought, but did not say.

His MA in international relations had been about justice

at the Nuremberg Trials, and his PhD was on *The Faerie Queene*. He adored Spenser's poetry, though he wasn't sure I was ready for it just yet. We were walking along Prince Albert Road, within earshot of London Zoo. He had finished his thesis over the summer, had it specially bound in hard covers with gold embossed title. It contained acknowledgements, abstract, footnotes, bibliography, index and four hundred pages of minute examination. Now it was a relief to contemplate the relative freedom of fiction. I talked about my own background and then for the length of Parkway and the top of the Camden Road, we fell into a companionable silence, odd between near strangers.

I was wondering about my sagging bed and whether it would support us. But I didn't really care. Let it go through the floor onto Tricia's desk, I would be in it with Tom when it went down. I was in a strange state of mind. Intense desire mixed with sorrow, and a muted sense of triumph. The sorrow was prompted by walking past my workplace, which had stirred up thoughts of Tony. All week I'd been haunted by his death again, but in different terms. Was he alone, full of blustering self-justifying thoughts right to the end? Did he know what Lyalin had told his interrogators? Perhaps someone from the fifth floor had gone out to Kumlinge to forgive him in exchange for all he knew. Or someone from the other side had arrived unannounced to pin on the lapel of his old windcheater the Order of Lenin. I tried to spare him my sarcasm, but generally I failed. I felt doubly betrayed. He could have told me about the two men who came in the chauffeured black car, he could have told me he was ill. I would have helped him, I would have done anything he asked. I would have lived with him on a Baltic island.

My small triumph was Tom. I'd received what I'd been hoping for, a typed one-line note from Peter Nutting upstairs thanking me for 'the fourth man'. His little joke. I had delivered the fourth writer to Sweet Tooth. I snatched a glance at him. So lean, loping along by my side, hands deep in his jeans, his gaze turned to one side, away from me, perhaps pursuing an idea. I already felt proud of him, and just a little proud of myself. If he didn't want to, he would never have to think of Edmund Spenser again. The Sweet Tooth Faerie Queene had delivered Tom from academic struggle.

So here we were, indoors at last, in my twelve feet by twelve bedsit, Tom in my junk-shop chair, and I perched on the edge of the bed. It was better to go on talking for a while. My housemates would hear the drone of our voices and soon lose interest. And there were many subjects for us because scattered about the room, piled on the floor and on the chest of drawers were two hundred and fifty prompts in the form of paperback novels. Now at last he could see that I was a reader and not just an empty-headed girl who cared nothing for poetry. To relax, to ease ourselves towards the bed I was sitting on, we talked books in a light and careless way, hardly bothering to make a case when we disagreed, which was at every turn. He had no time for my kind of women – his hand moved past the Byatt and the Drabbles, past Monica Dickens and Elizabeth Bowen, those novels I had inhabited so happily. He found and praised Muriel Spark's *The Driver's Seat*. I said I found it too schematic and preferred *The Prime of Miss Jean Brodie*. He nodded, but not in agreement, it seemed, more like a therapist who now understood my problem. Without leaving the chair he stretched forward and picked up John Fowles's *The Magus* and said he admired parts of that, as well as all of *The Collector* and *The French Lieutenant's Woman*. I said I didn't like tricks, I liked life as I knew it recreated on the page. He said it wasn't possible to recreate life on the page without tricks. He stood and went over to the dresser and picked up a B.S. Johnson, *Albert Angelo*, the one with holes cut in the pages. He admired this too, he said. I said I detested it. He was amazed to see a copy of Alan Burns's *Celebrations* – by far the best experimentalist in the country was the verdict. I said I hadn't yet made a start. He saw I had a handful of books published by John Calder. Best list around. I went over to where he stood. I said I hadn't managed to read further than twenty pages in a single one. And so terribly printed! And how about J.G. Ballard – he saw I had three of his titles. Couldn't face them, I said, too apocalyptic. He loved everything Ballard did. He was a bold and brilliant spirit. We laughed. Tom promised to read me a Kingsley Amis poem, 'A Bookshop Idyll', about men and women's divergent tastes. It went a bit soppy at the end, he said, but it was funny and true. I said I'd probably hate it, except for the end. He kissed me, and that was the end of the literary discussion. We went towards the bed.

It was awkward. We'd been talking for hours, pretending that we weren't thinking constantly of this moment. We were like pen friends who exchange chatty then intimate letters in each other's language, then meet for the first time and realise they must begin again. His style was new to me. I was sitting on the edge of the bed once more. After a single kiss, and without further caresses, he leaned over me and set about undressing me, and doing it efficiently, routinely, as though he were getting a child ready for bed. If he'd been humming to himself it wouldn't have surprised me. In different circumstances, if we'd been closer, that might have been an attractive tender moment of role-playing. But this was done in silence. I didn't know what it meant and I was uneasy. When he stretched across my shoulders to unfasten my bra, I could have touched him, I was about to, then I didn't. Supporting my head, he gently pushed me back on the bed and took off my knickers. None of this had any appeal for me at all. It was getting too tense. I had to intervene.

I sprang up and said, 'Your turn.' Obediently, he sat where I had been. I stood in front of him, so that my breasts were close to his face, and unbuttoned his shirt. I could see that he was hard. 'Bedtime for big boys.' When he took my nipple into his mouth I thought we were going to be all right. I'd almost forgotten the sensation, hot and electric and piercing, spreading up round the base of my throat and right down to my perineum. But when we pulled back the covers and lay down, I saw that he was now soft and thought I must have done something wrong. I was also surprised by a glimpse of his pubic hair – so scant it was almost non-existent, and what was there was straight and silky, like head hair. We kissed again – he was good at that – but when I took his cock in my hand it was still soft. I pushed his head down towards my breasts since that had worked before. A fresh partner. It was like learning a new card game. But he went down past my breasts, lowered his head and brought me off with his tongue beautifully. I came in less than a glorious minute with a little shout I disguised as a strangled cough for the benefit of the lawyers downstairs. When I came to my senses I was relieved to see how aroused he was. My pleasure had loosened his own. And so I drew him towards me and it began.

It was not a great experience for either of us, but we made it through, we saved face. The limitation for me was partly, as I've said, my awareness of the other three, who seemed to have no love lives of their own and who would be straining to hear a human sound above the creak of bed springs. And it was partly that Tom was so silent. He said nothing endearing or affectionate or appreciative. Even his breathing didn't change. I couldn't banish the thought that he was quietly recording our lovemaking for future use, that he was making mental notes, creating and adjusting phrases to his liking, looking out for the detail that rose above the ordinary. I thought again of the story of the false vicar, and Jean of the 'monstrous' clitoris, the size of a little boy's penis. What did Tom think of mine while he was down there measuring its length with his tongue? Too average to be worth remembering? When Edmund and Jean are reunited in the flat in Chalk Farm and make love, she reaches her orgasm and makes a series of *high-pitched bleats, as pure and evenly spaced as the BBC's time signal*. What then of my politely muted sounds?

Such questions bred other, unhealthy thoughts. Neil Carder delights in his mannequin's 'stillness', he thrills to the possibility that she was contemptuous of him and was ignoring him. Was this what Tom wanted, total passivity in a woman, an inwardness that *rolled back upon itself to become its opposite, a force that overwhelmed and consumed him*? Should I lie completely still and let my lips part as I fixed my gaze on the ceiling? I didn't really think so, and I didn't enjoy these speculations.

I added to my torments by fantasising about him reaching for a notebook and pencil from his jacket as soon as we were finished. Of course I would throw him out! But these self-harming thoughts were merely bad dreams. He lay on his back, I lay on his arm. It wasn't cold but we drew the sheet and blanket over us. We dozed lightly for some minutes. I woke when the front door slammed downstairs and I heard the receding voices of my housemates in the street. We were alone in the house. Without being able to see, I sensed Tom coming fully awake. He was silent for a while and then he proposed taking me out to a good restaurant. His Foundation money hadn't arrived, but he was sure it would come soon. I silently confirmed this. Max had signed off on the payment two days before.

We went to the White Tower at the south end of Charlotte Street and ate kleftiko with roast potatoes and drank three bottles of retsina. We could take it. How exotic, to be dining at the expense of the Secret Vote and not be able to say. I felt so grown up. Tom told me that during the war this famous restaurant had served spam *à la grecque*. We joked that soon those days would be back. He filled me in on the literary associations of the place while I smiled loopily, not quite listening because, again, some sort of music was playing in my mind, this time a symphony, a majestic slow movement on the grand scale of Mahler. This very room, Tom was saying, was where Ezra Pound and Wyndham Lewis founded their vorticist *Blast* magazine. The names meant nothing to me. We walked back from Fitzrovia to Camden Town, arm in arm and drunk, talking nonsense. When we woke the next morning in my room the new card game was easy. In fact, it was a delight.

15

Late October brought the annual rite of putting back the clocks, tightening the lid of darkness over our afternoons, lowering the nation's mood further. November began with another cold snap and it rained most days. Everyone was speaking of 'the crisis'. Government presses were printing petrol rationing coupons. There had been nothing like this since the last war. The general sense was that we were heading for something nasty but hard to foresee, impossible to avoid. There was a suspicion that the 'social fabric' was about to unravel, though no one really knew what this would entail. But I was happy and busy, I had a lover at last, and I was trying not to brood about Tony. My anger at him gave way to, or at least blended with, guilt for condemning him so harshly. It was wrong to lose sight of that distant idyll, our Edwardian summer in Suffolk. Now I was with Tom, I felt protected, I could afford to think nostalgically rather than tragically of our time together. Tony may have betrayed his country but he'd given me my start in life.

I revived my newspaper habit. It was the opinion pages that drew me, the complaints and laments, known in the trade, so I'd learned, as why-oh-why pieces. As in, why-oh-why did university intellectuals cheer on the carnage wrought by the Provisional IRA and romanticise the Angry Brigade and the Red Army Faction? Our empire and our victory in the Second World War haunted and accused us, but why-oh-why must we stagnate among the ruins of our former greatness? Crime rates were soaring, everyday courtesies declining, the streets filthy, our economy and morale broken, our living standards below those of communist East Germany, and we stood divided, truculent and irrelevant. Insurrectionary trouble-makers were dismantling our democratic traditions, popular television was hysterically silly, colour TV sets cost too much and everyone agreed there was no hope, the country was finished, our moment in history had passed. Why-oh-why?

I also followed the woeful daily narrative. By the middle of the month oil imports were right down, the Coal Board had offered the miners 16.5 per cent but, seizing the opportunity granted by OPEC, they were holding out for 35 per cent and were starting their overtime ban. Children were sent home because there was no heating in their schools, street lights were turned off to save energy, there was wild talk of everyone working a three-day week because of electricity shortages. The government announced the fifth state of emergency. Some said pay off the miners, some said down with bullies and blackmailers. I followed all this, I discovered I had a taste for economics. I knew the figures and I knew my way round the crisis. But I didn't care. I was absorbed by Spade and Helium, I was trying to forget Volt and my heart belonged to Sweet Tooth, my private portion of it. This meant travelling ex officio at the weekends to Brighton, where Tom had a two-room flat at the top of a thin white house near the station. Clifton Street resembled a row of iced Christmas cakes, the air was clean, we had privacy, the bed was of modern pine, the mattress silent and firm. Within weeks I came to think of this place as home.

The bedroom was just a little larger than the bed. There wasn't enough space to open the wardrobe door by more than nine inches or so. You had to reach inside and feel for your clothes. I sometimes woke in the early morning to the sound of Tom's typewriter through the wall. The room he worked in also served as kitchen and sitting room and felt more spacious. It had been opened up to the rafters by the ambitious builder who was Tom's landlord. That uneven tapping of the keys and the cawing of gulls – I woke to these sounds and, keeping my eyes closed, I'd luxuriate in the transformation in my existence. How lonely I'd been in Camden, especially after Shirley had left. What a pleasure it was, to arrive at seven on a Friday at the end of an arduous week and walk the few hundred yards up the hill under streetlight, smelling the sea and feeling that Brighton was as remote from London as Nice or Naples, knowing that Tom would have a bottle of white wine in the miniature fridge and wine glasses ready on the kitchen table. Our weekends were simple. We made love, we read, we walked on the seafront and sometimes on the Downs, and we ate in restaurants – usually in the Lanes. And Tom wrote.

He worked on an Olivetti portable on a green baize card table pushed into a corner. He would get up in the night or at dawn and work through until nine or so, when he would come back to bed, make love to me, then sleep until midday while I went out for a coffee and a croissant near the Open Market. Croissants were a novelty in England then and they made my corner of Brighton seem all the more exotic. I would read the paper cover to cover, minus the sport, then shop for our fry-up brunch.

Tom's Foundation money was coming through – how else could we afford to eat at Wheeler's and fill the fridge with Chablis? During that November and December he was doing the last of his teaching and working on two stories. He'd met in London a poet and editor, Ian Hamilton, who was starting up a literary magazine, the *New Review*, and wanted Tom to submit fiction for one of the early issues. He had read all of Tom's published stuff and had told him over drinks in Soho that it was 'quite good' or 'not bad' – high praise from this quarter, apparently.

   In the self-congratulatory way of new lovers, we had developed by now a number of smug routines, catch phrases and fetishes, and our Saturday evening pattern was well established. We often made love in the early evening – our 'main meal of the day'. The early morning 'cuddle' did not really count. In a mood of elation and post-coital clarity, we'd dress for an evening out and before leaving the flat we'd sink most of a bottle of Chablis. We would drink nothing else at home though neither of us knew a thing about wine. Chablis was a joke choice because, apparently, James Bond liked it. Tom would play music on his new hi-fi, usually bebop, to me no more than an arrhythmic stream of random notes, but it sounded sophisticated and glamorously urban. Then we would step out into the icy sea breeze and saunter down the hill to the Lanes, usually to Wheeler's fish restaurant. Tom had semi-drunkenly over-tipped the waiters there often enough, so we were popular and were shown with some flourish to 'our' table, well positioned to one side for us to observe and mock the other diners. I suppose we were unbearable. We made a thing of telling the waiters to bring us as a starter 'the usual' – two glasses of champagne and a dozen oysters. I'm not sure we really liked them, but we liked the idea of them, the oval arrangement of barnacled ancient life among the parsley and halved lemons and, glinting opulently in the candlelight, the bed of ice, the silver dish, the polished cruet of chilli sauce.

   When we weren't talking about ourselves, we had all of politics – the domestic crisis, the Middle East, Vietnam. Logically, we should have been more ambivalent about a war to contain communism, but we took the orthodox view of our generation. The struggle was murderously cruel and clearly a failure. We also followed that soap opera of over-reaching power and folly, Watergate, though Tom, like most men I knew, was so well up on the cast, the dates, every historical turn in the narrative and minor constitutional implication that he found me a useless companion in outrage. We should also have had all of literature. He showed me the poems he loved, and there was no problem with that – I loved them too. But he couldn't interest me in the novels of John Hawkes, Barry Hannah or William Gaddis, and he failed with my heroines, Margaret Drabble, Fay Weldon and, my latest flame, Jennifer Johnston. I thought his lot were too dry, he thought mine were wet, though he was prepared to give Elizabeth Bowen the benefit of the doubt. During that time, we managed to agree on only one short novel, which he had in a bound proof, William Kotzwinkle's *Swimmer in the Secret Sea*. He thought it was beautifully formed, I thought it was wise and sad.

Since he didn't like talking about his work before it was finished, I felt it was reasonable and dutiful to take a peek when he was out one Saturday afternoon researching in the library. I kept the door open so I could hear him coming up the stairs. One story, completed in a first draft by the end of November, was narrated by a talking ape prone to anxious reflections about his lover, a writer struggling with her second novel. She has been praised for her first. Is she capable of another just as good? She is beginning to doubt it. The indignant ape hovers at her back, hurt by the way she neglects him for her labours. Only on the last page did I discover that the story I was reading was actually the one the woman was writing. The ape doesn't exist, it's a spectre, the creature of her fretful imagination. *No.* And no again. Not that. Beyond the strained and ludicrous matter of cross-species sex, I instinctively distrusted this kind of fictional trick. I wanted to feel the ground beneath my feet. There was, in my view, an unwritten contract with the reader that the writer must honour. No single element of an imagined world or any of its characters should be allowed to dissolve on authorial whim. The invented had to be as solid and as self-consistent as the actual. This was a contract founded on mutual trust.

If the first was disappointing, the second piece amazed me before I started reading. It was over a hundred and forty pages long, with last week's date written in longhand below the last sentence. The first draft of a short novel, and he'd kept it a secret from me. I was about to start reading when I was startled by the door to the outside landing slamming shut, pushed by a draught through the leaky windows. I got up and propped the door open with a coil of oily rope that Tom had once used to haul single-handedly the wardrobe up the stairs. Then I turned on the light that hung from the rafters and settled down to my guilty speed-reading.

From the Somerset Levels described a journey a man makes with his nine-year-old daughter across a ruined landscape of burned-out villages and small towns, where rats, cholera and bubonic plague are constant dangers, where the water is polluted and neighbours fight to the death for an ancient can of juice, where the locals consider themselves lucky to be invited to a celebration dinner at which a dog and a couple of scrawny cats will be roasted over a bonfire. The desolation is even greater when father and daughter reach London. Among the decaying skyscrapers and rusting vehicles and uninhabitable terraced streets where rats and feral dogs teem, warlords and their thugs, faces done up in streaks of primary colours, terrorise the impoverished citizenry. Electricity is a distant memory. All that functions, though barely, is government itself. A ministerial tower block rises over a vast plain of cracked and weedy concrete. On their way to stand in line outside a government office, father and daughter cross the plain at dawn, passing over *vegetables, rotten and trodden down, cardboard boxes flattened into beds, the remains of fires and the carcasses of roasted pigeons, rusted tin, vomit, worn tyres, chemical green puddles, human and animal excrement. An old dream of horizontal lines converging on the thrusting steel and glass perpendicular was now beyond recall.*

This plaza, where much of the central section of the novel takes place, is a giant microcosm of a sad new world. In the middle is a disused fountain, the air above it is *grey with flies. Men and boys came there daily to squat on the wide concrete rim and defecate.* These figures *perch like featherless birds.* Later in the day the place teems like an ant colony, the air is thick with smoke, the noise is deafening, people spread their pathetic goods on coloured blankets, the father haggles for an ancient used bar of soap, though fresh water will be hard to find. Everything for sale on the plain was made long ago, by processes no longer understood. Later, the man (annoyingly, we are never told his name) meets up with an old friend who is lucky enough to have a room. She's a collector. On the table there is a telephone, *its wire severed at four inches and, beyond that, propped against the wall, a cathode ray tube. The television's wooden casing, the glass screen and control buttons had long ago been ripped away and now bunches of bright wires coiled against the dull metal.* She cares for such objects because, she tells him, they're *the products of human inventiveness and design. And not caring for objects is one step away from not caring for people.* But he thinks her curating impulses are pointless. *Without a telephone system, telephones are worthless junk.*

Industrial civilisation and all its systems and culture are fading from recall. Man is tracking back through time to a brutal past where constant competition for scarce resources allows little kindness or invention. The old days will not be back. *Everything has changed so much that I can hardly believe it was us who were there,* the woman tells him of the past they once shared. *This was where we were always heading,* one shoeless philosophical character says to the father. It's made clear elsewhere that civilisation's collapse began with the injustices, conflicts and contradictions of the twentieth century.

The reader doesn't find out where the man and the little girl are headed until the final pages. They have been searching for his wife, the girl's mother. There are no systems of communication or bureaucracy to help them. The only photograph they have is of her as a child. They rely on word of mouth,

195

and after many false trails, they are bound to fail, especially when they begin to succumb to bubonic plague. Father and daughter die in one another's arms in the rank cellar of the ruined headquarters of a once-famous bank.

It had taken me an hour and a quarter to read to the end. I replaced the pages by the typewriter, taking care to spread them as untidily as I'd found them, shifted the rope and closed the door. I sat at the kitchen table trying to think through my confusion. I could easily rehearse the objections of Peter Nutting and colleagues. Here were the doomed dystopia we did not want, the modish apocalypse that indicted and rejected all we had ever devised or built or loved, that relished in the entire project collapsing into the dirt. Here were the luxury and privilege of the well-fed man scoffing at all hopes of progress for the rest. T.H. Haley owed nothing to a world that nurtured him kindly, liberally educated him for free, sent him to no wars, brought him to manhood without scary rituals or famine or fear of vengeful gods, embraced him with a handsome pension in his twenties and placed no limits on his freedom of expression. This was an easy nihilism that never doubted that all we had made was rotten, never thought to pose alternatives, never derived hope from friendship, love, free markets, industry, technology, trade and all the arts and sciences.

His story (I made my phantom Nutting go on to say) inherited from Samuel Beckett a dispensation in which the human condition was a man lying alone at the end of things, bound only to himself, without hope, sucking on a pebble. A man who knows nothing of the difficulties of public administration in a democracy, of delivering good governance to millions of demanding, entitled, free-thinking individuals, who cares nothing for how far we have come in a mere five hundred years from a cruel, impoverished past.

On the other hand . . . what was good about it? It would annoy them all, especially Max, and for that alone it was glorious. It would annoy him even as it confirmed his view that taking on a novelist was a mistake. Paradoxically, it would strengthen Sweet Tooth by showing how free this writer was of his paymasters. *From the Somerset Levels* was the incarnation of the ghost that was haunting every headline, a peep over the edge of the abyss, the dramatised worst case – London become Herat, Delhi, São Paulo. But what did I really think about it? It had depressed me, it was so dark, so entirely without hope. He should have spared the child at least, given the reader a little faith in the future. I suspected my phantom Nutting might be right – there was something modish in this pessimism, it was merely an aesthetic, a literary mask or attitude. It wasn't really Tom, or it was only the smallest part of him, and therefore it was insincere. I didn't like it at all. And T.H. Haley would be seen as my choice and I'd be held responsible. Another black mark.

I stared across the room at his typewriter and the empty coffee cup beside it, and I considered. Might the man I was having an affair with prove incapable of fulfilling the moment of his earliest promise, like the woman with the ape at her back? If his best work was already behind him, I would have made an embarrassing error of judgement. That would be the accusation, but the truth was he'd been handed to me on a plate, in a file. I'd fallen for the stories and then the man. It was an arranged marriage, a marriage made on the fifth floor, and it was too late, I was the bride who couldn't run away. However disappointed I was, I would stick by him, or with him, and not only out of self-interest. For of *course* I still believed in him. A couple of weak stories were not going to dislodge my conviction that he was an original voice, a brilliant mind – and my wonderful lover. He was my project, my case, my mission. His art, my work and our affair were one. If he failed, I failed. Simple then – we would flourish together.

It was almost six o'clock. Tom was still out, the pages of his novel were convincingly spread around the typewriter and the pleasures of the evening lay ahead of us. I ran a heavily scented bath. The bathroom was five feet by four (we had measured it) and featured a space-saving hipbath in which you lowered yourself into the water and sat or crouched on a ledge in the manner of Michelangelo's *Il Penseroso*. And so I crouched and stewed and thought some more. One benign possibility was that this editor, Hamilton, if he was as sharp as Tom made out, was likely to turn both pieces down and give good reasons. In which case I should say nothing and wait. Which was the whole idea, to set him free with money, stay out of the way and hope for the best. And yet . . . and yet, I believed myself to be a good reader. I was convinced he was making a mistake, this monochrome pessimism didn't serve his talent, didn't permit him the witty reversals of, say, the false-vicar story or the ambiguities of a man making passionate love to a wife he knows to be a crook. I thought Tom liked me enough to listen. Then again, my instructions were clear. I should fight my interfering impulses.

Twenty minutes later I was drying myself by the bath, nothing resolved, thoughts still turning, when I heard footsteps on the stairs. He tapped on the door and came into my steamy boudoir and we embraced without speaking. I felt the cold street air in the folds of his coat. Perfect timing. I was naked, fragrant and ready. He led me to the bedroom, everything was fine, all troublesome questions fell away. An hour or so later we were dressed for the evening, drinking our Chablis and listening to 'My Funny Valentine' by Chet Baker, a man who sang like a woman. If there was bebop in his trumpet solo it was mild and tender. I thought I could even begin to like jazz. We chinked glasses and kissed, then Tom turned away from me and went with his wine to stand by the card table, looking down for some minutes at his work. He lifted one page after the other, searched the pile for a certain passage, found it and picked up a pencil to make a mark. He was frowning as he turned the carriage with slow meaningful clicks of the mechanism to read the sheet in the typewriter. When he looked up at me I was nervous.

He said, 'I've got something to tell you.'

'Something good?'

'I'll tell you at dinner.'

He came over to me and we kissed again. He had yet to put on his jacket and he was wearing one of the three shirts he'd had made in Jermyn Street. They were identical, of fine white Egyptian cotton, cut generously around the shoulders and arms to give him a vaguely piratical look. He'd told me that all men should have a 'library' of white shirts. I wasn't sure about the styling, but I liked the feel of him beneath the cotton, and I liked the way he was adapting to the money. The hi-fi, the restaurants, the Globetrotter suitcases, an electric typewriter on the way – he was shrugging off the student life, doing it with style, without guilt. In those months before Christmas he also had his teaching money. He was flush, and good to be around. He bought me presents – a silk jacket, perfume, a soft leather briefcase for work, the poetry of Sylvia Plath, novels by Ford Madox Ford, all in hardback. He also paid for my return railfare, which was well over a pound. At the weekends I forgot my scrimping London life, my pitiable food hoard in one corner of the fridge, and counting out the change in the mornings for my Tube fare and lunch.

We finished the bottle and fairly rolled down Queen's Road, past the Clock Tower and into the Lanes, pausing only for Tom to give directions to an Indian couple carrying a baby with a harelip. The narrow streets had a forlorn out-of-season air, salty-damp and deserted, the cobbles treacherously slick. In a good-humoured, teasing way, Tom was interrogating me about my 'other' writers supported by the Foundation. We'd been through this a few times and it was almost a routine. He was indulging sexual as well as writerly jealousy or competitiveness.

'Just tell me this. Are they mostly young?'

'Mostly immortal.'

'Come on. You can tell me. Are they famous oldsters? Anthony Burgess? John Braine? Any women?'

'What use are women to me?'

'Do they get more money than I do? You can tell me that.'

'Everyone gets at least twice what you get.'

'Serena!'

'OK. Everyone gets the same.'

'As me.'

'As you.'

'Am I the only one unpublished?'

'That's all I'm saying.'

'Have you fucked any of them?'

'Quite a few.'

'And you're still working through the list?'

'You know I am.'

He laughed and pulled me into the doorway of a jeweller's shop to kiss me. He was one of those men who are occasionally turned on by the idea of his lover making love to another man. In certain moods it aroused him, the daydream of being a cuckold, even though the reality would have sickened or wounded or enraged him. Clearly, the origin of Carder's fantasy about his mannequin. I didn't understand it at all but I had learned how to play along. Sometimes, when we made love, he would prompt me in whispers and I would oblige by telling him about the man I was seeing and what I did for him. Tom preferred him to be a writer, and the less probable, the more status-laden, the greater his exquisite agony. Saul Bellow, Norman Mailer, pipe-smoking Günter Grass, I went with the best. Or his best. Even at the time, I realised that a deliberate and shared fantasy was usefully diluting my own necessary untruths. It wasn't easy talking about the work I did for the Foundation with a man I was so close to. My appeal to confidentiality was one way out, this vaguely humorous erotic dream was another. But neither was enough. This was the little dark stain on my happiness.

Of course we knew very well the reason for our warm welcome at Wheeler's, for the nodding enquiries after Miss Serena's week, Mr Tom's health, our appetites, for the snappish drawing out of chairs, and napkins laid across our laps, but it also made us so very happy, and almost convinced us that we really were admired and respected, and far more so than the rest of the dull and ageing crowd. Back then, apart from a few pop stars, the young had not yet got their hands on the money. So the diners' frowns that stalked us to our table also heightened our pleasure. We were so special. If only they'd known they were paying for our meal with their taxes. If only Tom could know. Within a minute, while others who were there before us had nothing, we had our champagne, and soon after that the silver dish and its cargo of ice, and shells containing the glistening cowpats of briny viscera that we dared not cease pretending to like. The trick was to knock them back without tasting them. We knocked back the champagne too and called for a top-up. As on previous occasions we reminded ourselves to order a bottle next time. We could save so much money.

In the restaurant's moist warmth Tom had removed his jacket. He reached across the table to put his hand on mine. Candlelight deepened the green of his eyes, and touched his pallor with a faint, healthy tint of brownish-pink. Head as always slightly tipped to one side, lips as usual parted and tensed, not to speak so much as to anticipate my words or speak them with me. Just then, already tipsy, I thought I'd never seen a man more beautiful. I forgave him his tailored pirate's shirt. Love doesn't grow at a steady rate, but advances in surges, bolts, wild leaps, and this was one of those. The first had been in the White Tower. This was far more powerful. Like Sebastian Morel in 'Pawnography', I was tumbling through dimensionless space, even as I sat smiling demurely in a Brighton fish restaurant. But always, at the furthest edges of thought, was that tiny stain. I generally tried to ignore it, and I was so excited I often succeeded. Then, like a woman who slips over the edge of a cliff and makes a lunge for a tuft of grass that will never hold her weight, so I remembered yet again that Tom did not know who I was and what I really did and that I should tell him now. *Last chance! Go on, tell him now.* But it was too late. The truth was too weighty, it would destroy us. He would hate me forever. I was over the cliff edge and could never get back. I could remind myself of the benefits I had brought into his life, the artistic freedom that came with me, but the fact was that if I was to go on seeing him, I would have to keep telling him these off-white lies.

His hand moved up towards my wrist and tightened. The waiter arrived to refill our glasses.

Tom said, 'So this is just the moment to tell you.' He raised his glass, obediently I raised mine. 'You know I've been writing this stuff for Ian Hamilton. It turned out there was one piece that kept growing and I realised I was drifting into the short novel that I've been thinking about for a year. I was so excited and I wanted to tell you, I wanted to show it to you. But I didn't dare, in case it didn't work. I finished a draft last week, photocopied some of it and sent it to this publisher everyone's been telling me about. Tom Mischler. No, Maschler. His letter came this morning. I didn't expect such a quick reply. I didn't open it until this afternoon when I was out of the house. Serena, he wants it! Urgently. He wants a final draft by Christmas.'

My arm was aching from holding out my glass. I said, 'Tom, this is fantastic news. Congratulations! To you!'

We drank deeply. He said, 'It's sort of dark. Set in the near future, everything's collapsed. A bit like Ballard. But I think you'll like it.'

'How does it end? Do things get better?'

He smiled at me indulgently. 'Of course not.'

'How marvellous.'

The menu came and we ordered Dover sole and a red rather than a white wine, a hearty rioja, to demonstrate that we were free spirits. Tom talked more about his novel, and about his new editor, publisher of Heller, Roth, Marquez. I was wondering how I'd break the news to Max. An anti-capitalist dystopia. While other Sweet Tooth writers handed in their non-fiction versions of *Animal Farm*. But at least my man was a creative force who went his own way. And so would I, once I'd been sacked.

Preposterous. This was a time for celebration, for there was nothing I could do about Tom's story, which we were now referring to as 'the novella'. So we drank and ate and talked and raised our glasses to this or that good outcome. Towards the end of the evening, when there were only half a dozen diners left and our waiters were yawning and hovering, Tom said in a tone of mock reproach, 'I'm always telling you about poems and novels, but you never tell me anything about maths. It's time you did.'

'I wasn't much good,' I said. 'I've put it all behind me.'

'Not good enough. I want you to tell me something . . . something interesting, no, counter-intuitive, paradoxical. You owe me a good maths story.'

Nothing in maths had ever seemed counter-intuitive to me. Either I understood it, or I didn't, and from Cambridge onwards, it was mostly the latter. But I liked a challenge. I said, 'Give me a few minutes.' So Tom talked about his new electric typewriter and how fast he would be able to work. Then I remembered.

'This was going the rounds among Cambridge mathematicians when I was there. I don't think anyone's written on it yet. It's about probability and it's in the form of a question. It comes from an American game show called *Let's Make a Deal*. The host a few years ago was a man called Monty Hall. Let's suppose you're on Monty's show as a contestant. Facing you are three closed boxes, one, two and three, and inside

one of the boxes, you don't know which, is a wonderful prize
– let's say a . . .'

'Beautiful girl gives you a fat pension.'

'Exactly. Monty knows which box your pension is in and
you don't. You make a choice. Let's say you choose box one,
but we don't open it yet. Then Monty, who knows where the
pension is, opens a box he knows to be empty. Let's say it's
box three. So you know your fat pension for life is either in
box one, the one you chose, or it's in box two. Now Monty
offers you the chance of changing to box two or staying where
you are. Where is your pension more likely to be? Should
you move or stay where you are?'

Our waiter brought the bill on a silver plate. Tom reached
for his wallet, then changed his mind. For all the wine and
champagne he sounded clear-headed. We both did. We
wanted to show each other we could hold our drink.

'It's obvious. With box one I had a one in three chance
to start with. When box three is opened my chances narrow to
one in two. And the same has to be true for box two. Equal
chances that my fat pension is in either box. It makes no
difference whether I move or not. Serena, you're looking
unbearably beautiful.'

'Thank you. You'd be in good company with that choice.
But you'd be wrong. If you go for the other box you double
your chances of never needing to take a job again.'

'Nonsense.'

I watched him take out his wallet to settle the bill. It was
almost thirty pounds. He slapped down a twenty-pound tip,
and the looseness of the gesture revealed how drunk he was.
This was more than my weekly wage. He was trapped by
precedent.

I said, 'Your chance of choosing the box with your pension
remains one in three. The sum of probabilities has to add up
to one. So the chances of it being in one of the other two
boxes has to be two in three. Box three is open and empty,
so it's two in three that it's in box two.'

He was looking at me pityingly, as though I were an evangelical member of some extreme religious sect. 'Monty has given me more information by opening the box. My chances were one in three. Now they're one in two.'

'That would only be true if you had just come in the room after he opened the box and *then* you were asked to choose between the other two boxes. Then you'd be looking at odds of one in two.'

'Serena. I'm surprised you can't see what's there.'

I was beginning to feel a distinctive and unusual kind of pleasure, a sense of being set free. In a portion of mental space, perhaps quite a large portion, I was actually cleverer than Tom. How strange that seemed. What was so very simple for me, for him was apparently beyond comprehension.

'Look at it this way,' I said. 'Moving from box one to box two is only a bad idea if you'd made the right choice at the start and your pension is in box one. And the chances of that are one in three. So, one-third of the time it's a bad idea to move, which means that two-thirds of the time it's a good idea.'

He was frowning, struggling. He had glimpsed for a moment the truth, and then he blinked and it was gone.

'I know I'm right,' he said. 'I'm just not explaining it well. This Monty has chosen at random the box to put my pension in. There are only two boxes it can be in, so there has to be an equal chance it's one or the other.' He was about to get up and slumped back in his chair. 'Thinking about it is making me dizzy.'

'There's another way of approaching it,' I said. 'Suppose we have a million boxes. Same rules. Let's say you choose box seven hundred thousand. Monty comes along the line opening box after box, all empty. All the time he's avoiding opening the box that has your prize. He stops when the only closed boxes left are yours and, say, number ninety-five. What are the chances now?'

'Equal,' he said in a muffled voice. 'Fifty–fifty each box.'

I tried not to sound like I was speaking to a child. 'Tom, it's a million to one against it being in your box, and almost certain that it's in the other.'

He had that same look of fleeting insight, then it was gone. 'Well, no, I don't think that's right, I mean I . . . Actually, I think I'm going to be sick.'

He lurched to his feet and hurried past the waiters without saying goodbye. When I caught up with him outside he was leaning by a car, staring at his shoes. The cold air had revived him and he hadn't been sick after all. Arm in arm we headed for home.

When I thought he had recovered sufficiently I said, 'If it helps, we could test this empirically using playing cards. We could get . . .'

'Serena, darling, no more. If I think about this again I really will throw up.'

'You wanted something counter-intuitive.'

'Yes. Sorry. I won't ask you again. Let's stick with pro-intuitive.'

So we talked of other things and as soon as we got back to the flat we went to bed and slept deeply. But early on Sunday morning Tom, in a state of excitement, shook me awake from confused dreams.

'I get it! Serena, I understand how it works. Everything you were saying, it's so simple. It just popped into place, like, you know, that drawing of a what's-it cube.'

'Necker.'

'And I can *do* something with it.'

'Yes, why not . . .'

I fell asleep to the rattle of his typewriter keys next door and didn't wake for another three hours. We barely referred to Monty Hall during the rest of that Sunday. I made a roast lunch while he worked. It may have been the lowering effect of a hangover, but I was more than usually sad at the prospect of returning to St Augustine's Road and my lonely room, of turning on my single-bar electric fire, of washing my hair in the sink and ironing a blouse for work.

In sombre afternoon light Tom walked me to the station. I was almost tearful as we embraced on the platform, but I didn't make a big scene, and I don't think he noticed.

16

Three days later his story arrived in the post. Attached to the first page was a postcard of the West Pier and on the reverse was, 'Have I got this right?'

I read 'Probable Adultery' in the icy kitchen over a mug of tea before I left for work. Terry Mole is a London architect whose childless marriage is being steadily destroyed by the serial affairs of his wife Sally. She has no job and, with no children to attend to and a housekeeper to do the chores, she's able *to dedicate herself to constant and reckless infidelity.* She also applies herself each day to smoking pot and prefers a large whisky or two before lunch. Meanwhile, Terry puts in a seventy-hour week designing cheap high-rise council flats which will probably be pulled down within fifteen years. Sally has assignations with men she barely knows. *Her lies and excuses were insultingly transparent but he could never disprove them. He didn't have the time.* But one day a number of on-site meetings are cancelled and the architect decides to spend his free hours following his wife. *He was eaten away by sadness and jealousy and needed to see her with a man in order to feed his desolation and strengthen his resolve to leave her.* She's told him she's going to spend the day with her aunt in St Albans. Instead, she heads for Victoria station and Terry follows.

She boards a train for Brighton, and so does he, two carriages back. He tracks her through the town, across the Steine and into the back streets of Kemp Town until she comes to a small hotel in Upper Rock Gardens. From the pavement he sees her in the lobby with a man, fortunately a rather puny fellow, Terry thinks. He sees the couple take a key from the receptionist and begin to climb the narrow stairs. Terry enters the hotel and, unnoticed or ignored by the receptionist, also goes up the stairs. He can hear their footsteps above him. He hangs back as they reach the fourth floor. He hears a door being opened, then closed. He arrives on the landing. Facing him there are only three rooms, 401, 402 and 403. His plan is to wait until the couple are in bed, then he'll kick their door down, shame his wife and give that little fellow a hard smack to the head.

But he doesn't know which room they're in.

He stands quietly on the landing, hoping to hear a sound. *He craved to hear it, a moan, a yelp, a bedspring, anything would do. But there was nothing*. The minutes pass and he has to make a choice. He decides on 401 because it's the nearest. All the doors look flimsy enough and he knows a good flying kick will do the job. He's stepping back to make his run when the door of 403 opens and out step an Indian couple with their baby, who has a harelip. They smile shyly as they go past him and then they descend the stairs.

When they've gone Terry hesitates. Here the story becomes tense as it rises towards its climax. As an architect and an amateur mathematician he has a good grasp of numbers. He makes a hurried reckoning. There was always a one-in-three chance his wife is in 401. Which means that until just now there was a two in three chance she's either in 402 or 403. And now that 403 is shown to be empty, there must be a two in three chance she's in 402. *Only a fool would stay with his first choice, for the steely laws of probability are inflexibly true*. He makes his run, he leaps, the door of 402 smashes open and there are the couple, naked in bed, just getting going. He gives the man *a beefy slap round the chops, threw his wife a look of cold contempt*, then leaves for London, where he'll institute divorce proceedings and start a new life.

All that Wednesday I sorted and filed documents relating to one Joe Cahill of the Provisionals, his connection with Colonel Qaddafi and an arms shipment from Libya, tracked by Six and intercepted by the Irish navy off the coast of Waterford at the end of March. Cahill was on board and didn't know a thing until he felt the barrel of a gun in the back of his neck. As far as I could tell from paper-clipped addenda, our lot had been out of the loop and were irritated. 'This mistake', read one furious minute, 'must not be made again.' Interesting enough, up to a point. But I knew which location – the good ship *Claudia* or the inside of my lover's mind – interested me more. More than that, I was worried, fretful. Whenever I had a break, my thoughts returned to the doors on the fourth floor of a Brighton hotel.

It was a good story. Even if it wasn't one of his best, he was back on form, the right kind of form. But when I read it that morning, I knew at a stroke that it was flawed, built on specious assumptions, unworkable parallels, hopeless mathematics. He hadn't understood me or the problem at all. His excitement, his Necker-cube moment, had carried him away. Thinking about his boyish exultation and how I had drifted back to sleep and failed to discuss his idea when I woke made me feel ashamed. He had been thrilled by the prospect of carrying over into his fiction the paradox of weighted choice. His ambition was magnificent – to dramatise and give ethical dimension to a line of mathematics. His message on the postcard was clear. He depended on me in his heroic attempt to bridge the chasm between art and logic, and I had let him charge off in the wrong direction. His story couldn't stand, it made no sense, and it touched me that he thought it could. But how could I tell him that his story was worthless when I was, in part, responsible for it?

For the simple truth, self-evident to me, to him quite opaque, was that the Indian couple emerging from 403 could not possibly tip the odds in favour of 402. They could never replace the part that Monty Hall has in the TV game. Their emergence is random, while Monty's choices are constrained, determined by the contestant. Monty cannot be replaced by a random selector. If Terry had chosen 403, the couple and their baby couldn't magically transfer themselves to another room so they could emerge through a different door. After their appearance Terry's wife is just as likely to be in Room 402 as 401. He might as well kick down the door of his first choice.

Then, as I went along the corridor to get a mid-morning tea from the trolley, I suddenly understood the source of Tom's mistake. It was me! I stopped and would have put a hand over my mouth, but there was a man coming towards me carrying a cup and saucer. I saw him clearly, but I was too preoccupied, too shocked by my insight to take him in properly. A handsome man with protruding ears, now slowing down, blocking my way. Max, of course, my boss, my one-time confidant. Did I owe him another de-briefing?

'Serena. Are you all right?'

'Yes. Sorry. Head in the clouds, you know . . .'

He was staring at me in an intense way and his bony shoulders looked awkwardly hunched inside his over-sized tweed jacket. His cup clinked in its saucer until he steadied it with his free hand.

He said, 'I think we really ought to talk.'

'Tell me when and I'll come to your office.'

'I mean, not here. A drink after work, or a meal, or something.'

I was edging around him. 'That would be nice.'

'Friday?'

'I can't do Friday.'

'Monday then.'

'Yes, OK.'

When I was well clear of him, I half turned and gave him a little wave with my fingers, walked on and instantly forgot him. For I'd remembered clearly what I'd said in the restaurant last weekend. I'd told Tom that Monty chooses an empty box *at random*. And of course, two-thirds of the time that couldn't be true. In the game, Monty can only open an unchosen empty box. In two out of three occasions the contestant is bound to choose just that – an empty box. In which case there's only one box that Monty can go for. Only when the contestant guesses right and chooses the box with the prize, the pension, does Monty have two empty boxes to choose from randomly. Of course, I knew all this, but I hadn't explained it well. This was a shipwreck of a short story and it was my fault. It was from me that Tom had got the idea that fate could play the part of a game-show host.

With my burden of guilt doubled, I realised that I could not simply tell Tom that his story didn't work. The obligation was on me to come up with a solution. Instead of going out of the building, as I usually did at lunchtime, I stayed by my typewriter and took Tom's story from my handbag. As I threaded in a fresh sheet of paper I felt a stirring of pleasure, and then, as I started to type, even excitement. I had an idea, I knew how Tom could rewrite the end of the story, and let Terry kick down the door that doubles his chances of finding his wife in bed with another man. First of all, I got rid of the Indian couple and their harelipped baby. Charming as they were, they could play no part in this drama. Then, as Terry takes a few paces back, the better to run at the door of Room 401, he overhears two chambermaids talking on the landing below. Their voices drift up to him clearly. One of them says, 'I'll just pop upstairs and do one of them two empty rooms.' And the other says, 'Watch out, that couple are in their usual.' They laugh knowingly.

Terry hears the maid coming up the stairs. He's a decent amateur mathematician and realises he has a fantastic opportunity. He needs to think quickly. If he goes and stands close to any of the doors, and 401 will do, he will force the maid to go into one of the other two rooms. She knows where the couple are. She'll think he's either a new guest about to enter his room, or a friend of the couple, waiting outside their door. Whatever room she chooses, Terry will transfer to the other and double his chances. And that's exactly what happens. The maid, who has inherited the harelip, glances at Terry, gives him a nod, and goes into 403. Terry makes his decisive switch, runs and leaps at 402 and there they are, Sally and her man, *in flagrante*.

While I was in full flow I thought I'd suggest to Tom that he tidy up some other loose ends. Why doesn't Terry break down all the doors, especially now that he knows two are empty? Because the couple will hear him and he wants to preserve the element of surprise. Why not wait to see if the maid will clean a second room, at which point he'll know for certain where his wife is? Because it's established early on that he has an important site meeting at the end of the day and he has to get back to London.

I'd been typing for forty minutes and had three pages of notes to send. I scribbled a covering letter explaining in the simplest terms why the Indian couple would not do, found a blank envelope without an HMSO insignia, located a stamp at the bottom of my handbag and just had time to get to the letterbox on Park Lane and back before starting work again. How dull it was after Tom's story, to go through the *Claudia*'s illegal manifest, five tons of explosives, arms and ammunition, a relatively disappointing haul. One memo suggested that Qaddafi didn't trust the Provisionals, another reiterated that 'Six has overstepped the mark'. I couldn't care less.

That night in Camden I went to bed happier than I'd been all week. On the floor was my little suitcase, ready to be packed tomorrow night for my Friday-evening journey to Brighton. Just two days of work to get through. By the time

I saw Tom he would have read my letter. I'd tell him again how good his story was, I'd explain the probability once more, and make a better job. We'd be together with our routines and rituals.

Finally, the calculations of probability were mere technical details. The strength of the story was elsewhere. As I lay in the dark, waiting for sleep, I thought I was beginning to grasp something about invention. As a reader, a speed-reader, I took it for granted, it was a process I never troubled myself with. You pulled a book from the shelf and there was an invented, peopled world, as obvious as the one you lived in. But now, like Tom in the restaurant grappling with Monty Hall, I thought I had the measure of the artifice, or I almost had it. Almost like cooking, I thought sleepily. Instead of heat transforming the ingredients, there's pure invention, the spark, the hidden element. What resulted was more than the sum of the parts. I tried to list them: Tom had donated my grasp of probability to Terry, as well as consigning to him his own secret arousal at the idea of being a cuckold. But not before turning it into something more acceptable – jealous anger. Something of the mess of Tom's sister's life had found its way into Sally's. Then, the familiar train journey, the streets of Brighton, those impossibly tiny hotels. The Indian couple and their baby with the harelip were enlisted to fill a role in Room 403. Their pleasantness and vulnerability contrasted with the rutting couple in the room next door. Tom had taken control of a subject ('only a fool would stay with his first choice'!) which he barely understood, and tried to make it his own. If he incorporated my suggestions, then it would surely be his own. By a sleight of hand he made Terry far better at maths than his creator. At one level it was obvious enough how these separate parts were tipped in and deployed. The mystery was in how they were blended into something cohesive and plausible, how the ingredients were cooked into something so delicious. As my thought scattered and

I drifted towards the borders of oblivion, I thought I almost understood how it was done.

Sometime later, when I heard the doorbell, it featured in my dream as the culmination of an elaborate sequence of co-incidences. But as the dream evaporated I heard the bell again. I didn't move because I was hoping one of the others would go down. They were nearer the front door, after all. On the third ring I turned on the light and looked at my alarm clock. Ten to midnight. I'd been asleep for an hour. The bell rang again, more insistently. I put on my dressing gown and slippers and went down the stairs, too sleepy to question why I should be hurrying. My guess was that one of the other girls had forgotten her key. It had happened before. In the hallway I felt the chill of the lino penetrate the soles of my slippers. I put on the security chain before opening the door. Peering through a three-inch gap I could make out a man on the step but I couldn't see his face. He was wearing a gangsterish fedora and a belted raincoat on whose shoulders raindrops glistened from the street light behind him. Alarmed, I pushed the door shut. I heard a familiar voice say quietly, 'I'm sorry to disturb you. I need to talk to Serena Frome.'

I lifted the chain and opened the door. 'Max. What are you doing?'

He'd been drinking. He swayed a little and his tightly controlled features were slack. When he spoke I smelled whisky.

He said, 'You know why I'm here.'

'No, I don't.'

'I have to talk to you.'

'Tomorrow, Max, please.'

'It's urgent.'

I was fully awake now and knew that if I sent him away I wouldn't sleep, so I let him in and took him into the kitchen. I lit a couple of rings on the gas stove. It was the only source of heat. He sat down at the table and took off his hat. There

215

was mud on his trousers below the knee. I guessed he'd walked across town. He had a faintly deranged look, loose about the mouth, and under his eyes the skin was blue-ish black. I thought about making him a hot drink and decided not to. I felt some resentment that he was pulling rank on me, entitled to wake me because I was the junior. I sat down opposite him and watched while he carefully brushed the rain off his hat with the back of his hand. He seemed anxious not to appear drunk. I felt shivery and tense, and not just from the cold. I suspected Max had come to tell me more bad news about Tony. But what could be worse than being a dead traitor?

'I can't believe you don't know why I'm here,' he said.

I shook my head. He smiled at what he took to be a forgivable little lie.

'When we met in the corridor today I knew you were thinking exactly the same thing as me.'

'Did you?'

'Come on, Serena. We both knew it.'

He was looking at me earnestly, pleading, and at that point I thought I knew what was coming, and something inside me sagged with weariness at the prospect of hearing it, denying it, sorting it all out. And having to accommodate it somehow into the future.

Despite that I said, 'I don't understand.'

'I've had to break off my engagement.'

'Had to?'

'You made your own feelings clear when I told you about it.'

'So?'

'Your disappointment was obvious. I was sorry about it, but I had to ignore it. I couldn't let feelings get in the way of work.'

'I don't want that either, Max.'

'But each time we meet I know we're both thinking about what might have been.'

'Look . . .'

'As for all the, you know . . .'

He took up his hat again and examined it closely.

'. . . wedding preparations. Our two families have been busy with it all. But I couldn't stop thinking about you . . . I thought I was going mad. When I saw you this morning, it hit us both. You looked like you were going to pass out. I'm sure I looked the same. Serena, this pretence . . . this madness of saying nothing. I spoke to Ruth this evening and told her the truth. She's very upset. But this has been coming towards us, you and me, it's inevitable. We can't go on ignoring it!'

I couldn't bear to look at him. I was irritated by the way he conflated his own shifting needs with an impersonal destiny. I want it, therefore . . . it's in the stars! What was it with men, that they found elementary logic so difficult? I looked along the line of my shoulder towards the hissing gas rings. The kitchen was warming up at last and I loosened my dressing gown at the neck. I pushed my dishevelled hair clear of my face to help me think clearly. He was waiting for me to make the correct confession, to align my desires with his, to confirm him in his solipsism and join him in it. But perhaps I was being too hard on him. This was a simple misunderstanding. At least, that was how I intended to treat it.

'It's true your engagement came out of nowhere. You'd never mentioned Ruth before and I did get a bit upset. But I got over it, Max. I was hoping for a wedding invitation.'

'That's all over. We can start again.'

'No, we can't.'

He looked up sharply. 'What do you mean by that?'

'I mean we can't start again.'

'Why not?'

I shrugged.

'You've met someone.'

'Yes.'

The effect was frightening. He stood up quickly, tipping

over the kitchen chair behind him. I thought the din it made as it smacked against the floor was bound to wake the others. He stood in front of me unsteadily, looking ghastly, greenish in the yellow light of a single bare bulb, lips glistening. I was waiting to hear for the second time in a week a man tell me he was about to be sick.

However, he stood his ground, or swayed on it, and said, 'But you've been giving the impression that . . . that you wanted, well, to be with me.'

'Have I?'

'Every time you came to my office. You flirted with me.'

There was some truth in this. I thought for a moment and said, 'But not since I started seeing Tom.'

'Tom? Not Haley, I hope?'

I nodded.

'Oh God. So you meant it. You idiot!' He picked up the chair and sat heavily. 'Is this to punish me?'

'I like him.'

'So unprofessional.'

'Oh, come on. We all know what goes on.'

Actually, I didn't. All I knew was the gossip, which may have been fantasy, about desk officers taking up with female agents. What with the intimacy and stress and all, why wouldn't they?

'He'll find out who you are. Bound to happen.'

'No, it won't.'

He was hunkered down with his head propped on his hands. He blew noisily through his cheeks. It was hard to tell just how drunk he was.

'Why didn't you tell me?'

'I thought we didn't want feelings getting in the way of work.'

'Serena! This is Sweet Tooth. Haley's ours. And so are you.'

I was beginning to wonder if I was in the wrong, and it was for that reason that I went on the attack. 'You encouraged me to get close to you, Max. And all the while you were getting ready to announce your engagement. Why should I put up with you telling me who I can see?'

He wasn't listening. He groaned and pushed the heel of his hand into his forehead. 'Oh God,' he murmured to himself. 'What have I done?'

I waited. My guilt was an amorphous black shape in the mind, growing larger, threatening to suck me in. I had flirted with him, teased him, caused him to dump his fiancée, ruined his life. It would take an effort to resist.

He said abruptly, 'Have you got a drink here?'

'No.' Wedged behind the toaster was a miniature of sherry. It would make him sick, and I wanted him to go.

'Tell me one thing. What happened in the corridor this morning?'

'I don't know. Nothing.'

'You were playing games, weren't you, Serena. That's what you really like.'

It wasn't worth responding to. I just stared at him. There was a thread of saliva attached to the skin at the corner of his mouth. He caught the direction of my gaze and wiped it with the back of his hand.

'You're going to wreck Sweet Tooth with this.'

'Don't pretend that's your objection. You hate the whole thing anyway.'

To my surprise he said, 'Bloody right I do.' It was the kind of rough frankness that a drink brings on and now he wanted to inflict some damage. 'The women in your section, Belinda, Anne, Hilary, Wendy and the rest. Ever ask them what kind of degrees they got?'

'No.'

'Pity. Firsts, starred firsts, double firsts, you name it. Classics, History, English.'

'Clever them.'

'Even your friend Shirley got one.'

'Even?'

'Ever wonder why they let you in with a third. In *maths*?'

219

He waited but I didn't reply.

'Canning recruited you. So they thought, better to have you on the inside, see if you had someone to report to. You never know. They followed you for a bit, took a look at your room. Usual stuff. They gave you Sweet Tooth because it's low level and harmless. Put you in there with Chas Mount because he's a dud. But you were a disappointment, Serena. No one was running you. Just an ordinary girl, averagely stupid, glad to have a job. Canning must have been doing you a favour. My theory is he was making amends.'

I said, 'I think he loved me.'

'Well, there you are then. He just wanted to make you happy.'

'Has anyone ever loved you, Max?'

'You little bitch.'

The insult made things easier. It was time for him to go. The kitchen was tolerable now but the warmth off the gas rings felt clammy. I stood up, drew my dressing gown firmly around me and turned them off.

'So why leave your fiancée for me?'

But we hadn't quite reached the end, for his mood was taking another turn. He was crying. Or at least tearful. His lips were stretched tight in a hideous smile.

'Oh God,' he cried out in a squeezed high-pitched voice, 'I'm sorry, I'm sorry. That's the last thing you are. You never heard it, I never said it. Serena, I'm sorry.'

'It's fine,' I said. 'It's forgotten. But I think you should leave.'

He stood and groped in his trouser pocket for a handkerchief. When he was done blowing on it he was still crying. 'I've messed everything up. I'm a fucking fool.'

I led him back along the hall to the front door and opened it.

We had a final exchange on the steps. He said, 'Promise me one thing, Serena.'

He was trying to take my hands. I felt sorry for him but I stepped back. It wasn't the moment to be holding hands.

'Promise me you'll think about this. Please. Just this. If I can change my mind, so can you.'

'I'm awfully tired, Max.'

He seemed to be getting a hold of himself. He took a deep breath. 'Listen. It's possible that you're making a very serious mistake with Tom Haley.'

'Walk that way and you'll pick up a cab on the Camden Road.'

He was standing on a lower step, looking up at me, imploring and accusing me as I closed the door. I hesitated behind it, and then, even though I heard his retreating steps, I fixed the security chain before going back to bed.

17

One Brighton weekend in December, Tom asked me to read *From the Somerset Levels*. I took it into the bedroom and went through it carefully. I noted various minor alterations but, by the time I'd finished, my opinion was unchanged. I dreaded the conversation he was waiting to have because I knew I wouldn't be able to pretend. That afternoon we went for a walk on the Downs. I spoke of the novel's indifference to the fate of the father and little girl, of the assured depravity of its minor characters, the desolation of the crushed urban masses, the raw squalor of rural poverty, the air of general hopelessness, the cruel and joyless narrative, the depressing effect on the reader.

Tom's eyes shone. I couldn't have said anything kinder. 'Exactly!' he kept saying. 'That's it. That's right. You've got it!'

I'd picked up a few typos and repetitions for which he was disproportionately grateful. Over the following week or so he completed another draft of light revisions – and he was done. He asked me if I would go with him when he delivered it to his editor and I told him it would be an honour. He came up to London on the morning of Christmas Eve, the beginning of my three-day break. We met at Tottenham Court Road Tube station and walked together to Bedford Square.

He gave me the package to carry to bring him luck. One hundred and thirty-six pages, he told me proudly, of double-spaced typing on old-fashioned foolscap. As we walked along I kept thinking of the little girl in the final scene, dying in agony on the wet floor of a burned-out cellar. If I was really to do my duty I should have posted the whole thing in its envelope down the nearest drain. But I was excited for him and held the grim chronicle securely against my chest as I would my – our – baby.

I'd wanted to spend Christmas with Tom holed up in the Brighton flat, but I'd received a summons home and was due to take the train up that afternoon. I hadn't been back in many months. My mother was firm on the phone and even the Bishop had taken a view. I wasn't enough of a rebel to refuse, though I felt ashamed when I explained myself to Tom. In my early twenties the last threads of childhood still bound me. He, however, a free adult in his late twenties, was sympathetic to my parents' view. Of course they needed to see me, of course I should go. It was my grown-up duty to spend Christmas with them. He himself would be with his family in Sevenoaks on the twenty-fifth, and he was determined to get his sister Laura out of the Bristol hostel and unite her with her children around the festive table, and try to keep her off the drink.

So I hauled his package towards Bloomsbury, conscious that we only had a few hours together, and then we'd be apart for over a week, for I'd be going straight back to work on the twenty-seventh. As we walked he told me his latest news. He had just heard back from Ian Hamilton at the *New Review*. Tom had recast the climax of 'Probable Adultery' as I'd suggested in my notes and submitted it along with his talking-ape story. Hamilton had written to say that 'Probable Adultery' was not for him, he had no patience for the ins and outs of the 'logic stuff' and he doubted that 'anyone but a Senior Wrangler would'. On the other hand, he thought the garrulous monkey was 'not bad'. Tom wasn't sure if that was an acceptance. He was going to meet Hamilton in the New Year and find out.

We were shown into Tom Maschler's grand office or library on the first floor of a Georgian mansion overlooking the square. When the publisher came in, almost at a run, I was the one who handed over the novel. He tossed it on the desk behind him, kissed me wetly on both cheeks and pumped Tom's hand, congratulated him, guided him towards a chair and began to interrogate him, barely waiting for an answer to one question before starting the next. What was he living on, when were we getting married, had he read Russell Hoban, did he realise that the elusive Pynchon had sat in that same chair the day before, did he know Martin, son of Kingsley, would we like to meet Madhur Jaffrey? Maschler reminded me of an Italian tennis coach who once came to our school and in an afternoon of impatient jovial instruction rebuilt my backhand. The publisher was lean and brown, hungry for information, and pleasantly agitated, as though perpetually suspended on the edge of a joke, or a revolutionary new idea that might come to him through a chance remark.

I was grateful to be ignored and wandered up to the far end of the room and stood looking at the wintry trees in Bedford Square. I heard Tom, my Tom, say that he lived by his teaching, that he hadn't yet read *One Hundred Years of Solitude* or Jonathan Miller's book on McLuhan but intended to, and that no, he had no clear idea of his next novel. He skipped the question about marriage, agreed that Roth was a genius and *Portnoy's Complaint* a masterpiece, and that the English translations of Neruda's sonnets were exceptional. Tom, like me, knew no Spanish and was in no position to judge. Neither of us had read Roth's novel at that point. His answers were guarded, even pedestrian, and I sympathised – we were the innocent country cousins, overwhelmed by the range and speed of Maschler's references, and it seemed only right after ten minutes that we should be dismissed.

We were too dull. He came with us to the top of the stairs. As he said goodbye he said he might have taken us to lunch at his favourite Greek place in Charlotte Street, but he didn't believe in lunch. We found ourselves back on the pavement, a little dazed, and as we walked on spent a good while discussing whether the meeting had 'gone well'. Tom thought on balance it had, and I agreed, though I actually thought it hadn't.

But it didn't matter, the novel, the terrible novel, was delivered, we were about to part, it was Christmas, and we ought to be celebrating. We wandered south, into Trafalgar Square, passing on the way the National Portrait Gallery and, like a couple of thirty years' standing, we reminisced about our first meeting there – did we both think it was going to be a one-night affair, could we have guessed what would follow? Then we doubled back and went to Sheekey's and managed to get in without a booking. I was wary of drinking. I had to go home and pack, get to Liverpool Street for a five o'clock train, and prepare to throw off my role as secret agent of the State and become a dutiful daughter, the one who was sleekly rising through the ranks of the Department of Health and Social Security.

But well ahead of the Dover sole, an ice bucket arrived followed by a bottle of champagne, and down it went, and before the next one came Tom reached across the table for my hand and told me he had a secret to confess and though he didn't want to trouble me with it just before we separated, he wouldn't sleep unless he told me. It was this. He didn't have an idea, not even a scrap of an idea, for another novel and he doubted that he ever would. *From the Somerset Levels* – we referred to it as 'the Levels' – was a fluke, he had blundered into it by accident when he thought he was writing a short story about something else. And the other day, walking past Brighton Pavilion, an inconsequential line of Spenser had come to mind – *Put in porphyry and marble do appear* – Spenser in Rome, reflecting on its past. But perhaps it needn't only be Rome. Tom found himself beginning to map out an article about poetry's relation to the city, the city through the centuries. Academic writing was supposed to be behind him, there had been times when his thesis had driven him to despair. But nostalgia was creeping in – nostalgia for the quiet integrity of scholarship, its exacting protocols, and above all, for the loveliness of Spenser's verse. He knew it so well, the warmth beneath its formality – this was a world he could inhabit. The idea for the article was original and bold, it was exciting, it crossed the boundaries of disparate disciplines. Geology, town planning, archaeology. There was an editor of a specialist journal who would be delighted to have something from him. Two days before, Tom had found himself wondering about a teaching job he had heard was going at Bristol university. The MA in international relations had been a diversion. Perhaps fiction was too. His future lay in teaching and academic research. How fraudulent he had felt at Bedford Square just now, how constrained during the conversation. It was a real possibility that he would never write another novel again, or even a story. How could he admit such a thing to Maschler, the most respected publisher of fiction in town?

Or to me. I disengaged my hand. This was my first free Monday in months but I was back at work for the Sweet Tooth cause. I told Tom it was a well-known fact that writers felt emptied out at the end of their labours. As if I knew a thing about it, I told him that there was nothing incompatible about writing the occasional scholarly essay and writing novels. I cast about for an example of a celebrated writer who did just that, but couldn't think of one. The second bottle arrived and I embarked on a celebration of Tom's work. It was the unusual psychological slant of his stories, their strange intimacy in combination with his worldly essays on the East German uprising and the Great Train Robbery, it was that *breadth* of interest that marked him out, and was the reason why the Foundation was so proud to have an association with him, why the name of T.H. Haley was conjured in literary circles, and why two of its most important figures, Hamilton and Maschler, wanted him to write for them.

Tom was watching me throughout this performance with his little smile – it sometimes infuriated me – of tolerant scepticism.

'You told me you couldn't write *and* teach. Would you be happy on an assistant lecturer's salary? Eight hundred pounds a year? That's assuming you get a job.'

'Don't think I haven't thought of that.'

'The other night you told me you might write an article for *Index on Censorship* about the Romanian security service. What's it called?'

'The DSS. But it's really about poetry.'

'I thought it was about torture.'

'Incidentally.'

'You said it might even become a short story.'

He brightened a little. 'It might. I'm meeting my poet friend Traian again next week. I can't do anything without his say-so.'

I said, 'No reason why you shouldn't write the Spenser essay too. You have all this freedom and that's what the Foundation wants for you. You can do anything you like.'

After that he seemed to lose interest and wanted to change the subject. So we talked about the things that everybody was talking about – the government's energy-conserving three-day week, due to start on New Year's Eve, yesterday's doubling of the price of oil, the several explosions round town in pubs and shops, 'Christmas presents' from the Provisional IRA. We discussed why people seemed strangely happy conserving energy, doing things by candlelight, as though adversity had restored purpose to existence. At least, it was easy enough to think so as we finished the second bottle.

It was almost four when we said our goodbyes outside

Leicester Square Tube station. We embraced and kissed, caressed by a warming breeze wafting up the subway steps. Then he set off on a mind-clearing walk to Victoria station while I headed to Camden to pack my clothes and meagre Christmas presents, blearily aware there was no chance of making my train and that I would be late for Christmas Eve dinner, an occasion to which my mother gave selfless days of preparation. She wouldn't be pleased.

I took the six thirty, got in just before nine, and walked from the station, crossing the river then following by a clear half-moon the semi-rural path along it, past dark boats tethered to the bank, inhaling air icy and pure, blown in across East Anglia from Siberia. The taste of it reminded me of my adolescence, its boredom and longing, and all our little rebellions tamed or undone by the desire to please certain teachers with dazzling essays. Oh, the elated disap- pointment of an A minus, as keen as a cold wind from the north! The path curved below the rugger pitches of the boys' school, and the spire, my father's spire, creamily lit, rose up across the expanse. I cut away from the river to cross the pitches, passed the changing rooms that used to smell to me of all that was sourly fascinating about boys, and got into the cathedral close by an old oak door that never used to be locked. It pleased me that it was unlocked now, still squeaked on its hinge. It took me by surprise, this walk across an ancient past. Four or five years – nothing at all. But no one over thirty could understand this peculiarly weighted and condensed time, from late teens to early twen- ties, a stretch of life that needed a name, from school leaver to salaried professional, with a university and affairs and death and choices in between. I had forgotten how recent my childhood was, how long and inescapable it once seemed. How grown-up and how unchanged I was.

I don't know why my heart beat harder as I went towards the house. As I came closer I slowed. I'd forgotten just how immense it was and it amazed me now that I could ever have taken this pale-red brick Queen Anne palace for granted. I advanced between the bare forms of cut-back rose shrubs and box hedging rising from beds framed by massive slabs of York paving. I rang, or pulled, the bell and to my astonishment the door opened almost immediately and there was the Bishop, with a grey jacket on over his purple clerical shirt and dog collar. He would be conducting a midnight service later. He must have been crossing the hall when I rang, for answering the door was something that would never occur to him. He was a big man, with a vague and kindly face, and a boyish though entirely white forelock that he was always brushing aside. People used to say that he resembled a benign tabby cat. As he processed in stately manner through his fifties, his gut had swelled, which seemed to suit his slow self-absorbed air. My sister and I used to mock him behind his back and sometimes were even bitter, not because we disliked him – far from it – but because we could never get his attention, or never for long. To him our lives were distant foolish things. He didn't know that sometimes Lucy and I fought over him in our teens. We longed to have him for ourselves, if only for ten minutes in his study, and we each suspected the other was the more favoured. Her tangle with drugs, pregnancy and the law had permitted her many such privileged minutes. When I'd heard about them on the phone, despite all my concern for her, I felt a twinge of the old jealousy. When would it be my turn?

It was now.

'Serena!' He said my name with a kindly, falling tone, with just a hint of mock surprise, and put his arms about me. I dropped my bag at my feet and let myself be enfolded, and as I pressed my face into his shirt and caught the familiar scent of Imperial Leather soap, and of church – of lavender wax – I started to cry. I don't know why, it just came from nowhere and I turned to water. I don't cry easily and I was as surprised as he was. But there was nothing I could do about it. This was the copious hopeless sort of crying you might hear from a tired child. I think it was his voice, the way he said my name, that set me off.

Instantly, I felt his body tense, even though he continued to hold me. He murmured, 'Shall I fetch your mother?'

I thought I knew what he was thinking – that now it was the turn of his older daughter to be pregnant or lost to some other modern disaster, and that whatever womanly mess was now soaking his freshly ironed purple shirt was better managed by a woman. He needed to hand the matter over and continue to his study to look over his Christmas Day sermon before dinner.

But I didn't want him to let go of me. I clung to him. If only I could have thought of a crime, I would have begged him to summon down the magic cathedral powers to forgive me.

I said, 'No, no. It's all right, Daddy. It's just, I'm so happy to be back, to be . . . here.'

I felt him relax. But it wasn't true. It wasn't happiness at all. I couldn't have said precisely what it was. It had something to do with my walk from the station, and with coming away from my London life. Relief perhaps, but with a harsher element, something like remorse, or even despair. Later I persuaded myself that drinking at lunchtime had softened me up.

This moment on the doorstep could not have lasted more than thirty seconds. I got a grip of myself, picked up my bag and stepped inside, apologised to the Bishop, who was still regarding me warily. Then he patted my shoulder and resumed his route across the hall to his study and I went into the cloakroom – easily the size of my Camden bedsit – to douse my red and swollen eyes with cold water. I didn't want an interrogation by my mother. As I went to find her I was aware of all that used to suffocate me and now seemed comforting – the smell of roasting meat, the carpeted warmth, the gleam of oak, mahogany, silver and glass, and my mother's spare, tasteful arrangements in vases of bare hazel and dogwood branches, minimally sprayed with silver paint to denote a light frost. When Lucy was fifteen and trying, like me, to be a sophisticated adult she came in one Christmas evening and gestured at the branches and exclaimed, 'How positively Protestant!'

She earned herself the sourest look I ever saw the Bishop give. He rarely stooped to reprimands but this time he said coldly, 'You'll rephrase that, young lady, or go to your room.' Listening to Lucy intone contritely something like, 'Mummy, the decorations are truly wonderful,' gave me the giggles and I decided that I had better be the one who left the room. 'Positively Protestant' became an insurrectionary catchphrase for us two, but always muttered well out of the Bishop's hearing.

There were five of us at dinner. Lucy had come across town with her long-haired Irish boyfriend, six-foot-six Luke, who worked for the city council as a parks gardener and was an active member of the recently formed Troops Out movement. As soon as I knew this I made a quick decision not to be drawn into argument. It was easy enough because he was pleasant and funny, despite a phoney American drawl, and later, after dinner, we found common ground in a discussion, almost an outraged celebration, of loyalist atrocities, of which I knew almost as many as he did. At one point during the meal the Bishop, who had no interest in politics, leaned across and enquired mildly whether Luke would be expecting a massacre of the Catholic minority if he had his way and the army was to withdraw. Luke replied that he thought the British army had never done much for the Catholics in the north, who would be able to take care of themselves.

'Ah,' my father replied, pretending to be reassured. 'A bloodbath all round then.'

Luke was confused. He didn't know if he was being mocked. In fact he wasn't. The Bishop was merely being polite

231

and now was moving the conversation on. The reason he wouldn't be drawn into political or even theological debate was because he was indifferent to other people's opinions and felt no urge to engage with or oppose them.

It turned out to have suited my mother's schedule to serve up a roast dinner at ten o' clock and she was pleased to have me home. She still took pride in my job and the independent existence she had always wanted for me. I had boned up once more on my supposed department in order to be able to answer her questions. A good while back I'd discovered that nearly all the girls at work had told their parents exactly who they worked for, on the understanding that they wouldn't press for details. In my case my cover story had been elaborate and well researched and I had told too many unnecessary white lies. It was too late to go back. If my mother had known the truth, she would have told Lucy, who might never speak to me again. And I wouldn't have wanted Luke to know what I did. So I bored myself for a few minutes while I described departmental views on reforming the social-security system, wishing that my mother would find it as dull as the Bishop and Lucy did and would stop prompting me with bright new questions.

It was one of the blessings of our family life, and perhaps of Anglicanism in general, that we were never expected to go to church to hear or see our father officiate. It was of no interest to him whether we were there or not. I hadn't been since I was seventeen. I don't think Lucy had been since she was twelve. Because this was his busy time of year, he stood abruptly just before dessert and wished us all a happy Christmas and excused himself. From where I sat, it looked like my tears had left no stain on the ecclesiastical shirt. Five minutes later we heard the familiar swish of his cassock as he passed the dining room on his way to the front door. I had grown up with the ordinariness of his daily business, but now, returning home after an absence, from my London preoccupations, it seemed exotic to have a father who dabbled routinely in the supernatural, who went out to work in a beautiful stone temple late at night, house keys in his pocket, to thank or praise or beseech a god on our behalf.

My mother went upstairs to a small spare bedroom known as the wrapping room to see to the last of her presents while Lucy, Luke and I cleared away and washed the dishes. Lucy tuned the kitchen radio to John Peel's show and we toiled away to the kind of progressive rock I hadn't heard since Cambridge. It no longer moved me. Where once it had been the call sign of a freemasonry of the liberated young and promised a new world, now it had shrunk into mere songs, mostly about lost love, sometimes about the open road. These were striving musicians like any others, keen for advancement in a crowded scene. Peel's informed ramblings between the tracks suggested as much. Even a couple of pub rock songs failed to stir me. It must be, I thought as I scrubbed at my mother's baking dishes, that I was getting old. Twenty-three next birthday. Then my sister asked if I wanted to go for a stroll round the close with her and Luke. They wanted to smoke and the Bishop wouldn't tolerate it in the house, at least, not from family – an eccentric position in those days, and an oppressive one, we thought.

The moon was higher now and the touch of frost on the grass was light, even more tasteful than our mother's efforts with the spray can. The cathedral, lit from the inside, looked isolated and displaced, like a stranded ocean liner. From a distance we heard a ponderous organ introducing 'Hark! The herald angels sing' and then the congregation gamely belting it out. It sounded like a good crowd, and I was glad for my father's sake. But grown-ups singing in ragged unironic unison about *angels* . . . I experienced a sudden lurch in my heart, as though I'd looked over a cliff edge into emptiness. I believed in nothing much – not carols, not even rock music. We strolled three abreast along the narrow road that ran past the other fine houses in the close. Some were solicitors' offices, one or two were cosmetic dentists. It was a worldly place, the cathedral precinct, and the Church imposed high rents.

It turned out that it wasn't only tobacco my companions were wanting. Luke produced from his coat a joint the size and shape of a small Christmas cracker, which he lit as we walked along. He went in for a good deal of solemn ritual, inserting the thing between his knuckles and cupping his hands in order to suck between his thumbs with loud hissing intakes of air, and showy retention of breath and smoke while continuing to talk, making himself sound like a ventriloquist's dummy – a fuss and nonsense I'd completely forgotten about. How provincial it seemed. The sixties were over! But when Luke presented his cracker to me – in a rather menacing way, I thought – I took a couple of polite puffs in order not to come across like Lucy's uptight older sister. Which was exactly what I was.

I was uneasy on two counts. I was still in the aftermath of my moment at the front door. Was it overwork rather than a hangover? I knew that my father would never refer to the matter again, never ask me what was up. I should have felt resentful, but I was relieved. I wouldn't have known what to tell him anyway. And secondly, I had on a coat I hadn't worn in a while, and as we began our walk around the close I felt in the pocket a piece of paper. I ran a finger along its edge and knew exactly what it was. I'd forgotten about it, the scrap I'd picked up in the safe house. It reminded me of much else that was messily unfinished, a scattering of mental litter – Tony's disgrace, Shirley's disappearance, the possibility that I was only taken on because Tony was exposed, the Watchers going through my room and, messiest of all, the row with Max. We'd avoided each other since his visit to my place. I hadn't been to see him with my Sweet Tooth report. Whenever I thought of him I felt guilt, immediately displaced by indignant reflection. He dumped me for his fiancée, then, too late, his fiancée for me. He was looking out for himself. Where was my share of blame? But next time I thought of him I had the same guilty turn, and had to explain it away to myself all over again.

All this, streaming behind one piece of paper like the tail of a misshapen kite. We walked round to the cathedral's west end and stood in the deep shadow of the high stone portal that led through to the town while my sister and her boyfriend passed the joint between them. I strained to hear my father's voice above Luke's transatlantic drone, but there was silence from the cathedral. They were praying, surely. In the other pan of the scales of my fortunes, apart from the minor fact of my promotion, was Tom. I wanted to tell Lucy about him, I would have loved a sisterly session. We occasionally managed one, but set between us now was Luke's giant form and he was doing that inexcusable thing that men who liked cannabis tended to do, which was to go on about it – some famous stuff from a special village in Thailand, the terrifying near-bust one night, the view across a certain holy lake at sunset under the influence, a hilarious misunderstanding in a bus station and other stultifying anecdotes. What was wrong with our generation? Our parents had the war to be boring about. We had this.

After a while we girls fell completely silent while Luke, in elated urgent terms, plunged deeper into the misapprehension that he was interesting, that we were enthralled. And almost immediately I had a contrary insight. I saw it clearly. Of course. Lucy and Luke were waiting for me to leave so they could be alone. That's what I would have wanted, if it had been Tom and me. Luke was deliberately and systematically boring me to drive me away. It was insensitive of me not to have noticed. Poor fellow, he was having to overreach himself and it was not a good performance, hopelessly overdone. No one in real life could be as boring as this. But in his round-about way he was only trying to be kind.

So I stretched and yawned noisily in the shadows and cut across him to say irrelevantly, 'You're dead right, I

should go,' and I walked off, and within seconds felt better,
easily able to ignore Lucy calling after me. Freed from Luke's
anecdotes, I went quickly, retracing the route we had come
by, and then I cut across the grass, feeling the frost crunch
pleasantly underfoot, until I was right by the cloisters, well
out of the half-moon's light, and found in the near darkness
a stone protrusion to sit on and turned up the collar of my
coat.

I could hear a voice from inside, faintly intoning, but I
couldn't tell if it was the Bishop. He had a large team working
for him on occasions like this. In difficult moments it's sometimes a good idea to ask yourself what it is you most want
to be doing and consider how it can be achieved. If it can't,
move on to the second best thing. I wanted to be with Tom,
in bed with him, across a table from him, holding his hand
in the street. Failing that, I wanted to think about him. So
that is what I did for half an hour on Christmas Eve, I
worshipped him, I thought about our times together, his
strong yet childlike body, our growing fondness, his work,
and how I might help. I pushed away any consideration of
the secret I was keeping from him. Instead, I thought about
the freedom I'd brought into his life, how I'd helped him
with 'Probable Adultery' and would help with much more.
All so rich. I decided to write down these thoughts in a letter
to him, a lyrical, passionate letter. I'd tell him how I came
apart at my own front door and wept on my father's chest.

It wasn't a good idea to be sitting motionless on stone in
sub-zero temperatures. I was beginning to shiver. Then I heard
my sister calling me again from somewhere in the close. She
sounded concerned, and that was when I began to come to
my senses and realise that my behaviour must have seemed
unfriendly. It had been influenced by a puff on the Christmas
cracker. How unlikely it now seemed, for Luke to have been
wilfully dull in order to secure a few moments alone with
Lucy. It was difficult to understand one's own errors of judgement when the entity, the mind, that was attempting the

understanding was befuddled. Now I was thinking clearly. I stepped out onto the moonlit grass and saw my sister and her boyfriend on the path a hundred yards away, and I hurried towards them, keen to apologise.

18

At Leconfield House the thermostats were turned down to 60°F, two degrees lower than other government departments, in order to set a good example. We worked in our overcoats and finger gloves, and some of the better-off girls wore knitted woolly hats with pompoms from their skiing holidays. We were issued with squares of felt to put under our feet against the cold coming up through the floor. The best way to warm your hands was to keep typing. Now that the train drivers were on an overtime ban in support of the miners, it was reckoned that power stations could run out of coal by the end of January, just as the nation ran out of money. In Uganda Idi Amin was arranging a whip-round and offering a lorryload of vegetables to the stricken former colonial masters, if only the RAF would care to come and collect it.

There was a letter from Tom waiting for me when I got back to Camden from my parents. He was going to borrow his father's car to drive Laura back to Bristol. It wasn't going to be easy. She was telling the family that she wanted to take the children with her. There had been shouting scenes around the Christmas turkey. But the hostel only took adults and Laura, as usual, was in no shape to care for her kids.

His plan was to come to London so that we could see in the New Year together. But on the 30th he sent a telegram from

Bristol. He couldn't leave Laura yet. He'd have to stay and try
to settle her in. So I saw in 1974 with my three housemates at
a party in Mornington Crescent. I was the only one in the
teeming squalid flat who wasn't a solicitor. I was at some kind
of trestle table pouring tepid white wine into a used paper
cup when someone actually pinched my bottom, really hard.
I whirled round and was furious, possibly with the wrong
person. I came away early and was home in bed by one, lying
on my back in the freezing dark, feeling sorry for myself. Before
I fell asleep I remembered Tom telling me how superb the
support people were at Laura's hostel. If so, how strange it
was that he needed to stay in Bristol for two whole days. But
it didn't seem important and I slept deeply, barely troubled
by my legal friends coming in drunk at four.

The year turned and the three-day week began, but we
were officially defined as a vital service and worked the full
five. On 2 January, I was called to a meeting in Harry Tapp's
office on the second floor. There was no advance warning,
no indication of the subject. It was ten o'clock when I got
there, and Benjamin Trescott was on the door, checking names
off a list. I was surprised to find more than twenty people in
the room, among them two from my intake, all of us too
junior to presume to take one of the moulded plastic chairs
set out in a constricted horseshoe around Tapp's desk. Peter
Nutting came in, scanned the room and went out again. Harry
Tapp got up from his desk and followed him out. I assumed
therefore that this was a Sweet Tooth affair. Everyone was
smoking, murmuring, waiting. I squeezed into an eighteen-
inch gap between a filing cabinet and the safe. It didn't bother
me, as it once would have, to have no one to talk to. I smiled
across at Hilary and Belinda. They shrugged and rolled their
eyes to show me that they thought it was all a great wheeze.
They obviously had Sweet Tooth writers of their own,
academics or hacks who couldn't resist the Foundation's
shilling. But surely, no one with the lustre of T.H. Haley.

Ten minutes passed and the plastic chairs filled up. Max

came in and took one in a middle row. I was behind him, so he didn't see me at first. Then he turned and glanced round the room, looking for me, I was certain. Our eyes met only briefly and he turned to face forwards again and took out a pen. My sight line wasn't good but I thought his hand was shaking. There were a couple of figures I recognised from the fifth floor. But no Director General – Sweet Tooth was nowhere near important enough. Then Tapp and Nutting came back in with a short muscular man in horn-rim glasses, with closely cropped grey hair and a well-cut blue suit and silk tie of darker blue polka dots. Tapp went to his desk while the other two stood before us patiently, waiting for the room to settle.

Nutting said, 'Pierre's based in London and has kindly agreed to say a few words about the way his work may have some bearing on our own.'

From the brevity of this introduction and Pierre's accent, we assumed he was CIA. He was certainly no Frenchman. His voice was a see-saw tenor, pleasantly tentative. He gave the impression that if any utterance of his were to be disproved, he would change his view in line with the facts. Behind the owlish near-apologetic manner, I began to realise, was limitless confidence. He was my first encounter with an American of the patrician class, a man from an established Vermont family, as I learned later, and the author of a book on the Spartan Hegemony and another on Agesilaus the Second and the beheading of Tissaphernes in Persia.

I warmed to Pierre. He began by saying that he was going to tell us something about 'the softest, sweetest part of the Cold War, the only truly interesting part, the war of ideas'. He wanted to give us three verbal snapshots. For the first, he asked us to think of pre-war Manhattan, and quoted the opening lines of a famous Auden poem that Tony had read to me once, and I knew that Tom loved. It wasn't famous to me and it hadn't meant much up until this point, but hearing an Englishman's lines quoted back to us by an American was touching. *I sit in one of the dives/ On Fifty-second Street/ Uncertain and afraid* . . . and that was Pierre in 1940, nineteen years old, visiting an uncle in midtown, bored by the prospect of college, getting drunk in a bar. Except he wasn't quite so uncertain as Auden. He longed for his country to join the war in Europe and assign him a role. He wanted to be a soldier.

Then Pierre evoked for us the year 1950, when mainland Europe and Japan and China were in ruins or enfeebled, Britain was impoverished by a long heroic war, Soviet Russia was counting its dead in the many millions – and America, its economy fattened and enlivened by the fight, was waking to the awesome nature of its new responsibilities as prime guardian of human liberty on the planet. Even as he said this he spread his hands and appeared to regret it or apologise. It could have been otherwise.

The third snapshot was also of 1950. Here is Pierre, the Moroccan and Tunisian campaigns, Normandy and the Battle of Hurtgen Forest and the liberation of Dachau behind him, and he's an associate professor of Greek at Brown university, walking towards the entrance of the Waldorf Astoria hotel on Park Avenue, passing a crowd of assorted demonstrators, American patriots, Catholic nuns and right-wing nutters.

'Inside,' Pierre said dramatically, holding up an open hand, 'I witnessed a contest that would change my life.'

It was a gathering with the unexceptional title of Cultural and Scientific Conference for World Peace, nominally organised by an American professional council but in fact an initiative of the Soviet Cominform. The thousand delegates from all over the world were those whose faith in the communist ideal had not yet been shattered, or not completely shattered, by show trials, the Nazi–Soviet Pact, repression, purges, torture, murder and labour camps. The great Russian composer, Dmitri Shostakovich, was there against his will, under orders from Stalin. Among the delegates from the American side were Arthur Miller, Leonard Bernstein and Clifford Odets. These and other luminaries were critical or distrustful of an American government that was asking its citizens to treat a former invaluable ally as a dangerous enemy. Many believed that the Marxist analysis still held, however messy events were turning out to be. And those events were much distorted by an American press owned by greedy corporate interests. If Soviet policy seemed surly or aggressive, if it leaned a little on its internal critics, it was in a defensive spirit, for it had faced Western hostility and sabotage from its inception.

In short, Pierre told us, the whole event was a propaganda coup for the Kremlin. It had prepared in capitalism's capital a world stage for itself on which it would appear as the voice of peace and reason, if not freedom, and it had scores of eminent Americans on its side.

'But!' Pierre raised an arm and pointed upwards with a rigid forefinger, trapping us all for several seconds in his theatrical pause. Then he told us that way up on the tenth floor of the hotel, in a suite of luxury rooms, was a volunteer army of subversion, a band of intellectuals gathered together by an academic philosopher called Sidney Hook, a group of mostly non-communist leftists, the democratic ex-communist or ex-Trotskyist left, determined to challenge the conference and, crucially, not to permit criticism of the Soviet Union to be the monopoly of the lunatic right. Bowed over typewriters, mimeograph machines and recently installed multiple phone lines, they had worked through the night, sustained by generous room-service snacks and booze. They intended to disrupt proceedings downstairs by asking awkward questions in the sessions, particularly about artistic freedom, and by issuing a stream of press releases. They too could claim heavy-weight support, even more impressive than the other side's. Mary McCarthy, Robert Lowell, Elizabeth Hardwick, and international support at a distance from T.S. Eliot, Igor Stravinsky and Bertrand Russell, among many others.

The counter conference campaign was a success because it seized the media narrative and became the headline. All the right questions were insinuated into the conference sessions. Shostakovich was asked if he agreed with a *Pravda* denunciation of Stravinsky, Hindemith and Schoenberg as 'decadent bourgeois formalists'. The great Russian composer got slowly to his feet and mumbled his agreement with the article and was shown to be miserably trapped between his conscience and his fear of displeasing his KGB handlers, and of what Stalin would do to him when he got home.

Between the sessions, in the upstairs suite, Pierre, with a telephone and a typewriter of his own in a corner near a bathroom, met the contacts who would transform his life, eventually prompting him to leave his teaching job and devote his life to the CIA and the war of ideas. For of course, the Agency was paying the bills of the conference opposition and it was learning in the process how effectively this war could be waged at one remove by writers, artists, intellectuals, many of them on the left, who had their own powerful ideas drawn from bitter experience of the seduction and false promises of communism. What they needed, even if they did not know it, was what the CIA could provide – organisation, structure and, above all, funding. This was important when operations moved to London, Paris and Berlin. 'What helped us back in the early fifties was that no one in Europe had a cent.'

And so, in Pierre's description, he became a different kind of soldier, drawn again into many new campaigns in liberated but threatened Europe. He was for a while an assistant to Michael Josselson, and later a friend of Melvin Lasky's until a rift opened up between them. Pierre was involved in the Congress for Cultural Freedom, wrote articles in German for the prestigious periodical, *Der Monat*, which was CIA funded, and did back-room work with the setting up of *Encounter*. He learned the delicate art of stroking the egos of intellectual prima donnas, helped organise tours by an American ballet company, and orchestras, modern art shows and more than a dozen conferences that occupied what he called the 'hazardous terrain where politics and literature meet'. He said he was surprised by the fuss and naivety that followed on from

Ramparts magazine's 1967 exposure of the CIA funding of *Encounter*. Wasn't the case against totalitarianism a rational and decent one for governments to adopt? Here in Britain no one was ever troubled by the Foreign Office paying for the BBC World Service, which was highly regarded. And so was *Encounter* still, despite the hullaballoo and pretended surprise and nose-holding. And mentioning the FO reminded him to commend the work of IRD. He particularly admired what it had done in promoting Orwell's work and he liked its arm's-length funding of publishing lists like Ampersand and Bellman Books.

After almost twenty-three years on the job, what conclusions would he draw? He would make two points. The first was the most important. The Cold War was not over, whatever people said, and therefore the cause of cultural freedom remained vital and would always be noble. Although there weren't many left who held a torch for the Soviet Union, there were still the vast frozen intellectual hinterlands where people lazily adopted neutralist positions – the Soviet Union was no worse than the United States. Such people needed to be confronted. As for the second point, he quoted a remark by his old CIA friend turned broadcaster, Tom Braden, to the effect that the United States was the only country on the planet that didn't understand that some things work better when they're small.

This earned an appreciative murmur in the crowded room from our cash-strapped Service.

'Our own projects have gotten too big, too numerous, too diverse and ambitious and over-funded. We've lost discretion, and our message lost its freshness along the way. We're everywhere and we've become the heavy hand, and we've created resentment. I know you have your own new thing going here. I wish it luck, but seriously, gentlemen, keep it small.'

Pierre, if that was his name, was not taking questions and as soon as he finished he nodded curtly to the applause and let himself be guided by Peter Nutting towards the door.

As the room emptied, with the less senior automatically holding back, I was dreading the moment when Max turned and caught my eye and came over to tell me we needed to meet. For office reasons, of course. But when I saw his back and large ears among the crowd edging out of the door, I felt a mix of bewilderment and familiar guilt. I had hurt him so badly he couldn't bear to speak to me. The idea horrified me. As usual, I tried to summon up protective indignation. He was the one who had told me once that women couldn't keep their personal lives out of their work. Was it my fault that he now preferred me to his fiancée? I pleaded my own case all the way down the concrete stairs – I took them to avoid having to talk to colleagues in the lift – and my case intruded all day around my desk. Did I make a fuss, was I pleading and tearful when Max turned away from me? No. So why shouldn't I be with Tom? Didn't I deserve my happiness?

It was a joy two days later to be on the Friday evening train to Brighton, after a separation of almost two weeks. Tom came to the station to meet me. We saw each other as the train slowed, and he ran alongside my carriage, mouthing something I didn't understand. Nothing in my life had been so sweetly exhilarating as stepping off that train into his embrace. His grip was so tight it knocked the air out of me.

He said into my ear, 'I'm just beginning to realise how special you are.'

I told him in a whisper that I'd longed for this moment. When we pulled apart he took my bag.

I said, 'You look different.'

'I am different!' He almost shouted it, and he laughed wildly. 'I've got this amazing idea.'

'Can you tell me?'

'It's so weird, Serena.'

'Then tell me.'

'Let's go home. Eleven days. Too long!'

So we went to Clifton Street, where the Chablis was waiting in a silver ice bucket which Tom had bought in Asprey's. It was strange to have ice cubes in January. The wine would have been colder left in the fridge, but who cared? We drank it as we undressed each other. Of course, separation had stoked us, the Chablis fired us up as usual, but neither were sufficient to explain the hour that followed. We were the strangers who knew exactly what to do. Tom had an air of yearning tenderness about him that dissolved me. It was almost like sorrow. It brought out in me such a powerful feeling of protectiveness that I found myself wondering as we lay together on the bed and he kissed my breasts whether I would ask him one day if I should come off the pill. But it wasn't a baby I wanted, it was him. When I felt and squeezed the small tight roundness of his buttocks and drew him towards me, I thought of him as a child I would possess and cherish and never let out of my sight. It was a feeling I had long ago with Jeremy in Cambridge, but that time I was deceived. Now the sensation of enclosing and possessing him was almost like pain, as though all the best feelings I'd ever had were gathered to an unbearable sharp point.

This was not one of those loud sweaty sessions that follow a separation. A passing voyeur with a view through the bedroom curtains would have peeped at an unadventurous couple in missionary pose, barely making a sound. Our rapture held its breath. We hardly moved for fear of letting go. This particular feeling, that he was now entirely mine and always would be, whether he wanted it or not, was weightless, empty, I could disown it at any point. I felt fearless. He was kissing me lightly and murmuring my name over and over. Perhaps this was the time to tell him, when he couldn't get away. *Tell him now*, I kept thinking. *Tell him what you do.*

But when we came out of our dream, when the rest of the world poured back in on us, and we heard the traffic outside and the sound of a train pulling into Brighton station, and we started thinking about our plans for the rest of the evening, I realised how close I'd been to self-destruction.

We didn't go to a restaurant that night. Lately the weather had turned mild, to the government's probable relief and the miners' irritation. Tom was restless and wanted to walk along the seafront. So we went down West Street and set off along the broad deserted promenade in the direction of Hove, cutting inland to stop in a pub, and at another point to buy fish and chips. Even down by the sea there was no wind. The street lamps were dimmed to save energy, but they still smeared a bilious orange on the thick low cloud. I couldn't quite say what was different about Tom. He was affectionate enough, gripping my hand to make a point or putting an arm round me and drawing me closer to him. We walked fast and he talked quickly. We swapped Christmases. He described the scene, the terrible parting between his sister and her children, and how she tried to drag her little girl with the prosthetic foot into the car with her. And how Laura wept all the way to Bristol and said terrible things about the family, especially their parents. I recounted the moment when the Bishop embraced me and I cried. Tom made me go through the scene in detail. He wanted to know more about my feelings and how it had been, walking from the station. Was it like being a child again, did I suddenly realise just how much I missed home? How long did it take me to recover and why didn't I go and talk to my father about it later? I told him I cried because I cried, and I didn't know why.

We stopped and he kissed me and said I was a hopeless case. When I told him about my night walk around the cathedral close with Lucy and Luke, Tom was disapproving. He wanted me to promise never to smoke cannabis again. This puritan streak surprised me, and though it would have been an easy promise to keep, I simply shrugged. I thought he had no business demanding pledges from me.

I asked him about his new idea but he was evasive. Instead he gave me the news from Bedford Square. Maschler loved

From the Somerset Levels and was planning to bring it out by the end of March, a speed record in the publishing world and only possible because the editor was such a force. The idea was to meet the deadline for the Jane Austen Prize for Fiction, easily as prestigious as the new-fangled Booker. The chances of making it onto the shortlist were remote but it appeared that Maschler was telling everyone about his new author, and the fact that the book was being raced into print specially for the judging panel had already been mentioned in newspapers. This was how you got a book talked about. I wondered what Pierre would have to say about the Service funding the author of an anti-capitalist novella. Keep it small. I said nothing and squeezed Tom's arm.

We sat on a municipal bench, facing out to sea like an old couple. There was supposed to be a waning half-moon, but it had no chance against the heavy lid of tangerine cloud. Tom's arm was round my shoulder, the English Channel was oily calm and silent, and for the first time in days I felt peaceful too as I shrank against my lover. He said he'd been invited to give a reading in Cambridge at an event for new young writers. He'd be sharing a stage with Kingsley Amis's son Martin, who would also be reading from his first novel, which, like Tom's, would be published this year – and by Maschler too.

'What I want to do,' Tom said, 'I'll only do with your permission.' The day after the reading he would travel on by train from Cambridge to my home town in order to talk to my sister. 'I'm thinking of a character who lives on the margins, scrapes by, but quite successfully, believes in Tarot cards and astrology and that sort of thing, likes drugs, though not to excess, believes a fair number of conspiracy theories. You know, thinks the moon landings were in a studio. And at the same time in other spheres she's perfectly sensible, a good mother to her little boy, goes on anti-Vietnam war marches, a reliable friend and so on.'

'It doesn't quite sound like Lucy,' I said, and immediately

felt ungenerous and wanted to make amends. 'But she's very kind really and she'll like talking to you. One condition. You're not to talk about me.'

'Done.'

'I'll write and tell her you're a good friend who's broke and needs a bed for the night.'

We walked on. Tom had never given a public reading before and he was apprehensive. He was going to read from the very end of his book, the part he was most proud of, the grisly death scene of father and daughter in one another's arms. I said it would be a shame to give away the plot.

'Old-fashioned thinking.'

'Remember, I'm a middle-brow.'

'The end is already there in the beginning. Serena, there is no plot. It's a meditation.'

He was also wondering about protocol. Who should go first, Amis or Haley? How did one decide?

'Amis should. Top of the bill goes last,' I said loyally.

'Oh God. If I wake in the night and think about this reading, I can't sleep.'

'How about alphabetically?'

'No, I mean, standing up in front of a crowd, reading stuff people are perfectly capable of reading for themselves. I don't know what it's for. It's giving me night sweats.'

We went down onto the beach so that Tom could hurl stones into the sea. He was strangely energetic. I sensed again his agitation or suppressed excitement. I sat leaning back against a bank of shingle while he kicked the pebbles over, looking for the right weight and shape. He took little runs at the water's edge and his throw went far out into the light mist, where the soundless splash was a faint patch of white. After ten minutes he came and sat beside me, breathless and sweaty, with a taste of salt in his kisses. The kisses began to get more serious and we were close to forgetting where we were.

He squeezed my face between his palms and said, 'Listen,

whatever happens, you need to know how much I like being with you.'

I was worried. This was the corny sort of thing a cinema hero says to his girl before he goes off to die somewhere.

I said, 'Whatever happens?'

He was kissing my face, pushing me back against the uncomfortable stones. 'I mean, I'll never change my mind. You're very very special.'

I let myself be reassured. We were fifty yards across the beach from the railed pavement above and it looked like we were about to make love. I wanted it as much as he did.

I said, 'Not here.'

But he had a plan. He lay on his back and unzipped his fly while I kicked off my shoes, peeled off my tights and knickers and stuffed them into my coat pocket. I sat on him with my skirt and coat spilling around us, and each time I swayed slightly he groaned. We thought we looked innocent enough to any passer-by on the Hove promenade.

'Keep still a moment,' he said quickly, 'or it'll all be over.'

He looked so beautiful, with his head thrown back and his hair spilling over the stones. We stared into each other's eyes. We heard the traffic on the seafront road and only occasionally a wavelet tinkling on the shore.

A little later he said in a distant toneless voice, 'Serena, we can't let this stop. There's no way round it, I have to tell you. It's simple. I love you.'

I tried to say it back to him, but my throat was too constricted and I could only gasp. His words finished us, right there together, with our cries of joy lost to the sound of passing cars. This was the sentence we'd avoided saying. It was too momentous, it marked the line we were wary of crossing, the transition from an enjoyable affair to something weighty and unknown, almost like a burden. It didn't feel that way now. I brought his face near mine, kissed him and repeated his words. It was easy. Then I turned away from him and knelt on the shingle to rearrange my dress. As I did so, I knew that before this love began to take its course, I would have to tell him about myself. And then the love would end. So I couldn't tell him. But I had to.

Afterwards we lay with our arms linked, giggling like children in the dark at our secret, at the mischief we had got away with. We laughed at the enormity of the words we had spoken. Everyone else was bound by the rules, and we were free. We'd make love all over the world, our love would be everywhere. We sat up and shared a cigarette. Then we both began to shiver from the cold, and so we headed for home.

19

In February a depression settled over my section of the Service. Small talk was banished, or it banished itself. Wearing dressing gowns or cardigans as well as overcoats, we worked through tea breaks and lunches, as if to atone for our failures. The desk officer, Chas Mount, generally a cheerful, unflappable sort, hurled a file against the wall and another girl and I spent an hour on our knees putting the papers back in order. Our group counted the failure of our men in the field, Spade and Helium, as our own. Perhaps they had been too emphatically briefed on preserving their cover, or they simply knew nothing. Either way, as Mount kept saying in different ways, there was no point in such dangerous and expensive arrangements if we were to have a spectacular atrocity like this on our doorstep. It was not our place to tell him what he already knew, that we were dealing with cells that knew nothing of each other's existence, that according to a *Times* leader, we confronted the 'best organised, most ruthless terrorist outfit in the world'. And even in those days the competition was intense. At other times Mount muttered the ritual curses against the Met and the Royal Ulster Constabulary that among Service people were as common as the Lord's Prayer. Too many clodhopping coppers with no idea of intelligence gathering or analysis was the drift, though the language was generally stronger.

Our own doorstep in this case was a stretch of the M62 motorway between Huddersfield and Leeds. I heard someone in the office say that if it hadn't been for the train drivers' strike the servicemen and their families would not have been travelling on a late-night coach. But trade unionists had killed no one. The 25-pound bomb was in the luggage storage at the rear of the bus and it instantly eradicated an entire family sleeping on the back seats, a serviceman, his wife and their two children aged five and two, scattering their body parts across two hundred yards of road, according to one of the cuttings that Mount insisted on pinning on a noticeboard. He had two children of his own, just a little older, and that was one reason why our section was obliged to take this matter personally. But it still wasn't clear that the Service was primarily responsible for preventing PIRA terrorism on the mainland. We flattered ourselves by thinking that if it had been, none of this would have happened.

A few days later, the Prime Minister, exasperated, bloated by an undiagnosed thyroid condition, plainly exhausted, addressed the nation on TV to explain that he was calling a snap election. Edward Heath needed a fresh mandate and told us that the question facing us all was – who governs Britain? Was it our elected representatives, or a small handful of extremists in the National Union of Mineworkers? The country knew the real question was would it be Heath again or Wilson again? A Prime Minister crushed by events, or the Leader of the Opposition, who, according to rumours that even we girls heard, was showing signs of mental illness? An 'unpopularity contest', one wag wrote in an opinion column. The three-day week was well into its second month. It was too cold, too dark, we were too gloomy to think clearly about democratic accountability.

My immediate concern was that I couldn't go to Brighton that weekend because Tom was in Cambridge, and then

253

travelling on to see my sister. He didn't want me to come to hear him read. It would 'destroy' him to know that I was in the audience. I had a letter from him the following Monday. I lingered over the salutation – *My darling one*. He said he was glad I hadn't been there. The event had been a disaster. Martin Amis was pleasant, and perfectly indifferent on the question of the running order. So Tom took top billing and let Martin go first as the warm-up act. A mistake. Amis read from his novel called *The Rachel Papers*. It was obscene, cruel and very funny – so funny that he had to pause now and then to let the audience recover. When he was done and Tom came out on stage to take his turn, the applause kept on and on, and Tom had to turn back into the darkness of the wings. People were still groaning and wiping their eyes as he finally made it to the lectern to introduce 'my three thousand words of buboes, pus and death'. During his reading some of the audience left, even before father and daughter had slipped into unconsciousness. People probably needed to catch last trains, but Tom found his confidence undermined, his voice became thin, he stumbled over simple words, missed out a line and had to go back. He felt the whole room resenting him for undoing the merriment. The audience applauded at the end because they were glad the torment was over. Afterwards in the bar, he congratulated Amis, who did not return the compliment. Instead he bought Tom a triple scotch.

There was also good news. He'd had a productive January. His article on persecuted Romanian poets had been accepted by *Index on Censorship*, and he'd finished a first draft of his monograph on Spenser and town planning. The story I helped with, 'Probable Adultery', turned down by the *New Review*, had been accepted by *Bananas* magazine and, of course, there was the new novel, the secret he would not share.

Three days into the general election campaign I received a summons from Max. It was not possible for us to go on avoiding each other. Peter Nutting wanted a progress report on all the Sweet Tooth cases. Max had no choice but to see me. We'd barely spoken since his late-night visit. We had passed in the corridor, muttered our 'good morning's, taken care to sit far apart in the canteen. I'd thought a lot about the things he'd said. He'd probably spoken the truth that night. It was likely the Service had let me in with a poor degree because I was Tony's candidate, likely they followed me for a while before losing interest. By sending me, harmless me, Tony may have wanted, as a farewell gesture, to show his old employers that he was harmless too. Or, as I liked to think, he loved me, and thought of me as his gift to the Service, his way of making amends.

I'd been hoping that Max would go back to his fiancée and that we could continue as before. And that's how it seemed for the first quarter of an hour, as I got in behind the desk and gave an account of the Haley novella, the Romanian poets, *New Review*, *Bananas* and the Spenser essay.

'He's being talked about,' I said in conclusion. 'He's the coming man.'

Max scowled. 'I would have thought it would be all over between you by now.'

I said nothing.

'I've heard he gets about. Something of a swordsman.'

'Max,' I said quietly. 'Let's stick to business.'

'Tell me more about his novel.'

So I told him about the excitement in the publishing house, newspaper comment on the rush to meet the Austen Prize deadline, the rumour that David Hockney would design the cover.

'You still haven't told me what it's about.'

I wanted praise from upstairs as much as he did. But even more I wanted to get at Max for insulting Tom. 'It's the saddest thing I've ever read. Post-nuclear, civilisation regressed to savagery, father and daughter travel from the West Country to London looking for the girl's mother, they don't find her, catch bubonic plague and die. It's really beautiful.'

He was looking at me closely. 'As I remember it, this is just the kind of thing Nutting can't bear. Oh, and by the way. He and Tapp have got something for you. Have they been in touch?'

'No, they haven't. But, Max, we agreed we couldn't interfere with our writers.'

'Well, why are you so pleased?'

'He's a wonderful writer. It's very exciting.'

I was close to adding that we were in love. But Tom and I were secretive. In the spirit of the times, we'd made no plans to present ourselves to each other's parents. We'd made a declaration under the sky on the shingle somewhere between Brighton and Hove and it remained simple and pure.

What became clear in this short meeting with Max was that something had tilted, or shifted. That night before Christmas he'd forfeited some power along with dignity and I sensed he was aware of that, and he knew that I knew. I couldn't quite restrain the cockiness in my tone, he couldn't quite stop himself from sounding abject one moment and over-emphatic the next. I wanted to ask him about his intended, the medical woman he'd rejected for me. Had she taken him back or moved on? Either way, it was a humiliation and I knew enough, even in my elated state, not to ask.

There was a silence. Max had given up on the dark suits – I'd noticed this from across the canteen a few days before – and reverted to bristling Harris tweed and, a sickly new development, a knitted tie of mustard yellow against a check Viyella shirt. My guess was that no one, no woman, was guiding his taste. He was staring at his hands spread out palms down on the desk. He took a deep breath that whistled audibly through his nostrils.

'I now know this. We have ten projects, including Haley. Respected journalists and academics. I don't know the names, but I've an idea of the books they're taking time off to write.

One is about how UK and US plant biology is making the Green Revolution across the rice-growing countries of the Third World, another is a biography of Tom Paine, then there's going to be an account, first ever, of a detention camp in East Berlin, Special Camp Number Three, used by the Soviets in the years after the war to murder social democrats and children as well as Nazis, and now enlarged by the East German authorities to detain and psychologically torture dissidents or anyone they fancy. There'll be a book about the political disasters of post-colonial Africa, a new translation of the poetry of Akhmatova, and a survey of European utopias of the seventeenth century. We'll have a monograph on Trotsky at the head of the Red Army, and a couple more I don't remember.'

At last he looked up from his hands and his eyes were pale and hard.

'So, how the fuck is your T.H. Haley and his little fantasy world gone to shit adding to the sum of what we know or care about?'

I'd never heard him swear, and I flinched, as though he'd thrown something in my face. I'd never liked *From the Somerset Levels* but I liked it now. Usually I would have waited to be dismissed. I got to my feet and pushed the chair under the desk and began to edge out of the room. I would have left with a smart parting line but my mind was a blank. I was almost through the door when I glanced back at him sitting upright at his desk in the apex of his tiny room and saw on his face a look of pain or sorrow, a strange grimace, like a mask, and I heard him say in a low voice, 'Serena, please don't go.'

I could sense it welling up, another terrible scene. I had to get out. I went quickly down the corridor and when he called after me, I increased my pace, fleeing not only the mess of his emotions but my own unreasonable guilt. Before I reached my desk downstairs by way of the creaking lift I reminded myself that I belonged, I was loved and nothing Max said could touch me now and I owed him nothing.

Within minutes I was usefully immersed in the atmosphere of gloom and self-blame in Chas Mount's office, cross-checking dates and facts on a pessimistic memo the desk officer was sending up the chain of command. 'Notes on recent failures'. I hardly thought about Max for the rest of that day.

Which was as well, because it was Friday afternoon and Tom and I were meeting in a Soho pub at lunchtime the next day. He was coming up to see Ian Hamilton in the Pillars of Hercules in Greek Street. The magazine was due to be launched in April with mostly taxpayers' money – the Arts Council rather than the Secret Vote. Already there'd been some grumbling in the press about the proposed price of 75p for 'something we've already paid for', as one newspaper put it. The editor wanted some minor changes to the talking-ape story, which at last had a title – 'Her Second Novel'. Tom thought he might be interested in the Spenser essay or offer him some reviewing. There was to be no payment for articles, but Tom was convinced that this was going to be the most prestigious publication to appear in. The arrangement was that I would turn up an hour after him and then we'd have what was described to me as a 'chip-oriented pub lunch'.

On Saturday morning I tidied my room, went to the launderette, ironed clothes for the following week and washed and dried my hair. I was impatient to see Tom and left the house early and was walking up the stairs at Leicester Square Tube station almost an hour ahead of time. I thought I'd browse among the second-hand books on Charing Cross Road. But I was too restless. I stood in front of shelves, taking nothing in, then I moved on to another shop and did the same. I went into Foyles with the vague idea of finding a present for Tom among the new paperbacks, but I couldn't focus. I was desperate to see him. I cut through Manette Street, which goes along the north of Foyles and passes under a building, with the bar of the

Pillars of Hercules on its left. This brief tunnel, probably the remains of an old coaching courtyard, emerges into Greek Street. Right on the corner is a window with heavy wooden glazing bars. Through it I glimpsed Tom from an oblique angle, sitting right by the window, distorted by the old glass, leaning forward to talk to someone out of my view. I could have gone and tapped on a pane. But, of course, I didn't want to distract him from his important meeting. It was foolish to arrive so early. I should have wandered off for a while. At the very least, I should have gone in by the main door on Greek Street. Then he would have seen me and I would have witnessed nothing. But I turned back and went into the pub by a side entrance in the covered passageway.

I passed through the peppermint scent emanating from the gents' lavatory and pushed open another door. There was a man standing alone at the near end of the bar with a cigarette in one hand and a scotch in the other. He turned to look at me and I knew instantly that it was Ian Hamilton. I'd seen his picture in the hostile diary pieces. But wasn't he supposed to be with Tom? Hamilton was watching me with a neutral, almost friendly look, and a lop-sided smile that didn't part his lips. Just as Tom had described, he had the strong-jawed look of an old-fashioned movie star, the villain with a heart of gold in a black-and-white romance. He seemed to be waiting for me to approach. I looked through the blue-ish smoky light towards the raised corner seat by the window. Tom was sitting with a woman whose back was to me. She looked familiar. He was holding her hand across the table and his head was inclined, nearly touching hers as he listened. Impossible. I stared hard, trying to resolve the scene into sense, into something innocent. But there it was, Max's silly improbable cliché, *swordsman*. It had got under my skin like a burrowing parasite and released its neurotoxins into my bloodstream. It had altered my behaviour and brought me here early to see for myself.

259

Hamilton came over and stood by me, following the line of my gaze.

'She's a writer too. Commercial stuff. But not bad in fact. Nor is he. She's just lost her father.'

He said it lightly, knowing full well that I wouldn't believe him. It was tribal, one man covering for another.

I said, 'They seem to be old friends.'

'What'll you have?'

When I said I'd have a glass of lemonade he appeared to wince. He went to the bar and I stepped back behind one of the half-screens that were a feature of the pub, allowing drinkers to stand in privacy to talk. I was tempted to slip out of the side door, stay out of Tom's reach all weekend, let him sweat while I nursed my turmoil. Could it really be so crude, Tom's bit on the side? I peeped round the screen and the tableau of betrayal was unchanged, she still spoke, he still gripped her hand and listened tenderly as he dipped his head towards hers. It was so monstrous it was almost funny. I couldn't feel anything yet, no anger or panic or sorrow, and I didn't even feel numb. Horrible clarity was all I could claim.

Ian Hamilton brought me my drink, a very large glass of straw-yellow white wine. Exactly what I needed.

'Get this down you.'

He was watching me with wry concern as I drank, and then he asked me what I did. I explained that I worked for an arts foundation. Instantly, his eyelids looked heavy with boredom. But he heard me out and then he had an idea.

'You need to put money into a new magazine. I suppose that's why you're here, to bring me the cash.'

I said we only did individual artists.

'This way I'll be letting you back fifty individual artists.'

I said, 'Perhaps I could look at your business plan.'

'*Business* plan?'

It was just a phrase I'd heard and I guessed correctly that it would close down the conversation.

Hamilton nodded in Tom's direction. 'Here's your man.'

I stepped out from the shelter of the screen. Over in the corner Tom was already on his feet and the woman was reaching for her coat from the seat beside her. She stood too and turned. She was three stone lighter, hair straightened and almost touching her shoulders, her tight black jeans were tucked into calf-length boots, her face was longer and thinner, beautiful in fact, but instantly recognisable. Shirley Shilling, my old friend. The moment I saw her, she saw me. In the brief second that our eyes met, she began to raise a hand in greeting then let it drop hopelessly to her side, as if to acknowledge that there was too much to explain and she was in no mood for it. She went quickly out of the front entrance. Tom was coming towards me, smiling loopily and I, like an idiot, forced a smile back, aware that Hamilton at my side, now lighting another cigarette, was watching us. There was something in his manner that imposed restraint. He was cool, so we would have to be too. I was obliged to pretend that I didn't care.

So the three of us stood at the bar for a long time drinking. The men talked books and gossiped about writers, particularly the poet Robert Lowell, a friend of Hamilton and possibly going mad; and football, on which Tom was weak, but adept at making good use of the two or three things he knew. It didn't occur to anyone to sit down. Tom ordered pork pies with a round of drinks but Hamilton didn't touch his, and later used his plate and then the pie itself as an ashtray. I assumed that Tom, like me, dreaded leaving the conversation, for then we would have to have a row. After my second glass I chipped in occasionally, but mostly I pretended to listen while I thought about Shirley. So much change! She had made it as a writer, so no real coincidence in her meeting Tom in the Pillars of Hercules – he had told me it was already established as the *New Review*'s office extension, anteroom and canteen, and in preparation for the launch dozens of writers came through. She had shed her decency along with the fat. She'd shown no surprise at finding me here, so she must have known my connection to Tom. When the time came for me to be angry she'd get more than her share. I'd give her hell.

But I felt nothing now. The pub closed and we followed Hamilton through the afternoon gloom to Muriel's, a tiny dark drinking club where men of a certain age with jowly ruined faces were perched on stools at the bar, pronouncing loudly on international affairs.

As we came in one said loudly, 'China? Fuck off. China!'

We made a huddle on three velvet armchairs in a corner. Tom and Ian had reached that point in a drinking session when the conversation patrols endlessly the tiny perimeters of a minor detail. They were talking about Larkin, about some lines at the end of 'The Whitsun Weddings', one of the poems Tom had made me read. They were disagreeing, though without much passion, about an 'arrow shower/ Sent out of sight, somewhere becoming rain'. Hamilton thought the lines were perfectly clear. The train journey was over, the just-married couples were released to go their ways, into London, into their separate fates. Tom less laconically said the lines were dark, touched with foreboding, the elements were negative – a sense of falling, wet, lost, some-where. He used the word 'liquescence' and Hamilton said drily, 'Liquescence, eh?' Then they went around again, finding clever ways to make the same points, though I sensed that the older man may have merely been sounding Tom out for his judgement or agility in argument. I don't think Hamilton cared either way.

I wasn't listening all the time. The men ignored me and I was beginning to feel a bit of a writer's moll as well as a fool. I made a mental list of my possessions in the Brighton flat – I might not be going there again. A hairdryer, underwear, a couple of summer frocks and a swimsuit, nothing I'd seri-ously miss. I was persuading myself that leaving Tom would lift from me the burden of honesty. I could go with my secret intact. We were drinking brandy with coffee at this point. I didn't mind parting from Tom. I'd forget him quickly and find someone else, someone better. It was all just fine, I could take care of myself, I'd spend my time well, dedicate myself to work, read Olivia Manning's Balkan trilogy, which I had lined up by my bed, use the Bishop's twenty-pound note to take a week's holiday in spring and be an interesting single woman in a small Mediterranean hotel.

We stopped drinking at six and went down into the street and walked in freezing rain towards Soho Square. Hamilton was due to give a reading at the Poetry Society in Earls Court that evening. He shook Tom's hand, embraced me, and then we watched him hurry away, nothing in his gait to suggest the kind of afternoon he'd had. And then Tom and I were alone, not sure which direction to walk in. Now it begins, I thought, and at that moment, revived by the cold rain in my face, and understanding the true measure of my loss and Tom's treachery, I was overcome with sudden desolation and couldn't move. A great black weight was on me and my feet were heavy and numb. I stood looking across the square towards Oxford Street. Some chanting Hare Krishna types, shaven-head dupes with tambourines, were filing back into their headquarters. Dodging their god's rain. I detested every last one of them.

'Serena, darling, what's the matter?'

He stood unsteadily before me, pissed, but no less good an actor for that, his face puckered with theatrical concern.

I could see us clearly, as though from a window two flights up, with the view distorted by black-edged raindrops. A couple of Soho drunks about to have a row on the filthy slick pavement. I would have preferred to walk away, for the outcome was obvious. But I still couldn't move.

Instead, I started off the scene, and spoke through a weary sigh. 'You're having an affair with my friend.'

I sounded so plaintive and childish, and stupid too, as though an affair with a stranger would have been just fine.

He was looking at me in amazement, and a fine show of being baffled. I could have hit him.

'What are you . . . ?' Then, a clumsy imitation of a man struck by a brilliant idea.

'Shirley Shilling! Oh God, Serena. Do you really think that? I should have explained. I met her at the Cambridge reading. She was with Martin Amis. I didn't know until today that you once worked in the same office somewhere. Then you and I started talking with Ian and I forgot all about it. Her father's just died and she's devastated. She would have come over but she was too upset . . .'

He put his hand on my shoulder but I shook him off. I didn't like to be pitied. And I thought I saw traces of amusement around his mouth.

I said, 'It was obvious, Tom. How dare you!'

'She's written a soppy romantic novel. But I like her. That's all there is to it. Her dad owned a furniture store and she was close to him, she worked for him. I felt truly sorry for her. Honestly, darling.'

At first I was simply confused, suspended between believing and hating him. Then, as I began to doubt myself, I felt a delicious sulky obstinacy, a perverse refusal to let go of the obliterating idea that he had made love to Shirley.

'I can't bear it, my poor darling, you've been suffering all afternoon. That's why you were so quiet. And of course! You must have seen me holding her hand. Oh my sweetheart, I'm so sorry. I love you, only you, and I'm so sorry . . .'

I kept a closed face as he went on protesting, and comforting me. Believing him didn't make me less angry with him. I was angry that he was making me feel foolish, that he might be secretly laughing at me, that he would work this up into a funny story. I was determined to make him try all the harder to win me back. I was coming to the point where I knew very well I was only pretending to doubt him. Perhaps that was better than appearing such a dolt, and besides, I didn't know how to get out of it, how to change my entrenched position and look plausible. So I remained silent, but when he took my hand, I didn't refuse him, and when he drew me towards him I complied reluctantly and let him kiss the top of my head.

'You're drenched, you're shivering,' he murmured in my ear. 'We need to get you indoors.'

I nodded, signalling the end of my truculence, the end of my disbelief. Even though the Pillars of Hercules was only a hundred yards away along Greek Street, I knew that indoors meant my room.

He pulled me closer towards him. 'Listen,' he said. 'We said it on the beach. We love each other. It's meant to be simple.'

I nodded again. All I could think of now was how cold I was, and how drunk. I heard a taxi's engine behind us and felt him turn and stretch to wave it down. When we were installed and heading north, Tom turned on the heater. It produced a roar and a trickle of cool air. On the screen that divided us from the cabbie was an advertisement for a taxi like this one, and as the lettering was drifting upwards and sideways, I worried that I would be sick. At my place I was relieved to find that my housemates were out. Tom ran a bath for me. The scalding water sent up clouds of steam that condensed on the icy walls and ran down to puddle on the floral lino. We got in the bath together, topped and tailed, and massaged each other's feet and sang old Beatles songs. He got out long before me, dried himself and went off to find more towels. He was drunk too, but he was tender as he helped me out of the bath, and dried me like a child, and led me to the bed. He went downstairs and came back with mugs of tea and got in beside me. Then he took very special care of me.

Months, and then years later, after all that happened,

whenever I woke in the night and needed comfort, I'd summon that early winter evening when I lay in his arms and he kissed my face, and told me over and over again how silly I'd been, how sorry he was, and how he loved me.

20

A t the end of February, not long before election day, the Austen Prize judges announced their shortlist and on it, tucked among the familiar giants – Burgess, Murdoch, Farrell, Spark and Drabble – was a complete unknown, one T.H. Haley. But no one took much notice. The press release was badly timed because that day everyone was talking about Enoch Powell's attack on the Prime Minister, his own party leader. Poor fat Ted! People had stopped worrying about the miners and 'Who governs?' and had started worrying about 20 per cent inflation and economic collapse and whether we should listen to Powell, vote Labour and get out of Europe. This was not a good moment to ask the country to contemplate contemporary fiction. Because the three-day week had successfully prevented blackouts, the whole affair was now regarded as a fraud. Coal stocks were not so low after all, industrial production was not much affected and there was a general impression that we'd been frightened for nothing, or for political purposes, and that none of it should have happened.

And so, against all the predictions, Edward Heath, his piano, sheet music and seascapes were moved out of Downing Street and Harold and Mary Wilson were installed for a second spell. On a TV at work I saw the new Prime Minister standing outside Number Ten in early March looking stooped and frail, almost as weary as Heath. Everyone was weary, and at Leconfield House they were depressed as well as weary because the country had chosen the wrong man.

I'd voted for Wilson a second time, for that wily survivor of the left, and I should have been more cheerful than most but I was exhausted from insomnia. I couldn't stop thinking about the shortlist. Of course, I wanted Tom to win, I wanted it more than he did. But I'd heard from Peter Nutting that he and others had read *From the Somerset Levels* in a proof copy and considered it 'flimsy and pathetic' as well as 'fashionably negative and boring' – Nutting told me this when he stopped me one lunchtime in Curzon Street. He strode on, striking the pavement with his rolled umbrella, leaving me to understand that if my choice was suspect, then so was I.

Gradually, press interest in the Austen Prize picked up and attention fixed on the only new name on the list. No first-time novelist had ever won the Austen. The shortest novel to be honoured in its one-hundred-year history was twice the length of *The Levels*. A lot of coverage seemed to suggest there was something unmanly or dishonest about a short novel. Tom was profiled in the *Sunday Times*, photographed in front of the Palace Pier looking nakedly happy and vulnerable. A couple of articles mentioned that he had a grant from the Foundation. We were reminded of how Tom's book was rushed into print to make the Prize deadline. Journalists had not yet read his novel because Tom Maschler was tactically holding back review copies. An unusually benign diary piece in the *Daily Telegraph* said that it was generally agreed Tom Haley was handsome and girls went 'wobbly' when he smiled, at which I felt a vertiginous moment of jealousy and possession. What girls? Tom now had a phone in the flat and I was able to speak to him from an odorous phone box on the Camden Road.

'There are no girls,' he said cheerfully. 'They must be in the newspaper office, wobbling in front of my photograph.'

He was amazed to be on the list, but Maschler had phoned to say that he would have been furious if Tom had been left off. 'It's too obvious,' he'd apparently said. 'You're a genius and it's a masterpiece. They wouldn't dare ignore it.'

But the newly discovered writer was able to remain detached from the Austen fuss, even though he was bemused by the press. *The Levels* was already behind him, it was a 'five-finger exercise'. I warned him not to say so to any journalist while the judges were still making up their minds. He said he didn't care, he had a novel to write and it was growing at a pace that only obsession and a new electric typewriter could deliver. His output was all I knew of the book. Three or four thousand words most days, sometimes six, and once, in an afternoon and all-night frenzy, ten. The numbers meant little to me, though I took my cue from the croaky excitement down the phone.

'Ten thousand words, Serena. Do that every day for a month and I'd have an *Anna Karenina*!'

Even I knew that he wouldn't. I felt protective of him and worried that when they came, the reviews would turn against him and he'd be surprised at his own disappointment. For now his only anxiety was that a trip he'd just taken to Scotland for research had interrupted his concentration.

'You need a rest,' I said from the Camden Road. 'Let me come at the weekend.'

'OK. But I'll have to go on writing.'

'Tom, please tell me just a little bit about it.'

'You'll see it before anyone else, I promise.'

The day after the shortlist was announced I received, in place of the usual summons, a visit from Max. He went first to stand by Chas Mount's desk for a chat. As it happened we were frantic that morning. Mount had written the first draft of an internal report, a retrospective in which the RUC and the army also had a hand. The issue was what Mount bitterly referred to as 'the running sore', by which he meant internment without trial. Back in 1971 scores of the wrong people had been rounded up because the RUC Special Branch suspect lists were out of date and useless. And no killers from the loyalist side had been arrested, no members of the Ulster Volunteer Force. The detainees were kept in inadequate accommodation without being properly separated. And all due process, all legality abandoned – a propaganda gift to our enemies. Chas Mount had served in Aden and had always been sceptical of the interrogation techniques the army and RUC were using during internment – black hoods, isolation, restricted diet, white noise, hours of standing. He was keen to demonstrate that the Service's hands were relatively clean. We girls in the office took it on trust that they were. The whole sorry affair was heading towards the European Court of Human Rights. The RUC, at least as he explained it, wanted to drag us down with them, and the army was on their side. They weren't pleased at all by his version of events. Someone on our side higher up than Mount had sent his draft report back and told him to rewrite it to keep all factions happy. It was after all 'only' an internal report and would soon be filed and forgotten.

So he was calling for more files, and we were in and out of the Registry, and busy typing up inserts. Max chose a bad time to hover by Chas Mount and try to engage him in small talk. In strict security terms, with these dossiers open he shouldn't have stepped into our office at all. But Chas was too polite and good-natured to say so. Still, his responses were brief, and soon Max came over to me. In his hand was a small brown envelope which he placed ostentatiously on my desk and said in a voice loud enough for everyone to hear, 'Take a look as soon as you have a moment.' Then he left.

For a good while, perhaps as long as an hour, I decided that I didn't have a moment. What I dreaded most was a heartfelt declaration on office stationery. What I eventually read was a properly typed memo headed 'Restricted' and 'Sweet Tooth' and 'From MG to SF' and a circulation list that included the initials of Nutting, Tapp and two others I didn't recognise. The note, obviously written by Max for the record, began 'Dear Miss Frome'. It advised me of what I had 'likely already considered'. One of the Sweet Tooth subjects was receiving publicity and might well receive yet more. 'Staff are expected to avoid being photographed or written about in the press. You may well consider it to be in the line of duty to attend the Austen Prize reception, but you are best advised to avoid it.'

Very sensible, however much I resented it. I had in fact planned to be there with Tom. Win or lose, he needed me. But why this circulated letter rather than a word in my ear? Was it too painful for Max to talk to me alone? I rather suspected some form of bureaucratic trap was being set for me. The question then was whether I should defy Max or stay away. Doing the latter seemed safer since it was procedurally correct, but I felt cross about it and on the way home that evening I felt indignant, and angry with Max and his schemes – whatever they were. I was annoyed too at having to invent for Tom a good explanation for my absence. Illness in the family, a bout of flu for myself, an emergency at work? I decided on a morbidly mouldy snack – rapid onset, total incapacity, quick recovery – and this deceit naturally brought me back to the old problem. There had never been a right moment to tell him. Perhaps if I'd turned him down for Sweet Tooth and then had the affair, or started the affair and left the Service, or told him on first meeting . . . but no, none of it made sense. I couldn't have known at the beginning where we were heading, and as soon as I did know, it became too precious to threaten. I could tell him and resign, or resign then tell him, but I would still risk losing him. All I could think of was never telling him. Could I live with myself? Well, I already was.

Unlike its boisterous infant cousin, the Booker, the Austen didn't go in for banquets, or for having the great and good on its judging panel. As Tom described it to me, there was

271

going to be a sober drinks reception at the Dorchester, with a short speech by an eminent literary figure. The judges were mostly literary types, academics, critics, with an occasional philosopher or historian drafted in. The Prize money had once been considerable – in 1875 two thousand pounds took you a long way. Now it was no match for the Booker. The Austen was valued for prestige alone. There had been talk of televising the Dorchester proceedings, but the elderly trustees were said to be wary and, according to Tom, the Booker was more likely to make it onto television one day.

The reception was at six the following evening. At five I sent a telegram from the Mayfair post office to Tom, care of the Dorchester. *Am sick. Bad sandwich. Thoughts with you. Come to Camden after. Love you. S.* I slouched back to the office, loathing myself and the situation I was in. Once I would have asked myself what Tony would have done. No use now. It was easy enough to pass off my black mood as illness and Mount let me leave early. I arrived home at six, just when I should have been passing through the Dorchester entrance on Tom's arm. Towards eight I thought I should play my part in case he turned up early. It was easy enough to persuade myself that I was unwell. In pyjamas and dressing gown, I lay on my bed in a haze of sulkiness and self-pity, then I read for a while, then I dozed off for an hour or two and didn't hear the doorbell.

One of the girls must have let Tom in because when I opened my eyes he was standing by my bed, holding up by a corner his cheque and in the other hand a finished copy of his novel. He was grinning like a fool. Forgetting my poisonous sandwich, I leapt up to embrace him, we whooped and hollered and made such a din that Tricia tapped on the door and asked if we needed help. We reassured her, then we made love (he seemed so hungry for it), and straight afterwards took a taxi to the White Tower.

We hadn't been back there since our first date, so that was an anniversary of a sort. I'd insisted on bringing with me

From the Somerset Levels and we passed it back and forth across the table, flipped through its one hundred and forty-one pages to admire the typeface, rejoiced in the author photograph and the cover, which showed in grainy black and white a ruined city that may have been Berlin or Dresden in 1945. Suppressing thoughts about the security implications, I exclaimed over the dedication, 'To Serena', got up from my seat to kiss him, and listened to his account of the evening, of William Golding's droll speech and an incomprehensible one by the chairman of the judges, a professor from Cardiff. When his name was announced, Tom in his nervousness had tripped on the edge of a carpet as he went forward and hurt his wrist on the back of a chair. Tenderly, I kissed that wrist. After the Prize ceremony he gave four short interviews, but no one had read his book, it didn't matter what he said and the experience made him feel fraudulent. I asked for two glasses of champagne and we toasted the only first-time novelist to take the Austen Prize. It was such a wonderful occasion that we didn't even bother to get drunk. I remembered to eat carefully, like the invalid I was supposed to be.

Tom Maschler had planned publication with the precision of a moon landing. Or as if the Austen was in his gift. The shortlist, the profiles, the announcement helped build the impatient expectation, which was fulfilled towards the end of the week when the book appeared in the shops just as the first notices appeared. Our weekend plan was simple. Tom would carry on writing, I would read his press on the train down. I travelled to Brighton on Friday evening with seven reviews on my lap. The world mostly approved of my lover. In the *Telegraph*: 'The only thread of hope is that which binds father to daughter (a love as tenderly achieved as anything in modern fiction) but the reader knows soon enough that this bleak masterpiece cannot tolerate the thread uncut. The heart-piercing finale is almost more than one can bear.' In the *TLS*: 'A strange glow, an eerie subterranean light, suffuses

Mr Haley's prose and the hallucinogenic effect on the reader's inner eye is such as to transform a catastrophic end-time world into a realm of harsh and irresistible beauty.' In the *Listener*: 'His prose gives no quarter. He has the drained, level stare of the psychopath and his characters, morally decent, physically lovely, must share their fates with the worst in a godless world.' In *The Times*: 'When Mr Haley sets on his dogs to tear out the viscera of a starving beggar, we know we are being tossed into the crucible of a modern aesthetic and challenged to object, or at least to blink. In the hands of most writers the scene would be a careless dabbling in suffering, and unforgivable, but Haley's spirit is both tough and transcendent. From the very first paragraph you are in his hands, you know he knows what he is doing, and you can trust him. This small book bears the promise and burden of genius.'

We had already passed through Haywards Heath. I took the book, *my* book, from my bag and read random pages and, of course, began to see them through different eyes. Such was the power of this assured consensus that *The Levels* did look different, more confident of its terms, its destination, and rhythmically hypnotic. And so knowing. It read like a majestic poem as precise and suspended as 'Adlestrop'. Above the train's iambic racket (and who taught me *that* word?) I could hear Tom intone his own lines. What did I know, a humble operative who had once, only two or three years ago, made the case for Jacqueline Susann against Jane Austen? But could I trust a consensus? I picked up the *New Statesman*. It's 'back half', as explained to me by Tom, was important in the literary world. As the contents list announced, the arts editor herself presented a verdict in the lead review: 'Admittedly, there are moments of poise, a clinical descriptive power capable of generating occasional surges of disgust at humankind, but overall the impression is of something forced, a touch formulaic, emotionally manipulative and altogether slight. He deludes himself (but not the reader) that he is saying

274

something profound about our common plight. What is lacking is scale, ambition and naked intelligence. However, he may do something yet.' Then a tiny item in the *Evening Standard*'s Londoner's Diary: 'One of the worst decisions ever taken by a committee . . . this year's Austen judges, perhaps with a collective eye to a role in the Treasury, decided to devalue the currency of their prize. They opted for an adolescent dystopia, a pimply celebration of disorder and beastliness, thankfully not much longer than a short story.'

Tom had said he didn't want to see the reviews, so in the flat that evening I read out the choicest parts of the good ones and summarised the negative articles in the blandest terms. He was pleased by the praise, of course, but it was obvious that he had moved on. He was glancing at one of his typed pages even as I was reading out the passage that included the word 'masterpiece'. He was typing again as soon as I'd finished, and he wanted to go on working through the evening. I went out for fish and chips and he ate his at the typewriter, straight off the page of yesterday's *Evening Argus*, which contained one of his best notices.

I read and we barely spoke a word until I went to bed. I was still awake an hour later when he got in beside me, and again, he made love to me in this new, hungry way of his, as if he'd lived without sex for a year. He made far more noise than I ever did. I teased him by calling this his pig-in-a-trough mode.

The next morning I woke to the muted sound of his new typewriter. I kissed the top of his head as I passed him on the way out to the Saturday market. I did the shopping there, collected up the newspapers and took them to my usual coffee shop. A table by the window, a cappuccino, an almond croissant. Perfect. And here was a brilliant review in the *Financial Times*. 'Reading T.H. Haley is like being driven too fast round tight corners. But be assured, this sleek vehicle never leaves the road.' I looked forward to reading that to him. Next on the heap was the *Guardian*, with Tom's name and a photograph of him at the Dorchester on the front page. Good. A whole article about him. I turned to it, saw the headline – and froze. 'Austen Prize-winning Author Funded by MI5'.

I was almost sick right there. My first stupid thought was that perhaps he would never see it. A 'reliable source' had confirmed to the paper that the Freedom International Foundation, perhaps unknowingly, 'had received funds from another body that was partly financed by an organisation indirectly funded by the Security Service'. I scanned the piece at the speed of panic. No mention of Sweet Tooth or of other writers. There was an accurate summary of monthly payments, of how Tom had given up his post-grad teaching post on receiving the first, and then, less harmfully, a mention of the Congress for Cultural Freedom and its connection to the CIA. The old *Encounter* story was warmed up, then, back to the scoop. It was noted that T.H. Haley had written

> passionate anti-communist articles on the East German Uprising, on the silence of West German writers about the Berlin Wall and, most recently, on the State persecution of Romanian poets. This is perhaps just the sort of kindred spirit our intelligence services would like to see flourish on these shores, a right-wing author who is eloquently sceptical of the general left-leaning tendencies of his colleagues. But with this level of secret meddling in culture, questions are bound to be raised about openness and artistic freedom in our Cold War environment. No one yet doubts the integrity of the Austen Prize judges, but the trustees might be wondering just what kind of winner their learned committee has chosen, and whether champagne corks flew in certain secret London offices when Haley's name was announced.

I read the piece again and sat immobilised for twenty minutes while my untouched coffee cooled. Now it seemed obvious.

It was bound to happen: if I wouldn't tell him, someone else would. My punishment for cowardice. How loathsome and ridiculous I'd appear now, forced into the open, trying to sound honest, trying to explain myself. I didn't tell you dearest because I love you. I was frightened of losing you. Oh yes, a perfect arrangement. My silence, his disgrace. I thought of going straight to the station to get the next London train, fading from his life. Yes, let him face the storm alone. More cowardice. But he wouldn't want me near him anyway. And so it went round, even though I knew there was no escape, I would have to confront him, I would have to go to the flat and show him the article.

I gathered up the chicken, vegetables and newspapers, paid for my uneaten breakfast, and walked slowly up the hill to his street. I heard him typing as I came up the stairs. Well, that was about to stop. I let myself in and waited for him to look up.

He was aware of me and faintly smiled in greeting and was about to continue when I said, 'You'd better look at this. It isn't a review.'

The *Guardian* was folded at the page. He took it and turned his back on me to read it. I was numbly wondering, when it came to it, whether I should pack, or just leave. I had a small suitcase under the bed. I would need to remember my hairdryer. But there might not be time. He might simply throw me out.

At last he looked at me and said neutrally, 'It's terrible.'

'Yes.'

'What am I supposed to say?'

'Tom, I don't . . .'

'I mean, these money trails. Listen to this. Foundation blah blah, "had received funds from another body that was partly financed by an organisation indirectly funded by the Security Service".'

'I'm sorry, Tom.'

'Partly? Indirectly? Three organisations back? How are we meant to know about that?'

277

'I don't know.' I heard the 'we' but I didn't really take it in.

He said, 'I went to their office, I've seen all their stuff. It's completely above board. '

'Of course it is.'

'I suppose I should have asked to audit the books. Like a fucking accountant!'

He was indignant now. 'I just don't understand it. If the government wants to put over certain views, why do it in secret?'

'Exactly.'

'They've got friendly journalists, Arts Council, scholarships, BBC, information departments, royal institutions. I don't know what the fuck they've got. They run a whole education system! Why use MI5?'

'It's insane, Tom.'

'It's madness. This is how these secret bureaucracies perpetuate themselves. Some squirt of an underling dreams up a scheme to please his masters. But no one knows what it's for, what the point is. No one even asks. It's right out of Kafka.'

He stood up suddenly and came over to me.

'Listen. Serena. No one has ever told me what to write. Speaking up for a Romanian poet in jail doesn't make me right wing. Calling the Berlin Wall a pile of shit doesn't make me a dupe of MI5. Nor does calling West German writers cowards for ignoring it.'

'Of course it doesn't.'

'But that's what they're implying. Fucking kindred spirit! That's what everyone's going to think.'

Was it really that simple, that he loved me so much, felt so loved by me, that he couldn't begin to suspect me? Was *he* that simple? I watched as he began to pace up and down the small attic room. The floor creaked noisily, the lamp suspended from the rafters stirred a little. This surely would be the time, when we were halfway there, to tell him the truth. But I knew I couldn't deny myself this reprieve.

He was in a frenzy of indignation again. Why him? It was unfair. It was vindictive. Just when his career had made a decent start.

Then he stopped and said, 'On Monday I'll go to the bank and tell them to refuse any more payments.'

'Good idea.'

'I can live on the Prize money for a while.'

'Yes.'

'But Serena . . .' He came over to me again and took my hands in his. We looked into each other's eyes, then we kissed.

'Serena, what am I going to do?'

My voice, when I found it, was flatly inexpressive. 'I think you're going to have to put out a statement. Write something and phone it through to the Press Association.'

'I need you to help me draft it.'

'Of course. You need to say that you knew nothing, you're outraged and you're stopping the money.'

'You're brilliant. I love you.'

He put away the loose pages of his new book in a drawer and locked it. Then I sat at the typewriter and put in a clean sheet and we worked on a draft. It took me some minutes to adjust to the sensitive keys of an electric machine. When it was done I read it back to him and he said, 'You can also put, "I wish to make it clear that at no point have I ever had any communication from or contact with any member of MI5."'

I felt my knees go weak. 'You don't need that. It's clear from what you've already said. It sounds like you're protesting too much.'

'I'm not sure you're right. Isn't it good to make it clear?'

'It is clear, Tom. Honestly. You don't need it.'

Our eyes met again. His were red-rimmed from exhaustion. Otherwise, I saw nothing but trust.

'All right then,' he said. 'Forget it.'

I handed him the page and went next door to lie on the bed while he got the PA's number from the operator and phoned his statement through. To my amazement, I heard him dictate the sentence, or a version of it, that we had just agreed to drop.

'And let me make this clear. I have never in my life had contact with any member of MI5.'

I sat up, and was about to call out to him, but there was nothing to be done and I sank back into the pillows. I felt weary of thinking about the same thing all the time. *Tell him. Get it over with. No! Don't you* dare. Events were moving out of my control and I had no idea what I should be doing. I heard him put the phone down and go to his desk. Within minutes he was typing again. How extraordinary, how wonderful, to have such power of concentration, to be able to push on now into an imagined world. I continued to lie there on the unmade bed, devoid of motive, oppressed by the certainty that the week ahead would be disastrous. I would be in deep trouble at work, even if the *Guardian* story wasn't followed up. But it was bound to be. It could only get worse. I should have listened to Max. It was possible that the journalist who wrote the piece knew no more than he had written. But if there was more, and I was exposed, then . . . then I should tell Tom before the newspapers did. *That* again. I didn't move. I couldn't.

After forty minutes the typewriter stopped. Five minutes later I heard the boards creak, and Tom came in wearing his jacket and sat by me and kissed me. He was restless, he said. He hadn't been out of the flat for three days. Would I walk to the seafront with him, and would I let him buy me lunch in Wheeler's? It was balm, instant forgetfulness. We were out of the house in the time it took me to put on my coat, and walking arm in arm down the hill towards the English Channel as if it was just another carefree weekend. As long as I could lose myself in the present with him, I felt protected. I was helped by Tom's lively mood. He seemed to think that his statement to the press had solved the problem. On the front we walked east, with a fretful frothy grey-green sea on our right whipped up by a fresh north wind. We went past Kemp Town, and then through a knot of demonstrators with placards protesting against plans to build a marina. We agreed we didn't care either way. When we came back past the same place twenty minutes later the demonstration had dispersed.

That was when Tom said, 'I think we're being followed.'

If I felt a brief dip of horror in my stomach it was because I thought he was implying he knew everything and was mocking me. But he was serious. I looked back. The cold blowy day had deterred promenaders. There was only one figure in sight, perhaps two hundred yards away or even more.

'That one?'

'He's got a leather coat. I'm sure I saw him when we left the flat.'

So we stopped and waited for this man to catch up with us, but within a minute he was crossing the road and turning up a side street away from the seafront. And at that point we became more concerned about getting to the restaurant before they stopped serving lunch, so we hurried back towards the Lanes and our table, and our 'usual', then Chablis with our grilled skate wings and, finally, a pot of sickly syllabub.

As we were leaving Wheeler's Tom said, 'There he is,' and pointed, but I saw nothing but an empty street corner. He broke away and jogged over to it, and it was clear from the way he stood there with his hands on his hips that he could see no one.

This time our priority, even more urgent, was to get back to the flat and make love. He was more frenetic, or ecstatic, than ever, so much so that I didn't dare tease him about it. I wouldn't have wanted to anyway. I could feel the chill of the coming week. Tomorrow I would take the afternoon train home, wash my hair, prepare my clothes, and on Monday I would have to account for myself at work to my superiors, face the morning newspapers and, sooner or later, face Tom. I didn't know which one of us was doomed, or more doomed, if that made any sense. Which of us would be disgraced? Please let it just be me, not both of us, I thought as I watched Tom leave the bed, pick up his clothes from a chair and go naked across the room to the bathroom. He didn't know what was coming and he deserved none of it. Just bad luck, to have met me. With this thought I fell asleep, as so often before to the sound of his typing. Oblivion seemed the only reasonable option. I slept deeply, without dreams. At some point in the early evening he came back quietly into the bedroom, slipped in beside me and made love to me again. He was amazing.

21

Back at St Augustine's Road on Sunday I had another sleepless night. I was too agitated to read. Through the branches of the chestnut tree and a gap in the curtains, a street lamp threw a crooked stick of light across the ceiling, and I lay on my back, staring at it. For all the mess I was in, I didn't know how I could have done things differently. If I hadn't joined MI5, I wouldn't have met Tom. If I'd told him who I worked for at our very first meeting – and why would I tell a stranger that? – he would've shown me the door. At every point along the way, as I grew fonder of him, then loved him, it became harder, riskier to tell him the truth even as it became more important to do so. I was trapped and I always had been. I fantasised at length of how it might be, to have enough money and single-mindedness to leave suddenly without explaining myself, go somewhere simple and clean, far from here, like the island of Kumlinge in the Baltic. I saw myself in watery sunlight, divested of all obligations and connections, walking without luggage along a narrow road by a sandy bay, with sea thrift and gorse and a solitary pine, a road that rose to a promontory and a plain white country church in whose tiny cemetery was a fresh stone, and a jam jar of harebells left by the housekeeper. I would sit on the grass by the mound of his grave and think about Tony, remember how we were fond lovers one whole summer, and I'd forgive him for betraying his country. It was a passing moment of stupidity, hatched from good intentions and it caused no real harm. I could forgive him because everything could be resolved in Kumlinge, where the air and light were pure. Was my life ever better and simpler than those weekends in a woodsman's cottage near Bury St Edmunds, where an older man adored me, cooked for me, guided me?

Even now, at four thirty, right across the country, bundled newspapers bearing Tom's picture were being hurled from trains and vans onto platforms and pavements. All would carry his Press Association denial. Then he would be at the mercy of Tuesday's press. I turned on the light, put on my dressing gown and sat in my chair. T.H. Haley, lackey of the security state, his integrity blown before he'd even got started, and I was the one, no, it was us, Serena Frome and her employers, who brought him down. Who could trust what a man wrote on Romanian censorship when his words were paid for out of the Secret Vote? Our Sweet Tooth darling spoiled. There were another nine writers, perhaps more important, more useful, and not in the frame. I could hear the fourth floor saying it – *the project will survive*. I thought of what Ian Hamilton would say. My feverish insomnia was making my fantasies active on my retina. I saw in the dark a ghostly smile and shrug as he turned away. *Well, we'll have to find someone else. Too bad. The kid was bright*. Perhaps I was exaggerating. Spender survived the *Encounter* scandal, and so did *Encounter* itself. But Spender had not been as vulnerable. Tom would be taken for a liar.

I slept for an hour before the alarm rang. I washed and dressed in a fog, too exhausted to think about the day ahead. I could feel it though, a numbing dread. The house was damp as well as cold this time in the morning, but the kitchen was cheerful. Bridget had a big exam at nine, and Tricia and Pauline were sending her off with a fried breakfast. One of the girls passed me a mug of tea and I sat to one side, warming my hands on it, listening to the banter and wishing that I too was about to qualify as a conveyancing solicitor. When Pauline asked me why I looked so glum I answered honestly that I'd had a sleepless night. For that I received a pat on the shoulder and a fried egg and bacon sandwich. Such kindness almost made me tearful. I volunteered to do the washing-up while the others got ready, and it was comforting, the domestic order of hot water, froth and steaming clean wet plates.

I was the last to leave the house. As I approached the front door, I saw among the junk mail scattered across the lino a postcard for me. The picture showed a beach in Antigua and a woman with a basket of flowers balanced on her head. It was from Jeremy Mott.

Hello, Serena. Escaping the long Edinburgh winter. What a joy to get out of my overcoat at last. Nice mystery rendezvous the other week and much talk of you! Come up and see me some time. xxx Jeremy.

Rendezvous? I was in no mood for puzzles. I put the card in my bag and left the house. I was feeling a little better once I was walking quickly towards Camden Tube station. I was trying to be brave and fatalistic. It was a local storm, a funding story, there was nothing I could do anyway. I could lose my lover and my job, but no one was actually going to die.

I'd already decided to look through the press in Camden because I didn't want to be seen with a pile by somebody from work. So I stood in the icy gale that swept through the twin-entrance booking hall, trying to manage the flapping sheets of several newspapers. Tom's story was not on any front page, but it was inside all the broadsheets, the *Daily Mail* and the *Express*, with different photographs. All versions were repetitions of the original piece, with the addition of parts of his Press Association statement. All carried his insistence that he knew no one from MI5. Not good, but it could have been worse. Without fresh information the story might die. So twenty minutes later there was something like a spring in my step as I walked down Curzon Street. Five minutes later, when I reached the office, my pulse hardly varied as I picked up an internal mail envelope from my desk. It was as I'd expected, a summons to a meeting in Tapp's office at 9.00 a.m. I hung up my coat and took the lift up.

They were waiting for me – Tapp, Nutting, the greyish, shrunken-looking gentleman from the fifth floor and Max. I had the impression I was walking in on a silence. They were drinking coffee, but no one offered to pour me one as Tapp indicated with an open hand the only unoccupied chair. On a low table before us was a pile of press cuttings. By it was a copy of Tom's novel. Tapp picked it up, turned a page and read, 'To Serena'. He tossed the book onto the press cuttings.

'Well then, Miss Frome. Why are we in all the newspapers?'

'It didn't come from me.'

Some soft, incredulous throat-clearing filled a brief pause before Tapp said unemphatically, 'Really.' And then, 'You're . . . seeing this man?'

He made the verb sound obscene. I nodded, and when I looked round I met Max's stare. He was not avoiding me this time and I forced myself to return his look, and only glanced away when Tapp spoke again.

'Since when?'

'October.'

'You see him in London?'

'Mostly Brighton. At weekends. Look, he doesn't know anything. He doesn't suspect me.'

'Really.' It was said in the same flat tone.

'And even if he did, he'd hardly want to tell the press about it.'

They were watching me, waiting for me to say more. I was beginning to feel as stupid as I knew they thought I was.

Tapp said, 'You realise you're in serious trouble?'

It was a proper question. I nodded.

'Tell me why you think you are.'

'Because you think I can't keep my mouth shut.'

Tapp said, 'Shall we say we have reservations about your professionalism.'

Peter Nutting opened a folder on his lap. 'You wrote a report for Max, recommending we take him on.'

'Yes.'

'You were already Haley's lover when you wrote that.'

'Certainly not.'

'But you fancied him.'

'No. That came later.'

Nutting turned his head to show me his profile while he thought of some other way to make me look self-serving. At last he said, 'We took this man into Sweet Tooth on your say-so.'

As I remembered it they presented Haley to me and sent me away with a dossier. I said, 'Before I ever met Haley, Max told me to go down to Brighton to sign him up. I think we were behind schedule.' I could also have said that it was Tapp and Nutting who caused the delay. Then I added after a pause, 'But I certainly would have chosen him if it had been left to me.'

Max stirred. 'It's true in fact. I thought he was good enough on paper and clearly I was wrong. We needed to get a move on with a novelist. But my impression was she had her sights on him from the start.'

It was annoying, the way he spoke about me in the third person. But I'd just done the same to him.

'Not so,' I said. 'I loved his stories and when I met him they made it easier to like the man.'

Nutting said, 'It doesn't sound like there's much disagreement.'

I tried not to sound like I was pleading. 'He's a brilliant writer. I don't see why we can't be proud of backing him. Even in public.'

'Obviously, we're cutting him loose,' Tapp said. 'No choice. The whole list could be in trouble. As for that novel, the Cornish whatever—'

'Utter drivel,' Peter Nutting said, shaking his head in wonder. 'Civilisation brought down by the internal contradictions of capitalism. Bloody marvellous.'

'I have to say I hated it.' Max said this with the eagerness of the classroom sneak. 'I can't believe it won that prize.'

'He's writing another one,' I said. 'It sounds very promising.'

'No thanks,' Tapp said. 'He's out.'

The shrunken fellow stood suddenly and with a sigh of impatience went towards the door. 'I don't want to see any more newspaper stories. I'm meeting the editor of the *Guardian* this evening. You can take care of the rest. And I want to see a report on my desk by lunchtime.'

As soon as he was gone, Nutting said, 'That means you, Max. Make sure we're copied in. You'd better get started. Harry, we'll divide the editors in the usual way.'

'D notice?'

'Too late and we'll look stupid. Now . . .'

His *now* meant me, but first we waited for Max to leave the room. He made a point of meeting my eye as he turned right round at the last moment to step backwards through the doorway. In his blank expression I read some sort of victory, but I may have been wrong.

We listened to his footsteps recede along the corridor then Nutting said, 'The gossip is, and perhaps you can set the record straight, that you were the cause of his engagement falling apart, and that generally, being a nice-looking girl, you may be rather more trouble than you're worth.'

I could think of nothing to say. Tapp, who had been chain-smoking through the meeting, lit another. He said, 'We yielded to a lot of pressure and fashionable arguments to bring women on. The results are more or less as we predicted.'

By now I was assuming they intended to sack me and that I had nothing to lose. I said, 'Why did you take me on?'

'I keep asking myself that,' Tapp said pleasantly.

'Was it because of Tony Canning?'

'Ah yes. Poor old Tony. We had him in a safe house for a couple of days before he went off to his island. We knew we wouldn't be seeing him again and we wanted to be sure there were no loose ends. Sad business. There was a heatwave. He spent most of the time having nosebleeds. We decided he was harmless.'

Nutting added, 'Just for interest, we pressed him on motivation. He gave us a lot of guff about balance of power, but we already knew from our Buenos Aires source. He was blackmailed. 1950, just three months into his first marriage. Moscow Centre put someone irresistible in his path.'

'He liked them young,' Tapp said. 'Speaking of which, he wanted us to give you this.'

He held up an opened envelope. 'We'd have given it to you months ago but the technical boys in the basement thought there might just be some embedded code.'

I tried to appear impassive as I took the envelope from him and pushed it into my handbag. But I'd seen the handwriting and I was shaking.

Tapp noted this and added, 'Max tells us that you've been worked up about a small piece of paper. That was probably me. I jotted down the name of his island. Tony mentioned that the sea-trout fishing round there is exceptional.'

There was a pause while this irrelevant fact dissipated.

Then Nutting resumed. 'But you're right. We took you on just in case we were wrong about him. Kept an eye on you. As it turned out, the danger you posed was of the more banal sort.'

'So you're getting rid of me.'

Nutting looked at Tapp, who passed across his cigarette case. When Nutting was smoking he said, 'No, actually. You're on probation. If you can keep out of trouble, keep us out of trouble, you might just scrape through. You're to go down to Brighton tomorrow and tell Haley he's off the payroll. You'll keep your Foundation cover, of course. How you do it is your own business. For all we care you can tell him the truth about his atrocious novel. And you'll also break off relations with him. Again, do it however you like. You're to disappear into the woodwork as far as he's concerned. If he comes looking for you, you're to turn him away firmly. Tell him you've found someone else. It's over. Is that understood?'

They waited. Again, I had that feeling I sometimes used to have when the Bishop called me into his study for a talk about my teenage progress. The feeling of being naughty and small.

I nodded.

'Let me hear you.'

'I understand what you want me to do.'

'Yes. And?'

'I'll do it.'

'Again. Louder.'

'Yes, I'll do it.'

Nutting remained seated while Tapp stood and with a yellowish hand politely indicated the door.

I walked down one flight of stairs and went along the corridor to a landing where there was a view down Curzon Street. I looked over my shoulder before I took the envelope from my bag. The single sheet of paper was grubby from much handling.

September 28th, 1972

My dear girl,

I learned today that you were accepted last week. Congratulations. I'm thrilled for you. The work will give you much fulfilment and pleasure and I know you'll be good at it.

Nutting has promised to put this note in your hands, but knowing how these things work, I suspect that some time will pass before they do. By then, you will have heard the worst. You'll know why I had to go, why I had to be alone, and why I had to do everything in my power to push you away. I've done nothing so vile in my life as drive off, leaving you in that lay-by. But if I'd

290

told you the truth, I would never have been able to dissuade you from following me to Kumlinge. You're a spirited girl. You wouldn't have taken no for an answer. How I would have hated it, you watching me slide down. You would have been sucked into such a pit of sorrow. This illness is relentless. You're too young for it. I'm not being a noble and selfless martyr. I'm dead certain I can do this better alone.

I'm writing this to you from a house in London where I've been staying for a couple of nights seeing some old friends. It's midnight. Tomorrow I set off. I want to leave you not in sorrow but in gratitude for the joy you brought into my life at a time when I knew there was no way back. It was weak and selfish of me to get involved with you – ruthless even. I hope you'll forgive me. I like to think you found some happiness too, and perhaps even a career. Good luck in all you do in life. Please preserve a little corner in your memories for those summer weeks, those glorious picnics in the woods, when you delivered such kindness and love to a dying man's heart.

Thank you, thank you, my darling.

Tony

I stayed in the corridor pretending to look out of the window, and I cried for a little while. Fortunately, no one came by. I washed my face in the ladies' room, then I went downstairs and tried to lose myself in work. Our part of the Irish section was in a state of muted turmoil. As soon as I came in Chas Mount set me to collating and typing up three overlapping memos he had written that morning. They were to be made into one. The issue was that Helium had gone missing. There was an unconfirmed rumour that he'd been uncovered and shot, but as of late last night we knew this not to be true. A report from one of the officers on the ground in Belfast described Helium coming to an arranged meeting, but staying only for two minutes, long enough to say to his controller that he was getting out, going away, that he was sick of both sides. Before our man could apply pressure or offer enticements, Helium walked out. Chas was certain he knew the reason why. His memos were versions of a strong protest to the fifth floor.

When an undercover agent was considered to be no longer useful, he might find he was brutally abandoned. Instead of looking after him as promised, fitting him out with a fresh identity and a new location for him and his family and giving him money, it sometimes suited the security services to have the man killed by the enemy. Or at least, to make it look like that. Safer, neater, cheaper and, above all, more secure. At least, this was the rumour going about and matters weren't helped by the case of the undercover man, Kenneth Lennon, who'd made a statement to the National Council for Civil Liberties. He was caught between Special Branch, his employer, and the Provisionals, whom he'd reported back on. He had learned, he said, that Special Branch was finished with him and had tipped off the other side, which was pursuing him in England. If the Provisionals didn't get him, Special Branch would do the job. He told the NCCL he didn't have long to live. Two days later he was found dead in a ditch in Surrey, shot three times in the head.

'It breaks my heart,' Chas said when I handed him the draft to read. 'These chaps risk everything, we cut them loose, word gets round. Then we wonder why we can't sign up anyone else.'

At lunchtime I went out to a phone box on Park Lane and called Tom. I wanted to let him know to expect me the next day. There was no reply, but at the time it didn't bother me much. We'd arranged to speak in the evening at seven to discuss the press stories. I could tell him then. I didn't feel like eating and I didn't want to go back indoors, so I went for a melancholy stroll through Hyde Park. It was March but it still felt wintry, with no sign yet of the daffodils. The bare architecture of the trees looked stark against a white sky. I thought of the times I used to come here with Max and how I'd made him kiss me, right by that tree. Perhaps Nutting was right and I was more trouble than I was worth. I stopped in a doorway, took Tony's letter out and read it once more, tried to think about it but started to cry again. Then I went back to work.

I spent all afternoon on a further draft of Mount's memo. He'd decided over lunch to tone down his attack. He must have known the fifth floor would not be pleased by criticism from below and could be vengeful. The new draft contained phrases like 'from a certain perspective', and 'it could be argued that . . . though granted, the system has served us well'. The final version excluded any reference to Helium – or to any deaths of undercover agents – and simply made the case for treating them well, giving them good aliases when their time was up in order to make it easier to recruit. It wasn't until almost six that I left, taking the rickety lift down, calling goodnight to the taciturn men on the door, who had finally come round to not scowling at me as I passed by their station.

I needed to get hold of Tom, I needed to read Tony's letter again. It was impossible to think, I was in such turmoil. I stepped out of Leconfield House and was about to head off towards Green Park Tube when I saw a figure across the street, standing in the doorway of a nightclub, in turned-up coat collar and broad-brimmed hat. I knew exactly who it was. I waited by the kerb to let the traffic pass, then I called across the road, 'Shirley, are you waiting for me?'

She hurried over. 'I've been here half an hour. What have you been doing in there? No, no, you don't have to tell me.'

She kissed me on each cheek – her new bohemian style. Her hat was in soft brown felt and her overcoat was tightly belted around her freshly narrowed waist. Her face was long, daintily freckled and fine-boned, with delicate hollows beneath her cheekbones. It was such a transformation. Looking at her now reminded me of my bout of jealousy, and though Tom had persuaded me of his innocence, I couldn't help being wary.

She took my arm and steered me along the street. 'At least they're open now. C'mon. I've got so many things to say to you.'

We turned off Curzon Street down an alley where there was a small pub whose intimate interior of velvet and brass she would once have dismissed as 'poncey'.

When we were installed behind our half pints she said, 'First thing is an apology. I couldn't talk to you that time in the Pillars. I had to get out of there. I was no good in groups.'

'I'm so sorry about your dad.'

I saw the tiniest of ripples in her throat as she held down the emotion released by my sympathy.

'It's been terrible for the family. It's really knocked us back.'

'What happened?'

'He stepped out into the road, looked the wrong way for some reason and got hit by a motorbike. Right outside the shop. The only good thing they could tell us was he died straight away, didn't know a thing about it.'

I commiserated, and she talked for a while of how her mother had become catatonic, of how the close family had nearly broken up over funeral arrangements, of the absence of a will and what should happen to the shop. Her footballer brother wanted to sell the business to a mate of his. But now the shop, run by Shirley, was open again, her mother was out of bed and talking. Shirley went to the bar for another round and when she came back her tone was brisk. That subject was closed.

'I saw the stuff about Tom Haley. What a fuck-up. I guessed it had something to do with you.'

I didn't even nod.

'I wish I'd been in on that one. I could've told them what a bad idea it was.'

I shrugged and drank my beer, vaguely hiding behind the glass, I suppose, until I could think of something to say.

'It's all right. I'm not going to probe. I just wanted to say this, put a little idea in your head, and you don't have to answer me now. You'll think I'm running ahead of myself, but the way I read that story this morning, you stand a good chance of being kicked out. If I'm wrong, bloody marvellous. And if I'm right, and you're stuck for something, come and work for me. Or *with* me. Get to know sunny Ilford. We could have fun. I can pay you more than twice what you're getting now. Learn all there is to know about beds. These aren't great times to be in business, but people are always going to need somewhere to kip.'

I put my hand on hers. 'That's very kind, Shirley. If I need it, I'll think about it carefully.'

'It's not charity. If you'd learn how the business works, I could spend more time writing. Listen. My novel was in an auction. They paid a bloody fortune. And now someone's bought the film rights. Julie Christie wants to be in it.'

'Shirley! Congratulations! What's it called?'

'*The Ducking Stool.*'

Ah yes. A witch, innocent if she drowned, guilty if she survived, then sentenced to death by burning. A metaphor for some young girl's life. I told her I'd be her ideal reader. We talked about her book, and then her next, an eighteenth-century love affair between an English aristocrat and an actress from the slums who breaks his heart.

Then Shirley said, 'So you're actually seeing Tom. Amazing. Lucky girl! I mean, he's lucky too. I'm just pulp fiction, but he's one of the best. I'm glad he got the Prize, but I'm not sure about that funny little novel, and it's rough what he's going through now. But Serena, I don't think anyone believes he knew where his grant money came from.'

'I'm glad you think that,' I said. I'd been keeping an eye on the clock mounted above the bar, behind Shirley's head. My arrangement with Tom was for seven. I had five minutes to get clear and find a quiet phone box, but I lacked the energy to do it gracefully. Talk of beds had revived my exhaustion.

'I've got to be going,' I muttered into my beer.

'First you've got to hear my theory of how this got into the press.'

I stood and reached for my coat. 'Tell me later.'

'And don't you want to know why they threw me out? I thought you'd be full of questions.' She stood close to me, blocking my way out from behind the table.

'Not now, Shirley. I've got to get to a phone.'

'Perhaps one day you'll tell me why they put the Watchers on you. I wasn't going to start informing on my friend. I was really ashamed of myself for going along with it. But that's not why they sacked me. There's a way they have of letting you know. And don't call me paranoid. Wrong school, wrong university, wrong accent, wrong attitude. In other words general incompetence.'

She pulled me towards her and embraced me and kissed me on the cheeks again. Then she pushed a business card into my hand.

'I'll keep the beds warm for you. And you think about it. Be the manager, start a chain, build an empire! But off you go, darling. Turn left out of here and there's a phone box at the end. Give him my best.'

I was five minutes late getting to the phone. There was no reply. I replaced the receiver, counted to thirty and tried again. I phoned him from Green Park Tube station and again from Camden. At home I sat on my bed, still in my coat, and read Tony's letter again. If I hadn't been worrying about Tom, I might have seen the beginnings of some relief there. The slight easing of an old sorrow. I waited for the minutes to pass until it seemed right to go out to the box on the Camden Road. I made the journey four times that evening. The last was at eleven forty-five, when I asked the operator to check if there was a fault on the line. When I was back at St Augustine's Road and ready for bed, I came close to getting dressed and going out one last time. Instead, I lay in the dark and summoned all the harmless explanations I could think of in the hope of distracting myself from the ones I didn't dare frame. I considered going to Brighton right away. Wasn't there such a thing as a milk train? Did they really exist and didn't they come into London in the early hours rather than out of it? Then I kept my thoughts off the worst possibilities by dreaming up a Poisson distribution. The more often he didn't answer the phone, the less likely it was he would answer the next time. But surely the human factor made a nonsense of that, for he was bound to come home at some point – which was when my weariness from the night before overcame me and I knew nothing until my alarm rang at six forty-five.

I got all the way to Camden Tube the next morning before I realised that I'd left home without my key to Tom's flat. So I tried him again from the station, letting the phone ring for over a minute in case he was asleep, then gloomily walked back to St Augustine's Road. At least I wasn't carrying luggage. But what was the point of my mission to Brighton if he wasn't there? I knew I had no choice. I had to see for myself. If he wasn't there, the search for him would begin in his flat. I found the key in a handbag and set out again.

Half an hour later I was crossing the concourse of Victoria station against the flow of commuters pouring off the suburban trains from the south. I happened to glance to my right, just as the crowd parted, and I saw something quite absurd. I had a momentary glimpse of my own face, then the gap closed and the vision was gone. I swung to my right, pushed through the crush, got clear and ran the last few yards into the open shop front of Smith's newsagents. There I was, on the rack. It was the *Daily Express*. I was arm in arm with Tom, our heads lovingly inclined, walking towards the camera, with Wheeler's restaurant out of focus behind us. Above the photograph, the ugly block capitals shouted out, HALEY'S SEXY SPY. I grabbed a copy, folded it double and queued to buy it. I didn't want to be seen next to a picture of myself, so I took the newspaper to a public lavatory, locked myself in a cubicle and sat there long enough to miss my train. On the inside pages were two more photographs. One showed Tom and me coming out of his house, our 'love nest', and another was of us kissing on the seafront.

Despite the breathless tone of excitement and outrage, there was hardly a word of the article that didn't have an element of truth. I was described as an 'undercover agent', working for MI5, Cambridge educated, a 'specialist' in mathematics, based in London, given the task of liaising with Tom Haley to facilitate a generous stipend. The money trail was vaguely but properly described, with references to the Freedom International Foundation as well as Word Unpenned. Tom's statement that he had never had any connection with a member of the intelligence services was highlighted in bold. A spokesman for the Home Secretary, Roy Jenkins, told the newspaper that the matter was of 'grave concern' and that the relevant officials had been called to a meeting later today. Speaking for the Opposition, Edward Heath himself said that, if true, the story showed that the government had 'already lost its way'. But most significant of all, Tom had told a reporter that he had 'nothing to say on the matter'.

That would have been yesterday. Then he must have gone into hiding. How else to explain his silence? I came out of the cubicle, binned the paper and just made the next train. All my journeys to Brighton lately had been on Friday evenings, in the dark. Not since that first time, when I travelled to the university in my best outfit to interview Tom, had I crossed the Sussex Weald in full daylight. Staring at it now, at the charm of its hedgerows and bare trees just thickening in early spring, I experienced again the vague longing and frustration that came with the idea that I was living the wrong sort of life. I hadn't chosen it for myself. It was all down to chance. If I hadn't met Jeremy, and therefore Tony, I wouldn't be in this mess, travelling at speed towards some kind of disaster I didn't dare contemplate. My single consolation was Tony's farewell. For all its sorrow, the affair was put to rest and I had at last my token. Those summer weeks were not my private fantasy, they were shared. It had meant as much to him as to me. More, in his dying days. I had evidence of what had passed between us, I had given some comfort.

It had never been my intention to obey Nutting and Tapp's order to break off with Tom. The privilege of ending the affair belonged to Tom. Today's headlines meant my time with the Service was over. I didn't even need to be disobedient. The headlines also meant that Tom had no choice but to be shot of me. I almost hoped that I wouldn't find him in the flat, that I'd be spared the final confrontation. But then I'd be in agony, it would be intolerable. And so I went round my problem and my scrap of consolation and I was in a daze until the train stopped with a jolt in the lattice steel cavern of the Brighton terminus.

As I climbed the hill behind the station I thought the cawing and keening of the herring gulls had an emphatic falling note, a far stronger terminal cadence than usual, like the predictable final notes of a hymn. The air, with its taste of salt and traffic fumes and fried food, made me feel nostalgic for the carefree weekends. It was unlikely that I would ever come back. I slowed as I turned into Clifton Street, expecting to see journalists outside the building where Tom lived. But the pavements were empty. I let myself in and began to climb the stairs to the attic flat. I passed the sound of pop music and the smell of cooked breakfast on the second floor. I hesitated on his landing, gave the door a hearty innocent knock to scatter the demons, waited, then I fumbled with the key, turned it first the wrong way, cursed in a whisper, and shoved the door wide open.

The first thing I saw were his shoes, his scuffed brown brogues, toes pointing slightly inwards, a leaf stuck to the side of a heel, laces trailing. They were under the kitchen table. Otherwise, the room was unusually neat. All the pans and crockery had been put away, the books were in tidy piles. I went towards the bathroom, heard the familiar creak of the boards, like an old song from another time. My small inventory of cinema suicide scenes included a corpse collapsed considerately over the bath with a bloodied towel around its neck. Fortunately, the door was open and I didn't have to go in to see that he wasn't there. That left the bedroom.

The door was shut. Again, stupidly, I knocked and waited because I thought I heard the sound of a voice. Then I heard it again. It was from the street below, or from a radio in one of the flats downstairs. I also heard the thud of my own pulse. I turned the handle and pushed the door open, but remained where I was, too frightened to go in. I could see the bed, all of it, and it was made, and the Indian print bedspread was smoothly in place. It was usually in a tangle on the floor. The room was too small for there to be anywhere else to hide.

Feeling sick and thirsty, I turned back into the kitchen for a glass of water. It was only as I came away from the sink that I saw what was on the kitchen table. The shoes must have distracted me. There was a parcel done up with brown paper and string, and, lying on top of it, a white envelope with my name on it in his writing. I drank the water first, then I sat down at the table, opened the envelope and began to read my second letter in as many days.

22

Dear Serena,
   You may be reading this on the train back to London,
but my guess is that you're sitting at the kitchen table. If so,
my apologies for the state of the place. When I started clearing
out the junk and scrubbing the floors I convinced myself
I was doing it for you – as of last week your name is on
the rent book and the flat may be of use. But now that I've
finished, I look around and wonder if you'll find it sterile, or
at least unfamiliar, stripped clean of our life here together,
all the good times wiped away. Won't you miss the cardboard
boxes filled with the Chablis empties and those piles of newspapers we read in bed together? I suppose I was cleaning up
for myself. I'm bringing this episode to an end, and there's
always a degree of oblivion in tidiness. Consider it a form of
insulation. Also, I had to clear the decks before I could write
this letter, and perhaps (do I dare say this to you?) with all
this scrubbing I was erasing you, you as you were.
   I apologise too for not answering the phone. I've been
avoiding journalists, and I've been avoiding you because it
didn't seem the right time for us to be talking. I think by now
I know you well enough and I'm confident that you'll be here
tomorrow. Your clothes are all in one place, at the bottom of
the wardrobe. I won't tell you my state of mind as I folded

your things away, but I did linger over the job, as one might over an old photo album. I remembered you in so many guises. I found at the bottom of the wardrobe, screwed up in a ball, the black suede jacket you wore in Wheeler's the night you tried to explain the Monty Hall problem to me. Before I folded it, I did up all the buttons with a sense of locking something down, or locking it away. I still don't understand probability. Similarly, under the bed, the short pleated orange skirt you wore to our rendezvous at the National Portrait Gallery, the skirt that helped kick the whole thing off, as far as I was concerned. I've never folded a skirt before. This one wasn't easy.

Typing 'folded' reminds me that at any point before I've finished you could put this letter back into its envelope, in sorrow or anger or guilt. Please don't. This is not an extended accusation, and I promise you it will end well, at least in certain respects. Stay with me. I've left the heating on in order to tempt you to remain here. If you become weary, the bed is yours, the sheets are clean, all traces of our former selves lost to the launderette opposite the station. It was a service wash, and the kind lady there agreed for an extra pound to do the ironing. Ironed sheets, the uncelebrated privilege of childhood. But they remind me too of the blank page. The blank page writ large and sensual. And that page was certainly large in my thoughts before Christmas, when I was convinced that I would never write fiction again. I told you about my writing block after we went to deliver *The Levels* to Tom Maschler. You were sweetly (and ineffectually) encouraging, though I know now that you had good professional reasons. I spent most of December staring at that blank page. I thought I was falling in love, but I couldn't summon a useful thought. And then something extraordinary happened. Someone came to see me.

It happened after Christmas, when I'd taken my sister back to her hostel in Bristol. I was feeling emptied out after all the emotional scenes with Laura and I wasn't looking forward to the dull drive back to Sevenoaks. I suppose I was a little more passive than I am usually. When a stranger approached me as I was getting into the car, my defences were down. I didn't automatically assume he was a beggar or a con artist. He knew my name and he told me he had something important to tell me about you. Since he seemed harmless and I was curious, I let him buy me a coffee. You'll have guessed by now that this was Max Greatorex. He must have tailed me all the way from Kent, and perhaps before that, from Brighton. I never asked. I own up to lying to you about my movements. I didn't stay down in Bristol to spend time with Laura. I listened to your colleague for a couple of hours that afternoon, and I stayed in a hotel for two nights.

So we sat in this dim evil-smelling relic of the fifties, tiled like a public lavatory, drinking the worst coffee I've ever tasted. I'm sure Greatorex told me only a fraction of the story. First, he told me who you and he worked for. When I asked for proof he produced various internal documents, some of which referred to you, others were notes in your handwriting on headed paper, and two included photographs of you. He said he'd taken these papers from his office at great risk to himself. Then he laid out the Sweet Tooth operation for me, though he didn't tell me the names of other writers. Having a novelist in the scheme was, he said, a whimsical afterthought. He told me he was passionate about literature, knew and liked my stories and articles and that his own principled opposition to the project hardened when he heard that I was on the list. He said he was concerned that if it ever came out that I was funded by an intelligence agency, I would never outlive the disgrace. I couldn't know it at the time, but he was being less than honest about his motives.

Then he talked about you. Because you were beautiful as well as clever – actually, the word was cunning – you were considered ideal for the job of getting down to Brighton and signing me up. It wasn't his style to use a vulgar locution like honeytrap but that was what I was hearing. I got angry and had a shoot-the-messenger moment and almost popped him one on the nose. But I have to hand it to him – he took care not to appear to relish what he was telling me. His tone was sorrowful. He gently let me know that he would far rather be enjoying his short holiday break than discussing my squalid affairs. He was risking his prospects, his job, even his freedom in this breach of security. But he cared for openness and literature and decency. So he said.

He described your cover, the Foundation, the precise sums and all the rest – in part, I suppose, as corroboration for his story. And by this time I had no doubts. I was so worked up, so hot and agitated that I had to go outside. I walked up and down the street for a few minutes. I was beyond anger. This was a new dark place of hatred – for you, for myself, for Greatorex, for the Bristol Blitz and the grisly cheap horrors the post-war developers had heaped upon the bomb sites. I wondered if there was a single day when you hadn't told me an outright or implicit lie. That was when I leaned into a doorway of a boarded-up shop and tried and failed to throw up. To get the taste of you out of my gut. Then I went back inside Kwik-Snax for more.

I felt calmer when I sat down and was able to take in my informant. Even though he was the same age as me, he had an assured, patrician manner, the touch of the smooth civil servant about him. He may have been talking down to me. I didn't care. He had an extra-terrestrial look, the way his ears were mounted on mounds of flesh or bone. Since he's a scrawny fellow, with a thin neck and a shirt collar a size too big for him, I was surprised to learn that you were once in love with him, to the point of obsession, to the point at which his fiancée walked out on him. I wouldn't have thought he was your type at all. I asked him if bitterness was his motive for talking to me. He denied it. The marriage would have been a disaster, and in a way he was grateful to you.

We went over the Sweet Tooth stuff again. He told me that it wasn't at all unusual for intelligence agencies to promote culture and cultivate the right kind of intellectuals. The Russians did it, so why wouldn't we? This was the soft Cold War. I said to him what I said to you on Saturday. Why not give the money openly, through some other government department? Why use a secret operation? Greatorex sighed and looked at me, shaking his head in pity. He said I had to understand, any institution, any organisation eventually becomes a dominion, self-contained, competitive, driven by its own logic and bent on survival and on extending its territory. It was as inexorable and blind as a chemical process. MI6 had gained control over a secret section of the Foreign Office and MI5 wanted its own project. Both wanted to impress the Americans, the CIA – which over the years had paid for more culture in Europe than anyone would ever realise.

He walked with me back to the car and by this time it was raining hard. We didn't waste much time in parting. Before he shook my hand he gave me his home phone number. He said he was sorry to be the bearer of such news. Betrayal was an ugly matter and no one should have to deal with it. He hoped I would find a way through. When he was gone I sat in the car with the ignition key drooping from my hand. The rain was coming down like it was the end of the world. After what I'd heard I couldn't face the drive or my parents or coming back to Clifton Street. I wasn't going to see the New Year in with you. I couldn't imagine doing anything but watch the rain clean the filthy street. After an hour I drove to a post office and sent you a telegram, then I found a hotel, a decent one. I thought I might as well use up the last of my suspect money on luxury. In a mood of self-pity, I ordered up to my room a bottle of Scotch. An inch of that with an equal amount of water was enough to persuade me that I didn't want to get drunk, not at five in the afternoon. I didn't want to be sober either. I didn't want anything, even oblivion.

But beyond existence and oblivion there's no third place to be. So I lay on this silky bed and thought about you, and

305

replayed the scenes that would make me feel worse. Our earnest and inept first fuck, our brilliant second, all the poetry, fish, ice buckets, stories, politics, the Friday evening reunions, playfulness, shared baths, shared sleep, all the kissing and stroking and touching tongues – how accomplished you were at appearing to be no more than you seemed to be, no more than yourself. Bitterly, sardonically, I wished meteoric promotion on you. Then I wished for more. I should tell you that in that hour, if your lovely pale throat had appeared upturned on my lap and a knife had been pushed into my hand, I would have done the job without thinking. It is the cause, it is the cause, my soul. Unlike me, Othello didn't want to shed blood. He was a softie.

Don't walk away now, Serena. Keep reading. This moment doesn't last. I hated you all right, and loathed myself for being the dupe, the conceited dupe who easily convinced himself that a cash fountain was his due, as was the beautiful woman on his arm as we promenaded on the Brighton seafront. As was the Austen Prize, which I took without much surprise as my rightful possession.

Yes, I sprawled on my four-poster king-sized bed, on a silk counterpane with medieval hunting motifs, and I pursued all the pain and insult that memory could flush from the thickets. Those long dinners in Wheeler's, the raised glasses chinked, literature, childhood, probability – all of it congealed into a single fleshy carcass, turning over slowly like a good spit-roast. I was thinking back before Christmas. Weren't we permitting into our conversation the first hints of a future together? But what future could we have had when you hadn't told me who you were? Where did you think it would end up? Surely you didn't intend to keep this secret from me for the rest of your life. The Scotch I drank at eight that night tasted better than the Scotch at five. I had a third without water, and phoned down for a bottle of Bordeaux and a ham sandwich. In the forty minutes that it took for room service to arrive, I continued with the Scotch. But I didn't get roaring drunk, didn't trash the room or make animal noises or raise curses against you. Instead, I wrote you a savage letter on hotel stationery, found a stamp, addressed the envelope and put it in my coat pocket. I drank one glass of wine, ordered up a second sandwich, had no more coherent thoughts and was meekly asleep by ten.

I woke some hours later into total darkness – the curtains in that room were thick – and entered one of those moments of untroubled but total amnesia. I could feel a comfortable bed around me, but who and where I was lay beyond my grasp. It lasted only a few seconds, this episode of pure existence, the mental equivalent of the blank page. Inevitably, the narrative seeped back, with the near details arriving first – the room, the hotel, the city, Greatorex, you; next, the larger facts of my life – my name, my general circumstances. It was then, as I sat up and groped for the bedside light switch, that I saw the whole Sweet Tooth affair in utterly different terms. This brief, cleansing amnesia had delivered me into common sense. This wasn't, or wasn't only, a calamitous betrayal and personal disaster. I'd been too busy being insulted by it to see it for what it was – an opportunity, a gift. I was a novelist without a novel, and now luck had tossed my way a tasty bone, the bare outline of a useful story. There was a spy in my bed, her head was on my pillow, her lips were pressed to my ear. She concealed her real purpose, and crucially, she didn't know that I knew. And I wouldn't tell her. So I wouldn't confront you, there'd be no accusations or terminal row and parting of ways, not yet. Instead, silence, discretion, patient watching, and writing. Events would decide the plot. The characters were ready-made. I would invent nothing, only record. I'd watch you at work. I too could be a spy.

I was sitting upright in bed, mouth open, staring across the room, like a man watching his father's ghost step through the wall. I'd seen the novel I was going to write. I had also seen the dangers. I would go on receiving the money in the full knowledge of its source. Greatorex knew that I knew.

307

That made me vulnerable, and gave him power over me. Was this novel conceived in the spirit of revenge? Well, no, but you did set me free. You didn't ask me if I wanted to be part of Sweet Tooth, I wouldn't ask you if you wanted to be in my story. Ian Hamilton once told me of a writer friend who'd put intimate details of his marriage into a novel. His wife was outraged to read their sex lives and pillow talk minutely reproduced. She divorced him and he regretted it forever, not least because she was very rich. No such problem here. I could do as I pleased. But I couldn't sit here for long with my mouth agape. I dressed hurriedly, found my notebook and filled it in two hours. I merely had to tell the story as I saw it, from the moment you came to my office at the university, to my rendezvous with Greatorex – and beyond.

The next morning, buzzing with purpose, I went out before breakfast and bought three exercise books from a friendly newsagent. Bristol, I decided, was a decent place after all. Back in my room I ordered coffee and set to work, making notes, setting out the sequences, trying out a paragraph or two for taste. I wrote almost half of an opening chapter. By mid-afternoon I was feeling uneasy. Two hours later, after a read-through, I threw down my pen with a shout and stood up suddenly, knocking over the chair behind me. Fuck! It was dull, it was dead. I'd covered forty pages, as easily as counting. No resistance or difficulty or spring, no surprises, nothing rich or strange. No hum, no torque. Instead, everything I saw and heard and said and did was lined up like beans in a row. It wasn't mere clumsy surface ineptitude. Buried deep in the concept was a flaw, and even that word sounded too good for what it was trying to name. It simply wasn't interesting.

I was spoiling a precious gift and I was disgusted. I took a walk through the city in the early evening darkness, and wondered whether I should post that letter to you after all. The problem, I decided, was me. Without thinking, I was presenting myself in the guise of the typical hero of an English comic novel – inept and almost clever, passive, earnest, over-explained, urgently unfunny. *There I was, minding my own business, thinking about sixteenth-century poetry, when, would you believe it, this beautiful girl walks into my office and offers me a pension.* What was I protecting with this veneer of farce? All the heartache, I supposed, that I hadn't yet touched on.

I walked to the Clifton Suspension Bridge, where, it was said, you could sometimes spot a prospective suicide casing the joint, calculating the fall. I crossed and stopped halfway to stare down into the blackness of the gorge. I was thinking again about the second time we ever made love. In your room, the morning after the White Tower. Remember? I lay back on the pillows – what luxury – and you swayed above me. A dance of bliss. As I read it then, your face as you looked down showed nothing but pleasure and the beginnings of real affection. Now I knew what you knew, what you had to conceal, I tried to imagine being you, being in two places at once, loving and . . . *reporting back.* How could I get in there and report back too? And that was it. I saw it. So simple. This story wasn't for me to tell. It was for you. Your job was to report back to me. I had to get out of my skin and into yours. I needed to be translated, to be a transvestite, to shoehorn myself into your skirts and high heels, into your knickers, and carry your white glossy handbag on its shoulder strap. On my shoulder. Then start talking, as you. Did I know you well enough? Clearly not. Was I a good enough ventriloquist? Only one way to find out. I had to begin. I took from a pocket my letter to you and tore it up, and let the bits drift down into the darkness of the Avon Gorge. Then I hurried back across the bridge, eventually waved down a taxi and spent that New Year's Eve and part of the next day in my hotel room filling another exercise book, trying your voice. Then I checked out late and drove the car home to my anxious parents.

Do you remember our first meeting after Christmas? It must have been January 3rd or 4th, another of our Friday evenings. You must have noticed how I made a point of coming to meet your train. Perhaps it crossed your mind that it was unusual. I'm a hopeless actor and I was worried that it would be impossible to behave naturally in your company, that you'd see through me. You'd know that I knew. Easier to greet you on a crowded platform than in the silence of the flat. But when your train came in and I saw the carriage containing you slide by, with you reaching so prettily above your seat for your bag, and seconds later, when we went into that powerful embrace, I felt such desire for you that I didn't need to fake a thing. We kissed and I knew it was going to be easy. I could want you and watch you. The two weren't mutually exclusive. In fact, they fed each other. When we made love an hour later, you were so sweetly and inventively possessive, even as you carried on with your usual pretence – I put this at its simplest: it thrilled me. I almost passed out. So it began, what you kindly termed my 'pig-in-a-trough mode'. And it multiplied my pleasures, to know that I could retreat to the typewriter to describe the moment, from your point of view. Your duplicitous point of view, which would have to include your understanding, your version, of me, lover and Sweet Tooth item. My task was to reconstruct myself through the prism of your consciousness. If I gave myself a good press, it was because of those nice things you said about me. With this recursive refinement, my mission was even more interesting than yours. Your masters did not require you to investigate how you yourself appeared through my eyes. I was learning to do what you do, then better it with one extra fold in the fabric of deception. And how well I took to it.

Then, a few hours later, Brighton beach – strictly, Hove, which doesn't chime romantically, despite the half-rhyme with love. For only the second time in our affair I was on my back, now with damp shingle cooling my coccyx. A passing policeman on the promenade would have done us for public indecency. How could we have explained to him those parallel worlds that we spun around us? In one orbit, our mutual deceit, a novelty in my case, habitual in yours, possibly addictive, probably fatal. In the other, our affection bursting through ecstasy to love. We reached the glorious summit at last and traded our 'I love you's even as we each reserved our secrets. I saw how we could do it, live with these sealed compartments side by side, never letting the dank stench of one invade the sweetness of the other. If I mention again how exquisite our lovemaking became after my rendezvous with Greatorex, I know you'll be thinking of 'Pawnography'. (How I regret now that punning title.) The foolish husband lusting after the wife who stole his stuff, his pleasure sharpened by his secret knowledge of her deceit. All right, she was a rehearsal for you before I knew of your existence. And I don't deny the common root is me. But I have in mind my other story, the one about the vicar's brother who ends up loving the woman who'll destroy him. You always liked that one. Or how about the writer driven to her second novel by the spectre of her apish lover? Or the fool who believes his lover is real when in fact he's dreamed her up and she's only a counterfeit, a copy, a fake?

But don't leave the kitchen. Stay with me. Let me exorcise this bitterness. And let's talk about research. By the time you came to Brighton that Friday, I'd had a second meeting with Max Greatorex, at his place in Egham, Surrey. Even at the time, I was surprised how open he was, filling me in on the Sweet Tooth meetings, your various encounters in the park and in his office, his late-night visit to St Augustine's Road and, generally, the workplace. As I learned more, I wondered if he was longing, in a self-destructive way, to become the Fourth Man, or if he was in sexual competition with your Tony Canning. Max assured me that Sweet Tooth was so low level that it hardly mattered. I also got the impression that he'd already decided to leave the Security Service and go into something else. Now I know from Shirley Shilling that his purpose in meeting me in Bristol was to break up our affair.

He was indiscreet because all he cared about was destroying you. When I asked to see him again, he thought I was driven by angry obsession, which he was happy to feed. Later, he was surprised to discover that I was still seeing you. He was furious when he heard you intended to come to the Austen event at the Dorchester. So he called his press contacts and threw us to the dogs. In all, I've met him three times this year. He gave me so much, he was so helpful. It's a pity I detest him. He told me Canning's story, how he was interviewed one last time in a safe house before he went off to the Baltic to die, how he had a nosebleed, which ruined a mattress and nourished some lurid fantasies of yours. Greatorex was much entertained by all that.

At our last meeting he gave me an address for your old friend Shirley Shilling. I'd read about her in the papers, how a clever agent had lined up five publishers to bid for her first novel, how they were queuing up for the movie rights in LA. She was on Martin Amis's arm when we were reading together in Cambridge. I liked her, and she adores you. She told me about your pub-rock crawls around London. After I said I knew about your work she told me about your time together as cleaning ladies, and how she was asked to snoop on you. She also mentioned your old friend Jeremy, so while I was in Cambridge I went to his college and got a forwarding address for him in Edinburgh. I also visited Mrs Canning. I told her that I'd been a student of her husband. She was polite enough, but I didn't learn much. You'll be pleased to hear that she knows nothing about you. Shirley had offered to drive me to the Canning cottage in Suffolk. (She drives like a maniac.) We peered into the garden and went for a stroll in the woods. By the time we left I felt I had enough to reconstruct the scene of your secret affair, your apprenticeship in secrecy.

From Cambridge, remember, I went on to see your sister and her boyfriend Luke. As you know, I dislike getting stoned. It's such a mental constriction. That prickly, electric self-consciousness just doesn't suit me and nor does a joyless chemical appetite for sweet things. But it was the only way Lucy and I could really get along and talk. The three of us sat in low light on cushions on the floor of their flat, incense smouldering from homemade clay pots, a sitar raga leaking onto our heads from unseen speakers. We drank purifying tea. She's in awe of you, poor girl, desperate for her big sister's good opinion, which I think she rarely gets. At one point she said forlornly that it wasn't fair that you were cleverer *and* prettier. I got what I had come for – your childhood and teenage years, though I might have forgotten most of it in a haze of hash. I do remember that we ate cauliflower cheese and brown rice for supper.

I stayed the night in order to go on Sunday to the cathedral to hear your father. I was curious, because you'd described to me in a letter how you collapsed into his arms on your front doorstep. And there he was, in distant splendour, saying nothing at all on that particular day. Underlings, grand enough in their own right, undeterred by the feeble turn-out, conducted the service with all the brio of unshaken faith. One fellow with a nasal voice preached the sermon, a sure-footed exegesis of the Good Samaritan parable. I shook your father's hand on my way out. He looked at me with interest and asked in a friendly way if I'd be coming back. How could I tell him the truth?

I wrote to Jeremy to present myself as your good friend who was passing through Edinburgh. I told him that you'd suggested I get in touch. I knew you wouldn't mind a lie, and I also knew I was taking a chance. If he mentioned me to you my cover would be blown. This time, I had to get drunk to make real progress. How else would I have got the story of how you came to write for *?Quis??* It was you who told me about his elusive orgasm, his peculiar pubic bone and the folded towel. Jeremy and I had the sixteenth century, its history and literature, in common too, and I was able to bring him up to date on Tony Canning as traitor, and then your affair, which shocked him. And so our evening sped along beautifully and I thought it was money well spent when I picked up the bill at the Old Waverley Hotel.

But why trouble you with details of my research? First, to let you know I took this matter seriously. Second, to be clear, that above all it was you who were my principal source. There was, of course, everything that I saw for myself. And then the small cast among whom I wandered in January. That leaves an island of experience, an important fraction of the whole, that was you alone, you with your thoughts, and sometimes you invisible to yourself. On this terrain, I've been obliged to extrapolate or invent.

Here's an example. Neither of us will forget our first meeting in my office. From where I sat, when you stepped through the door and I took in your old-fashioned peaches-and-cream look, and your summer-blue eyes, I thought it was just possible that my life was about to change. I've imagined you minutes before that moment, making your way from Falmer station, approaching the Sussex campus filled with the snobbish distaste you've expressed to me since for the idea of a new university. Sleek and fair, you strode through the crowds of long-haired bare-foot kids. Your scorn was barely fading from your face by the time you introduced yourself and started telling me your untruths. You've complained to me about your time at Cambridge, you've told me it was intellectually stultifying, but you defend your place to the hilt and look down on mine. Well, for what it's worth, think again. Don't be fooled by loud music. I reckon my place was more ambitious, more serious, more enjoyable than yours. I speak as a product, an explorer, of Asa Briggs's new map of learning. The tutorials were demanding. Two essays a week for three years, no let-up. All the usual literary studies, but on top compulsory historiography for all newcomers, and then for me, by choice, cosmology, fine art, international relations, Virgil, Dante, Darwin, Ortega y Gasset . . . Sussex would never have allowed you to stagnate the way you did, would never have permitted you to do nothing else but mathematics. Why am I bothering you with this? I can hear you say to yourself, He's jealous, he's chippy about his plate-glass learning emporium, about not having been at my place with the snooker-table lawns and honey limestone. But you're wrong. I only wanted to remind you why I painted a curl on your lips as you passed under the sound of Jethro Tull, a sneer I wasn't there to see. It was an informed guess, an extrapolation.

So much for research. I had my material, the wafer of gold, and the motivation to hammer it out. I went at it in a frenzy, more than a hundred thousand words in just over three months. The Austen Prize, for all the excitement and recognition, seemed like a monstrous distraction. I set myself a target of fifteen hundred words a day, seven days a week. Sometimes, when my invention ran out, it was near impossible, and at others it was a breeze because I was able to transcribe our conversation minutes after we'd had it. Sometimes events wrote whole sections for me.

A recent example was last Saturday, when you came back to the flat from shopping to show me the *Guardian* story. I knew then that Greatorex had upped his game and things were going to move fast. I had a ringside seat for the deception, yours and mine. I could see you thought you were about to be exposed and accused. I pretended to love you too much to suspect you – it was easy to do that. When you suggested making a statement to the Press Association, I knew it was pointless, but why not? The story was writing itself. Besides, it was time to renounce the Foundation's money. It touched me when you tried to dissuade me from claiming to know no one from the intelligence service. You knew how vulnerable I was, how vulnerable you'd rendered me, and you were in agonies as you tried to protect me. So why did I make the claim anyway? More story! I couldn't resist it. And I wanted to seem like an innocent in your hearing. I knew I was about to do myself a lot of harm. But I didn't care, I was reckless and obsessed, I wanted to see what happened. I thought, correctly as it turned out, that this was the endgame. When you went to lie on the bed to brood on your dilemma, I set about describing you reading the newspapers in your cafe near the market, and then, while it was still fresh, our entire exchange. After our Wheeler's lunch we made love. You fell asleep and I worked on, typing and revising the recent hours. When I came into the bedroom in the early evening to wake you and make love to you again, you whispered as you took my cock in your hand and brought me into you, 'You're amazing.' I hope you won't mind. I've included that.

Face it, Serena, the sun is setting on this decaying affair, and the moon and stars are too. This afternoon – your yesterday, I expect – the doorbell rang. I went down to find standing on the pavement a woman from the *Daily Express*. She was pleasant and frank as she told me what was going to be in the next day's paper, how I would be presented as a mendacious, greedy fraud. She even read me passages she'd written. She also described the photographs and asked politely if I'd care to give her a quote. I had nothing to say. As soon as she'd gone I took notes. I won't be in a position to buy a copy of the *Express* tomorrow but it won't matter because this afternoon I'll incorporate what she told me, and have you read the story on the train. Yes, it's over. The reporter told me her paper already had quotes from Edward Heath and Roy Jenkins. I'm headed for public ignominy. We all are. I'll be accused, and rightly, of lying in my statement to the Press Association, of taking money from an inappropriate source, of selling my independence of thought. Your employers foolishly meddled where they don't belong and they've embarrassed their political masters. It can't be long before the list of other Sweet Tooth beneficiaries comes out. There'll be derision and blushes and a sacking or two. As for you, you have no chance of surviving tomorrow's press. You appear stunning in the photographs, I was told. But you'll be looking for a job.

Soon I'm going to ask you to make an important decision, but before I do, let me tell you my favourite spy story. MI5 had a hand in it, as well as Six. 1943. The struggle was starker and more consequential than it is now. In April that year the decomposing body of an officer of the Royal Marines washed up on the coast of Andalucia. Attached to the dead man's wrist by a chain was a briefcase containing documents referring to plans for the invasion of southern Europe through Greece and Sardinia. The local authorities contacted the British attaché, who at first seemed to take little interest in the corpse or its luggage. Then he appeared to change his mind and worked frantically to get both returned. Too late. The Spanish were neutral in the war, but generally more favourable to the Nazi cause. The German intelligence community was on to the matter, the documents in the briefcase found their way to Berlin. German High Command studied the contents of the briefcase, learned of the Allies' intentions and altered their defences accordingly. But as you probably know from *The Man Who Never Was*, the body and the plans were fake, a plant devised by British intelligence. The officer was actually a Welsh tramp, retrieved from a morgue and, with thorough attention to detail, dressed up in a fictional identity, complete with love letters and tickets to a London show. The Allied invasion of southern Europe came through the more obvious route, Sicily, which was poorly defended. At least some of Hitler's divisions were guarding the wrong portals.

Operation Mincemeat was one of scores of wartime deception exercises, but my theory is that what produced its particular brilliance and success was the manner of its inception. The original idea came from a novel published in 1937 called *The Milliner's Hat Mystery*. The young naval commander who spotted the episode would one day be a famous novelist himself. He was Ian Fleming, and he included the idea along with other ruses in a memo which appeared before a secret committee chaired by an Oxford don, who wrote detective novels. Providing an identity, a background and a plausible life to a cadaver was done with novelistic flair. The naval attaché who orchestrated the reception of the drowned officer in Spain was also a novelist. Who says that poetry makes nothing happen? Mincemeat succeeded because invention, the imagination, drove the intelligence. By miserable comparison, Sweet Tooth, that precursor of decay, reversed the process and failed because intelligence tried to interfere with invention. Our moment was thirty years ago. In our decline we live in the shadow of giants. You and your colleagues must have known the project was rotten, and doomed from the start, but your motives were bureaucratic, you kept going because the order came down from on high. Your Peter Nutting should have listened to the chairman of the Arts Council, Angus Wilson, another novelist with connections to wartime intelligence.

I told you that it wasn't anger that set me writing the pages in the parcel in front of you. But there was always an element of tit for tat. We both reported back. You lied to me, I spied on you. It was delicious, and I thought you had it coming. I really believed that I could wrap the matter up between the covers of a book and write you out of my system and say goodbye. But I reckoned without the logic of the process. I had to go to Cambridge to get your terrible degree, make love in a Suffolk cottage to a kind old toad, live in your Camden bedsit, suffer a bereavement, wash your hair and iron your skirts for work and suffer the morning Tube journey, experience your urge for independence as well as the bonds that held you to your parents and made you cry against your father's chest. I had to taste your loneliness, inhabit your insecurity, your longing for praise from superiors, your unsisterliness, your minor impulses of snobbery, ignorance and vanity, your minimal social conscience, moments of self-pity, and orthodoxy in most matters. And do all this without ignoring your cleverness, beauty and tenderness, your love of sex and fun, your wry humour and sweet protective instincts. To recreate you on the page I had to become you and understand you (this is what novels demand), and in doing that, well, the inevitable happened. When I poured myself into your skin I should have guessed at the consequences. I still love you. No, that's not it. I love you more.

You may think we're too mired in deceit, that we've told each other enough lies to outlast a lifetime, that our deception and humiliation have doubled the reasons for going our separate ways. I prefer to think they've cancelled out and that we're too entwined in mutual surveillance to let each other go. I'm in the business now of watching over you. Wouldn't you like to do the same for me? What I'm working my way towards is a declaration of love and a marriage proposal. Didn't you once confide to me your old-fashioned view that this was how a novel should end, with a 'Marry me'? With your permission I'd like to publish one day this book on the kitchen table. It's hardly an apologia, more an indictment of us both, which would surely bind us further. But there are obstacles. We wouldn't want you or Shirley or even Mr Greatorex to languish behind bars at Her Majesty's leisure, so we'll have to wait until well into the twenty-first century to be clear of the Official Secrets Act. A few decades is time enough for you to correct my presumptions on your solitude, to tell me about the rest of your secret work and what really happened between you and Max, and time to insert those paddings of the backward glance: in those days, back then, these were the years of . . . Or how about, 'Now that the mirror tells a different story, I can say it and get it out of the way. I really was *pretty*.' Too cruel? No need to worry, I'll add nothing without your say-so. We won't be rushing into print.

I'm sure I won't always be an object of public contempt, but it may take a while. At least the world and I are now in agreement – I need an independent source of income. There's a job coming up at University College London. They want a Spenser specialist and I'm told I have a decent chance. I'm feeling a little more confident that teaching needn't prevent me writing. And Shirley told me she may have something for you in London, if you're interested.

Tonight I'll be on a plane to Paris to stay with an old school friend who says he can give me a room for a few days. When things have quietened down, when I've faded from the headlines, I'll come straight back. If your answer is a fatal no, well, I've made no carbon, this is the only copy and you can throw it to the flames. If you still love me and your answer is yes, then our collaboration begins and this letter, with your consent, will be Sweet Tooth's final chapter.

Dearest Serena, it's up to you.

Acknowledgements

I owe particular thanks to Frances Stonor Saunders for her book, *Who Paid the Piper? The CIA and the Cultural Cold War*; and also to Paul Lashmar and Oliver James's *Britain's Secret Propaganda War: 1948–1977*, and to Hugh Wilford's *The CIA, the British Left and the Cold War: Calling the Tune?* The following were also extremely helpful: *Writing Dangerously: Mary McCarthy and her World* by Carol Brightman; *The Theory & Practice of Communism* by R.N. Carew Hunt; *Operation Mincemeat* by Ben MacIntyre; *Reluctant Judas* by Geoffrey Robertson; *Open Secret: The Autobiography of the Former Director-General of MI5* by Stella Rimington; *The Defence of the Realm: The Authorized History of MI5* by Christopher Andrew; *Spooks: The Unofficial History of MI5* by Thomas Hennessey and Claire Thomas; *Spy Catcher: The Candid Autobiography of a Senior Intelligence Officer* by Peter Wright; *State of Emergency: The Way We Were: Britain, 1970–1974* by Dominic Sandbrook; *When the Lights Went Out: Britain in the Seventies* by Andy Beckett; *Crisis? What Crisis? Britain in the 1970s* by Alwyn W. Turner; *Strange Days Indeed* by Francis Wheen.

I am grateful to Tim Garton Ash for his thoughtful comments; to David Cornwell for irresistible reminiscences; to Graeme Mitchison and Karl Friston for stripping out the Monty Hall problem; to Alex Bowler, and, as always, to Annalena McAfee.